AT CERTAIN POINTS
WE TOUCH

AT CERTAIN POINTS WE TOUCH

Lauren John Joseph

BLOOMSBURY PUBLISHING

LONDON · OXFORD · NEW YORK · NEW DELHI · SYDNEY

BLOOMSBURY PUBLISHING
Bloomsbury Publishing Plc
50 Bedford Square, London, WC1B 3DP, UK
29 Earlsfort Terrace, Dublin 2, Ireland

BLOOMSBURY, BLOOMSBURY PUBLISHING and the Diana logo
are trademarks of Bloomsbury Publishing Plc

2 4 6 8 10 9 7 5 3

Typeset by Integra Software Services Pvt. Ltd
Printed and bound in the U.S.A. by Berryville Graphics Inc., Berryville, Virginia

To find out more about our authors and books visit www.bloomsbury.com
and sign up for our newsletters

For Peter

PART ONE

'I write entirely to find out what I'm thinking, what I'm looking at, what I see and what it means.'
— JOAN DIDION

Prologue

When did you know you were dead?

I'm asking you a question that I know you can never answer.

It is now ten years since we met, six years since we last spoke, four years since your death, and I'm writing you this from Mexico City, under grave obligation. It is not a letter, since I know you cannot reply; maybe it's another monologue, certainly it does not require a second voice; let's call it plainsong then. This is the chant recalling your life, it is fiction, it is biography, it is a transfiguration.

Last night I was walking home through my neighbourhood of Tacubaya, a few hours before dawn. I was with a very handsome American boy whom I had picked up at a house party, we were on our way to get breakfast at the all-night taqueria. Because we were drunk, and because we were high, and because Tacubaya is quite dicey at 4.30 a.m., we picked up the pace of our flirtatious stroll so that it became more of a determined tramp. It was chilly, and it seemed like we were getting lost, but we were stubborn, and both unwilling to pull out a phone for guidance, preferring to show off to each other with how well we knew the city.

My new American friend and I took several wrong turns, and found ourselves suddenly stumbling out of the crumbling residential streets, onto a massive six-lane highway which told us we had gone too far. Gargantuan heavy goods vehicles, massive petroleum tankers and enormous Coca-Cola trucks thundered across the dying night, bellowing diesel through the city, causing the pavement to rumble beneath our feet. We stood stock-still, dazed, in shock, in front of a shuttered mechanic's shop, agog at the sight of this impenetrable traffic, regarding each other with an attitude of, *Well, what now?*

A few doors down, a pharmacy slept under an illuminated emerald cross, bolted to its facade and spilling lurid green into the easing darkness. Text skated over the horizontal axis of the crucifix – *¡Medicamentos, suplementos, descuentos y más!* – the infinite scrolling jargon of drugstore commerce, cordially punctuated at the end of each round by a very civil proclamation of the time, date and temperature.

I stand and watch the information pass by several times, quite stupefied, before I find the wherewithal to ask out loud, 'Is that right?'

The American boy says, 'Yeah, I know. Feels colder than twelve degrees, right?'

I shake my head, 'No. The date. Is that today's date?'

He nods, 'Yeah, it's the twenty-ninth.'

'Of February?' I ask.

'Yeah,' he replies.

'It can't be,' I say, incredulous.

'I guess it's a leap year,' he says, and laughs nervously. That was when I felt it.

'I have to go,' I say.

'Where?' he asks.

'Home,' I say. 'Do I have your number? I'll call you tomorrow, later, tonight.'

He looks confused, and says, 'OK…'

I can see that he is put out. He thought he was going to get a fuck, but I don't much care, I'm already hurrying away.

You see, it came over me like a compulsion, like food poisoning, like a scream in the dark tearing me violently from a dream: the exhortation to finally put this down on paper.

I crash into my apartment, drop my coat to the floor and skitter, still drunk, towards the kitchen table. I know that I have to begin right here and now, at 5.15 a.m., at least to make a start, if I am to ever to crawl up out of this perdition. With a clean sweep of my right hand I clear a mess of mail and half-read magazines from the tabletop, grab for my computer with my left, and began to write.

Disinterred, exhumed, hauled up from such an early grave comes the writer I had all but abandoned, here to type out the opening line, *When did you know you were dead?* The writer who has held silent all these years, sticking to the shadows of shame and fear, the writer who has watched the other players wear themselves out running amok, the psychic I is now coming into her legacy. Who else has the dominion and tenacity to accept the many months of solitude which will be required to perform this commission? Only the writer. Only the writer can tell the story of our life, and your sorry death. The priest, the painter, the soprano I might have been don't have it in them. Only the writer.

The significance of the day's date has opened like a portal onto mania. The phantasmagoric nature of its revelation, materialising before me on that lonely neon crucifix, driving me into a frenzy of desperation, contrition, and rage. *And what is there to be gained now, after all this time? Am I hoping to perform some act of penance here on the page?* I can't answer. I simply sit and write, I give myself over. I turn inwards, and try to remember the first time I saw you, back when you were just one in a multitude of sweat-streaked golden boys.

I write straight through to lunchtime when the drugs and alcohol finally wear off, leaving only a headache. I go to my room around 1 p.m. and take out the cache of your letters from under my mattress, only to find my eyes are too sore to read them. Frustrated, exhausted, I throw myself into bed but I don't undress, I don't even draw the curtains; I simply sink into the low light of a room which never fully catches the sun, to snatch some rest, though I know I won't really be able to sleep until this is finished, until it is all out and down, and staring back at me. As I doze, I dream of council tower blocks being dynamited, collapsing down into ascending clouds of hot grey smoke. In my dream I'm watching from a safe distance but still I am afraid and I say so, out loud from my sleep.

Above my body, across the street, a neighbour flings open a window and the sun's momentary reflection on the glass lights up the bedroom like a camera flash. I snap awake, startled and disorientated, so confused by my lack of sleep that, for a few seconds upon waking, I believe that I am back in London, that I am coming to on that irreversible afternoon four years ago, when I woke up alone and found out that you were dead. Only this time I somehow know what has happened instinctively, without having to be told; briefly I believe that I have been woken by a pythonic vision. Slowly, I sit up, ragged and bemused, the letters fall from my bed, casting my eyes about the room, only very gradually understanding where I am. Then I begin to panic. I don't know how long I've slept, I'm terrified that I've lost the whole of this precious day. I scramble about on the floor looking for the alarm clock, and am desperately relieved when I see that it is only 1.45 p.m. – I have barely dented sleep. It is still today, thank God, it is still 29 February. Nauseous, dehydrated and sore, I return to the kitchen. I spread out your letters on the table and begin to work again on this book, this exertion, this panegyric. It is for you, just for you, leapling, happy birthday.

I

You were infamous, even before we met you held space in my imagination. You appeared out of nowhere, you came into view fully formed like that old Joan Baez ballad, and just like that you were everywhere, a hyperobject. I saw you at parties, at openings, on the runway, modelling for a mutual friend in his last season before he got the big job in Paris, plodding in the way that you did. *How could anyone so slender be so heavy?* I wondered. It was as if the pavement had always been calling your name. I had seen you read poetry at galleries and cabarets and other murky late-night gatherings, heaving your gangly build, unwieldy as a bicycle frame, up on a makeshift stage. In an unironed shirt and a cartoon character tie, you'd declaim verse with something like zeal. Some of it was yours, some of it was liberally borrowed, and all of it was spliced together in the Kathy Acker mode, uncredited in any case, as you tore through it all, shuffling slightly back and forth in the spotlight. We had occasionally shared a bill, and I think those readings were the only times I saw passion stir you, not that you lacked emotion, but it almost always came out in clouds of schoolboy sulking, rather than in bursts of ecstasy or animation. In that way you were like a cat, needy but incapable of admitting it. The written word seemed to hold some animating power over you though, it made your corpse dance.

You were not flash, no, almost impossibly casual, but you seemed to know everyone, or rather everyone knew you. You were ineluctable. How many times? I couldn't count. How many times before we ever spoke had we locked eyes? Across a dance floor, in the scrum at a bar, sat wilting on a comedown in opposite corners of an acquaintance's bedroom, but still we were strangers. And from this safe remove I indulged with distinct voyeuristic pleasure in your cruel beauty, your Greek nose, messy blond hair and blue eyes, each distinguishing feature a clue towards decoding the warning, *Avoid this handsome bastard*. Not that I had to do much to keep out of striking distance, your time was very well filled with a revolving cast of sprightly admirers. I watched as they flocked about you.

You always looked as though you had been violated; you were like a found photograph, black and white, black and white, of a little boy, bundled onto the Kindertransport by his desperate mother. You looked as though you had been dressed by the charity of a refugee relief organisation, all obscure football kits, acrylic granddad sweaters, cheap formalwear and nineties sports gear (as yet still not back in), helpless, impuissant, like you'd walked through the unspeakable. In truth, it was this aura of sadness that you radiated, as much as your physical allure, which drew these lovers to you, the anger and the pain that played across your face involuntarily. Or rather it was the tragic combination of the two, the defiled and the carnal, which spoke to the devoted masochists who offered themselves to you. In turn you toyed with each one a while, all of them so pumped full of speed and ego, each so sure that they were the one you were waiting for. Like big cat lovers, every one of them believed that they possessed the touch that would keep them safe from harm, and each one willingly shoved their head into your mouth; you had hardly to do a thing.

We had many mutual friends, and at twenty-one and twenty-three respectively, we were communards hell-bent on seizing the night, liberating it for ourselves, appearing at every party deserving of our self-regarding brilliance, dressed to kill, or fight at least. Me in Elsa's black fur coat and a purple balcony bra, you in your cycling shorts and slogan T-shirts, fumbling our way in the darkness towards the people we were growing into, towards each other. We partied at a companionable distance for years, on boats, and in squats, in nightclubs, on rooftops, surrounded by every imaginable kind of attention-seeking behaviour, with photographers never ceasing, with our drug-fucked contemporaries stagger-ing around in abandon, in clothes from three nights earlier, and the occasional supermodel, or movie star, drifting by and winking, 'Love the look babes.'

Amongst all these tabloid icons and underage pill-heads we circled each other a drawn-out while; ours was a long, slow courtship, an incendiary device with a spolette fuse. We didn't in fact speak until it was almost too late, until the very end of my final term at univer-sity, barely a month or so before I was due to leave London for good. We almost missed each other entirely, leapling, isn't that a strange thing to think about now? The retrospective shudder I feel, when I think that we might never have met, can make this connection seem almost mystical; but then, every lover was once a stranger. Really the only detail of our first meeting that stands out as perverse or prophetic is the fact that it was Lulu who first introduced us.

It's late but not that late. We're all at a party for a magazine, at a restaurant in Mayfair, a plush affair but a tedious one, too far into summer for a party indoors not to be simply stifling. Lulu says, 'Tom, this is JJ,' then she cracks a broad, very satisfied grin and continues with cool intent, 'And JJ, *this* is Thomas James.' She presents you like the star prize on a TV game show, she wants a reaction, maybe she wants to cause a scene simply to liven things up, but none of us are really in the mood for drama. It's too warm, we're all fading. I smile politely, you don't register any particular interest in me, just give a brief nod, looking vaguely irritated, and the three of us stand about scuffing the carpet for a while, mildly embarrassed. It's boring, but we haven't heard of anything better yet, and the bar is still free, so we linger awkwardly.

Lulu excuses herself a few minutes later, promising a swift return. You watch her cross the shag of the carpet, she's so imperious and graceful, only the briefest flutterings of her fingers give away her butterflies, her nerves. Maybe out of boredom, maybe out of simple spite, you try it on with me, of course you do. I'm aware that you try it on with everyone, if only to ensure you are desired, so I'm not flattered, though seeing you here with Lulu I admit that I am intrigued. You tower over me, even with that terrible slouch of yours, and give me a few soggy lines about redheads being good in the sack. I roll my eyes, and understand that your reputation as a disco lothario is largely owing to conversation in a nightclub being almost always inaudible. You're out of your element, but honestly so am I, we're together in that.

I cast my eyes about the room hoping to see Elsa or Jovian maybe, to be spared this experience, but neither have arrived, they've probably heard what a dud this party is. It is officially too late now to hope for any improvement here tonight, I decide to cut my losses and split.

'Will you say goodbye to Lulu for me?' I ask.

You don't reply, just sort of shrug, coarsely.

A week later, at a party on the Thames, as you casually brush up against me you tell me that you intend to become the leader of a major political party, it doesn't really seem to matter to you *which*. I never could see you as the coherent product of all your composite parts, but then maybe that's because I couldn't ever tell when you were being serious. You say that you're going to set the country straight, you tell me the nation needs a strong man, you're showing me the outlines of your thinking, you've changed tactic.

Having spent my collegiate summers living communally in acid-soaked Northern California, participating in experimental performances as political protest, I thought you were unforgivably out of touch, that all your ideas were half-baked, though obviously I was completely blind as to how embarrassingly anachronistic my own worldview was. We both suffered from a millennial cognitive dissonance, believing that the mass-market political remedies offered up by the twentieth century could yet ease the explosive new ills of the twenty-first. We were clinging to the fading glory of parliamentary democracy, global capitalism and liberal socialism with a fervour not unlike that with which I now cleave to your letters, to your evaporating memory.

When I met you, I was myself primed to disappear. I was intent on heading back there, into the past. I wanted to return to California, to stay forever wrapped in the feel-good flower-power dream of art as transformative. It was the summer in which I was supposed to escape the mortification of my childhood and adolescence for good, and ride off into a golden future of acclaim and self-actualisation, a tomorrow only the United States of half a century ago could offer. And you, you were only ever supposed to be a minor figure, just someone I knew back in London, a handsome boy I used to see around, with whom I once shared an awkward ten minutes shortly before I left the old country.

And yet.

I had a respectable second-class degree pending confirmation, and a relentless desire to get out of England. I felt an expanding fear that if I didn't leave as soon as I could, I would be eaten up like all the other kids I grew up with, clever but unconnected, swallowed whole by bad drugs or dream-killing jobs in supermarkets. That I had made it to university was miracle enough. My early life had been characterised by the quality of poverty and violence you might find in Marguerite Duras's writing on Saigon: all of the scarcity, all of the dashed illusions, though none of the sunset glamour. I even had a depressive schoolteacher for a mother, well, part-time classroom assistant, but why interfere with such an upright fantasy?

Very early on I came to know that indigence was the one unforgivable sin; that I would have to divorce myself from it through education, through distance, through my work, or succumb to its vices totally. I think my mother had an inkling of this too, which is why, after her second divorce, she moved us from Liverpool to a nameless town in Lancashire where she could recreate herself again, and where my disaffection could more fully blossom. This feeling of alienation ran through my life, looming like the Berlin Wall, separating everything I knew from everything I wanted. The inscrutable grey concrete of class, connections, power, it seemed utterly insurmountable. I could only get on, I figured, if I got out, tunnelled under the wall, smuggled myself across the border in the boot of a Trabant, used what I had to greater advantage, in a more flattering context.

I went to study in London, but the capital was only ever the first stop on a longer voyage. Ever since I was a child looking west over the Mersey, my eyes had always been drawn to the Atlantic, and America beyond. It could have been the Stonewall riots, or David Hockney's swimming pools, the image of Bogie and Bacall sharing a smoke, or all those canned nineties sitcoms. I didn't puzzle it out, I just accepted it; as all butterflies abide by their predestined migrations, it was in my queer genes. I was looking for a place to be reborn, why else choose San Francisco? Why not mainline NY or LA, if not for that city's reputation (so Wilde had it) as the place where everyone who disappears is said to be seen again?

I had spent each academic year in London biding my time, attending far more parties than lectures, coasting by doing the bare minimum, completing only the work that was required in order for me to attend summer school at the University of California, Berkeley. If I had not found that exchange scheme, funded by frozen food philanthropists to encourage underprivileged international students to expand their career horizons, I don't think I would ever have believed in the future. It wasn't the classes in sociology and American history that made me believe, Lord knows. It wasn't the good cheer of the campus, or the stoned coalitions of marriage equality activists that gave me faith either. No, hope was the effect of the psychedelicised souls I met there; the dropouts, the dreamers and the comeback queens I encountered, shuttling back and forth across the Bay on the BART train each day.

The minute I was done with my academic requirements in London I was determined to get back there, although since I had now graduated, there wouldn't be any more summer school, but then that had never really been the point of the exercise, had it? Before the ink was even dry on my final theology paper, I left London to begin the journey back to California. I walked out of the Gower Street examination room and over to Euston train station, skipped out on my rent, left the distractions, the assurances of friendships to be continued, and the years of all-night parties where I had found you, and countless others like you, behind. I'm sure I didn't spare a thought for you, and if I did, I was certainly not weighed down with any regret or distress at the idea of letting you slip forever into the bygone. Why should I be? We'd barely shared a drink.

I went home to my mother's house in the broken Northwest, and sat waiting in a sort of penurious limbo for my final student loan cheque (which always arrived, somewhat illogically, after classes had ended) so that I could buy my ticket back to America. My mother was unconvinced.

'What about a teacher training qualification? That's a good job,' she said.

'It's just not what I want,' I replied.

She grew impatient, 'Why do you always have to make it so hard on yourself? You never could just accept what you've got and be grateful, could you?'

I didn't respond.

'Anyways, what do they have there, in California, that we don't have here?' she asked, but she wasn't being ironic.

I wanted to answer, 'Good drugs,' or 'Hope,' but I didn't. I just said, 'Avocados.'

At the time I thought my mother's resistance to my aspirations was something selfish and unimaginative, and so I was angry, in much the same way I had been when I told my family that I didn't want to be a boy anymore, and Auntie Viv said, 'I'll pray for you.' She wasn't praying for the forgiveness of my soul, she wasn't asking God to undo this affliction, she was praying that my difference wouldn't make my life more difficult, but being full of unearned pride, I refused to understand her prayer. Likewise I couldn't credit my mother with the experience required to legitimately question my choices, to ask whether someone like me would ever face anything but intolerance and indifference when setting off on such an implausible path through life.

My brothers and sisters were very young then, primary school age, and so I would pick them up at three each afternoon, four little blond beauties, who looked more like your children than my siblings. I walked them home, my arms full of backpacks and blazers, watching them skip on ahead of me in the brilliant mid-afternoon sun, calling after them at thirty-second intervals, 'Watch the road! Don't go too far – do you hear me?' At the main intersection, between the petrol station and the discount supermarket, while we waited for the orderly green man, I would listen to them squabble about whose turn it was to feed the guinea pigs, and imagine how beautiful it would be, if only I could accept that this was my life. If I could smile and bow to an unremarkable existence in this worn-out town in Northern England. If I could kiss goodbye to my filthy ambition, perhaps happiness would be my reward.

I gave the children batons of carrot and peanut butter, most of which I guessed would go straight to Bert and Ernie, and I watched them from the kitchen window as they tumbled in the garden, perfect and golden and unspoiled. I tapped on the window when their play turned too rough, and when they found something exciting in the grass they'd wave to me and hold it up, the stick, the forgotten bucket and spade, the snail. I knew that I was witnessing something precious, that these summers would never come again, that soon they'd be too big, too cool, too stoned to want me to cut up carrots for them, and even then, the images seen through the glass seemed to me already like memories revisited, when the family camcorder footage is finally digitised. Why couldn't this be enough?

I usually had just enough baseless optimism to see me through until sunset, until bedtime. Afterwards however, as I watched the sky evolve steadily from blue through purple to black, panic would set about me – all my little incubi and succubi creeping out to tease and torment me. The night has always been my kingdom, ever since I was a sinful teenager slipping out from my bedroom unnoticed at 11 p.m., but here, now, far from the big smoke, having long outgrown one-horse night-life, sunbed tans, older men and 1 a.m. closing times, I felt deposed.

Lying on the couch, in the thickening dusk I grew so horribly aware that I had nowhere to go. Agonised by the endless wait on funds, bored and without any other stimulation besides incessant children's television shows populated by nightmarish singing puppets, and a few illicit backseat fucks with a local copper, I grew agitated. Palpitating, almost insane with impatience, calling to check my bank balance every night at midnight to see if the money was there yet, if I had the funds to leave, turning crimson in the face when those mocking robot zeros taunted me over the phone. 'I can't stay here a minute longer,' I muttered to myself, grandiose and piss-elegant. 'My life can't be all potato waffles and bedtime tantrums! I'm a person of ambition and drive.'

I wanted to be a writer; it had replaced my child-hood dream of taking holy orders before I even started secondary school. My mother shook her head and despaired, and you, with your relentless middle-England attitude, would only ever ask, 'And what will you do for money, eh Bibby?' Although I had more or less ignored you in person, given you the cold shoulder and the slip in public, we struck up an easy rapport when at a distance again, during this purgatorial period after graduation. The connection there was so flimsy that I would have to walk over to the library if I wanted to successfully compose and dispatch a message to you. They started out as mean-ingless how-are-yous, sandwiched between searches for cheap flights and taps on the shoulder from the elderly librarian, reminding me that my allotted half-hour was almost up. But quickly and deliberately my emails grew more and more blue.

I promise at first it was just for my own amuse-ment, but you responded with something so enticing that I was taken in by my own game. It's likely that I seduced myself, reading your messages under my breath in the library, in my own voice, imbuing your words with my choice of intonation. In person you were so unappealingly self-aware, but here onscreen you were unpretentious and direct.

You wrote, 'When are you coming to see me then Bibby? When you gonna put your money where your mouth is?', and my body came alive.

I told my mother that I was going back down to London, to look for a job. I said I'd be back in a week or so. She said, 'Oh here we go again, the frigging wandering star! I never know if I'm coming or going with you.' But she wasn't upset, no, something like amusement played on her face as she waved me off again.

The inevitability of it all.

The Megabus to London took seven and a half hours, approximately the flight time across the Atlantic, but it only cost eight quid. This impulse, to pack up and go extemporaneously, on the spur of the moment, to throw all my plans out of the window and do the exact opposite of what I had set out to do, has come to define me. This and my insistence on running straight towards the thing most likely to do me harm.

I wasn't going to London explicitly to see you, it was just that I figured it would be as easy to eat toast and fret about money on Elsa's couch in Westminster as it was at home, and besides, maybe I would benefit from a few final weeks in the capital. There was an exhibition of costumes worn by the Supremes at the V&A, and the BFI were showing *Vertigo* on the big screen, though of course in my heart I had accepted that I wouldn't make it to either. I was heading to your bed and I knew it.

Elsa had been my first friend in London. We met a few months after I started at university, on a shoot for a jeans label, which neither of us should ever have been booked for. I felt as uncomfortable in the studded denim jackets as she looked in the tasselled miniskirts, and the whole discomfiting thing bonded us immediately. She'd spent her own childhood cutting her hair short with paper scissors, trying to look more like a boy; she spoke Swedish, Spanish, French and Italian; she'd been a model since she was fourteen and had picked up languages as other beautiful girls pick up fiancés. Her flat was in a very sedentary block, otherwise populated by members of Parliament and well-to-do old ladies. A friend of a friend owned it and let her have it for £400 a month; she had that kind of life, comic and sad, we spoke the same language. The whole place was full of canvases and half-finished collages, bits of costume, and tear sheets from magazines that hadn't yet been slotted into her portfolio. She was the only twenty-something resident in that inscrutable old building, which always gave her life there shades of *Eloise at the Plaza*.

When she saw me arrive from the window, she flung it wide open, singing the Queen of the Night aria out into the late June sky.

'Liza Minnelli!' she shouted. 'Listen to my song of rage and seduction!'

I chuckled and went inside. I don't know when it started or why, but as far back as I could remember we had always called each other Liza Minnelli. It was very confusing for a lot of people.

Every afternoon Elsa went to Costcutter to buy the same handful of ingredients. Baba behind the till was in love with her; he would light up each time he saw her, thrusting a pot of Onken into her arms and saying, 'Here! Your favourite yoghurt.' She cooked the same pasta dish each evening too, arrabbiata; she'd learnt the recipe when in Milan, skipping castings in favour of sketching in Da Vinci's vineyard. She welcomed me back to London with a bowl of this famed pasta; it was spicy and fragrant and I've never been able to eat it since without thinking of Elsa stuffing pillows up her shirt and pretending to be an elderly soprano called Victoria Plum as she cooked.

After dinner, I wrote a message to tell you I was in town, and promptly, as if you'd been waiting to hear this, you invited me over, you said, to watch the football. When I told Elsa that I was going out to see a friend, she said, 'Mon Dieu, Liza! You are an absolute tart,' kissed me on both cheeks and then sat back down at her sketchbook.

Perhaps it was the World Cup, or maybe the FA Cup final? Regardless, the game was of no interest to me. I only wanted to see if you could cut it head-to-head, devoid of the kaleidoscopic backdrop of nightlife, if you were as competent without the smokescreen of email free verse. You weren't, and sitting there upright and self-conscious in front of your tiny portable TV, I began to feel a little silly for having obeyed your summons to this fruitless conclave.

Your apartment was enormous. I think you said it had previously belonged to a radio station that had outgrown the place. It was one big room, which you had shoddily partitioned with plywood into a kitchen, two tiny bedrooms that you rented to unlucky acquaintances, and your own room, much larger. There was a photocopier in the kitchen and shelves of photographic prints, market stall garbage and old vivisected video cameras strewn about the place. The linoleum floor tiles were turquoise and worn through, the furniture was uncomfortable and mismatched, bulky and old-fashioned, and there was a taxidermied bird in a glass box scowling at the sight of it all. It was cool, even in summer it was chilly, but then your roommates had gone out, so we had the place to ourselves, and the slapstick, hangdog, outworn nature of it all was almost romantic.

You offered me cheese and cider, like we were in a pub in Kent, sitting nervously through the game, through the commentary after the first half, through the second half, through extra-time, through the post-match discussion, and every move you made towards me was more cumbersome than the last. I regarded you and your obvious discomfort from somewhere else, I was outside of myself observing from a distance. I could have said, 'Look! All you have to do is lean slightly *this* way, then that hand there will naturally fall *here*, it's that easy!'

But I didn't, I left you to your own devices, and I was quite sure that, come a little after midnight, I'd be making my excuses and heading over to Aldgate to catch the last train. Maybe you sensed that, though I know it's worthless now to try and decode what you had deduced back then, but all the same you took on a sudden pose of frankness, and reclaimed the tone I had gobbled up in your emails. Standing up and indecorously adjusting your junk, which being forever half-cocked was always jammed too tightly in your underwear, you shot me a look deep and inquisitive. You popped your head back, chin up, eyebrows raised, offering me for the first time this nod in reverse which I would come to know so well.

You said, 'So, what's the vibe then, eh Bibby?'

You never used my first name, you had upper-class pretensions, and besides my name was too masculine for what you considered me to be, or too Catholic perhaps, because though God rarely troubled your thinkings, my being a Roman always struck your good

Anglican self as ludicrous and Irish and peasantly. I felt similarly contemptuous of your trademark argot, and replied with a derisory snort, 'The *vibe?*'

'The vibe,' you continued, and your head gestured towards your bedroom door in two little spasms. Or rather, the lack of a bedroom door because all you had was a doorway, which I followed you through all the same. You sealed the cave by dragging another piece of plywood over the abyss, like the rock rolled over Christ's tomb, and we disappeared into the twilight of shed inhibitions. There were no curtains, only a cantankerous set of vertical blinds that would never descend, so the room was never more than murky, with light spilling in from all the restaurants in the streets below. I think it was Ramadan, so they were all full with late-night merrymaking, much to your obvious and immediate chagrin.

Your bed was very high and the sheets were pretty dirty. You seemed to pride yourself on being slovenly, it was your own little way of kicking over the apple cart, futile and unoriginal as it was. You kissed me like an amateur, graceless, breathing too heavily, but connecting your mouth to mine much too timidly, until I curled up my fingers in your hair and forced you to kiss me harder. That seemed to work, and you clambered backwards into your bed pulling your clothes from your long limbs with a lithesome dexterity I had not at all expected. Naked with your cock hard and already spilling something syrupy, you lay on your back and pulled me towards you, on top of you; now I towered over you.

My clothes came off with equal expediency, hitting the floor in a cascade of fabric, discarded pins and brooches, and I lay flat upon you. I felt your hips tilt, your bony pelvis rising violently from the left and the right, and, still totally silent, I felt you reach for my dick, wrapping your hand around it and squeezing it, almost painful, seeming quite satisfied with yourself, smirking in your caliginous bedroom. Your legs spread, your hairy ass crack rubbing deliberately on my stiff cock, you fingered yourself with your spit, and I started to fuck you with no niceties or formalities.

I could see that your mouth was open and murmuring, mouthing something, but still you stayed dumb and noiseless. It was like that throughout, as I fucked you hard and fast, then slow and tender, pulling out all the way to slam back inside you remorselessly. I knew you were enjoying it, you wanked your cock furiously, vigorously, and squeezed your hole tighter to drain as much pleasure as you could from me, and when I told you I was going to cum you opened your mouth wide and stuck out your tongue and I knew what you meant. Pulling out of your ass only just in time, I unloaded a copious stream of semen across your face and into your open mouth, splattering your cheeks and plastering your blond hair to your forehead. I kissed you as you continued to jerk off, and with merely a whimper in my mouth and four white jets, you decorated your own torso with another coffee cup full of spunk.

There was nothing sentimental about any of it, nothing romantic, no tender doe-eyed gazing, and yet I slept so soundly next to you, and you were dead to the world too. Even when daylight crept in, announcing another period of fasting for the neighbours you so scorned, we barely stirred until the high June sun began beating down on the bed, causing you to kick aside the duvet, causing me to marvel at your marble naked body.

Inevitably I began to run my fingers through your fair pubes, and you lying still as if asleep, let me play with your immediately hardening cock. Your balls, I noticed, were tight; I hadn't been able to scope you out properly in the demi-darkness of the night before. You had a funny little paunch above your hips, though the rest of your body was almost skeletal. I kissed you, regardless of your atrocious morning breath, and you responded hungrily, wanting not just my tongue in your mouth, but to feel me as deep as I could go inside you again.

So I lifted up your legs and put your feet in my face, I wanted to smell them, they were sweaty and dirty and made me as hard as I'd ever been. I went next to your asshole, taken aback by how perfectly pink it was, and licked it with all the tenderness that had been missing eight hours earlier. You never did have any patience though, and my amorous touches were wasted, trampled by your desire, your pressing need to be penetrated. Again I fucked you, with your calves on my shoulders, and your big beautiful feet poking out behind me like the Devil's own unfurled wings. This time you came first, spilling it all on your stomach, then rolling over to let me fuck you like a dog before I came all over your downy arse. Panting, I watched my cum trickle and dribble down towards the mattress as you stretched out languidly face-down on the bed in the sun, on those sheets for which the morning light did no favours.

I didn't shower, we didn't make plans to see each other again, I don't think you even offered me breakfast, anyway I would have declined. When I hit the street below, the windows of the secretarial college opposite your room burst open, and an almighty gale of screams came forth. Ten or fifteen business-casual ladies had been gathered at the window, watching as I fucked you, and (our foreign desire obscured to them when viewed through the fixed lens of their own rigid sexuality) they yelled out: 'We saw ya!! What were you doing to 'er, eh? Eh? We saw ya!'

They were laughing uproariously and not unkindly. It was jarring, flattering somehow, and alienating since usually I am the one read as a woman. I gave them an idiotic frat boy thumbs-up, sparking another riotous wave of hilarity which I heard all the way to the end of your street, 'We saw ya!', ringing out all the way to the tube, seemingly the whole way back to Elsa's apartment.

How many times? How many times did I leave your apartment after similar nights over the course of our incomprehensible acquaintance? How many sunny mornings did I walk into with a smirk on my face, how many evenings did I kick my way out of there molten with illogical rage? Numberless. There was no middle ground with you, which makes your own endless moral ambivalence all the more frustrating now I come to review it. You had no steady code of ethics yet you dealt in absolutes. There were only those you esteemed and those you detested, and I had the dubious luck of being pitched between the two like loose cargo on deck, thrown between prow and stern on turbulent seas. I'm not sure what I ever did to earn your desire or deserve your contempt, but I took comfort in knowing that this was how you acted with any number of people. I know I wasn't the only person who left your presence seething and cursing, and to quote my mother, calling you *fit to burn*.

Looking about me now, ten years since we met, six years since we last spoke, four years since your death, acknowledging this indefatigable era of puerile talking heads who have clawed their way to infamy, with a litany of manufactured outrages stoking their phony moral panics, I can't help thinking that you were a sort of John the Baptist for them all. I don't mean that as a compliment, only a thought that comes to mind when I think of the world we're left to deal with now.

But these aren't the things that are most pronounced when you are in love, they are truths which reveal themselves over time, like the bones of a skeleton as the flesh rots away. Somehow it's been a decade since that first fuck and I don't know where all the time has gone. Perhaps the heat of the affair has burned it all up? It's like that sad scene in *The Blue Angel* where the once-dignified Emil Jannings serves Marlene Dietrich as her handmaid, testing the temperature of her curling tongs on the pages of a wall calendar. He clamps the jaws of the tongs down on the date, scorching away day after day, month after month, until years are elided in a montage that lasts no more than a minute. This is how the years have gone by.

The gap between that morning, when I left your bed for the first time, and this extrasolar evening, from where I sit at my kitchen table in Mexico City trying to write it out, is bridged by a love story so white-hot as to burn my hands even as I attempt to put it down on paper.

Our letters are the only real archive. So affected, so antiquated; who else even wrote letters after the year 2000, besides you and me, and you and him, and him and me? They're unsophisticated and at points pretty embarrassing to revisit, but I kept them all, of course I did. I'm a natural hoarder, I'm horribly sentimental, and I always have one eye on the idea that someday these things might prove useful. So, I stashed your letters with my birth certificate, my change of name deeds, my passport, and the letters I wrote to you, which found their way back to me, along with drafts of other missives and unconnected pages, addressed to me but somehow forgotten on your desk until after your death. Now they're all spread out on this table together, both sides of the conversation, an endless tundra speckled with cigarette ash and dotted with cans of Coke.

Reading back over them now, I am beginning to discern the course they plot, from that first stolen morning to the fatal instant when I heard the news. To that afternoon when I lay squandering my final moments of innocence, in another unmade bed, staring at the screen, learning the horrible truth. And in such pedestrian words, nothing that carried the spirit of your Brutalist personality, or the sting of your infantile ire, or the sadistic poetry you threw around. Just an unpunctuated phrase, barely a sentence, tossed out into the world by a friend of a friend who had somehow heard the news before me. When did you know you were dead?

Of course, I didn't believe it, of course I thought it was a joke, a mix-up. I scrambled, naked and automatic, for my phone, and called the only person I knew had the authority to confirm it. Shaking, hardly able to breath, all I said was, 'Is it true?'

In the ragged way his own breath came, in the sorrow that filled the silence as he tried to speak, I knew that it was.

'Yes,' he said. 'Thomas is dead.'

With that single line came the mission to write this story out, it descended in totality, flickering like the tongue of the Holy Spirit above my head. But I would not accept it. I didn't believe I had either the talent or the moral sovereignty, and so I ran in the opposite direction, away from this nomination, to the Middle

East, Far East, to South America. But in every place I arrived I found some remembrance of you, an inscription or a legend, like the Viking graffiti carved into the marble at the Hagia Sophia, which told me you had been there before me. Pursued by these illusions, I kept on going, trying to find a plot of unspoiled earth, some place that wouldn't try to enslave me to your story. I roamed until I found myself waiting out the winter here in Mexico City, a place which I believed lay undisturbed by your spectral presence. And I was happy here, happy and complacent, until last night, when you rose up before me as if to say, *Come on then*, and I knew I could deny you no longer.

II

You were a photographer, you were a creep. Architecture is what you studied but photography is what you loved. You paid the same slavish Rabelaisian devotion to images of post-war buildings (which are now canonical but were then only ugly) as you did to pictures of young boys sliding off their underwear. You had a disorganised, xeroxed collection of both, dog-eared and stacked up, falling to the floor, an upheaval of your twin obsessions, a mess which would have become an archive I'm sure, had you lived that long, had you become that famous photographer.

You took pictures, all the time, sneaky snapshots at parties on cheap compact cameras, blinding people in nightclubs with those incandescent flashes, throwing a shadow up the wall, exposing reddened eyes, capturing revellers mouth-open, mid-revelation. Of course you never asked first.

You took pictures of the circles we inhabited, and the globe you travelled. You visited Iceland, South America, the coast of China; yes, you voyaged far and wide in your short life. Meanwhile, I managed to to-and-fro from California once a year, imagining that I was the one seeing the world. How hindsight embarrasses us.

It's almost as if that's her sole function – not reflection, not contextualisation, no, just a note to let you know, in private moments of contemplation, just to say, 'Oh dear, look what an idiot you were then.'

I've seen some of the places you photographed first-hand now. Sometimes, especially when passing through the capitals of Latin America, I almost thought I might discover you there, that maybe you'd faked it like a Nazi general and fled to Buenos Aires. It gave me the same uncanny sensation of nauseous comprehension, when I recognised a building from one of your pictures, as when I first saw the photograph of *The Falling Man*, plunging from the North Tower of the World Trade Centre, and remembered that I had been up there myself as a child in the nineties. Everything disparate rushes together in moments like that, and makes me feel like there is nothing beneath me anymore, as though I'm hurtling downwards too, like that falling man striking his beautiful pose, like an arrow, like a dancer, his final seconds now forever suspended outside of time.

You took pictures with cameras of dubious workability, on film of untrustworthy character, even when you were photographing a friend's wedding, or some other important moment that didn't seem well suited for pranks. Yes, it was irresponsible, it was selfish even (and that was motivation enough for you), but more than that, it was an experiment in seeing the world. The pictures might come out in strange ghostly greens, or as double exposures, as spectral blurs, or else they might not come out at all, leaving you only with twenty-eight black and shiny canvases of nothingness, streaked occasionally with red trails like an eyeball stricken with uveitis.

You photographed strange street scenes, tricks and lovers, the jungle, and always those same square ineluctable buildings, Brutalist, Bauhaus, which to my underclass eye could only ever speak of council estates and tower blocks, but which seemed to you (born of Kent's cricket fields) so bold and clean and honest, free of any frivolity, masculine, authoritative.

My own tastes have always been baroque, florid even; I always wanted everything in gold leaf, on Louis heels, candied fruits and marzipan, pencil eyebrows, turquoise walls, tea on the lawn, antique pearls, sadism in lipstick and rouge, jazz-age desolation, crumbling hauteur, genteel contempt, and a rococo attitude to accessorising. Clearly then your enthusiasm for stark grey buildings was lost on me. I couldn't appreciate these concrete hulks any more than I could salivate over your cache of slender, hairless boys posing nude for unseen, unknown pornographers.

I lived in one of those unforgiving slabs of modernity you adored until I was primary school age, until we were burgled by junkies, and the council moved us to a new estate near the docks. My grandparents lived in one too, on the fourteenth floor of a shoddy 1960s tower block. From their living room you could see out over the Mersey, and as a child I dreamed of flying from the window to somewhere new. I would stand, resting my chin on the window ledge, hypnotised by the sublime terror of being so far above the little houses below, panic-stricken in case I should somehow be taken by a gust of wind and dropped onto the street. Torpid in terror, but comforted by some proto-erotic sensation, I stared for hours out of the window, imagining how long it would take me to hit the ground.

I would ask my nanny in alarm and delight, what would happen if there was a fire at night? Knowing that we were forbidden to use the lift in case of emergency, I was paralysed with the holy fear of being trapped up there, with nanny in her wheelchair and my grandfather, still sprightly in his late fifties but hardly fit to carry her down a thousand blazing stairs.

'You'd have to go down with your granddad,' she said, knitting pragmatically, 'and send the fire brigade up for me.'

'I couldn't do that!' I exclaimed, disgusted at the idea. 'We couldn't leave you.'

'You'd have to, love,' she said, and changed the channel in time to shout her answers out at a favourite TV quiz show.

Having lived in them, having feared dying in them, I couldn't love those buildings like you did; that aesthetic of social uplift through moral discipline was not at all photogenic to me. I think of my nanny often, combing her waist-length grey hair, like a jukebox Rapunzel with her Doris Day records on display, dying of a heart attack, waiting for the ambulance, and I wonder now whose story I'm trying to tell. The way all of this comes together, every previous sorrow paving the way to you, as Agnes Varda put it, *the most cherished of the dead*.

You liked to amalgamate your collected softcore stock images of skinny naked boys with the photographs you'd taken of grave Soviet architecture. The boys were torn from magazines, ripped from the internet and printed on A4 home office paper, photographed from photographs, photocopied in greyscale. They were forever striking attitudes of such lascivious naivety that they seemed doubly lewd. That moment in front of the leering lens that memorialised their innocence (and concurrently the destruction of it) was surely where you found the erotic located. They were underage, or at least looked to be, and so you loved to flaunt them, enlarge them, and pin them to your wall, cut them out and glue them to envelopes, collage them in with pictures you'd found of long-defunct Ukrainian scientific institutes. Boys posing unconvincingly as soldiers or boxers, xeroxed with the contrast turned way up, or bleached and so drained of detail, slapped together, then copied again and blown up, so the whole monolith of soft dicks and dour concrete looked monumental and ridiculous.

The young boys and the Brutalist buildings have become inseparable now, and when I think about you, these fixations of yours rush to the front of my mind, vying for priority against images of your own naked body, your bike, your blue plastic comb, your handwritten letters, your VHS tapes, your erratic emails, your little tile of eczema, your Morrissey records, your cocked eyebrow, your crooked smirk, your insouciant swagger. A memory of you eating a bagel on Brick Lane one lost Saturday morning, whilst sorting through tables of junk, loses priority to the snapshots you found there, discarded 8 x 4s of vintage teens in their undies, taken by some other long-forgotten degenerate.

These images, these acts of twink-worship came from a tradition I wasn't a part of: a golden gay boy lineage, like a cool enticing stream, which I stood alongside but not in. I felt alienated by your desire for them, because I knew I wasn't a boy, surely, but didn't I feel envious too? Certainly I was uncomfortable when you showed me these pictures, but I saw how it made you smirk when I looked askance, so I tried to make my face register disinterest. I didn't want to seem prudish, like I didn't get it. Can I chalk that obsession with adolescent boys up to an immature desire (omnipresent with you) to stick out your tongue at conventional mores, and to do so using imagery we've all been conditioned to wilt at, to shrink in silent indignation when faced with? I'm not even sure it was sexual to you. It could have just been another stupid joke, another way to get a rise out of people. Or am I just an apologist now, has time made me an apostle for your paederasty and nothing more? Have I become president of your fan club, willing to bend over backwards, to pull off gravity-defying feats of logic to scrub your name clean? Like an old Peronista, weeping at the grave of Evita decades later, ignoring the despotism, forgetting the financial ruin, mourning the spiritual leader of the nation under the Andrew Lloyd Webber lyrics which actually, *ludicrously*, adorn her tomb.

Perhaps it's as simple as this: my flagrant, Romantic aesthetic is built as much on sentimentality as decadence (surely they're flipsides of the same coin), and now that you're gone everything that made you the curt, antagonistic bastard you were has gone with you, and all that's left behind is the narrative we want to circulate in your absence. Or maybe it's because after I read what the newspapers wrote about you I desperately wanted to resuscitate you, by scraping the insidious sensationalising homophobia (which introduced you briefly to a wider public) from your reputation. All of that trash, all of that *GAY FASHION PHOTOGRAPHER PARTY DRUG DEATH FALL SEX SHOCK* is what you get if you die young and handsome at a party in a house owned by someone very famous. Maybe you would've thought it was funny, maybe you would've got a kick out of the insinuation that your sexual desire was directly responsible for your death. But spare a thought for those of us who had to read it, suffer it, knowing there was nothing we could do to unwrite those tabloid lies. Those of us who took to scuttling about, beatifying you, petitioning for your canonisation, and adding you to that very, very long list of bastards raised to sainthood.

None of it makes sense. I'm trying to stitch these scenes from a life together, I am trying to master the art of cinematic collage, but I find the material has become amorphous. I can no longer tell what is true apart from what I want to be true anymore. It's like a movie I watched when I was high. The images shimmer somewhere in the murky depths, I know I have watched this film before, but I can't pull up anything I would trust as a real, true detail, because everything has been embellished by these years of grief, guilt and remorse. The celluloid has tarnished, it wasn't ever deemed to be worth much, it wasn't stored properly, so now the writer can't even decipher the director's name on the film can. I can no longer separate what happened onscreen from the stoner wisecracks I made whilst watching it. All I know is that I'm sorry.

How many times have I told you that? Prompted to sob by some asinine song playing in a department store, catching myself absentmindedly staring at a picture I've googled up, straining from the window of a bus to keep in vision a passerby who looks like you, muttering under my breath when I'm convinced you're in the room with me. It feels so different to write it down, though; it's somehow official, 'I'm sorry.' It's too late, I know that these words can't amount to anything more than artifice now, but maybe I can find some shelter for myself in that fabrication, in Nietzsche's maxim, *We have art in order not to die of the truth.*

You, Lulu, Finley, Morgan, Elsa; I have always been drawn to artists, to talented people, perhaps I was hoping that one of you might reveal my own gifts to me. In her living room, in between castings for modelling assignments, Elsa painted my portrait. Her world, with its bedroom views of Westminster Abbey, was so very different to yours, which opened up onto mosques and market stalls. She made colourful, almost tropical abstract paintings, sometimes sensual, always touched with something eerie, combining the verdant and the mordant, the way the old art school, Parque Lage, in Rio does, with its solemn, Italianate architecture sitting at the foot of the rainforest. And like you, Elsa collaged her own private universes, mocking up Victorian-looking spirit photography, pasting her face onto assorted mysterious beauties, and compositing the assembled chimera onto a swirling background of monstrous hand-illustrated foliage. Though your lives and works seemed light years apart (and I think I'm right in saying you never really liked each other) her fancies and yours commingled, came alive for me, like little devils. Ignis fatuus, populating my meditations and infiltrating my sleep all through that first summer; a parade of mirthless Slavic twinks gyrating against hulking pink Soviet observatories and dancing the rhumba with plumed phantoms through the Amazon.

William Burroughs said writing is always fifty years behind visual art but I think he was being too generous. I scrabbled behind you all, always envying you artists your freedom from the need to entertain, your independence from the onlookers. A collage or an illustration can gather dust in a frame, and still it goes on breathing, whereas a book and a reader are wasp and orchid, they depend on each other for existence; it's the act of reading which defines the written word, as Minae Mizumura put it. I have often longed to find another talent, something flashier, more instantaneous, to put before the public and leave to hang there. I tried to paint, I tried to dance, I even tried calligraphy, but nothing ever quite worked, it always felt like I was simply fighting against my own nature. I guess in penning this book I've come to accept the terms of my sentence; writing is the responsibility of the survivors.

A few months after you'd died I went with Elsa to the Whitechapel Gallery, right across the street from your flat. I saw a Hannah Höch cut-up, a strange turquoise-black whirligig called *Der Unfall*, which seemed to be comprised of four wagons colliding (though equally it could have been one wagon flying outwards in four directions). And looking at it, with its impossible logic and centrifugal force, I felt quite sickened again, overwhelmed by that same terrifying recognition, panicked as if the ominous white figure-eight at the centre of the accident were a void into which I was hurtling head-first. Elsa said that afterwards she went home and painted for five hours straight, 'Right up until the light went, like I used to.'

I remember that first summer of knowing you as being one extended sunset, eternally crepuscular. And if I recall it as being intensely warm (though it was probably just an average English crossfade from June to July) that's simply because it never rains in the past. Sometimes it snows when we look back, sometimes there are thunderstorms and heatwaves, but never drizzle. It's as though the extreme weather of climate change has already found a home in memory, and so I recall all the days of our first acquaintance as being sweltering, and all the nights as torrid.

There was always one more party, one more fuck, one more hangover to be had. I probably should have gone back to my mother's after a week or so on Elsa's couch, but it never seemed quite the right time to quit. I told myself that of course it wasn't for your sake I was sticking around, your delicious nearness was just coincidental, just a convenience to enjoy whilst I waited on the money to buy my plane ticket to California.

Each day I watched Elsa working at her easel, all the way to sundown, dozing on and off on her couch, until it was time for us to find the evening's entertainment. In truth we lived for the night, dressing up and crashing parties, assuming a new alter ego every twilight, and vying with each other to see who could get photographed for which magazine. We'd share a Toblerone, gifted by Baba at Costcutter, and dig about in my suitcase and in Elsa's wardrobe, putting together outfits comprised of hand-me-downs from her glamorous grandmother, shoplifted cocktail gowns and party shop schmatter. Thick as thieves, high as kites, we went roaring into the beautiful unknown. We would be out all night causing havoc, coming back against the flow of early morning commuters, having walked from Soho or Hoxton in our clown white and lunatic dress. We'd scare Elsa's unsuspecting, highly respectable neighbours witless, falling out of the lift, one shoe on, one shoe off, waving a polite, 'Good morning,' and stumbling down the corridor giggling in buoyant exhaustion.

Those nights had no end, we'd turn up at whichever party seemed most important, skip the line and air kiss the queen on the door. Sometimes it was Lulu, sometimes Tina, often Kalika.

'Girl, you look f-a-b,' I'd say. 'You know Elsa, don't you?'

'Sure,' she'd say. 'Go in.'

I went to my first gay clubs at thirteen, they have been the only real home I've ever known. They've always made me feel free and weightless, as though dancing in outer space. I can't think of any other explanation for how suddenly, after simply passing through a door and descending a spiral staircase, I find myself somewhere so different, other than if, by stepping inside the club, I'd actually stepped onto the surface of a forbidden planet.

The rules are all so different there, and not just those of decorum and morality – the very order of time and space changes. A disconcerting masquerade of half-recognised faces dazzle under strobing lights, making me dizzy with a cacophonous freedom, even while I'm still sober. A night at a party can last a lifetime, or flash by in the space of three songs; the dance floor can take a month to cross in a crush, or contract to the head of a pin, when 'Like a Prayer' plays and the whole club gives praise. Looking out onto the crowd, seeing no horizon to give the place a sky above or earth below, watching the waves of ecstatic bodies peaking like mountains, the lights flecking them all with gold leaf, making it impossible to see who is floating up, and who is coming down. You appear just as I'm thinking of you, or rather thinking of a picture of you in Brazil with a camera around your neck, wearing something you'd seemingly slept in.

We found each other every time, on the shaded outskirts of the scrum; though we always skirted each other a few times at first, neither of us wanting to seem too eager, too interested. We went through this reiterative mating dance countless times. Usually a mutual friend would bring us together with a wave, like an air traffic controller. I'd leave Elsa chatting in French to a girl from her agency, you'd leave whomever you were with, and we would pair off for a while. You'd say something infuriating just to get a rise from me, and I'd skulk off again across the dance floor, only to find you standing silently over my shoulder a few minutes later. We didn't go home together every time we saw each other, only most times, sometimes your petty provocations pushed me too far.

You were honestly so completely maddening, even the way you dressed was antagonising. I myself have always loved to seem a little anachronistic, old-fashioned, never knowingly underdressed, to look as though I'd found my clothes accidentally; but you, with your love of obnoxious slogan T-shirts and your irrational fear of the iron, simply took things too far. Nothing ever seemed to fit you, everything you owned was too big or too small, T-shirts that swam around your torso, sports shorts that seemed too brief, jackets that were just a little too short in the sleeves, and trousers that were baggy in the arse. Every ensemble cut through with a very deliberate attempt to exasperate, like you were trolling the very idea of getting dressed up.

You wore white vest tops, but not like an Old Compton Street rent boy; you were too skinny, you looked more like you'd left your sports kit at home and had been forced to do P.E. in your undershirt. There was a pair of purple polyester shorts that you wore in a way I can only call obscene, accessorising them with a little ribbon tied above your knee like a garter, which made them wholly indecent. Your Bart Simpson tie, your US collegiate T-shirts, those pornographically tight little boy Y-fronts you always wore, every outfit you wore had one element of Lolita to it, one touch of the infantilising and erotic (perhaps in homage to the low-budget twinks on your walls), each costume rendering you a giant kinky baby.

You had a solid collection of stupid things to wear on your head, picked up on your trips to find old cameras at still unfashionable markets in South London. I remember that you had a large hat in the shape of a pint of Guinness, the sort of thing pubs give away on St Patrick's Day, which you would wear with an entirely straight face to warehouse parties and private views. Since you always looked so downbeat and sorrowful (like a chastised public schoolboy), it didn't ever seem like you were wearing it for a laugh, but then you couldn't exactly be taken seriously in it either. I never told you that you looked like a twat, though often you *really* did look like a twat. For the record, I don't feel bad criticising your taste like this now, because I know you did the same to me. For example, that wide-brimmed wool fedora from Liberty, which I wore constantly in imitation of Bowie in *The Man Who Fell to Earth*. You rode past me when I was wearing it once; Lulu told me that you said, 'I saw Bibby yesterday, at the bus stop wearing a big stupid hat.'

'Sounds about right,' she said she had replied.

In the club, you watch me break off from my friends and head to the bar. You squeeze next to me in the scrum, flick my lapels, and say, 'Aren't you a picture of elegance, eh, Bibby?' Tired of your lamentable digs, I tell you to go and fuck yourself (which I now recognise as the whole point of the exercise) only to find myself on a night bus with you back to Aldgate an hour later.

III

That summer, when we were first lovers, I felt the sly smirk of a great social victory creep across my lips, spiteful yes but delicious. I felt it spread into a thin, narrow smile when I regarded you from across the bar or the pool table, pint glass in your right hand, the left snaking beneath the waistband of your football shorts, with only the thumb still visible. That little digit hooked over the elastic as if it were the line that bisected indecency into its two opposing fragments. Leaving your thumb to hang there seemed to keep things clean, somehow made you seem more timid than lewd. That lingering fifth finger was the one foot the Hays Code insisted stay upon the floor, when 1930s movie stars went to bed.

You'd catch my eye, screw up your mouth as if to say *hmmmm*, take a slug of your pint then turn back to your conversation. And that was enough. I knew that people would be talking about us, asking how on earth you and I had gotten involved in the first place, straining their suppositions to comprehend how it worked, squinting to see if they could bring us into focus, saying, 'I thought she'd gone off to America anyway?', frustrated maybe that there were no outpourings of public affection, no bust-ups to confirm what everyone somehow knew. It felt like a court romance, didn't it? But then London's social scene always was so nosy and provincial, full of such silly gossip. What did I care anyway? I was just biding my time until I had my ticket out of there.

Was there really any need for us to be so discreet? I think maybe you were just naturally uptight, though if I had asked you to hold my hand I like to think you would have. Or maybe these cold public poses allowed us a more fevered private experience? Knowing that I could do whatever I wanted with you and your fine blond body excited me immensely, almost as much as it thrilled me to act as though it was of no interest, until you took me home. I think it added a certain glamour to it all, this erotic nonchalance, and the feeling that we had a secret that people wanted in on. I liked the game, it felt like role play, I suppose I wanted to keep you on your toes too. I didn't want you ever to think that you had won me, that it was all in the bag. And I was more than aware that for you, the thrill was in the kill, not the feast. In that way at least we were very alike.

But looking at you, leaning on your pool cue like Doryphoros in a cycling jersey, looking so threadbare and vainglorious, I felt something like love course through me. Surely I had stars in my eyes, certainly my heart raced whenever we met, so perhaps I was simply steadying myself with my cool composure and haughty banter. It's too late now to ask, but would you have held my hand? Questions never asked become just like all the other flotsam and jetsam, tossed about on the tide, all things done and all things not done carried by the same currents, ever further out.

From an ocean of incidents I might choose to look back on now, one night remains lodged in the forefront of my memory. I can't say why. Disturbing and peculiar as it was, it was only one in a hundred such scenes I might reminisce about. But then, memory is electric: the images that come back to us most frequently are the ones we visit most often – it's like a self-fulfilling prophecy.

We're at the Joiners Arms, in that murky era between the times when punters stabbed each other behind the fruit machines, and when they fucked quite openly in the bathroom, a golden age between two tussling impulses: death drive, sex drive. I arrive late, it isn't very busy, a couple of people are at the bar, a few playing pool, another larger huddle on the dance floor, already wasted and *really* into it. We're there (like all the rest of them) because it's 2 a.m. and everywhere else is already closed. I've been performing, and so I'm dressed as some sort of nymphomaniac Christ; I have on a pink bra and a crown of gold laurels, strappy high-heeled sandals, and a burgundy sash which I've fashioned from a bedspread, or a curtain. I also have a streak of fake Halloween blood from a tube under my nose, though I don't know why. You regard this ensemble quite apathetically, with that upwards bob of your chin, the same kind of gesture you see from an otherwise static buyer bidding on antiques at an auction house.

'Alright Bibby?' you offer, in no hurry.

I nod, 'Yeah, good – you?'

With your right hand, you extend what at first I read as a gesture of a gun towards me, then you wrap the two straightened fingers around the twisted strap of my bra and say, 'What's all this then?'

It's a tender remark but one left unanswered because we're swiftly interrupted by a pair of junkies. A sallow, broken man in a grey baseball cap, chewing at his lips as

45

his eyes dart about in their sockets, escorts in a lamentable, excessively thin woman with yellow hair and blackened, insomniac eyes. He says to us, 'Eh guys! Can yous two look after my girl, yeah?'

We look at each other, already by this point in our lives imperturbable, and agree to do so.

'Sure,' I say, 'we'll look after your girl.'

As he disappears towards the back of the pub, I notice that this poor woman, now in our care, is bleeding profusely from a nasty gash across her thigh. The blood has soaked through her makeshift bandage, allowing it to slip freely down her leg into the carmine pooling at her feet. Startled, I think to myself, *I'm dressed as Jesus*, and wonder if this makes the scene all the more fitting or all the more perverse.

'Did he go to call an ambulance?' I ask you.

'Yeah, I guess, I dunno,' you say, and you seem irked, more by his bad manners than anything else.

I try to talk to our wounded charge. I'm amazed that she's still standing, but I can't get any sense from her. I don't know if she's high, or in shock, but it doesn't seem as though she's feeling any pain. I begin scanning the room for help, looking to see if I can find her companion, hoping he's been able to call 999 in his corrupted state. He hasn't. The wholly unnecessary strobe light picks him out on the dance floor amongst all the other mid-week ravers, he's pressed up at the centre of their throng, occasionally punching the air, out of time with the music.

'He's just dancing,' I say redundantly.

You look over your shoulder, then back at the dumbstruck bloodied body between us; your upper lip curves back at the corner in a comical snarl, as if to say, *What the fuck?*

Beverley, the landlady, clocks the situation and signals to the doormen. A purple-faced bouncer, with no love lost for any of the pub's clientele, wades into the small crowd of dancers with his neon vest popping in the laser lights. He grabs hold of this dissociated man by his T-shirt, and hustles him unceremoniously towards the door, in spite of his squirming and his protestations.

'Eh! Eh! Eh!' he shouts, pointing towards us, 'That's my girl!'

The bouncer turns on the spot, and for a moment I'm afraid the doorman will think it's me he's indicating. Instead he swings an arm out and snatches up our ward. He growls, 'The both of you. Out!' And the two of them are pushed back through the door and out onto Hackney Road.

'Drink?' you say, unmoved, already heading to the bar.

I trail behind you, all at once thinking, *Thank goodness that's over,* and also, *Did that just happen?* You have a pint, I think *Maybe I'll have one too? No, just a Coke.* Mainly I'm lost in my marvelling at the gathering on the dance floor, they're still going, oblivious. We don't stay much longer. We sip our drinks just slowly enough to put time between us and them, then we split, heading back to your house. The pool of blood is still there on the floor when we leave.

In a sweet act of chivalry, you wheel your bike alongside me, all the way back home. It's late when we get there, and you carry the bike up the cement staircase to your apartment, like a drowsy virgin bride. I think maybe I'm a bit envious of that bicycle, even though it seems ridiculous to say so. You're the first person I've ever known who cycles everywhere, and you cherish biking as an opportunity to splash some aggression about. When someone cuts you up or clips you, you milk it for every possible drop of aggro, it makes you feel more like a man to pick fights with strangers in a socially acceptable sort of way.

'You love that bike, don't you?' I say, with a little shake of my head, trying for an expression of resigned indulgence.

'Yeah,' you say, and you run your tongue along your bottom lip as you fiddle with the front door key. 'But not as much as I love a big dick up my arse.'

You make me snigger and I begin to ache for you.

'Come on then,' you say, and step inside.

One of your roommates is still up, sitting at the kitchen table fiddling with Logic or Pro-Tools, headphones half on, half off.

You give him a nod and then gesture in my direction, 'This is Bibby.'

Your roommate smiles the dopey-eyed smile of a stoner, and sighs a soft, 'Hey.'

'I need a piss,' you say, and disappear into the bathroom.

I sit down in the one chair that isn't piled full of records or VHS tapes. I can hear a muddy bassline seeping out from your roommate's headphones, it blends surprisingly well with the insistent hum-buzz of the fluorescent lights overhead, an accidental bricolage, only slightly unsettling. The whole place, well worn and overlit, has the feeling of a GDR interrogation room, Teflon and irascible, I feel sure that the mirror on the wall must be two-way glass.

That kitchen always felt more real than real, the way a film set does, when you pick a banana up from a fruit bowl and realise that it's plastic, it's a prop. The clutter and the reflective quality of the turquoise lino under the too-bright strip lights I found so profoundly disorienting. Like the time we went and stood in the middle of that Kader Attia installation with all the books and telescopes and engravings of medieval astronomers; looking down into a mirrored surface, catching another mirror above us, light bouncing back and forth, opening up a tunnel of illumination, breaking out through the gallery ceiling, spiralling up in eternal reflection, *The Light of Jacob's Ladder*.

The toilet flushes, you come out so quickly I know you can't have washed your hands. You stride across the living room, walk straight into your bedroom, turn aggressively to give me a short upwards nod, that gesture of insistence. I stand up and say goodnight to your roommate. He grins knowingly back at me, and I wonder what you've told him, or what he's heard through the thin-as-cardboard walls. I follow you into that familiar room, pulling the sheet of plywood over the doorway behind me.

IV

Yesterday I got an email from Finley, a friend from California. He is passing through London on his way to Berlin. He wanted to know if I was in town, obviously I am not. Finley is six hours into the future: his message reaches me at lunchtime in Tacubaya, but I understand that it was sent from Hoxton at twilight. It's strange to think of Finley there. When I picture him bustling down Old Street it's like catching a late-night movie in a hotel room and spotting a beloved star playing a bit part, years before the role that gained them fame. I haven't yet replied.

I don't often travel to that little slice of East London anymore, in my mind I tend to wander further out, Bow, Mile End, occasionally south of the river, Southwark, Waterloo, where memories are skimpier, if no less forgiving. There's something too painful in remembering how full of potential everything seemed back then when the world was ours. I find myself flinching from even happy memories now, for fear of discovering new ways to wound myself in amongst the rubble of a glorious past. *But such is the task in hand*, I tell myself, *the psychic I must remain open.*

When we were lovers we spent much of our time in Hoxton and Shoreditch, at the parties Jovian threw, he was something of a lightning rod for those of us who believed ourselves to be underground sophisticates. He had enjoyed a brief pop career in the nineties, in a band which had been hyped beyond hyperbole before disappearing from view after one lonely CD single, with barely anyone noticing. His events catered to those of us with shared interests in French literature of the 1880s and the Downtown scene of New York in the 1980s, we were all very much still enthralled by Rimbaud, the Blitz Kids, the Club Kids and Weimar Berlin; real entry-level stuff, though we quite earnestly thought we were reinventing the world.

Before I knew Jovian, my life in London was unremarkable; I lived in drab student accommodation, I drank too much cheap booze, a story so familiar, so pathetic I need hardly recount it. Our introduction was facilitated in the most byzantine fashion by a photographer I met quite by chance at the Covent Garden post office, who told me I had a look of Dietrich across the eyes and asked me if I'd sit for him.

'I take very tasteful portraits,' he said, 'I'm very serious about my work. I even have a website.'

The pictures were highly stylised black and white Hollywood glamour shots, he posed me draped over dining chairs, smothered in ancient furs, eyes rolled back like an orgasmic Madonna.

'Oh yes,' he said, 'Lili Marlene herself would approve!'

He was plainly fixated with the great star, he seemed to see her in everything. His tiny flat on Floral Street was a reliquary to her, an ageless obsession which had dominated him as far back as he could remember. As a little boy, he read in a gossip magazine that she was ill in bed at home, alone in Paris. He felt so terribly sorry for her that he asked his father if he could send her a sheepskin blanket, to keep her warm in bed whilst she recovered. Being the most upright of all movie queens, Dietrich wrote back to thank him for such a thoughtful gift.

'It brought her a great deal of comfort,' he said.

They'd kept up a correspondence all through the seventies, and he had her neatly typed letters bound in an oxblood volume, naturally I was quite dazzled.

'If you're interested in all of this,' he said, 'there's a few soirées you might like to try.'

He scribbled down some addresses on a sheet of Smythson notepaper, showed me out, then vanished back inside his grotto for good. I never saw him again after that strange encounter, but I took his suggestion and went to one of Jovian's parties that same weekend. I followed his advice to the letter and there opened up a mirror world of counterculture, it was really and truly life-changing, and all thanks to this peculiar meeting at the oversized parcels window.

The parties in petrol stations, the salons at the Savoy, the performances in church graveyards, the kind of affairs I'd read about in Derek Jarman's diaries, the scenes where I first saw you and your impossibly straight nose; it had all been waiting for me. I arrived and was accepted; in the chaos and uproar it was simply assumed that everyone who was there was there for a reason, no questions asked, no answers needed. And as the context changed my market value changed in relation to it; I was no longer a gawky, effeminate embarrassment to be seen with, I was a stylish, photogenic, charming androgyne. On the other side of the looking glass, everything I had always been reviled for became exactly what people desired from me; London was lotusland for a while.

When I saw Jovian for the first time, he was wearing a top hat and carrying a riding crop. I recognised him from one of the prints in the photographer's portfolio, so I introduced myself by saying, 'I think we have a mutual friend.' Everything was so easy then, doors seemed to open without my even having to knock. Jovian asked me what I did, I told him I was studying but that I wanted to be a writer.

He said, 'I'm sure you're very good, but I think you need a more *visual* medium. Have you ever been onstage?'

As a child I'd been too shy even to audition for roles in school musicals, so all I could do was shake my head.

'You must!' he said, 'Everybody must really, but you, especially.'

I didn't quite know if I should be flattered or not but I didn't have a great deal of time to puzzle it out.

'Look,' Jovian continued, '*As it happens* I've written a piece about Valerie Solanas' attempted murder of Andy Warhol, and *you'd* make a fantastic Jackie Curtis.'

He told me there was no need to audition, all of that was so old-fashioned, he believed in personality above all else. It wouldn't even be necessary for me to learn any lines, because the whole thing was pre-recorded.

'You just have to go onstage and *be*,' he said. 'I'm sure you can manage that now can't you?'

Jovian threw a cabaret every Friday night, in the back room of a very modish restaurant. Nestled in amongst all the artists' studios and Turkish cafes, the place had implausibly become a little Max's Kansas City, drawing pop stars, fashion editors and artists to the minuscule stage at the end of the bar, with its promise of extreme and original performance.

Crammed into the dressing room on any given Friday you might see Lulu painting her face like a Dada masterpiece, or Leo ripping up his tights, Helen and Dixie quiet and assiduous, like a pair of agnostic monks, Tina squaring up to whoever had strayed onto her bad side that day. No, it wasn't always entirely genial, there was a lot of jealousy and bitching, as is often the way in a company of such mixed ability, but Jovian did his best to keep us all from each other's throats.

I held Jovian in playful parental affection, even though he was a terrible gossip, but then that was half the fun. We told people ridiculous stories, that he was my father, or that we were working together, ghost-writing the memoirs of the last great Warhol starlet, Jackie Jackie Pizza Hut. Although he was less than ten years older than me, and although Jackie Jackie Pizza Hut obviously didn't actually exist, people were taken in, and would often ask me, 'How's your dad?', and would often ask him, 'Will Jackie Jackie come over for the book launch?' Jovian and I grew to be very close largely because of these silly games. I never knew how you ended up in that dressing room though, perhaps he thought his cabaret needed a dash of casual misogyny?

Backstage was really just a strip of cement corridor, with a few chairs pressed around the plywood plank which acted as a make-up table. It was cold and impractical, and to get to the stage you actually had to push your way out through the audience, a feat very few managed with anything approaching grace. The room was full of old wigs and dresses, a few disembodied vacuum cleaners, mops, buckets, props and lipstick-kissed bottles of red wine bought cheap at the offie, with empty cans of hairspray set rolling around the floor as one of us perennially scuttled about on their knees, looking for a lost eyelash, a safety pin, the back of an earring. It was never very clear what amongst the clutter was part of the act, and what belonged to the long-abandoned detritus of the place. Frequently the distinction was erased when some half-cut queen or inspired mime snatched up an old mop head and took it onstage as a final flourish, a finishing touch, saying, 'Well, it's a look innit?'

I'd done well enough with my mute Jackie Curtis bit to be offered a semi-regular slot on the bill.

'Doing what?' I asked.

'Oh anything, whatever you want,' said Jovian, 'As long as it's *visual*. And seven minutes or less.'

I remember arriving in a fluster to get ready to perform, one evening early in our affair, and finding Lulu there before me. It was the first time I had shared a dressing room with her, she was the acknowledged star, and I was very much the ingénue. She was in high demand; I'd watched her perform everywhere from after-hours clubs to Christmas parties on Bond Street, she was in fact only on the bill that night en route to a better-paying gig in Soho, naturally I was nervous.

When I came in she was already half made-up, and I felt as though I were trespassing, witnessing Diana at her bath. She paused her grooming and regarded me in the mirror with a very deliberate stare. I panicked that she might pick a fight with me, but instead she offered a vague smile, then returned to her reflection, to assess her progress in the time-streaked mirror. Emboldened, I sat beside her, and began to lay out my make-up and brushes. Maybe she didn't know.

'I hear you're off on your travels again soon, eh la?' she said quietly, turning her face from profile to profile with her fingertips to inspect the glow of the highlighter powder.

Caught off-guard, I asked, 'How did you know?'

'Jovian,' she said.

'Honestly,' I said, trying to force a breezy smile, 'I do wish she'd keep her gob shut sometimes!'

I always told Jovian everything. Until now, until writing this all out, I'd say that he was the only person I'd ever been completely honest with, about you. His status as den mother made him the natural repository for all of our secrets, and I felt a great need to spill the beans, to gush. I told him because, unlike a lot of people who knew you, he liked you. I told him all about you and me and the women across the road who saw me fuck you. I told him everything, really *everything*, how you infuriated me, how you infatuated me, and how the money to buy my plane ticket had finally come in.

'And is it love?' he had asked.

My cheeks coloured though I didn't reply.

'Well, he's a lucky boy,' Jovian said. 'A lucky, lucky boy.'

I swept a make-up brush distractedly across the crumbling surface of a doleful green eyeshadow, whilst next to me Lulu blotted her lips. Watching her deft touches, transfixed by how she could bring any persona alive with a ten-quid make-up palette and a party shop wig. She was a walking stretched canvas, the painter and the painted.

Pausing for a moment, she said, 'Tom's outside,' almost under her breath.

'Is he?' I asked, aiming for nonchalant but landing instead on self-conscious.

'At the back,' she said, 'He's reading later. Or so I gather.'

I wanted to be finished with my face quickly, but not too quickly; I didn't want it to seem like the news that you were there had propelled me to hurry along. If anything, I slowed things down, sharpened a few eye pencils which weren't all that blunt, taking long steadying breaths, still absentmindedly admiring Lulu.

She stood up and put on a red raincoat, then began to wrap bandages carefully around her industriously made-up face, leaving an artful gap for her bright red lips to bleed through. From the costume, I recognised the act she was preparing as one I'd seen before, a sort of plastic surgery parody number. I liked it, it was a segment of a longer show that I'd seen right there, at Jovian's cabaret, a few weeks earlier on my first evening out with Adam.

You were away in Kent that weekend visiting your parents, and Adam seemed like a tender distraction. We'd been flirting online for a while, he was from the North too, he seemed like the kind of boy who would ask before he kissed you. I thought, *Why not? He's cute and I don't owe anybody anything,* so I went out with this stranger from the internet. From our first embrace it seemed impossible that we hadn't known each other since childhood, we had almost identical birth dates, he had grown up poor and Catholic too. He gave me Colette's *Flowers and Fruit* and complimented me on the harlequin scarf I had borrowed from Elsa for the occasion, he was immediately a part of my life.

I brought him to the cabaret expressly to see Lulu; I had wanted to share a secret with him, the first, I hoped, of many. I could flatter myself that I knew her somewhat, exaggerate our closeness and offer up her brilliance to Adam as one might pop the cork on a magnum of Krug, pour a glass for everyone in the bar and say with only a smile, *Think nothing of it.* I took him there, to be suave, to be chic, to prove to myself that I could love not just fuck. Besides, where else could I have invited him? Onto Elsa's couch whilst she was at a casting?

Adam liked the show. Watching Lulu onstage with him on my metaphorical arm made me feel like Proust's narrator watching La Berma; I was hoping to be bathed in her reflected splendour, hoping that she would act on him like an aphrodisiac, like a can-can girl, that he would fall willingly into my arms. She had after all thrown her light on you and transformed you from a lurking presence into something very desirable, so I believed she could cast the same lustre on me. I was clearly so taken by Lulu that it begs the question now, *Well why didn't you just go home with her then?* Though at the time I could no more have propositioned her than I could have seduced the Venus de Milo, and anyway I think she thought of me only as one more wide-eyed admirer. Ultimately I wanted to be up there with her, I wanted to have that power for myself, to wield it over suitors without any unnecessary intercession.

Adam commented that he'd never seen anything like Lulu's show before. It was a series of clever little vignettes, sometimes quite daft, sometimes quite daring, each set to pre-recorded music in a style some clever soul later called vocal masking, but which back then we knew as lip-synching. Like all the great silent stars, Lulu remained mute. At one point she climbed up a perilous stack of dinner plates in her platform shoes, then later on did her bit with the surgical bandages. When I saw this section for the first time with Adam, there were actually two of them onstage. I remember that Lulu brought a partner out and made it a duet, they were dressed identically in gauze and red raincoats, black bob wigs and sunglasses. In synchronicity, to the tune of 'You're So Vain', the two bodies snapped their fingers, swung their hips, and stripped off their bandages, a burlesque of Burlesque, dancing neatly rather than passionately in their knickers and bras. From inside each lacy cup they pulled half an orange, which they squeezed on the beat overhead, juicing the fruit straight into their mouths.

I suppose that evening was what one might affectionately call a first date, but that too seems so impossible now; that two people who aimed ultimately to get each other naked would set a time and a place to meet, and spend the evening sharing some cultural experience, as a sexual Vorspeise. Of course you, my fuckable Frankenstein, you my postmodern neanderthal, you preferred to cut to the chase. I always had the very distinct feeling that you considered romance effete, inessential, too gay for you to waste your time on, when you could get a shag just by looking your intended dead in the eye, massaging your crotch and shrugging, *Come on then*.

It's a funny thing how all these memories now entangle themselves like snakes fucking. Whenever I hear 'You're So Vain' I think of Adam, then I think of you, then I think of Lulu dressing backstage, putting on her bandages to re-stage that routine, the two of us sharing the greasy mirror, and Tina casually cursing the bastard who had moved her wig. I remember how Lulu repeatedly smoothed over the creases in her raincoat to no real effect. I don't think I had ever imagined that before curtain-up she might well be as anxious as anyone else. I was still skittish myself, hanging back, knowing that you were outside. I suddenly wanted to remain in the dressing room forever, to extend the moment with some casual chit-chat, and so, off the cuff I asked Lulu, 'What happened to whats-her-name who used to do the "You're So Vain" bit with you?'

Unmoved and impatient, from behind her bandages she said, 'Gone. I got sick of her always stealing my material.'

I took what felt like a hint, zipped up my make-up bag, and went outside into the audience. Not to look for you, but to bump into you. The first performers were already sequestered behind the curtain, the show was about to start. I sat down next to you in the corner, incuriously, just as Leo came onstage, screaming over a Yoko Ono track, black make-up smudged down his face.

'Shit,' you said, issuing your one-word judgement.

You and Leo were on the outs, I surmised, maybe he'd brushed you off, had enough? It was possible, he was frenetic and restive, and only sixteen. You sat low in your chair, slumped and sprawled, always too big for the furniture, sipping a pint. We'd complicity agreed to meet there, an arrangement provided with good cover by the coincidence that we were both performing that evening, amongst the ambrosia salad of our peers. Neither of us had directly told the other we'd be there, and I sometimes wonder if we were ever really that different.

After Leo came Jovian in a white tux singing Duran Duran, then Tina who made a pancake and did the splits, then Helen who sang 'Where Is My Mind?' with absolute sincerity, then Lulu herself. She performed her number, peeled off her bandages, calling me, like a painting of a painting in a painting, mise en abyme, backwards to that night I brought Adam as an offering into her temple. Sat beside you, I watched myself watching this same routine a few weeks earlier with him. Remembering how Lulu's magic had worked like a charm on him, how there was clearly something serpentine to our interactions, because while he was at the bar, Dixie had asked, 'Who's your new fella then la?' and made me blush.

At the end of that night, the end of our date, out in the purple haze of deep summer, when we had strolled back to the tube station, Adam had said, 'Do you want to keep on walking?' What would you have thought of that I wonder? Would you have been jealous? I hadn't asked myself that question, instead I had said, 'Yes.'

We walked for hours, all through the city, as far as Tate Britain. When we stopped to rest on a bench outside the museum the sun was rising, and the flowers above our heads were beginning to drip nectar. Am I right to think there were lilac bushes outside the Tate then? Or was that a mirage? Adam said to me, 'I think it's time for someone to kiss someone now,' and I was giddy with the saccharine rush of the situation, as that someone became me, leaning in, musing, *So this is love?*

We kissed for a long time, and until now that has always been where my memory of that morning has ended, with a romantic close-up and fade-out. But here in the full light of recollection, I recognise a new detail. I have pressed too heavily on the plasterboard wall of the past, have fallen through, this text is beginning to surprise me. I realise now that this dawn scene wasn't always destined to end with a kiss.

Adam had said, 'Do you want to come home with me?'

Uncharacteristically coy, I had said 'No,' and there never again came a second chance, try as I did for as long as I did. Isn't that sad? Not a great tragedy, but a sorrow at least. I would've liked to see him tender and sweat-stained, cunt-struck and exhausted. It would've been one more rose on your grave if nothing else.

All this time I have believed myself the passive agent, seen myself as the slighted, the victim swept aside by forces I could but acquiesce to, what an idiot, what a child! *I played it that way.* And why did I decline? Adam was suffused with a quiet sexuality; he was well mannered and polite yes, but I recognised these niceties as simple royal icing, frosting over an evident sexual prowess. I knew from his kiss that he'd be dynamite in the sack. Was it modesty, then, that persuaded me to bow out? Was I simply tired? Or was it in actuality, when the morning sun rose and cleared away all those nocturnal hidey-holes and half-truths, that I was already too lost to you?

Stripped of her final bandage, Lulu takes a bow, you clap loudly and nudge me to say, 'Nice.' Then Jovian comes back on to introduce you, and without ceremony, without any *wish me luck* chintzery, you stand up and walk directly to the microphone, a patina of applause greets you, then the soft soundscape of gentle expectation, cleared throats and resting glasses as you begin.

You look so tall up there, clutching the loose leaves of your poems, so long and impassive. The spotlight quite often reduces a person to half-size under the collective scrutiny of an audience, but on you it acts like a magnifying glass, enlarging you, distorting you. The incongruity of seeing you in this context, in your crumpled attempt at formalwear, flanked in time by extravagant femininities, Lulu and Leo. This, along with your pale height, and your indecipherable facial expression, gives me the wildest feeling of déjà vu. You look like nothing more than that rigid gentleman, captured midway to an oratorial pose by Manet in his painting of a triptych on a balcony. You're so pompous, that cheesy oversized necktie of yours flailing around at your waist, as you toss off nasty, angry, brutal lines of poetry without any sign of pain troubling your face. Your words divorced from your actions, an occasional smirk, almost sociopathic, incandescent and irrepressible in your ire, a ridiculous enigma. *Why were you so angry all the time?* and other unanswered questions.

The stage is barely raised (like standing on a pair of old phonebooks maybe) yet you seem three storeys high, 2D and tabular, pushed back against the wall of the shallow stage behind you, upright, almost flat, like Manet's three figures. It is an impossible painting: I have stood before it, almost eye-to-eye with that mournful threesome, yet they're supposed to be up high on a balcony, so how can this be? Am I floating in mid-air? Looking at you onstage, you seem so far above me, yet I know you are really only raised a quarter of a metre, and I'm equally perplexed. Are *you* floating in mid-air? Before you're finished I leave you on your nimbus, and quietly return backstage to grab what I need because I'm up next.

I shiver in the dressing room, listening to your final lines muffled through the wall. There's some more tepid applause, and then Jovian's voice returns to the microphone. I open the door a crack, so I won't miss my cue, and Jovian introduces me, lavishes me. He tells the audience that they're in for something special, and asks, 'Are you all having a good time?'

Waiting for the introductory rites to be over so I can get on with it already, I gasp, am quite aghast, when I hear him say, 'This is Miss JJ's final performance here, or anywhere in London, for quite some time, because on Tuesday she's back off to sunny California!'

'Shit!' I say to myself. 'Shit, why is he saying that? Shit!' And then a gentle ripple of cheers carries me onstage.

It's supposedly an honour to close the show, but you see I've always been set a little on edge by secular traditions (I find them as sinister as convention) so I come out holding an ice cream in silence, a spectacular non-event. I take the audience in, trying to make out faces for a moment, but when the light is shining on you, everything in front of you is obscured, and so the room remains populated with unnameable figures. I blink, waiting for it to happen, and slowly enough it does. The opening refrain of 'Everyday Is Like Sunday' rolls out of the speaker system, and the audience giggles in the dark. I regard the ice cream cone in my hand, as it starts to melt under the lights and dribble down my wrist like a satiated cock. I let the white whipped cloud of sickly, foamy Mr Whippy tilt wildly in the wafer cone, like a drunk leaning on the bar, with the flake heaving over to a 45-degree angle, a single-mast schooner about to capsize. I watch it collapse, I watch it liquefy, just as I had watched Leo thrash about, and Lulu strip, and you recite, and Helen sing. I watch it melt, but I do nothing. The song continues to play but doesn't prompt me to any action other than observation, the ice cream overflows the cone and begins splashing to the floor in thick pearly drops, a sticky little puddle forming at my feet, and the song goes on.

I know that track is three minutes thirty-five, but I also know that time is just a pick-up line, just an advertising gimmick some dot com bro made up. For the duration of the song wristwatches stop working, the melting of this ice cream cone is the thawing of an ice age, the blink of an eye is the fracturing of Pangaea in three acts. All time is already here anyway, it's only that we don't readily have the equipment, or the life span, to see it from above as an omniscient God must. For a housefly a second is a year, time is measured by the heartbeat; for a whale a year is a moment too brief to notice, and they mourn their dead too. Time is just the passing of heat towards cold (purely by chance, it's not a fixed law), the changing of states.

How can I explain myself? I have an incalculable wealth of time in these three minutes thirty-five, to look at myself on this precipice and ask if walking off the edge of the continent again is the right thing to do, but I don't reach anything like a conclusion before the ice cream falls sadly to the floor, with an anticlimactic splat. The track fades out and the bemused applause of the restless audience brings the present moment onstage, like an understudy who never got her chance to shine, finally allowed to take a bow with the company on closing night. I curtsy and step out of the footlights. In the dressing room Lulu looks at me dryly and says, 'Oh la, you've got strawberry sauce all over your slingbacks!'

Changing took some time, the confined conditions of the dressing room made the whole process infuriatingly slow. I packed up, posed for a few group photographs, and shuffled out into the empty performance space, it looked so unkind. The house lights were on, the ambience and the audience gone, the grey cement of the floor looked slimy in its thin coating of ticker tape and broken glass. You had waited. I was surprised. I'd thought you would for sure have been at the Joiners already, trying your luck with some easy mark, but you had waited, leapling, you had waited.

You looked pissed. You said, 'Nice of you to tell me,' with snotty, ironic disdain.

'I know,' I said. 'I'm sorry. I couldn't find the right time.'

A taxi arrived, and beeped its horn.

Jovian came out from the dressing room, pulling a suitcase, with a suit carrier slung over his arm, his face wet-wiped of most of its make-up, his bulging Bette Davis eyes a little red from scrubbing too hard, but his charisma barely smudged.

You looked at him angrily, and said, 'Bibby's going to California on Tuesday,' as if you hadn't just heard him say that.

'I know,' said Jovian, puzzled, 'I know that.'

You said, 'Oh you know do you, yeah? Cool, you already know,' but only to antagonise.

Jovian looked at the two of us, taking our measure, his eyes passing from my cheeks, stained with a flush of shame, to your almost quivering bottom lip, and back again. He said, 'My cab's here.' Then he squared his bag on his shoulder and said calmly, pragmatically, 'You two should go home together.'

He blew a camp little kiss back at us over his shoulder, as he pulled the suitcase behind him out into the hallway that led into the street.

'Alright,' you said, still shirty but somehow soothed. 'Come on then.'

I knew I should be getting back to Elsa's, to begin the process of cramming everything back into my suitcase because it always takes me days to pack, but instead I followed you out onto the desolate garbage-pocked street, in the direction of your flat, with my bags of costume and make-up dragging behind me. We didn't make it very far. Just a few streets over, you veered off course, gestured for me to follow, and disappeared down an alley behind a mechanic's shop, obviously a spot you'd visited before. Straight away, you kissed me, hot and breathless, tugging at my belt with one hand, unzipping your fly with the other, but I didn't know what to do with my bags amongst all the unseen trash of the street. While you slapped your hard cock on my belly, I flailed about in the dark, trying to kiss you and keep my belongings off the grimy pavement. Impatiently, you took the bags from me and promptly dropped them to the ground, saying, 'Fuck's sake Bibby.' But that is who you were.

Overcome, and with both hands freed, I reached for the firm globes of your arse, and pulled you closer up against me, and you dry-humped me like a randy little dog, rubbing your hard dick on mine. I parted your arse and slid my fingers, middle and index, down over your hole. With just the slightest pressure I was inside you, and your dick jolted upright, you broke off from chewing my bottom lip and grunted. The moon materialised again, briefly, and revealed your face to me, twisted with the same ecstatic expression St Sebastian wears in all those salacious paintings of his martyrdom. You drove your hips back hard against my hand, forcing my fingers deeper into you, grazing my knuckles on the wall behind you, throwing back your head with your blond hair all askew in the tender moonlight. My God you were beautiful, my backstreet Endymion, with your pants around your knees and your foreskin drawn back in perfect excitement, leaning against the brick-work like the sort of boy Thomas Eakins was always pining to paint.

'You gonna fuck me?' you said.

'Here?' I asked.

'Yeah, course,' you said.

And you turned around to show that you were serious, spread your legs as far apart as your trousers would allow and tilted yourself forward at the pelvis. Resting your forearms on the wall, you arched your back up, and I didn't hesitate. I forced my cock into you, pressing against the surprise and resistance of your hole, forcing a groan from you that stuck in the back of your throat, and sounded like the low moan of a man who had been wounded. This new timbre turned me on, and so I was not gentle, I was rough, but I was also scared, so I fucked you hard to be done with it. I took hold of the back of your head, grabbed a fistful of your hair, careful to keep your face from smashing against the wall as I hammered away at your arse.

You turned to look at me over your shoulder, and in between a few soft low groans, you asked, 'Will you be back?'

'What?' I asked, not breaking my stroke.

'Will you be back from America?' you repeated.

'Yes,' I said, 'Of course I will.'

You pushed back against me harder and harder, taking the very last inch up your arse with a whimper, wanking your own dick madly. You moaned, 'Cum. Cum, cum in me.'

I let myself go, throwing all the energy I had into fucking you, you perfect slut, as hard as I could, until I emptied myself into you, filling the mystery inside you with spunk, as your body contracted around my cock and you buckled at the knees. After a moment of silence, I pulled my dick out of you, you gave a little yelp of discomfort. You straightened up slowly, and turned towards me. Your cock was still at half mast, dripping cum onto your pants and your shoes. You kissed me again, without pulling up your trousers, and I put my fingers back in your hole to feel the warmth and wetness of my semen inside you.

You repeated the question, 'Will you be back?'

'Of course,' I replied.

But I don't know if either of us really believed it.

PART TWO

'It's impossible for the human mind to dominate
the things which haunt it.'

— IRIS MURDOCH

I

Waking up on a plane, in the cool blue transatlantic air of panic and confusion, lost and alert to the sure knowledge that any moment could be my last. Inflight slumber, deep and fitful, knocked out by the cabin pressure, the reduced saturation of oxygen into haemoglobin, the attendant emotions that accompany international travel, exhaustion, excitement, equanimity all taking their sleepy toll. Suspended in a limbo of imperceptible movement at 40,000 feet, cruising between states of being, European and American. The impermeable silence of the cabin, like a shroud drawn over a corpse, the palpable terror of waiting for it to happen. Waiting for someone to pull out a foldable utility knife, a can of mace, to detonate a shoe bomb, to stand up and yell, 'Stay in your seats! Do *not* move.' The sound of the aircraft's engine roaring, the passengers screaming, as we drop seven miles down towards the ground. Terror-stricken, I wake from this recurring nightmare and, taking brief comfort in the stillness of the flight, immediately fall back into the cold sweat of a new dream.

I arrived in California, in what now seem impossibly uncomplicated circumstances: sunshine, second-hand clothes, and communal living. You didn't really care for Yanks, for psychobabble, for PC culture, for flag-waving, or people who spoke second languages, and there I was taking up residence on 26th and Mission, San Francisco. If I'd have wanted to rub salt into the wound of my abrupt departure, I couldn't have chosen a better address.

After buying my ticket I had around $200, maybe $250 but no more, and I steadfastly clung to the belief that this would see me through until at least September. What was there to pay for anyway? I was sharing Robert's room, above a laundromat in the Mission, drugs were relatively cheap, and I ate almost nothing but M&Ms. I didn't need luxury, I didn't need comfort even. I was there to dash myself on the rocks of the city's subculture, to combine myself body and soul with a literary heritage that could claim the work of Ginsberg and Didion, Mark Twain and JT LeRoy as but a small part of its gift to the world. I didn't intend to do so through any devised course of study or network of agents and publishers, no, but simply by turning up and being more relentless, more demented, and more ambiguous than anyone else. Surely this would lead swiftly and effortlessly to at least a modest fortune before fall came in? I recount all of this now and somehow the mood I write in catches your own tone of detached disdain, resurrects your slight sneering at my endeavours long after the fact of your death.

Robert was your all-American counterpart, only taller, more affable, with better teeth. On a trip to LA he'd been scouted as a menswear model and had declined (politely) on the grounds that he didn't feel it was necessary for him to replicate the great white beauty standard any further. I thought his response was at once fantastically self-aggrandising and absolutely right on – he had such an appealing lack of self-aware-ness. I couldn't ever picture Robert in fashion, posing in underwear, advertising sunglasses; he was too inno-cent. Instead he worked at a call centre, part-time, while he finished up collecting the missing credits he needed to officially graduate from Berkeley, that great academic alcazar across the Bay where he and I and Morgan had all met. I don't think my presence in Robert's bedroom helped his lackadaisical scholastic ambitions any; certainly it made him almost eternally late for work, which was foolish, as we depended on him as the sole breadwinner.

Morgan had the small room off the kitchen, just big enough to fit a single bed and a suitcase of clothes. A beaded curtain hanging in the empty doorway, it reminded me of your room, only hers caught the full weight of the late-morning sunlight and so always felt like the cabin of a small yacht. The uneven floorboards and the not-too-distant rumblings from the laundro-mat below added to this feeling of being at sea, riding the crest of a wave, bobbing on the rolling ocean.

While Robert was at work, Morgan and I spent our time trawling the internet for odd jobs, $50 here and there to sit for artistic photographers, or proof-read sophomore essays. Morgan had also never quite graduated, she'd served her time but there was some un-filed paperwork, some incomplete requirement, which prevented her from obtaining the full and public blessing of the University of California. I reflected that by the time I had arrived in San Francisco, my own degree certificate was probably being posted out to my mother's house, and this bureaucratic achievement made me feel somewhat distinguished, there on the breadline.

Morgan had read my writing. I'd never shared it before, I'd barely even spoken about it with anyone else. I'd tried to keep it from her too, but she was so full of curiosity, and so little curbed by boundaries that my psychic armour quickly buckled. I had been sitting and scribbling one morning whilst she scoured for jobs online, trying to conceal my actions, closing the book each time she tried to peek.

'Oh just show me already, you silly tart,' she said.

I shook my head, sighed, and vacated my seat so she could sit and read from my notebook.

'The passive voice is used a little too often,' she said, 'but you really are quite good.'

I thanked her, and she continued, 'The problem is, no one is really just a writer anymore. You have to be a slashie, you know? A writer slash activist, writer slash filmmaker, writer slash performance artist. Or whatever Miranda July calls herself. You need to get eyes on you.'

'Do you think so?' I asked.

'Yes of course,' she said, 'This isn't La Belle Époque darling, attention is currency! Perhaps we can tell people you're Tracey Emin's godchild. People love proximity to scandal.'

She handed me my notebook and turned back to the search for odd jobs, leaving me to puzzle on the accuracy of her assessment and her diagnosis of my condition.

'Oh look,' she said, 'there's an old lady in Alameda who needs help digitising her black and white photos. We could do that, it's $25 an hour too. I'll write.'

After panning for gold online all morning, occasionally turning up alluvial nuggets, more often just pulling up wild onions, Morgan and I would walk the Spanish streets of the Mission. All of the world's great cities are more truthfully confederations of small villages banded together by asymmetric geography, and none more so than San Francisco, where each neighbourhood is also distinguished by its own microclimate. The Latin bohemian heart of The City (never *San Fran*) is gifted with an almost Central American weather system, with long, hot, dry afternoons, in dreamy comparison to the famous foggy scenes of Outer Sunset or Ocean Beach.

'This was New Spain,' Morgan said. 'Before California was Mexico.'

This seemed self-evident; San Francisco had never felt like America to me. People always talk about how European the city is, I suppose because it's not done there, to openly carry a gun or tattoo a swastika on your forearm, but really San Francisco doesn't belong to North America, or to Europe either. SF is not a place, not really, it's more a state of mind, an overlapping, a fault line from where you can hear the sighs of the unavenged Ohlone, Asia's golden gates swinging open, the last startled gasp of the Viceroy.

In evoking these memories of how vividly life throbbed for me in San Francisco, I ask myself if this is why I came to settle, to rest, to write this out in Mexico? Did this country become home for me because I had, in a way, lived here before? Surely it's no mere coincidence. I remember the insatiable sunshine pouring down on the perpetual streets of San Francisco, how they ran on and on for thirty city blocks, making me feel delirious, faint in the brilliant light, like I was coming up on MDMA. Morgan and I, two dispossessed Catholic children making our way past rows of dollar stores, taquerias, beauty shops and bodegas, and always to the mesmeric soundtrack of the same reggaeton cuts, played loudly from the windows of the same cars circling the same streets as aimlessly as us, ambling amongst the camp and holy curios, the glow-in-the-dark Virgins, the Jesus Christ clocks and the bemused faces of all those glossy statuettes of Saint Francis himself. Morgan was adopted, I was far from home, this promenade was imbued with solace and solemnity for us; we came to recognise the children playing in the street, and the mendicants, and the mystic who camped out on the pavement near the social security office and shouted to me, 'Don't you be ashamed of those freckles, child! Don't you dare! Because they're kisses from the angels, and when you get to Heaven they'll know. My God they'll know!'

At a point we'd turn off Mission and walk up two blocks, onto the corridor of murals that ran down Valencia, where the sophistication had already set in, had started to manifest in tattoo parlours, vintage stores, and coffee shops with chic and elaborate brewing methods. This was our day then, settling in to an iced coffee and masquerading as members of the fraternity of solvent San Franciscans, who either talked loudly on their cell phones, or else read otherwise overlooked tomes on US culpability for coups across Latin America, with amassed self-satisfaction.

Our goal was always the same, to meet new people, people who might hook me up with a gig or better yet, give Morgan a job. She had skills and citizenship and she was undeniably gorgeous, perhaps the most beautiful woman I'd ever known. She wore her hair up in a loose, messy chignon, above her great doe eyes and tiny pinched nose, her glossed lips and her distinguished cocktail-party shoulders. Her adopted mother had been a socialite from one of the city's first families, before she went back to the land, alongside her nobody construction-worker fiancé, with whom she spent all the money she had buying acres for utopian development, right before the big financial crash that left her broke and ostracised from polite society. Morgan grew up amidst European furniture and fine marble fittings, in a house which forever remained a testament to the highest fashions of 1972, on acres and acres of empty, barren, undeveloped land. Her best friends were the packs of stray dogs she found running around, and it was quite apparent that she'd learnt how to behave as much from the hounds as from her genteel, *No, no dear, don't sit like that* mother.

We devised a system to meet people, in which one of us would strike up a conversation with whichever stranger the other wanted to talk to. I'd chat casually with someone who we had overheard talking on the phone about hiring at their new boutique, making charming feel-good small talk. Some way into the conversation, as if by perfect coincidence I'd add, 'Oh! And have you met my friend Morgan? She's just graduated from Berkeley and she's looking at jobs in fashion.'

In return Morgan would ask to borrow a lighter from any of the club kids, curators or party promoters we might see outside the cafe, waving me over mid-smoke, with the introduction, 'This is JJ, my dear friend from London – a very talented artist working with text, and looking to get involved with things out here.'

I'd grin awkwardly, shake hands with a line of strangers like the Princess of Wales at a movie premiere, and Morgan would continue inventing new ways to talk me up.

'All the work is about gender,' she'd say to these people she barely knew, flashing her dazzling hostess' smile. 'I think you'd *really* like it.'

It seemed so much nicer like that, and it covered our tracks a little. In this way, though we never landed any real opportunities besides the isolated suggestion of an interview at a start-up, or the promise of an email exchange with someone who knew someone with a new space opening, we did score a much wider social circle than we might have otherwise enjoyed. Kip, the barefoot poet who lived in a caravan in a friend's garden; Uni, who dressed up as a unicorn and played love songs in shop windows on the ukulele; and Rumi Missabu, the septuagenarian drag queen who had ossified in low-level celebrity since his stint as part of the legendary Cockettes, around about the same time that Morgan's mother had forever despoiled the family name. And of course would-be lovers. Morgan would also send me up to the counter to ask a question to which I already knew the answer, which I could convey into an offhand quip to the customer behind me, from where it was only a short step on to, 'Oh! And have you met my friend?' Never was so much optimism raised against so little hard capital, but we were quite happy.

Once our welcome was truly worn out, once the ice cubes had melted down to two inches of water at the bottom of our glasses, when there was nobody left to casually bump into, Morgan and I would head back towards the BART station, to pick up Robert and make our daily pilgrimage to El Farolito. Robert spoke Spanish, he always ordered for us all, two burritos and a side of guacamole. Morgan and I shared a veggie burrito, and Robert (being a working man) had his own; besides, he was paying. We'd recount our exploits to him, as he leant, exhausted from the tedium of the call centre, on the restaurant's less than pristine wall. Morgan and I would unwrap all of our stories for him, and lay them out on the table, the people we'd met, the contacts we'd made, the conviction we felt that any day now, practically any minute now, we'd both be gainfully employed, and hunkering down on lucrative creative assignments. Stuffed full on half of a burrito each, we were assured by his tender disposition that yes, anything might be possible the next day.

Into this honeyed world your letters came with promptness and regularity, breaking up my panhandling and remorseless joie de vivre. It's funny but the further apart we were, the more we were compelled to commit words to paper, to turn away from the utility of contemporary communications, to forget the expediency of the internet in favour of the romance of the postal service. Or perhaps it was simply a question of the time difference? Maybe at a certain point time flattens, and the seven-hour delay of an email attains the same weight as the five-day hold-up of a letter?

You sent me love letters in which I thought I could detect the faintest echo of your question, 'Will you be back?', though the incipient tenderness was always palliated with a cold sadism. No opportunity for a pot shot was overlooked in your missives; if there was a slight to make, you'd make it. 'Those crusty Cali punks might be good for a fuck,' you wrote, 'but don't expect them to be able to read or write.'

'Who is Thomas James?' Robert called out, reading from the back of an envelope, and bouncing into the room with the mail.

'A guy,' I said.

He frisbied a letter from you across the room, I think he may have even added a fruity little 'Oooh-oooh!' sound, too. The letter fluttered briefly mid-air then twirled down, landing on the bed between us.

'Sorry,' he smirked.

I shrugged.

He went to work saying, 'See you later JJ.'

I had to be alone to open them because my heart would skip about in my chest and all the blood rushed to my crotch. I always needed the assured stillness of an empty house to read what you wrote, because your letters were like little jack-in-the-boxes, little parcel bombs. I'm not saying I was trying to protect anyone else from whatever ricin powder or anthrax dust might swirl out of the envelope, rather I wanted to keep the thrill of it all for myself, to fall back in my chair, choking and spasming on the floor, alone. I wanted the freedom to masturbate on Robert's bed, when the letter took that turn.

When they came, your sporadic emails contained too little to cling to, besides some explicit self-portraits. One was headed *my fit bod* and had no text, only three pictures you'd taken of yourself, with your digital camera set to timer. They were all suggestive, one extremely graphic, another became famous, across the width of a circle at least. It showed you in a medium shot, in your bedroom, in a blue T-shirt and pink underpants. Your chin was slightly lowered as if you were trying to stoop into frame, your left arm was bent sharply at the elbow, shepherding your hand to your crotch where it squeezed tight around your balls, causing the rigid, I imagined throbbing, line in your underwear to flex harder and longer. It was as if you were trying to taunt me, to say, *See what you're missing?* As if you were inviting me to come back home. Maybe, if I had felt that I was the only recipient of these images, I would have found more succour in them.

I'm not saying that your emails failed to provide any sustenance, simply that it was your letters which kept

us close. They always arrived in hand-crafted envelopes, the paper inside a size too big, folded not neatly,
forming a margin down the left-hand side of the page
which intersected the horizontal pleat. Usually there
would be a boy inside, in black and white, loitering in
tight underwear. Often you would tape poems you'd
copied by hand onto the page, as collage, as punctua-
tion to stories of the turnings of the scene in London
(in which I remained very invested). I remember how
Mervyn Peake and Billy Bragg would be pasted in
there, between paragraphs about Paulette, a girl you'd
been fucking, and more contempt-laden tirades, telling me not to put it about too much in LA (sic), on
account of all the 'Diegos with bad Morrissey tattoos'.

The letters were very like being in your presence,
they made all the hairs on my body stand up, they made
me want to sock you one (like you deserved) and fuck
you hard (like you desired). This tangle of yearning and
conflicting possibilities comprised my life at that time,
so it's fitting now to have your name forever stamped
all over it. I used to imagine that the ink on the page
was akin to the blood in your veins, an epistolary tran-
substantiation that would fall through the letter box.
That ink had been expressed from the pen held in your
hand, hadn't it? And the hand was driven by cracks of
the whip of the brain, pumped full of blood from the
heart, wasn't it? I thought of the electrical impulses
that had caused your fingers to curl around the pen,
as they did around my cock, and it seemed impossible
that you wouldn't in some way be transferred onto the
paper on which you scribbled out your manic ejacu-
lations. If I ran my fingers over the page with my eyes
closed, I could just about feel the depressions formed
by your biro over there in London. I saw you chewing

it, I saw the saliva slide down it, as it did down my dick, to smudge the ink a little.

Elsa sent me a few postcard-sized sketches, and Adam too wrote all summer long. He was the most diligent, but I guess it's clear that I loved you best. I'm sorry to say it now (because the loss causes me pain) but he was becoming one of my dearest of friends. His letters were jolly and encouraging, he was pleased to hear that I was going for it, whatever it was, he didn't quite understand, but he sent me a CD of his favourite arias as inspiration, all the same. I listened to it all through the hottest months, stretched out in my underwear on the wooden floor of the living room, allowing the sunlight streaming through the window to have its way with me. I would turn up the volume until it was almost uncomfortably loud and, enraptured by the warmth and the music, splay across the floorboards, my every muscle engorged with ardour and adoration, a letter from you moist in hand. I consented to let these impossible, unnatural voices lavish me, yes, but it was you I watched cavorting in my mind's eye. It was your contemptuous torso, your ravenous, dishevelled, contrary affection I imagined myself ravished by; it was you, my uncouth ever-ready concubine that I longed for, despite being clear in the knowledge that in California I had a real sense of self, a belief in the future, and the pleasure of belonging. I had all of that, and yet still I craved you, isn't that perverse?

These letters are the last surviving traces of my willing submission to that strange passion, to the euphoric entanglements of the fatally immature, to the ties that bound us. I've reread them all, endlessly of course, I know them by heart, but though I can practically recite them from memory, sometimes even now they reveal something new when I look at them. They show me a bit more of you, but still not you. You spent time with them, I can feel that. A little while after you were killed, when I was quite literally staggering around in my grief, a friend told me to write you a letter and mail it without an address. I did that, but even as I listened to it drop into the guts of the post box, I knew it was nonsense. It didn't feel like a weight off my mind to write out everything I felt, and send it off blindly. It only felt like a waste of paper, like a magic trick from a Christmas cracker, like a wellness exercise from a fashion glossy. And yet, I've tried frequently to contact you, I've gone on writing to you, what other reason is there for this book?

I know for sure, even as I write it, that this book has possessed me. I felt it just now as I was walking back from lunch at the fondita, waiting for a break in the traffic so I could dash across the road. I felt it as insistently as I had felt it in front of the drugstore's neon cross, when this mission settled on my brow. I understood immediately that I am now entirely at the mercy of this story, compelled to write it out, to keep dancing until I fall into a dead faint with the red shoes still on my feet. Maybe then I can rest. This is the only story I can write, even when I try to scratch out something else, something pleasant, this story expands in the line breaks. In the silences when the keyboard is resting still between thought and image, I hear your voice saying, *That's how it is, eh Bibby?*

It's not like you were my first love, not at all. I'd been fucking my classmates, older men in public toilets, and other people's boyfriends since I was thirteen. I'd known my way around nightclubs and bedrooms since my second scholarship year of secondary school, and known love's thrills and spills for practically as long. I'd broken up households, I'd lived with boyfriends, and in one sanctimonious set of circumstances had even been engaged, when the idea of gay marriage was little more than a lightning rod for debate around tolerance and equality. So why then am I left with you? I didn't ever commemorate any of those other affairs with anything more than a few melodramatic scenes in Pret A Manger, a couple of catty remarks and some ill-advised but perfectly enjoyable post-break-up sex. What is this hold you have over me? How can I ever possibly hope that in hammering all of this out at my keyboard, I could speak to you across the great divide (as though my desktop were a ouija board), and break that hold? I feel sticky and sinister when I think about it, my desires become necrophile, and I see you now, like Marilyn Monroe found in the nude, the back of her blonde head, her shoulders rising like polished Thassos marble above the crisp white sheets, her bedroom untidy, cluttered and in disarray.

Even when you were living you had me compelled, I think, because the nastiness that always existed between us, the barely concealed cruelty, the flared tempers, the irreconcilable differences made me feel, well, grown up. Before you I had only known the bitterness to come in at the end of the affair, as a spoilt harvest resulting from negligent or unskilled farming, from irreversible changes to the climate, from infestation of parasites, or just plain bad luck. But with you the unkindness was sown with the seeds out in the fields, and tended to with such malicious care that indecorous resentment, red-earth hatred, would have to be the crop we reaped.

We didn't ever talk of the future, of monogamy, of joint gym memberships, though we did talk of love, in letters and in person. I suppose I thought of you as Nelson Algren there on the wrong side of the ocean, and myself as Simone de Beauvoir, refusing to set up house and relishing the sparks that flew when we sparred. I went around for a while calling myself Simone de Boudoir, you would've suited the name *Nelson*, but I can't say we chose the patron saints of our relationship very wisely, when you look at them, him and her, and you and I. I'm sorry that you didn't ever get to have your moment in the sun. Surely you would have earned it by now. I'm sad that I'll never get to see you in the newspapers collecting an award, and strike up a cigarette, startle my maid and mutter to myself, 'Putain!' with my eyes still full of desire.

Often Morgan and I wasted whole days in Dolores Park whilst Robert was at the call centre. We were quite inseparable. We wore each other's clothes: cartoon slogan T-shirts, high-waisted seventies polyester slacks from Salvation Army, far too much Dior mascara (the one indulgence we could never do without), taking turns to carry about the oversized gold clutch we shared. In the park, amongst the sinewy guys cruising each other, the filthy, dreadlocked activists, the business-casual jocks, the Latter-day Saints and the boom box *reinas*, we looked lost. We looked like two little cosmic waifs who had come to San Francisco in '78, following the trail of peace and love all the way to where the corpse of the hippie dream lay face-down in the dirt, knifed to death by the Manson family, punk rock and smack.

But why should the parade which had long passed by bring us shame? Rumi, our golden-aged drag mother, said we made her feel like she was kicking it up at Haight-Ashbury again, and that was enough of a reason to *keep on keepin' on*. Certainly my bohemian, psyche-delic, Marxist delusions of sexual, political and economic revolution were no more ridiculous than your outdated flirtations with Mark E. Smith and Morrissey, and fundamentally weren't we dreaming the same dream to the same end? The dream of freedom; only you would have called it *individual liberty*, or something quasi-Thatcherite like that, whilst at the same time hating the woman, the way you ultimately hated all women.

I wonder would you have come to hate me if I had left the final residuals of maleness behind me during your lifetime, during our love affair? Or would you, in participating in this transformation, have come to love me better? Over time (ten years since we met, six since we last spoke, four since you died) I've come to hypothesise that if I could have shown you more of me, you would have shown me more of you, and perhaps we might have come to a less brittle understanding.

So, let me tell you about this one day, this perfect little opalescent cliché, which I never shared with you because I didn't want you to mock me. I didn't want to seem less desirable to you because of my truly juvenile nature. I'm trying to be honest about who I am, but here at the kitchen table, I can still hear you say, *And that's the sort of thing you call fun is it, Bibby?*

On an anonymous weekday afternoon, around about the time the sun starts to sink behind the horizon, but before it was quite fully gone, Robert arrived to meet me and Morgan in Dolores. Upbeat, he bought us a magic truffle each from the shirtless dude who wandered the park all day, selling them out of the two bronzed bowls hung from the milkmaid's yoke he carried on his shoulders. We appreciated his generosity.

'If I have it to share, I should share it,' Robert said magnanimously. 'That's how to live if we want a fairer world.'

'Far out,' Morgan giggled. She was at once teasing him and lionising the sentiment, the foundational clause on which the whole city's countercultural pose was laid.

With the sunset came the inevitable chill, so we left the park and we walked back to the house. We felt cold but we felt loose, and by the time we were home we felt that familiar feeling of luscious, soggy calm and bliss creep in from the truffles. Morgan had discovered a Tiny Tim YouTube playlist, and the three of us rolled about the floor for a while indulging in that, and our increasing hysterics. Then we played the game we had devised to help us write texts collectively, which we called *English Lessons for the Foreign Artist*. In deepest mock-solemnity we tossed a balloon back and forth between us, calling out an improvised proverb each time we caught it, generating bon mots as profound as, *If one eats gooseberries one is in effect a goose* and *Sharks really do attack! Look! I don't have the legs to prove it!* With the drugs, the chanting, and the dryers tumbling away below, the whole place seemed to vibrate ominously, and we stood for a while, braced for an earthquake that never came. Eventually it passed, replaced by another feeling, and I sang a phrase that was the shared leitmotif of the period, 'I'm actually totally starving.'

'Me too,' Robert agreed.

'Me three,' added Morgan. Then, spying a letter, from you, which had fallen to the floor from my pocket, she said, 'I'm so hungry I could eat all the love letters our little JJ gets sent by her British floozies!'

She pounced on it and made as if to stuff it in her mouth, she licked her lips cartoonishly, then held the letter between her teeth like a rambunctious puppy. I let out a nervous squeak, unsure if I was amused or not. Swiftly, Robert snatched the letter from Morgan's fangs saying, 'Bad girl! Bad! Down!' and she pretended to whine and held up her paws under her chin. I wiped the saliva from the envelope on my sleeve, stashed the letter in my notebook, and Robert said, 'Let's go get donuts.'

Since our walk home earlier had been quite chilly, we fell under the communal hallucination that it must be very, very cold outside by now, so before we left we wrapped up well. It was mid-August in Northern California, but the truffles persuaded us that we'd need long pants and sweaters, scarves, gloves and hats. I think Robert even suggested I wear a scuba mask, just in case it rained. He himself pulled a green patent raincoat over his multiple sweatshirts, so tight in the arms he could barely bend his elbows.

We had the great fortune of living close to a 24-hour donut shop. Why such a thing was really necessary I never knew, but nor did I question it, I was simply grateful that it was only a few minutes' walk away, and always very happy to get there. The ancient proprietress was never at all shocked by the condition in which anyone arrived. She looked like had been slinging donuts to stoners since the Spanish-American War; losers like us were probably the very core of her business model.

We marvelled at the endlessly imaginative combinations one could create with sugar, flour and sprinkles: the looping donuts, the twisted donuts, the glazed donuts, the filled donuts, the ring donuts, the donut holes and the crumb donuts, a cathedral of carbohydrates and saturated fats, your very own America at $1.25 a pop. It took us forever to decide what to get because they all just looked *so good*. We stood there mumbling and drooling, until eventually Robert grew bored and impatient, and asked the lady at the counter to give us three of her favourites each. She obliged, and we took our swag and slumped down at a table in the window.

Finally peaceful, slobbering over the selection, we chewed with careful greedy purpose, like a small herd of cows, senseless and slow. Robert sang an old Eurovision hit to himself, Morgan absentmindedly stared out of the window, joining him for the chorus. She was wearing a white Mod faux fur hat on her head and had flipped down the tips of her pink heart mittens, to make eating a little easier. Her face was powdered with icing sugar, her green eyes disappearing below heavy lids. She smiled a big dopey grin out into the warm night, and waved at a couple passing by.

'Who are they?' asked Robert in his jelly reverie.

'I don't know who the guy is,' she replied, her mouth half full of masticated frosting and dough, 'but that's the chick I had the job interview with last week.'

'Oh cool,' he said, nodding and chewing, his eyes also half shut. 'Do you think she'll call you back?'

Later, being ever careful not to waste a resource, we took the remains of our feast up nearby Bernal Hill, like real San Franciscans. We sat on a bench, dreadfully aware of all the rats scrambling about in the bushes, somewhat horrified, somewhat charmed, full of resplendent empathy all the same. The city in the purple of night tessellated out before us, lights on in homes and hotels, the horizon a chequerboard of irregular squares, static but jostling with each other, seeming to buzz at the points where their geometries collided. The occasional triangular crown of a skyscraper making itself known like the golden towers in Klee's *Architecture*, and sure enough I thought about you.

'So who is this Thomas James dude with the letters?' Morgan asked, her head resting on my shoulder, Robert's head in her lap. 'Is it a thing?'

'I don't know,' I said.

'You do know, you liar.' She chuckled, and reached into the brown paper bag for a final few crumbs. Licking her fingers and imitating me, she said, 'You can't kid a kidda la. You can't kid a kidda.'

II

Like my red hair, my green eyes and my tendency towards depression, I inherited my love of the written word from my mother. When I was a child she almost never allowed me to watch TV because it distracted her from the reading which seemed like the one lone comfort in a life otherwise exclusively peopled by abusive men, and disparaging officers from the Department of Social Services. I see how alike we are now, when I remember taking *Crime and Punishment* back into Robert's bed with me at three in the afternoon, because I was hungry and all out of cash. Morgan sat on the end of the bed, shaking her head and saying, 'You have to admit there's a certain beautiful irony in reading that book in *these* circumstances.'

When I had announced my vocation at age eight, my dream of writing books and plays and acting them out onstage, my grandfather, a striking docker, shook his head resolutely and said, 'That's not for the likes of us.' He'd been to Germany, he'd broken his foot and shattered his own dream of playing football for Everton, so I took his verdict very seriously. I didn't question its validity. If I hadn't met Morgan and Robert, I honestly don't think I ever would have.

In London I had taken a few tentative steps, with my ice cream cone and my strawberry sauce-splattered slingbacks, towards the life of the artist I believed I could become, but the quality of my dreams was always overshadowed by this native class pessimism. There wasn't a dole cheque big enough to sustain my delusions of grandeur, and I couldn't see how it would ever be permissible for a person to be working class, transgender and successful all at once. My own immediate past was just too close at hand.

In California though, I felt that I'd broken the hypnotic spell of that old hegemony – even if I were promptly falling under another. If I was only kidding myself that America is less economically unjust than the UK, well, isn't such a fallacy the essence of the USA? California, the Golden State, where kids with no means but plenty of hustle go to be reworked as household names. You arrive as a good-looking nobody, as Lucille LeSueur, and you come out as Joan Crawford, right? None of us really knew what we were going to do with our lives, we couldn't figure out where our interests, talents and opportunities overlapped in any profitable way. We just knew we were searching for something more than the hand dealt us offered.

Morgan, Robert and I spent most weekends at the performance salons Rumi invited us to, at the Anarchist Bookstore, or the Center for Sex and Culture. Frail and majestic, Rumi had overseen these cabals as far back as anyone could remember, shepherding a bunch of the original Beats and acidheads onstage, keeping the spotlight focused on the talents of assorted insurrectionist senior citizens. We were often fifty years younger than anyone else present, but that's what I loved most about California: when I went looking for my future, I always found the past. Carl with Records, who wore a lamp-shade decorated with cut-outs of Judy Garland on his head, and sang songs about busty chorus girls, his lyrics hooted over long-forgotten Broadway instrumentals, which were only ever coincidentally in the same key or time signature; Vin C, another giant kinky baby, who posed in solo tableaux costumed with ruffles, hoop skirts and huge lollipops; and Bambi Lake, the original San Franciscan icon of glittering penury.

Rumi would always joke that no one ever knew how to contact Bambi, because no one ever knew where she was sleeping at any given time. 'But,' she would smile, her remaining few teeth on proud display, 'Bambi always says, "Honey if you want me to do a show, you just put my name on the poster and I'll be there!"' And lo, though her life was so completely parlous, she would be summoned by the black magic of showbiz. Fashion-model thin at seventy, blonde hair streaming about the spaghetti straps of her gown, Bambi would stride in off the street and head with deathly accuracy to the mic to decimate with her *chanson*.

We were agog, under this influence; and it was quite a revelation to see that nobody really knew what *it* was, this *it* that we were all chasing. Seemingly there were no rules in the Wild West, you just put on your Stetson (or your lampshade), jumped on your horse (or your donkey piñata) and rode over the edge. You could be pushing eighty and dressed like a dollar store Christmas tree, but if you were still alive, then good for you for writing political satire to be screamed onstage, straight in the face of a hatstand dressed as President Bush. What choice did we have when this doorway appeared but to step through it? It felt as though we had fallen down a storm drain, descended beneath the city, splash-landed in some underground river of transcendental stimulation.

Once Rumi let us up onstage to perform *English Lessons for the Foreign Artist* for the first time, we considered ourselves to truly have arrived, we needed very little encouragement. We began turning up at private views and readings in kimonos and clown white, carrying mangoes, introducing ourselves as Simone de Boudoir, Jean Paul Tarte and Manual Kunt, telling people we were a troupe of Dada mimes.

'Only we speak too,' said Robert.

'A lot!' I said.

'I made the costumes out of old sofa cushions!' added Morgan, deliberately tangential.

We didn't necessarily have an act, so we didn't really need a stage. We'd simply pick a spot, the more crowded the better, and recite our co-authored mantras. 'The Baby Flew Too Close To The Sun!' we chanted, with passion ever increasing, tearing at our pillowcases until we were naked and screaming like three flaming maniacs. There were no rehearsals, because as now confirmed radical situationists, we believed that rehearsal was bourgeois and counterrevolutionary. Instead we ran around galleries naked in powdered wigs, or on roller skates, dressed as vampire daisies, throwing up cans of pea soup on each other, holding sacred as our mission statement a slur once slung at our spiritual antecedents, the Cockettes: 'Having No Talent Is Not Enough'.

Of course, it was at first a joke, that the three of us would become performance artists, but in the post-Warholian world where everybody is a superstar, nobody ever was as gauche as to question our authenticity. Besides, supercharged by our anarchic foremothers, we believed we were actively engaged in the destruction of so regressive a concept as *the authentic*. Ineluctable, we turned up everywhere for the entirety of that summer, whether or not we were invited, presenting this performance at bookshops, cafes, cinemas, house parties, museums and theatres, with Morgan declaring, 'It isn't a party without us darling!' Eroded, people eventually decided that it was better to be in on the joke, and so, gradually we were legitimised on the very fringes at least, with invites to perform for modest fees, from gallerists and promoters. A sort of hush money in effect.

'You see?' said Morgan. 'Attention is currency!'

If it all seems a little silly now (and it does) I can excuse myself (to some extent) by accepting that my becoming a writer was an awkward, gradual process, not unlike coming out of the closet. To borrow a thought from Daniel Lavery, *How will I know when I've dipped into fabulism if I don't keep in contact with my past selves?* In the same way that I have passed from bisexual, to gay, to queer, to trans, I had to move through various disingenuous mutations as an artist, before I could become that which I really am. It would have been as impossible for me to declare myself a serious writer back then as it would have been to definitively stake a claim on femininity; neither seemed attainable modes of being, except through disdainful irony. Weighed down with as much shame as I had on my shoulders, I had to mock myself for a long time, strike counterfeit poses to see how they felt, before I could admit that the gag was just a cover. *Well*, I tell myself, *better late than never.*

Obviously, we wasted all of the money we made from our performances on jugs of Long Island iced tea, and of course we were thrown out of most of the places we performed in, but even that did not dampen our spirits. If anything it energised us; hadn't Bambi Lake herself been eighty-sixed from practically every bar in town? What could be better than horrifying, mystifying what at times felt like an entire city? All those mouths hanging open in incredulity, concurrent mumbles of 'They can't be for real!' and '*Are* they for real?'

It was the kind of ecstasy that can only be experienced before life's base metal is tempered by the heat of real tragedy, before a person becomes tougher but less hard. Back then, on those nights climbing out of club windows, half-cut and licentious, I was so insulated by ignorance that nothing could touch me. Not the reality of the situation, not the thin ice of people's patience which I could practically hear cracking beneath my feet, not the hangovers and not the hunger, which we just laughed off, going to bed if it was too uncomfortable, joking, 'Is this what they did in the Great Depression?' I hadn't yet been dealt the knock-out blow of your loss, our separation seemed still only temporary, so I was unable to conceive that things wouldn't always be glorious if threadbare, somehow. I didn't know how many windows would open onto sorrow, I didn't know that there wouldn't always be a tomorrow. If I did, I would never have left home; would anyone?

We received (and quickly forgot about) an invitation to perform at the city's big drag night in early September. We were bemused, we couldn't really understand why we had been asked, we weren't really drag queens, we wondered if they had any idea of what we actually *did* onstage? One of us must have agreed to the invite (though I can't say who) because a follow-up email arrived a few weeks later, detailing stage times and venue protocols.

Morgan was flat out on the couch, checking the collective email account to distract from period pains.

'Oh-oh,' she said, 'this is tonight…'

'What? No!' I scowled. 'It can't be.'

'Uh-huh,' said Morgan. 'It's tonight. Look! The theme is *Memory! Barbara Streisand Through the Years.*'

'Fuck!' I said in irritation. 'Why does it always have to be Streisand? Ugh, this town! Why is it still 1977 here?'

Robert was away in Fresno, asking his father to lend him some money, Morgan was laid up with cramps, I was hungover and had no patience for any of it.

I said, 'I guess we'll just have to cancel then.'

My head ached from too much liquor, I was not at all unhappy to skip it.

Morgan shrieked, 'No way! This pays $200!'

'Well,' I began, 'I can't see what we're supposed to do about it.'

She sighed with frustration, 'Just find a clip on YouTube, and lip-synch to it. It can't be that hard.'

The club was a San Francisco institution, they'd packed a thousand people into that intimate, some said infamous, leather bar every week for twenty years already. I'd seen those queens in flawless face, dressed to kill in custom gowns paid for with day-job salaries, and I did not think our papier-mâché pastiche was going to cut it. Morgan explained to me (not for the first time) the precarity of our financial situation, and promised me a Vicodin for my nerves.

'Besides,' she said, patting my head, 'what's three minutes of your life, when the rent's this far overdue?'

From the sofa, Morgan took the shears to an emerald-green jumpsuit we'd found in the street, and fashioned me a Flintstones-style evening gown with a big zigzag hemline. I dug about in Robert's room until I found a matching wig, stolen from the Walgreens' party section, picked a gummy worm out from among the synthetic curls, and began to feel optimistic, the way one always does in the calm surrender, after the tension of conflict has passed. We got stoned, sifting through Streisand playlists, settling on 'Don't Rain on My Parade', and devising a routine which seemed hilarious to us, though it amounted to nothing more than some fumblings with an old, unwilling umbrella, which once erected, opened up in a canopy of tatters.

Because Robert was away we skipped burritos and ate a dinner of Lucky Charms, orange juice and tequila, out of plastic tumblers.

'It's good,' Morgan said, 'but it could do with a little grenadine.'

She gave me the promised Vicodin, and took one herself for her cramps.

In spite of the medication and an afternoon of such serious preparation, the menacing prospect of the grandes dames of drag still coated me with sweaty anxiety. Here were these men masquerading as women, and there was me masquerading as them, on a meta slip and slide, on course for collision with either the dysphoria associated with being seen as a drag queen, or the ensuing disappointment when it became clear I wasn't one (both, potentially). One Vicodin was not enough, I needed two to even get in the cab, and despite Morgan's assurances that I would be fine, that's about as far as the video cassette of my memory runs, before the tape gets caught in all the moving parts of the camera, before the film chews itself up, and gives me nothing but abstract haze. I was not there, sat in the make-up chair, as Morgan did my face.

'Let's go green!' she said, considering the available options in her palette, 'because green is good! And green is what we've got.'

I must've agreed.

When I come to, Morgan is shaking me by the shoulders, and reassuring the disgruntled club hostess, 'She's fine, look — she's totally fine!'

The hostess, who seems to me at least ten feet tall, a demonic voice in a towering inferno of fabricated hair, gives me a poke in the ribs with her press-on and says, 'You good, girl? Good, you on, girl.'

Morgan stands me up, holds a drink out for me to sip through a straw, turns me to look at myself in the mirror, and says, 'Ta-da!'

I see that she has painted not just my eyelids, but my entire face green, down to the very décolletage. She seems quietly impressed with herself, the way somebody might be if they'd perfectly arranged a thousand little rocks in a miniature Zen garden.

'And look!' she exclaims, holding up my hand in front of my face. 'Nails!'

The fingernails are eight inches long, and made from green glittered cardboard.

'Did you superglue these on?' I ask, groggy, slowly surfacing to the realisation that this is really happening.

'Uh-huh!' she smiles, and I see that she is clearly strung out too.

I look like a microwaveable spaghetti dinner for one, I look like a box of broken biscuits, like an undercooked chicken breast, like I've been eaten by a dog, thrown up, and eaten again. Certainly nobody could mistake me for a drag queen. My polished contemporaries themselves strike double-takes in horror, as the mistress of ceremonies hustles me towards the stage. She shepherds me thoroughly, as though she believes I am capable of suddenly thinking better of it all and absconding, leaving a sloppy hole in her schedule.

'OK then!' the hostess smiles a pasteboard grin at the side of the stage. 'What was your name again?'

'Barbara Streisand-a-saurus!' declares Morgan, and I nod.

'And you're British, right? The crowd loves Londoners here.'

'Yes siree,' I slur, 'yes sireee, ma'am.'

And then, I go on, somehow.

How it felt to be there, in front of a thousand people fiddling with an umbrella dressed like a kindergartener's doodle of a dinosaur, I have no recollection. I must have filled my slot well enough because we weren't asked to leave, and we did get the $200, though we were obviously never invited back again. The only reason I know that it happened at all is because Morgan filmed it on a camcorder we called Baby (another psychic I), which we bought with Robert's credit card, intending to return it at the end of summer. I've seen the footage, so I know that I didn't fall down in a stupor, or freeze up in terror, I've watched myself back and I look totally unaffected. What takes over in moments like that? Adrenaline, some self-preservation instinct, joy? Or was I held together, like the protagonist in *The Ministry of Fear*, by the credo that one would rather die than cause a fuss by breaking with convention, however bananas the context?

Yes, I've watched myself back, I've watched myself induce a few guffaws from the crowd with my slapstick and (dare I say it?) a slice of personality even. I've watched myself back, but just like reading over my letters to you again, I can't reconcile myself to the body that made those motions, wrote those words. It's as though it were all pre-programmed, like I was hexed or hypnotised, like every choice I thought I had ever made had been made for me, like free will were only a funfair hall of mirrors, like the performance we think we're improvising is more tightly scripted than we'll ever know.

The past is fixed, we know. That's the consensus all of us physicists, Catholics, Buddhists and classicists have agreed upon. The real shocker is that the future seems to be so too, and all of these gestures we make, all of these cave paintings are just ways of killing a few hours before bed. All time is here. The dissociation becomes quickly terrifying, when you consider that you maybe aren't the driver, just the car.

I've looked back on that bumpy, out-of-focus, less than amateur footage, and tried to imagine other endings, imagine what might have happened had I pulled off the wig, thrown down the umbrella, and screamed out *Stop this train! I want to get off!* Because when I watch myself back on video tape now, even at half-speed, I'm watching time run out for you too, leapling, that's how tightly this is wound. Even if it is not predestined, even if it is all arbitrary images, and haphazard connections, all time is here. It's simply that our experience (yours and mine) differs now, although it shouldn't because, lover, I'm dead too. Even on that stage staggering about to Streisand, I can see that I'm already dead. Watching it back, I'm watching you rushing towards your sudden, unnecessary death. It's all up there, your life, mine, the cum I pumped out of your cock, your last moments, the blood coming out of your nose, all our fights, all our letters, *Come on then*, and that green thing obliterated onstage, reaching out to the audience to take the dollar bills proffered as tips, but failing in every swoop, forgetting and re-forgetting those nightmarish cardboard nails superglued to her nail beds.

III

In one of your letters you threatened to come out to California yourself, if I stayed away any longer. I sat blushing, reading and rereading that line, alone and hungover, late one morning with Robert at work and Morgan out, at another job interview maybe.

You recounted to me your struggles to become someone; it always felt like you were wrestling with yourself, your obvious insecurity and your outsized ego rolling in the dirt together, less Jacob and the Angel, more Hulk Hogan vs. Rick 'the model' Martel, having at it with no-holds-barred camp on the WrestleMania stage circa 1994. You laid out your plans to do *something*, to be *something* several times over, without really specifying what, and followed each statement with the question, '*But how?*' Weren't we on the same quest? I was chasing some ambiguous *it* too. I wonder now how things might have been different, if either of us had had a champion behind us, cheering them on, someone who really believed that we might amount to something one day. How might we have blossomed had we had even one such person in our lives, offering genuine encouragement, supporting us to act on our most secret ambitions, rather than turn them in on ourselves to linger as the source of shame? It's doubly doleful, now I come to consider it, that of all the people in the world, we couldn't even offer this to each other.

As often, you were worried about money, you were angry with your family, and disparaging of people around you who seemed to be doing better. I empathised, really I did. I was as envious, impecunious and resentful as you, only I had the barrier of the great wide American continent between me and all of that, which at least gave the illusion of progress, healing and financial security, and sometimes the illusion is what's most important. Certainly people respond and react to what they imagine you to be, to the person they've projected onto you, far more than the person you actually are, or else how could our tender connection have survived for so long?

You broke off writing midway through, and returned to your letter saying, 'Back now', as if we were on the phone, as if I could have somehow known that you'd left off to change your shorts, take a piss, or open the door to another lover. *Back now*, I note, *that's a very authorial device. Let's keep a hold of that one.*

In this little break in the letter, like an ellipsis in time, you took off on a divagation away from the page; maybe something on the radio caught your attention, maybe someone you knew passed below in the street, maybe a cloud rolled over the sun and reminded you to buy some stilton before the shops shut? That leaving off is preserved there on paper, it opens up expansively now. How long were you away from your desk? I don't know. What were you doing? It's unimportant.

Time can be bent and time can be punctured (we call these punctures black holes), time happens according to the equipment we have to measure its passing, and it moves faster two floors up than it does at street level. When I thought that I might only have a few more weeks left in San Francisco in which to file for a visa extension or else pack up again, the days became fleet in their running shoes, sprinting out ahead of me, so quick I couldn't keep up. But reading your letter, and thinking that if I did put my papers in order, it might be six months, more, before I saw you next, the days suddenly became a slow-moving multitude, sad and long.

A letter is itself a little sliver of eternity, incorporating a multitude of present moments; the present moment of writing and posting, the present moment of delivery and reading, the present moment of archiving and opening up again, and all at the same time. I saw a letter in the British Library with Elsa, written by Ealdorman Ordlaf and sent to King Edward the Elder in the ninth century, marked 'useless' by a clerk in Canterbury in the twelfth century, and now prized as the earliest surviving letter in English. Even though I couldn't make out more than two words of the minuscule, illegible script, I remember thinking – *that proves loop quantum gravity right, doesn't it?* And I remember a very upright, slick, groomed gallerist asking me, 'Oh, so do you make time-based work?' and telling her, 'All art is time-based, surely?' And I remember being taught the essential life skill of letter-writing in school at age nine, and how by the time I was a teenager letters had become almost entirely obsolete.

Your letter brought me up to speed with your sex life, with details of Anders who had played you and gone back to Scandinavia, with Paulette who seemed to like you a needless amount, and Lucy Dear, who seemed more like your own twin than your lover, more you than you, an equal. You were planning a trip with her, maybe. I was not jealous, I think in fact all your other lovers helped keep my interest keen, as if I had to prove myself distinguished amongst them.

And yet I already felt myself to be somehow prominent, that I was held in high esteem, because I knew that you weren't telling all of them about each other. They were all stumbling about in the dark asking, *Does he love me? Does he even like me?*, unaware that they weren't alone in that thick tenebrosity, whilst I had all of these letters signed, *Love Tom*.

I liked your honesty, you were brutal, frank, I liked that you didn't baby me, or pull your punches. I felt that in levelling with me you trusted I could handle it, and it gave me such a sophisticated thrill. *Let the children play*, I smirked to myself. I didn't think I had anything to worry about from this assortment of dilettantes; this parade of holes and protuberances didn't threaten me. You yourself wrote revolting short poems (not among your best) about the various participants in your fuck parade, comparing the most unappealing aspects of 'shitty arses' and 'ycasty hoods'. And I, in spite of the nose on my face, which impulsively scrunched up when I read these repulsive little details, took delight in your expansive sexual tastes. I can't ever imagine you calling yourself queer (though your sexuality definitely was), and there's no way you would ever have allowed yourself to be spoken of as pansexual, or marched under any nom de guerre that carried hints of discourse or wafts of patchouli. *Bisexual*, though it felt outmoded, was loaded with a certain erotic kick for me, and again I felt terribly grown up, thinking of you with your boys, and with your girls. I felt worldly, like I might start speaking with a mid-Atlantic drift, like I might walk over to my studio and cast a new bronze, like I might roll my own joints and read John Kennedy Toole just for fun. I felt like your amorphous mistress, like a voyeur watching you in a brothel through our designated peephole, like Patrick White's Eadith Trist, like Donald Sutherland's Casanova. I was sure that in between thrusts and moans, you would spy my hiding place, stare dead at me, and unload your sperm into the willing body beneath you, without us ever breaking eye contact. Moreover your ambivalence, when it came to the specifics of the body you were attending to, made my own gender, for the first time, feel weightless and irrelevant, and I'm so grateful to you for that, my blue-eyed bastard.

To quote the distanced, disinfected language of the sexual health centre, I knew that you were *playing the active role with partners of both sexes*. You were topping both (so silly), but bottoming for me; did this give me an inflated sense of importance? As if knowing the next time I saw you I would penetrate you meant I had a legitimate and greater claim on you. How ridiculous of me to think that by plunging myself into you up to the hilt, I would be safe from what came next, how masochistic, how dualistic, how Catholic, how macho, even.

Hidden here, inside my own lickerish replies, was the perfect opportunity to casually mention that I was thinking about coming back soon. To suggest that if the Australian boy whom you hated was really moving out of your apartment, that I could take over his room, just for a little while of course. I could've done that, I could've asked without risking any loss of face. If you'd have said no, well then, I'd have just extended my visa, no harm done, knowing where I stood.

It wouldn't have been living together; we would have been, I don't even know how to put it, *live-in lovers*, as I remember it to have had been coded by TV shows in the sarcoma-ravaged nineties. We could have participated in that grand lineage of fruity flatmates, Morecambe and Wise, Laverne and Shirley, Phoebe and Joey, only I'd insist that you never hung a bedroom door, so that I might have free rein to watch you screw your rag-tag lovers, and maybe occasionally avail myself of them too. You had even hinted at it yourself, some nebulous situation like this, and yet I could not bring myself to write the words, 'Can I come and stay with you?'

Not now, I thought, *not yet. One day he and I will have our chance to share a cage, but no, not now, not yet.*

That is about as much planning for the future as I ever did. There never seemed to be any time to sit down and think about what was the most pragmatic thing to do, to stay or to go. And anyway, surely it was the kind of situation that would simply resolve itself? One that I could allow the universe to decide on my behalf. There always seemed to be something in the way of making an appointment at the consulate: a hangover, a coffee date, the opening of a new thrift store, a protest, a last-minute gig, countless weightless obligations silently eating up all of my time. And of course there was also the question of money: who did we know who might lend me enough to file the correct papers? We thought we might save a little something from our performances, but it all seemed to go, we never quite knew where. On taxis maybe, on huevos rancheros at Boogaloos and matinees at the Roxie? Robert even went back to Fresno on his day off to ask his father for more money, but returned with a sheepish look on his face, saying, 'Sorry baby, I tried,' and that was sort of that. Perhaps it had only ever really been a bluff, a way to stall the inevitable, to take the decision off my hands, to spare myself from choosing between two impossible utterances; 'I'm staying' or 'I'm going'. Ultimately, no decision is a decision. I let myself go on a current of irresponsibility, and recorded it all for posterity, on the camcorder, that other psychic I, which we never did get around to returning to Walmart.

From the middle of July to the middle of October, it's all there suspended on mini-DV, in no particular order, because we kept losing tapes, finding them again, accidentally taping over them when we were stoned, and occasionally trying to reconstruct those moments we'd lost, which seemed so vital to us, in our frequent states of delirium. It's all there now, like a collage in motion, expertly spliced by dabblers, so a night in October appears midway through an afternoon in September, and Rumi's performance salons rupture footage of sunset over the Bay, and Bambi Lake bursts into song midway through a trip to the grocery store. On the same video cassette that had captured my evening of misadventures as that hybrid of mythical creatures, Barbara Streisand-a-saurus, you will also find many further ramblings in night vision. Images captured at a club, all in green and grey, footage taken six weeks, a month later, at a party after a performance. If you have the means of watching mini-DV tapes, or maybe a way of transferring this analogue incongruity to a digital format in the afterlife, you will see me with my hair backcombed out like a lion's mane, standing on end, in breast bindings of pink gaffer tape. Morgan is filming a man in a baseball cap who is pivoting his attention from her to me, though I do my best to ignore him. I look harassed from certain angles, bored from others, clearly bombed and not in the mood for this dude. On the tape you can hear me reply to one of his numerous lines with, 'I don't speak English,' and then you see him say, 'What? Really?' and then I repeat, deadpan, 'I don't speak English.'

He looks astonished, his eyes big and black in the nightcam setting, and he says to the camera (by which I mean Morgan), 'Is that true? She doesn't speak English?'

And Morgan chuckles, 'Yeah, no, it's true. She doesn't speak English.'

Later that evening we all went up to the top of one of San Francisco's tallest hotels, and fell into a huge cuddle puddle on the bed of a friend from college who was back in town for the weekend with an expense account. There's erratic footage of us, so high that we could see over the curtain of fog that was rolling into the city. Through the window we watched it come in like a semi-solid wall towards us, beneath us, engulfing everything below, leaving us suspended on the fortieth floor, looking down into a carpet of vaporous cloud. The fog was in action but perfectly still, it was solid but intangible, I felt I could have walked on it but that if it chose to, the fog could drop me to the ground. It had the texture of albino cotton candy, of a foam bath, of the bubbles pumping out of David Medalla's *Cloud Gates*, an enigmatic, evolving monument collapsing in on itself as it created itself. It was an effortless thing of terrifying beauty, which left us cut off from everyone everywhere else, and we marvelled at it. Maybe this is how the people of Pompeii felt when they saw their liquid deaths come rolling down the hillside, maybe they had been fixed to the spot in sublime surrender. Or maybe (more likely) they had run screaming in all directions, not being as high on ecstasy as we were.

Robert had scored from a colleague at the call centre, and we had decided that this was the night for it, that it would be even more fun than the evening he pushed me around an abandoned frat house in a shopping trolley, and bought us acid from a boy called Flower.

Around dawn we went home, messy with impotent desire and sloppy loving kisses, him and me falling into bed and really knowing the meaning of the word *ecstatic*. I thought to myself *Now this a beautiful morning*, and in my gooey state I made a note to tell you all about it, leapling. I wished my mouth could melt into Robert's mouth forever, I wished that I could get hard, and as the sun rose higher, I wished that, at any point in the past three months, we had taken the time to put his bedroom curtains back up.

We fell asleep, Robert and I, in a tangle of limbs, and half-unravelled clothing, drooling on each other, yo-yoing in and out of consciousness. I don't remember when the filming stopped but the camera was lying beside us flickering blue grey green when I woke up. We must have slept all day, because it was dark again when I came round, and Morgan was standing over me saying, 'Hey, hey sleepyhead, hey! Wake up. I made you tea. Hey, wake up! You have to pack, silly. Your flight is in six hours.'

IV

I don't think I shared any specific details of my travel plans with you, I might've said I was coming back in October but I'm sure I didn't say when exactly. I wanted to keep you hungry, sure, but I had also begun to panic, once it was clear I was headed back to London, that maybe this entire affair was only the product of my imagination. The closer I got to you the more I wanted to put the space back between us, and if there was no longer distance, then time would have to do. Arriving back in England, I made plans to see Elsa, to see Jovian, to see my mother even, but not to see you. I said to myself, *If he really wants to see me, he won't wait for an invite.*

I stayed with Adam, in his rented one-bedroom pre-war council flat near Waterloo. He seemed genuinely excited to have me back home, said he was happy to make space for me, and I felt comforted knowing plan B was so lean and lithe and enticing. A conservatoire graduate, a soprano called Sarah, had the bedroom proper. As is now typical, the living room had been rezoned as a second bedroom, and Adam slept on a fold-out sofa, jammed under the windowsill, next to his desk, perpendicular to a now-defunct fireplace.

All of his belongings were as meticulously organised and arranged as they needed to be in such a succinct space. But he was a person of such ineffable charm, such blithesome good humour, that his tiny room felt like a Wunderkammer, not a prison cell. One whole buttercup-yellow wall (surely not his choice of colour) was decorated with a lovely exhibition of photographs and postcards (some of which I recognised as mine, though there was no trace of you there yet) and fairy lights which were illuminated at dusk. An arrangement of pictures, delicate, comforting, rolling on to offer recollections of tender adventures, of strolls on sunny days, classical concerts, and excessive, somewhat out of character sessions in cheap chain pubs, images like a deconstructed movie, fragmented in freeze-frames across the wall.

It reminded me of a party I went to in the loft above an old warehouse in Brooklyn, with Jonny and Morgan, the whole place filled with netting and balloons, light shows, and partygoers all dressed up according to some not quite apparent theme. The Dirty Projectors were playing a secret set amongst all the glam rock moon dust.

But wait, this hadn't happened yet, this is a memory too. A memory from the future, itself provoked by the memory of Adam's stroboscopic wall.

I remember the chick on the door at that party letting me pass, but telling Jonny, 'Sorry it's costume only,' and Jonny pointing to me and saying, 'Costume? That's not costume, that's what she always wears!'

'OK, cool,' she said. 'You can all go in.'

But no, this hadn't happened yet, time is running away with me. I lived this as a zigzag, so how can I now share it as an arrogant straight line? Let's compromise then, on an S-shaped curve, on a narrative which flows to the inevitable sea, yes, but not without opportunity to double back on itself, when immoveable memory forces our waterway to reconsider its route.

Adam made me a boiled egg and sausages, which now seems an odd combination of things for anyone over the age of eight to eat, but at the time we were both quite satisfied with this German breakfast for lunch. Somewhere along the way he'd been absorbed into the name game Elsa and I played, so he called me Liza, and I called him Liza too. It was a flagrant sort of code we had between us, which didn't shield our communications from anyone in any way, only made things circular and frustrating for everybody else.

I didn't unpack my suitcase for the twelve long weeks that I was there; there wasn't any room to, but I wasn't uncomfortable. Unhappy yes, but not uncomfortable. I knew I would have to get a job, I would have to find my own place, I would have to think about how I could keep things going without my collaborators in California, but later, later. For now there was still time, and we spent that time, Adam and I, catching up and looking forward to what we might achieve, schemes and dreams, babe.

Adam had graduated (how upstanding) with a master's in composition from the Royal Academy of Music; he was looking for a way to straddle the classical and contemporary, and Heaven knows he had the body at least for straddling. He would practise the violin with biceps and pectorals flexing wildly inside his T-shirt, standing to look out of the window, with the hazy autumn sunlight haloing him, nostrils flaring with concentration. He seemed to be made of a flexible marble, his skin so smooth, creamy and unblemished, and his crown garnished with a thick head of brown curls, some bricolage of the Apollo Belvedere and a cappuccino. I remember the first time I saw him shirtless, him resplendent in a towel, and me feeling like a bloated skeleton in comparison. I remember feeling panic, arousal and hard-to-suppress giggles rising all at once, thinking, *You can't look at him like that!* and also *Why the fuck did I pass that up?* His polished Carrara torso, with impossible abdominal detailing and blue veins, his big round nipples the same shade of pink, I noticed, as your beautiful asshole. He turned discreetly, let the towel drop and stepped into a pair of white undies, drawing them slowly up his leg. His arse was exceptional, pornographic, divine, I was struck still at the sight, bashful but unable to look away, as a glorious voice from Heaven filled the afternoon air with the sweet trills of Rossini.

'Sarah's rehearsing for *The Barber of Seville*,' he said.

It all felt like a Fragonard painting, frothy but correct, slightly conservative even, when compared to San Francisco. Adam even had a job in West London, teaching rich brats their scales. He taught three days a week, which cramped our social life a bit, but not horribly. He took the day of my return off, but the following day he was away again to Kensington, leaving me to my jet lag, and to the dozen or so snack packs of pretzels I'd snatched from the plane.

I lay on his sofa-bed munching, regarding his mosaic of a life at twenty-four on the wall, behind which Sarah's extraordinary voice swooped and reverberated, so different from the constant hum of tumble dryers, and I thought for a disloyal moment, *This isn't so bad now is it?*

I wrote to Morgan, I wrote to Robert: *I made it back to London, somehow. Do you miss me yet? I'm staying with*

*Adam and I don't even have to sleep on the kitchen floor —
I've made it! I haven't seen anyone else, I think I sort of want
to lay low for a while, I don't know if I'm ready to jump back
into all of this yet. Ciao 4 now, call me every five minutes!
x JJ x*

There was the suspicion of a chill in the air, but the
afternoon was still bright and golden, and I felt safe, yes
really. I felt like the earth beneath my feet had stilled for
a minute, or rather that I'd acclimatised to its endless
spinnings. Such a bold romantic statement like this is
typical of a Gemini; had anything really changed besides
the weather?

I scrolled through job postings half-heartedly, flashing
back to all of my unsuccessful attempts at finding work
under the table in California, and hoping that things
would be easier (if less desirable) here. Here, where my
passport said I was entitled to work for a living, as long
as I contributed my share of taxes so the government
could continue arming and then overthrowing dicta-
torships in the Middle East.

I was very unproductive, though. I hardly moved in
fact. I was barely dressed when Adam returned from
teaching that afternoon. He said, 'Have you eaten dinner?'

Obviously I hadn't, so he made more sausages and
boiled eggs, and I never did have the heart to say that I
had given up eating meat. Afterwards he said, 'Oh Liza,
I almost forgot! Do you want to go to a party tonight?'

Of course I did.

One weekend, while away at the seaside at Aldeburgh,
workshopping a new composition, Adam had formed
a fast friendship with a famous actor. A grande dame
of British theatre, a woman with one foot onstage at
the National and one on-set in Hollywood. Maybe it
was the shared straddling that sparked their friendship,

or their bent sexualities, or maybe it was just a plain mutual love of opera. Who knows? They decided before the weekend was out that they'd write one together, an opera about a nineteenth-century surgeon who was *unmasked* as a woman after death. They were both inexplicably drawn to this story, without quite knowing why. Even when she was away in New York or Los Angeles, she would keep Adam up to date with ideas that came to her while she was working on those $200 million movies, giving blockbusters that hint of sophistication which Hollywood always has to buy in. One such note she had dashed off, invited Adam to her girlfriend's birthday party, at their home in High Holborn, and that is where we headed to that evening.

We walked all the way from Southwark. I think most all of my memories of Adam are of us walking through the city, sometimes for considerable distances, never really feeling it a chore, delighting in each other's company. We took Blackfriars Bridge, which allowed me a glimpse over the Thames for the first time since I'd been back, and I admired that lustrous cityscape, London looking like a jewellery box spilled open on the river bank. We both wore bow ties, I don't know where our overlapping appetite for them came from, but at the time we didn't feel right going out without one. I have always maintained a conviction of my robust, selfish sense of style, but from this vantage point it seems more accurate to say that I have always had a talent for squeezing into other people's wardrobes, adapting to available resources.

The night was warm, warmer than some San Francisco evenings even, and we skipped through that ghostly deserted strip of London, east of the West End, which empties out entirely at sunset. Skirting the financial district, taking Fleet Street and Kingsway, we didn't seem to encounter more than a handful of people all the way, so when we arrived in the foaming party atmosphere, it was quite a contrast.

Of course I knew our hostess from her work, but in person she was more vivacious than in the roles I'd seen her play. Perhaps sensibly, she kept this warmth and affability for her real life, off-screen, off-stage, if indeed this is what you could call real life. Her girlfriend was a bona fide celebrity beauty who played in action adventures against the ageing A-list leading men of Hollywood, and the party was well stocked with famous faces, the kind of people you would recognise instantly. It felt a little like walking into a wax museum hired for a corporate function, as if we were attending a private shindig at Madame Tussauds where everyone was allowed time enough to loiter with the waxworks, free of the crush and hubbub of the general public.

I asked Adam, 'Is that... ?'

'Yes, it is,' he answered before I'd even finished my question.

The star of the world's biggest sitcom arrived, bringing a six-pack of Evian with him, citing contractual commitments and digestive sensitivities. The birthday girl was hanging on the arm of the mega-watt co-star of her latest flick, and the face of Elizabeth Arden was wandering about with a birthday cake. Over where the table had been pushed back to make a little dance floor, I saw a novelist who had famously been under a fatwa for most of the nineties, shuffling about semi-rhythmically. I felt drugged. It wasn't that I was starstruck (the only time I've ever felt like that happened years later when Derek Jarman's muse asked if I wanted to dance), rather, I couldn't quite comprehend how all of these people had come to be in the same sphere. They seemed to have little in common (in their work at least) besides success. Is it just that at a certain level you have to hang about with people who are as famous as you, I wondered, or else you'd simply be embarrassed by your own greatness? Everyone seemed so beautifully out of place, like all those ancient bronze statues arranged in a field of flowers in Godard's *Contempt*, gorgeously incongruous.

Through this melange of household names and gossip mag icons came our hostess, dishing out more sausages (with mash this time) to her guests, who all looked utterly delighted by this homely touch. She was all grace, and if she was aware that she was standing on top of the world, she didn't appear affected by it.

'How are you?' she asked me, though we'd only just met. 'Not bored, I hope? Having a good time? Adam's told me a lot about you.'

I blushed and said, 'Oh likewise! And what a lovely home you have.'

I could feel you over my shoulder smirking, snorting, mimicking me, *Oh likewise I'm sure! Fuck's sake Bibby.* Suddenly I felt very guilty that I hadn't called you. I wanted to, but honestly the whole thing had been so intense, I was a little afraid of it, of the heat of it. Or if I'm being really truthful, afraid of the possibility that it might have burnt itself out. I didn't feel ready to be consumed again, by anything, not passion, not disappointment, I wanted to live in the moment, especially when the moment was turning out to be so very unexpected, still pregnant with possibility.

From his modest, homely letters over the summer I would never have imagined Adam had been keeping this sort of company, but then I guess you never really know anybody, do you? It was an unreal occasion, spectral even, but it felt like a fitting welcome back to London, back to this haunted house, back home, if I could ever have considered London home. Or at least it made me feel that I hadn't entirely left all that was magic and unpredictable behind me in California. I was confused, I was jet-lagged, I couldn't really make much sense of any of it, but perhaps I was glad to be back?

When we picked up our coats and said our goodbyes, thanking our lady of the bangers and mash sincerely for the hospitality, we saw that on the thinning dance floor, the writer was still at it. He danced alone and awkwardly, like an uncle drunk on Carling at your First Holy Communion. He bopped about, out of time, but seemingly quite happy, and I recognised the song as 'I Will Survive'.

I couldn't resist texting my mother on the way home, to share what I'd seen, and even though it was after 1 a.m. she wrote back straight away saying, 'Well he did survive didn't he?'

V

You don't need a watch to tell the time, you can look at the sun; you don't need a diary to tell you where you are in the year, just look at the colour of the priests' robes. Right now they're wearing purple for Lent. A pick-up truck drives through Tacubaya, my neighbourhood, every day at breakfast time and then again at twilight, broadcasting a slurred, pre-recorded message through an antediluvian speaker system. The voice of an eternally young woman calls out, *Lavadoras, microondas, estufas, artículos domésticos no deseados.* She's offering to buy any unwanted household goods for a fair price. I follow this birdsong, as others follow the adhan or the barechu; I use it to begin and end my writing each day. Something of the eternal is stored up in the old girl's recorded, distorted voice, as it is in the Lenten chasubles, and the sun's steady pilgrimage across the brilliant sky. Her chant gives me borders, making it possible for me to fall backwards and forwards through time, I find myself carried on a series of concentric circles. Truly time is ever circulating, and our great challenge is how to square this gospel with the comforting fiction of a linear narrative.

Father Ignacio dresses in accordance with the Church's calendar, in and out of ordinary time, the amplified voice of this rag'n'bone child weaves away from, and then returns to my neighbourhood. 'Back now,' you once wrote without explaining where you'd been. Sometimes when I reread that old letter I wonder if you hadn't coyly omitted a word, 'Come.' I puzzle on whether it wasn't in fact an imperative, 'Come back now.'

Once I had left Robert's room and installed myself in Adam's, I found that your letters had taken on a new meaning, they had become souvenirs from California, occasionally flecked with donut crumbs, stained with iced coffee. I studied them to see if, in this new context, they might give up their secret and tell me where I stood, but as always they refrained coquettishly.

I set about finding a job, a hustle of some sort to bring me back into the rhythm of life in London; but I'm a very impatient person, I get bored quickly, and so a week of classified ads proved very tiresome, even when I seemed to be making progress. I got an interview pretty quickly, but for a job I knew I didn't really want, all I really wanted was to remain free. I attended dutifully, hoping that they wouldn't hire me, tired out by the whole charade of plastering a smile on my face, and nodding fallaciously to try and win over a bunch of corporate morons. When the weekend rolled in I was ready for it.

At that time the weekend meant Raymond's Revue Bar on Friday, Bar Music Hall on Saturday, and Hoxton Bar and Grill on Sunday, parties to be attended with all the propriety once reserved for the opera, the ballet and the theatre. Was it a compulsion or an obligation, the paralysing fear of missing out, or the desire to get our faces in one more magazine before they all moved online, that drove us so fastidiously out? I don't think I ever thought about why I made the rounds so religiously; it must've been the feeling of reprieve that parties always gave me, a sense that anything might still happen, and because I love dancing. I didn't have a job yet, I didn't have a room, but I still had faith that nightclubs could change my life, and so I was putting all my chips on that.

It was a ridiculous way to live, not all that different to how Robert and Morgan and I had managed to coast on our slim San Franciscan social credit for so long, with free meals at a brasserie on Market Street. Morgan's friend was the maître d' and wanted to give the place a sexy, crazy frisson, so she invited us to drink and dine on the house any time we wanted – an offer we very readily accepted. We arrived ravenous every evening for two weeks straight, ate octopus and knocked back Bellinis, threw up in the toilets, and heckled the paying guests until we were put in a taxi home. We'd sleep it off, wake up again at 3 p.m., dress for dinner and walk back over to the restaurant. That we kept this up for a fortnight, before we were thanked for our services with one final round of cocktails, is both miraculous and testament to just how far I am capable of pushing my luck. I've never really known when enough is enough. Ironically over the years this has come to make me very wary of starting new things up, because once something gets going, be it drugs, or sex, or writing this out to you now, I know that it's pretty much impossible for me to pull back, to quit, to stop.

On Sunday night in Shoreditch, highly energised, and knowing your best friend was amongst the DJs, I went out with Adam to see and be seen. I remember how new this all still was to him, and how well he took to it, as though he too had spent his own adolescence in gay clubs, rather than in serious musical study. When

I first met him he owned one non-classical CD, Mariah Carey's *Music Box*, sitting alone, ostracised on a shelf full of Mozart, Britten, Chopin and the adored Ligeti.

When we first started dancing together, to techno or pop, I'd ask, 'Do you like this?'

And he'd say, 'I love it! What is it?'

Arriving a little late, we could see the crowd at the door from across Hoxton Square, a line of people so long it was clear that they would never all get in, not if the party ran until 6 a.m. and had twice the space.

'Liza!' Adam said. 'That queue is massive!'

But I hadn't got all dressed up and skipped paying the bus fare just to wait in the street with a bunch of hopeful amateurs. We swerved away from the line, towards the guest list scrum.

'Are we on the list, Liza?' he asked.

'No,' I said, 'but don't you worry your curly head about that.'

Better than the list was Kalika, a roving hungry ghost, who could cross over from the realm of the rave into the streets to snatch up sorry souls huddled on the pavement, if they looked good enough. Resplendent in the regalia of the undead club kid (latex, blue face, outrageous headpiece), she saw us, came forth and waved, 'Come in girl – come in!'

She yelled to the always present skinny bitch with the clipboard, 'These two have *got* to come in.'

No questions asked, a couple of air kisses shared, and Kalika was back off, on her phone, calling to an unknown presence, 'Where are you? I'll get you. I don't see you. Where are you?'

As anyone who had grown up on *Party Monster* will tell you, the first thing to do after arriving at a club is to make the rounds, scope out who's there, wearing what, who's cruising who, who's being trailed by a camera crew, and why. Everyone who wanted to soak up a bit of kudos or flaunt their hard-earned cachet was in that crowd. I remember watching the old guard and the new wave squaring up, when a renowned make-up artist came in with a photographer to shoot a style story for Italian *Vogue*. Some recent Central Saint Martins graduate, some new designer, hissed, 'Don't let her take your picture, she'll steal your look!'

With the voice of Hera, she quipped back, 'Ha! Mother did that look years ago.'

We saw Helen and Dixie plotting something, kneedeep, we saw Elsa taking Polaroids of two painters from Florence, we saw Jovian dancing with the editor of *i-D*, we saw Leo roll about on the dance floor with lipstick all over his face, writhing under a blanket of camera flashes. It was as if I'd never been away, like I'd simply gone to the bathroom for five minutes, and not to California for three months. The world keeps turning, it pays you no mind, things tick over almost as if you were never there, so how can we ever know that we ever *were* there? Theoretical physicists say that nothing exists, besides the relationships between things, that is to say particles which are sometimes there and sometimes not, fluctuating in the space-time field. Looking out over the overdressed and underwhelmed, at these blessed children, the ones chosen by the Gods of art and fashion and music to represent them here on Earth, I could almost buy that theory. I watched them bump and grind, or stand about posing, embrace each other, blank each other, feeling that I was right at the heart of it, and simultaneously relegated to the sidelines. I saw them as a heaving encyclopaedia of nightlife, the shades of Studio 54, the Blitz Club, Le Chat Noir and Chez

Romy Haag all bustling forth from the past and onto the dance floor.

Your new lover, Paulette, materialises out of a dark corner. I recognise her from a photograph you've sent me, of the two of you pulling tongues in Piccadilly Circus of all places. But how does she know who I am? She comes towards me with both hands outstretched, like a handmaiden, like a priestess, like a witch.

'You're back,' she says.

'I am,' I say.

She gives me a smile, a genuine smile, it's almost as if she's the first person to notice in fact that I am here. As if I'd been a spectre stalking the disco, and everyone else I'd waved to and blown kisses at had looked right through me. As if I am dead already, but no, Paulette can see me, I must still be living. How lovely she is, the perfect architecture of her body, the incomparable combination of aristocrat and dominatrix she carries. And the warmth she effuses, no hint of unkindness or of jealousy, but no submission or capitulation either, just something I might even call kindness, were I to value such a workaday concept.

'Thomas hasn't seen you yet,' she says, with a little grin.

She leads me by the hand into a quieter area opposite the bar, an awkward little corner in which there are no chairs to sit on, and where the ceiling slopes so as to make standing difficult. Of course this is where I find you, in this halfway house of discomfort, of not quite knowing, neither one thing nor the other. I know this is where she will lead me, so why don't I turn away and head towards the dance floor? Instead I come, with Adam, into your infernal throne room. It's bare and hardly welcoming, you're flanked as always by a few strung out admirers, some of whom I recognise, and smile to.

'Alright Bibby,' you say, matter of fact.

'Hello Thomas,' I reply, not knowing what tone to strike here in front of your gorgeous lover, and my best friend. 'Do you know Adam?' I ask, thinking that I can at least buy myself a minute with social etiquette.

'Dunno,' you say, sizing him up. 'Maybe.'

Adam excuses himself almost immediately from your evaluating glare. He says, 'Liza, I'm just going to pop to the loo,' and slips out of this overcrowded homecoming, and back into the party.

'Who's that?' you ask.

'Adam,' I repeat, 'I just said that, two seconds ago.'

'You shagging him?'

'No I'm not,' I blush, 'I'm just staying with him.'

And just like that, like walking drunk straight through a French window (without even noticing that I'm cut up and decorated with shards of sparkling glass), just like that I'm back. I had wanted to believe that if I could put off seeing you for long enough, that when we met again it would be a non-event, that I wouldn't find it impossible to say, *Nice to see you Thomas, I'll call you next week.* That it would be in my power to follow Adam back across the dance floor, to go and get lost amongst the preening crowd, to forever be forgotten by you. But it is not so; the flame of my infatuation hasn't yet burned down, or perhaps I just haven't kept away long enough.

Leo comes over laughing like a madman, offers a quick hello and begins to regale everyone with some ludicrous anecdote, making it easy for you and I to peel off into private conversation. We lower our voices a little, as if they weren't already masked by the music, as if everybody didn't already know about this.

'How's things?' I ask.

You say, 'This place is a shithole – everyone here's a cunt.'

'Harsh,' I say.

You slouch against the slanted ceiling, you look like you're squatting a doll's house, you tap your can of beer against my ribcage and say, 'Want a bit?'

'Yeah mate,' I say, borrowing your laddish affectations, 'I want a bit alright.'

You crack the tip of a smile, and say, 'You're quite dirty aren't you Bibby? Bibby, the flamboyant homosexual, is actually quite a dirty bastard.'

'Something like that,' I say. 'Only I don't see why I can't be both. Why do I have to be one or the other? I don't believe in binaries.'

'Oh, no Bibby,' you recoil, 'not this California *deconstruction* bollocks Bibby, please. Not from an Englishman.'

'God, you are a nightmare,' I say, incredulous at how quickly you have slipped under my skin, to fill me with that familiar flush of anger and desire. I break off. I say, 'I want to find Lulu.'

You don't bat an eyelid. You say, 'She's probably out the front smoking.'

I stalk back out into the party, looking for Lulu, who has apparently already gone home. At a loss, I string a few words of conversation together with Tina whom I bump into near the cloak room. For some reason it's even more difficult than usual to talk sense with her. She keeps asking, 'Do you think I'm the most beautiful drag queen in the room? Do you think I'm too fabulous?'

I assure her she is, but she goes on, gabbing, 'You're just saying that to shut me up, aren't you? Because I'm getting on your nerves and you want me to be quiet, don't you? Well guess what? I am TOO fabulous.'

And then, as usual, you stroll apathetically back into my eyeline and say 'Alright?', as if we haven't just been talking.

Automatically I point to Tina and say, 'Oh, do you two know each other?'

'Yes,' she says, 'he's a twat,' and leaves.

'What's that about?' I ask, though it's hardly surprising that two such difficult people should antagonise each other.

You shrug, and say, 'Dunno. Probably doesn't like me because she's a shit Northern drag queen.'

It's not even a good joke, not even a fair read, but I laugh, and I know I am done for as soon as you prise that out of me. You take a step closer towards me. In my heels I am as tall as you, but the heat of your breath on my face makes me feel minute and powerless, and the hand that you slip in your shorts tells me that I should lay down my resistance, make it easy on myself.

Leapling, you predator, you murderer. I'm lost, I think, I'm already dead.

'Am I going to get a fuck then?' you ask.

'Dunno,' I reply, aping you.

You smirk, 'Dickhead.'

Although the party will keep on going for another hour or so, it feels like the right time to be thinking about taxis and night buses, before things start to get too crazy out on the street. Elsa comes running towards me, ahead of Adam, singing, 'Liza! Here you are, Liza Minnelli! Where have you been all night, you absolute tart?'

She embraces me, ignores you, and says, 'I missed you, you sexy croque madame, how was San Francisco? No, don't tell me now, I have to go because I have a casting at 10 a.m.! *Madre de Dios!* Let's meet for a celebrity cappuccino this week though, yes?'

'Yes, Liza,' I say. '*Tout de suite.*'

Adam says he'll walk with her, as far as the Tate, and asks if he should leave the light on for me at home.

'Maybe,' I say, 'I might stay out a while longer though.'

'OK Liza,' he says, softly, and kisses me on the cheek, 'I'll see you tomorrow then.'

And they go, leaving us alone again, to play our silly game of cat and mouse.

VI

Whilst I had been away Elsa had enrolled at Central Saint Martins, I admired her for that. She was taking steps towards actualising her potential by studying for a degree in time-based art at the Charing Cross campus. That notable old edifice is now a block of luxury flats, and the creative high jinks which once defined the place have been not exactly erased, but subsumed into the building's new life of live-in nannies and thirty-quid hand soap. I'm sure the people who live there tell their guests (and probably themselves when they jerk off) *Alexander McQueen developed his skills right here!* Generations of great British talent had poured out their souls there in order to stare down whichever demons drove them to the creative arts, and naturally, to increase the property value in the area while they were at it.

Because Elsa had worked in fashion since she was fourteen, the womenswear students in the building all pounced on her, paying her the princely sum of £25 a pop to act as a fit model. They tacked their toiles to her in order to see their designs on her flesh before they cut the garment in velvet, leather or brocade. Being an art student working undercover in the fashion department gave Elsa a deeply inverted voyeuristic thrill, she'd turned the tables. She thought that if nothing else she'd get some good material out of it for her own work.

'And the twenty-five quid always come in handy too, Liza,' she said.

We met for coffee, a few days after our brief reunion at the club. She entertained me at length with tales of what went on at the storied school, she spoke for so long in fact that she missed her afternoon class. The womenswear design MA was overseen by a woman who, for many people, *was* the British fashion industry. An old-school professor who told it like it was, and would've thrown a glossy coffee-table book (signed and dedicated to her, naturally) at anyone who spoke back to her, though no one on record had ever dared to. As is the way in such a cruel business as fashion, the most merciless bullies are lauded and applauded for their straight talk, by designers who go on to become billionaire businessmen with drug problems which lead them to suicide.

Elsa said, 'Liza! You wouldn't believe it! They took me up to the great lady herself yesterday. She asked me to turn around in the dress, so she could see the detailing at the back. So I did, and she said, "Horrible! Terrible! What have I been teaching you all? And who is this model? This fat cow with the hooker's cleavage? Get her out of here!"' Elsa snorted with laughter, 'Can you believe it? She actually said that, Liza!'

She was beside herself; it took a while for her to regain her composure. 'Hooker's cleavage!' she repeated, squeezing her really rather modest breasts together, and then cracking up again. When her giggles finally subsided, she said, 'Oh Liza, I haven't asked about you! Is it strange to be back?'

'It is,' I said, 'I miss the sun.'

I told her in some detail about how I'd misspent my time in San Francisco, much of which she knew from emails, and from details Adam had shared, but she sat through the retelling quite patiently. It was really only a prelude to the present day anyway, a prologue to set up the now. Surely enough we reached the topic forever on my mind, the seemingly insurmountable subject of love.

'Thomas James?' she asked.

'He's a fucking nightmare,' I said.

'Oh Liza,' she sighed half-seriously, 'If he's such a pain, why don't you get rid of him and date Liza instead? You and he would be great together! You two could write beautiful operettas, and I could sing them all!'

And she gave a little improvised performance of a soprano at full tilt, in the coffee shop, singing, 'Liza Minnelli should marry Liza Minnelli and write an opera for me – Liza Minnelli!'

She had a beautiful voice, but then everything about her was beautiful. I say I'm not a jealous person, but perhaps I am, jealous of talent though, not of possessions, if, that is, we can't claim to own our gifts, but merely share a body with them.

'I think that moment has passed for us now,' I told her. I said, 'There are some opportunities which only offer themselves once,' and I felt regret arrive.

'Oh Liza,' she said, 'this does all seem like a bit of a mess.'

'Uh-huh,' I said. 'You know, when I told my mother that I was gay, the first thing she said was, "After all the trouble I've had with fellas?" I'm beginning to think she's wiser than I ever gave her credit for.'

I spoke with a smirk, but I couldn't convince either of us that I was as blithe as all that, so I switched tracks, and told Elsa about the job I'd found, at a perfumers in the City.

'You know, I can't imagine you with a job,' she said, then stopped, embarrassed. 'I'm sorry Liza, that sounded rude. I'm not saying you aren't capable, it's just, well…' she trailed off.

I knew well what she meant. My own feigned enthusiasm for this new career was itself wafer-thin.

'I know,' I said, 'this isn't where I thought I was headed either. I feel like a late-term abortion, like I've been ripped out of my own life.'

But Elsa brightened. 'Maybe it will be fun,' she said. 'Maybe you'll meet a few sexy croque madames. You know, working in the City could be quite glamorous. Maybe you'll be whisked away by a financier, or the CEO of Pepsi even, like Joan Crawford herself!'

Elsa was always so enthusiastic, even about the most hopeless of lost causes. Like a Truman Capote character, she had a sort of genius for spinning elaborate fantasies around irremediable circumstances; it was as if she thought she could keep her own sadness at bay by believing so deeply in other people's inevitable happiness.

'Yes, yes,' she said, 'I can see you married to a banker, with a little dog under your arm, in furs and diamonds! You look a bit like a young Lady Astor, actually.'

'Lady Astor?' I asked.

'Oh yes, Liza,' she said, 'I learned all about her while I was standing around in those half-made dresses. Apparently she was Pierre Balmain's favourite model in the sixties before she got married, but then she got caught up in some big high-society sex scandal, which I think is also very you, Liza Minnelli. And then her husband died and so she converted to Catholicism, and now she's a psychotherapist. Such a strange life.' She gazed over the rim of her coffee cup, out of the window, disappearing for a moment into a sombre consideration of the Viscountess's turbulent existence.

Personally, I wasn't sure I could move from fragrance counter to country seat quite as quickly as Elsa believed possible, but I was certainly a little cheered up by her ebullience. And at least the job was something. Some suggestion of roots anchoring me into the still spongy ground beneath my feet. You see, leapling, I had to find a way, any way really, to nail myself down, or else I'd have been taken out by the current, far from London, far from you, and in all likelihood carried back in ignominy to teacher training and my mother's house. I couldn't, I wouldn't. So I accepted this life selling perfume in the City. *Just for a while*, I told myself. *Until I see how things work out.*

I hadn't told you about this new job. I was afraid you'd tease me, either for being reduced to a shop girl, or else for working at such a snotty establishment. I didn't know if this news would bring out the Tory or the Commie in you, no one could ever tell from which direction your jeers might come. This ambivalence seems now to have been the foundation of our mutual attraction, neither of us ever seemed willing to openly declare where we stood on the matters of core identity, or depth of feeling.

The last time we had woken up together in your bed, you had been busy with other concerns, mainly pouring cases and cases of vitriol over Jovian, a friend, I'd thought, for life. I hadn't seen much of him myself since I'd been back. His cabaret had been cancelled by the restaurant over accusations of theft and damage to the property, though the reality of the situation was that the owners had realised they could turn a bigger profit putting tables where the stage once was. Jovian had retreated into himself, until he could find a new venue, and by all accounts was in a very blue mood.

Remembering the many pleasant afternoons the three of us had shared in his flat, I said, 'We should go over and visit Jovian one day.'

'He's a cunt,' you said curtly.

This was because the boy he'd suggested to replace your hated Australian roommate had proved to be even worse, and you held him personally responsible.

'He can fuck off,' you said. 'He's shown his true colours with his poor choice of *friends*.'

Unrequested, you gave me the lay of the land as it now stood, brought me up to speed with how things had changed in my absence, without explicitly saying so. You still saw Lulu, you still held an affection for her, and for Leo too, strangely. He was the only person I knew to blatantly take the piss out of you, and maybe that's why. No mention of Anders or Lucy, whom I presumed had either committed no outrage of note, or else had long gone on the bonfire. Paulette was who I thought you were most unfair to. When I asked you about her, asked rather delicately if you were still intimate, you laughed and said, 'My brief foray into snatch? Yeah, that's over.'

'You seemed quite chummy last time I saw you together,' I protested.

'Yeah well, I'm a nice guy,' you said. 'It's finished but I'm not being a cunt about it.'

'You're mad,' I snorted. 'She's *unbelievably* gorgeous.'

'Well, unfortunately, in her weakness as a woman,' you said with visceral disdain, 'she decided to fuck that Australian dickhead too, didn't she? Foolishly coinciding with Jovian's poor judgement.'

'Wow!' I gasped, 'You're brutal.'

We were naked in your bed. I rolled away from you, but you pressed up behind me, reached your hand under the duvet and towards my cock. It was already semi-hard, and you said, 'What's all this then?'

I blushed, a little embarrassed.

Caressing my arse with one hand and rolling my balls in the palm of the other, you asked, 'What about your mate anyway?'

'Who?' I said.

'The one you're staying with. Shagged him yet?'

I was stiff in your hands now. I flushed further, and said, 'Oh Adam? No. No, it's not like that.'

You noticed that talking about him like this was making me harder still, and you sniggered a little sadistically at my self-consciousness.

'Not like you Bibby,' you said, taking on a mock Yankee accent, 'not like you to pass up *a fine piece of ass.*'

'Stop it,' I said meekly, my face pink and open.

You were enlivened by how obviously ill at ease this line of chat had made me; you were hard too. You moved in one long seamless motion, vaulting over me like a lithesome competitive gymnast, pinning me flat on my back. You looked into my eyes, searching for the source of my growing humiliation, and when you found it you smirked, but didn't break off your study. Maintaining this hypnotic glare, this domineering gaze, you straddled your legs either side of me and started to rub your arse up against my cock. You let the head of my dick rest against your hole, briefly, torturously, toying with me, as if weighing up whether or not you would let me back inside you. Then roughly, aggressively, as if you had to have it, you spat in your hand and reached behind you to slather your saliva on my cock.

'Come on then,' you said and slipped my dick inside you. You grunted loudly as it opened you up wide, you bucked up on it, riding me like a cowboy. We didn't normally fuck very verbally but your mood that morning was slanderous, merciless, so you pressed your face right into mine and said, 'I bet you'd fucking love to do this to your mate wouldn't you? Fucking love to.'

I didn't respond, I couldn't. I was paralysed with this intoxicant, this coalescence of lust and lechery and shame.

You said, 'Imagine it's him you're fucking now. Adam. Imagine it's his arse you're fucking.'

You leant back, eyes closed, teeth together, grinding my girth against your prostate, stroking your cock and forcing mine deeper and deeper within you. Groaning, you dropped your head back over your shoulders in deep pleasure, and with your face towards Heaven, and a weak rim of late autumn sunlight glancing off your cheek, you looked like nothing more than that Wolfgang Tillmans portrait of Damon Albarn in the shower. Then, quite abruptly, without any warning, you came hard all over my body. You shot your load in rapid spurts across my stomach, my chest, as far as my throat. I felt your arse contract around me violently, and very quickly it was over. You pulled my dick out with a sharp intake of breath between your teeth, saying, 'Fuck! I was really horny.'

Then, you stood up, threw yesterday's boxers over to me so I could wipe up the cum and said, 'I've got to get ready to go.'

I looked out of the window, searching the sky for a hint of blue, waiting for my hard-on to subside, listening to you sing 'For Tomorrow' from the kitchen.

VII

A few unremarkable weeks passed by. You went away on a trip to Copenhagen; I told myself that was fine, I had other things to worry about, you'd be back. Winter made herself known and I wrote with increasing frequency to Morgan and Robert: *This place is freezing, and so grey, it's like a Sherlock Holmes film. Why didn't I just overstay my visa and live on with yous two, become the illegal immigrant I was born to be? I guess that you were probably quite glad to get rid of me for a while though, right? I've dragged the full weight of my dependency onto Adam's bed now, for better or worse. It's literally insane, we share the same bed and I lie there all night with a huge erection. I have to make sure I face the wall because I don't want my dick to rub up on him in my sleep! I'd be mortified, he's like my brother now. Only my brother is in a young offenders' institute, so maybe that's not a fair comparison. Seriously though, I miss yous, when will I see you both?*

The ache that accompanied writing those emails and waiting for a response, like sending a begging letter to a lover, *Take me back, I've changed.* Who knew that technology could have such a bite, such a sting? That it's not just some neutral network of swift messages, that it can dish out retribution as easily as a meek 'how are you?' Technology, the loathsome thing, worse even than books. At least people have largely given up reading now, but the sprawl and spam of the internet goes on, ad infinitum holding us prisoner in the suspended illusion of freedom.

Away from the computer, in what remained of my offline imagination, San Francisco had already been anthologised for me as the Valley of No Tears, where we all lived off Little Debbie snack cakes and never gained weight, where freedom was a reality, and frivolity was an inalienable right. The weeping comedowns, the sunburnt necks and the squabbles over the last of the Pop-Tarts were not recorded as part of this myth. Involuntarily the unpleasant details sank like sediment in the still waters of my memory. Even when I was forced, by the fragile nature of my present situation, to face up to the imperfect truth of the past, I refused to assess with any seriousness the eggshell-fine, breakable nature of the future, or the delicate situation I was in.

I had my job at the perfumers, selling eau de cologne to hurried businessmen as last-minute gifts for their secretaries, wives and mistresses, but had yet to see my salary clear. The road to Hell is paved with good intentions, yes, but it's unpaid wages and clerical errors that cement the gaps in between the flagstones. I was working close to fifty hours a week and still I was flat broke. It was a humiliating time, to admit that I was helpless, and a short step from homeless, even though I was employed in a job as meaningless, degrading and unrewarding as was expected of someone of my background.

Adam was doing his best to love me in spite of having been forced, at the gunpoint of his own generosity, to share a house, to share a room, to share a bed with me for six weeks already, and for no real recompense.

Because it was approaching Christmas and he was looking for some extra cash to buy gifts, he took a part-time
job in the City too, at a mid-level luxury shoe shop, just
around the corner from where I worked. I myself was
going to gift everyone I knew with looted bottles of
bath oil, taken in lieu of the interest accrued on unpaid
earnings.

'Your revolution will be finely fragranced, Liza,' he
had said. He was always so tender, so rarely judgemental.

I was talking with him one day after work, about
the holy trinity of Warhol queens, Jackie, Holly and
Candy. He was fresh out of the shower, I was waiting to
go in, he stood there pink and moist, a towel wrapped
around his waist, slung low, the thick curved outline of
his cock clear and calling.

I looked away timidly, and blabbered on, 'Who was it?
Fran Lebowitz? Or Julie Newmar, who had that great
line in the documentary? You know, "Candy Darling
was the most glamorous person I've ever met – but she
was always sleeping on somebody's couch!"'

'I can't remember,' he said with an easy open smile,
'but it sounds like someone else I know.'

Intrigued by this response, I turned my body to
mirror his, holding my own towel lightly by the loose
knot which kept it closed. He was perhaps an arm's
length away. I let my eyes skim over his near-nakedness,
quite flagrantly. He was still smiling so I stepped closer,
he didn't say anything.

Sarah's angelic voice filled the room with golden
notes, Adam held my gaze and ran his hand through
his wet curls, exposing the hair of his armpit and the
thick, pearlescent musculature of his biceps, triceps
and lats. Steam was rising from his broad shoulders,
droplets of water running down his throat, between

his pecs, over his rippled abdomen and into the bush of hair just visible over his towel. I took another step closer, he didn't move. I smirked and asked, 'Don't you think it's funny that after all this time living together, we haven't ever seen each other naked?' I paused, my breath coming quickly now, and said, 'We've never even once been naked together.'

But I'd overplayed my hand. A cloud passed over his face, his expression lost all of its light.

'Yeah,' he said, 'and I'd like to keep it that way.'

I blushed scarlet, and he turned to the wall, sliding a pair of white Gap undies up under his towel, like a prudish tourist on a Greek beach.

Over his shoulder he said, 'I just don't see you like that.'

I felt completely ashamed. I saw myself as he saw me for the first time, my nail polish, my cinematic hairdo, my smooth legs and torso, saw how deeply unerotic my whole mode of being was to him. Crimson-faced, I hurried to the bathroom, to shower and hide my shame. From under the running water I heard him leave the flat, with an uncharacteristically curt, 'I'm going out – I'll be back late – see you.'

It wasn't the sound of his endurance failing, not yet, but it suggested tensions, undeniably. He didn't ever mention the incident again, we just set it aside and we went on much the same, as friends, as good friends. But something had changed, a confidence had been betrayed. After that, if I was home, Adam would change in the bathroom. He gave up the ritual of holding me in his arms for a little while, each morning after his alarm went off, and I was most of all sorry for that. Sex you can find anywhere, but a warm connection like ours was is a rarer thing, and one that I felt the loss of profoundly.

Quite why I feel so compelled to write out all of these little mortifications now, I don't know. Am I attempting to be comprehensive, or am I hoping to perform some act of self-flagellation with the page? I can't say. I feel that I am now just two hands in motion over a keyboard, barely sentient, animated by a power greater than myself, a vessel, as Martha Graham called herself, for something I don't necessarily understand. 'We do not know how to pray as we ought,' wrote St Paul to the Romans, 'but the Spirit himself intercedes with inexpressible groanings.' So I trust to this text to reveal itself to me, disgrace, abasement and all.

You announced your return from Copenhagen, with a text that read, *I'm back what's the vibe Bibby?* I imagined you'd sent a few such messages out, casting about to see who was ready to receive you now that you were home, so it hadn't cheered me much. It appeared as I waited for Adam on a bench outside the Royal Exchange, we had plans to share an overlapping lunch hour. I read it back a few times, willing myself to just delete it. Then Adam arrived, and the pathetic way I fumbled to get my phone back into my pocket made the contents of the message grievously clear.

He kissed me on the cheek, things were still a little awkward after our ignominious misunderstanding, but not painfully so; he disliked conflict, he wasn't the type to revisit these things out loud. We had said that we would talk about it, but of course we never did. He dropped down on the bench next to me, looking hearty. Clearly I hated my job much more than he hated his. I felt crushed into insignificance by the financial district's neo-classical bulk; it was perverse that we earned minimum wage there in the shadows of fortune, empire and slavery. Adam seemed to enjoy selling shoes to executive secretaries, but

I had such contempt for my job, such loathing, that still I can hardly bear to speak about it now. As a writer I have that power, I can decline to say any more about that job, and I do so, because it was a miserable waste of time, and because it is unnecessary to the story I am trying to tell. Like Sheila E. said, *The discipline is when not to play.*

I sat chewing an egg mayo butty, and slugging corporate chain coffee. The diminishing sunlight made me pine for happier afternoons, at home, watching my little sisters play in the garden. I tried (and failed) to be thankful for life's small mercies.

'This place really is the end,' I said.

'I quite like it,' Adam replied.

'But you like everything and everyone,' I said.

'Not everyone,' he said pointedly, and added, 'if you hate it so much here, why stay?'

'I'm trying to get it together, believe me,' I said, frazzled by the caffeine and too many early mornings falsifying stock checks. 'It's not easy.'

'It never is, Liza.'

I sighed. 'Well I can't just up and leave everything behind again, can I?'

'Everything?' he asked.

'You know what I mean, Liza. I have friends here.'

'Right,' he said, and shook his head. 'Only some of your friends just don't seem very nice.'

'Yeah, I know,' I replied, 'but neither does meth until you've smoked it, and even then it still seems like a horrible idea, only then you're jonesing for it.'

He frowned.

'I'm joking!' I said.

'Well, you're not painting a very pretty picture,' and here he screwed his face up a little, as though he were about to sneeze. 'You don't seem very happy.'

'I don't think I am,' I said and sighed.

'Will you be seeing Thomas James tonight?' he asked.

'No – I don't know,' I said, as though I had yet to make up my mind. 'Maybe.'

'And does that make you happy?' he asked, but only rhetorically.

'No,' I said. 'Not really.'

'So then why go?'

I couldn't answer that, but as sure as night follows day I did go. I came to you after shutting the shop and cursing my luck. All the grammar, all the tenses of my life were at odds. I don't know why, but I went, I came, like a non-native speaker who mixes up their verbs and asks, 'Shall I go to you now?'

My God, I was tired that evening, as tired as I am now, throwing all of this down on digital paper, struggling away at my kitchen table, before my wrists give way to RSI, or seize up entirely. I had never seen your apartment in winter. It was cold, and yet seemingly no more than usual, as though your place were a principality independent of the rest of London's weather. Perhaps I had just acclimatised to the chill or maybe my crashing mood had disengaged my thermostat. Regardless of the reasoning, I kept my coat on. It was a claret oversized jacket, cut to look like a shirt, a beautiful thing from Helmut Lang. It had previously belonged to a friend of a friend; it was his prized possession, until he told his boyfriend it was over, that he was leaving him for a mutual acquaintance. In retaliation his hot-headed boyfriend slashed the jacket with a pair of scissors, across the back and along the sleeves, and left it dangling on the hanger, with the stuffing popping out like cotton candy clouds of vapour. The mutual friend had patched it up, with very visible stitches, a love token to say, *Don't worry baby*, to show that he could fix the damage. He couldn't, of course, and they split soon afterwards too. I inherited the jacket, but didn't learn their lesson.

'Nice coat,' you said, and for once I don't think you were even taking the piss.

You weren't drinking beer or ale but instead you had a big bottle of Copella apple juice on the table, and I thought to myself that your picking it over the supermarket own-brand carton was a polished touch.

'So then, Bibby,' you said again, as always, 'what's the vibe?'

There was no need for anything elaborate, anything laborious, we both knew why I was there and there were no audience members to pantomime for anymore. Besides, I was too exhausted to front, worn down by a job I despaired of, by my empty pockets, and by sharing that platonic sofa-bed. I sat next to you on your couch, right thigh to left thigh close. I don't think we'd ever been in such proximity before, besides when we fucked. You liked to pace, you liked to keep a bit of space, but that night you were all stillness. In contrast, I felt the sort of palpitations you get when you're about to say 'I love you' for the first time, the same nervousness that must accompany a marriage proposal, if you really care for your intended. I was wary that you might pull away or throw me a disgruntled look, or say, 'What's all this then Bibby? Getting soppy, eh?' But you didn't. You let me drop my head on your shoulder and sit with you quietly, no wisecracks, no shifting uncomfortably where you sat, just softness and silence.

Later you showed me the treasures you had added to your trove, records and posters and videos you'd scooped up dirt cheap, at car boot sales and markets, and it felt a little like we were picking out baby clothes, didn't it? These are the first, probably the last, maybe the only gentle moments we spent together in all the time I knew you. We didn't trade insults, we didn't rib each other, or drop any unkind remarks, we just spent the evening drinking apple juice, and talking about Morrissey.

It's funny now (now that he has been unmasked as the internationally embarrassing bovver-boot closet case he is) to think of how much he meant to the two of us then. His nasty sense of humour, his self-pity, I guess we could have seen it coming. But at that time we could all take comfort in the idea that he was being ironic, or satirical, that of course he didn't really mean England for the English, when he sang 'England for the English', how could he? Someone I love very much now has a tattoo made up of Smiths' lyrics on his chest, he sometimes talks about having it removed, though he's unsure if there's really any point. It wouldn't take away the shame Morrissey has heaped on all his former fans, and nor would it undo the sentiment the words once held for him (and us) at the time. All it could possibly result in was more pain and blood and bruising. Unlike tattoos, the past cannot be covered over.

There's an impossibly small colour TV in your room, and a VHS player, picked up from a market too, I'm sure. It seems only fitting that we should regress to such antiquated technology to indulge in this adored but outdated pop star, and our own juvenile, teenage love. We watch *Morrissey Live in Dallas* on that tiny screen. There he is, back in 1991, bunches of flowers smacking him in the face as he sings, frantic college boys climbing onstage with him and ripping off their shirts; but none of it seems of much interest to the man in the spotlight. In comparison to more contemporary performers, he seems out of breath and out of tune, his schtick consists of flailing and pouting, a charismatic mess. I see at least why you loved him, though I still can't explain myself. Remember of course, this happened long before the internet made us all perfect.

He starts to sing 'November Spawned a Monster', and I am totally spellbound. I say out loud, 'I love this one. This one is from my favourite of his albums,' but then I fumble for the name of the record, I can't call it up.

'Can't remember the name of your so-called favourite album eh, Bibby? Oh dear,' you smirk. 'It's *Bona Drag*, I thought you would've remembered a name like that.'

'Dickhead,' I say, but without any malice now, without any intention to wound.

You smile, deadpan, and kiss me with a force that says, *It's getting late, come on, I want it,* and as always I give way. I stand up and hold out my hand to walk you over to the bed, to leave Morrissey serenading his fans over on the TV set, only you don't rise. You stay in your seat, but reach to unbutton my fly. The doorway is uncovered, either of your flatmates could walk by and look in, but you don't seem to care, and it's thrilling. You take my pants down to my knees, and my already hard cock in your hand, licking the viscous liquid from the tip.

'Pre-cumming in your pants already eh, Bibby?' you say with a big self-satisfied grin on your face.

The video cassette runs its course, and then once the concert is over plays on to black and white static, spilling a gentle fuzz and a low-level hiss into the otherwise noiseless room. You work your way all the way down my cock, so your nose is in my pubes, and my balls are in your face. You pull off, and use your left hand to stroke it where you kissed it, and your right hand yanks out your own stiff prick. I feel myself carried away, I push your head down deeper, so you will choke a little, you splutter, break free, spit on the floor, and then get right back to it. I watch your blond head bob, with skills gleaned through relentless practice, and I am grateful to the owners of all the other cocks you've sucked, you flawless amoral slut.

Is it common to feel madly in love every time you approach orgasm? With your lover, with life, with the universe? I can't believe this is something I'm alone in. Surely it's universal? Robert once told me that in sex he saw the face of God, and I laughed, and I'm ashamed of that laugh now. I feel my balls tighten, and that age-old feeling of surrender in me, the sensation that I am lost to a vortex of pleasure, a black hole which will consume me, in a flash of joy, a blinding momentary loss of consciousness. Wanking my cock studiously, and jerking yourself off below, you look up at me, giving me the full power of your eyes in the most flattering of lights (love) and half moan, half drool, 'Are you going to cum?'

'Yeah,' I nod, breathlessly, 'I am,' and then to illustrate my point, I begin to arch my back, and fold at the knees.

You wrap your mouth back around me and I feel my cum shoot deep down your throat, you're mumbling and spasming yourself, unloading your own big load of spunk on the floor.

Afterwards, once the blood that has rushed away returns to our heads, once we have wiped up all the spilled semen, and I have pulled up my pants, you say, with an earnestness I've never seen in you before, 'You can stay here you know. I mean, I just got back, and it's late and everything.'

I thank you and say, 'I appreciate that, but Adam would worry.'

'Adam, yeah,' you said with a shade of contempt. 'Well then, see you, Bibby.'

'See you, Tom,' I say and kiss you good night.

VIII

I was pulled out of my dreams by a coruscating agony emanating from my groin. Adam didn't wake; he snored softly on the sofa-bed, and I tiptoed in torment to the bathroom to piss away the vexation of what at first I thought was merely an overfull bladder. Pain of exceptional quality poured out with the golden stream of urine. Pain, and slime the colour and consistency of ranch dressing, accompanied by the sensation that my urethra was filled with broken glass – that I was pissing out a pogrom. The shock of standing, blinking in the bathroom light, cold, sore, water weeping from my eyes and my cock, witnessing the arrival of adulthood. I thought back to my little sister calling out to my mother from the bathroom saying, 'Mum! Mum! Something's wrong,' and my mother going in to attend to her, comforting her, saying, 'It's OK love, you're just growing up.'

Now I was coming of age with this gift from you, leapling! I was a fertile site of life at a microscopic level. Barely twenty-four hours since you'd taken my semen down your throat, here I was showing the first signs of pregnancy. Time moves so quickly at a microbial level.

I went back to bed, quietly, wincing. From the foothills of his dreams Adam asked, 'Are you OK, Liza?'

'Yes,' I said, 'fine.'

I lay in some discomfort, trying to ignore the constant burning irritation. I was a mother now and gestation is always a trial for one's physical body. Of course, I knew I couldn't keep the baby, even though I am Catholic, but I knew God would forgive me for terminating the life of this bunch of unconscious, multiplying cells. Until the morning though, I would remain the bearer of your child. I spoke to that congealing ooze within me, feeling its molecules replicate, this parasitical sludge, our child, until the sun came up.

At dawn I made use of what privacy the kitchen offered to look up the number of a clinic who could give me an abortion, and I phoned to make an appointment that very day. I called my boss to tell her I was ill, and said I would try to make it in after lunch. Undoubtedly she thought I was just getting home from a bender, but I honestly didn't care. Then I texted you, *Hey, sorry to wake you with bad news but I think you might have an STI. I'm going to the clinic, you should probably make an appointment too. I'll let you know what they say X*

The clinic offered the routine I knew from my semi-regular check-ups over the past decade or so, including the perennial question, impossible to answer, 'Are you Male (M) or Female (F)?' Just one of the components of the experience which made my visits less frequent than they should have been. When I was fourteen I had accompanied my best friend to get an HIV test in Liverpool. We spent the whole afternoon in silent panic, hanging around the hospital waiting for results, so those clinics also held a compound residue of nineties AIDS panic, and moral damnation, which I did my best to elude. But in this case it was unavoidable. I was seen pretty quickly, given the diagnosis of gonorrhoea, and the medication to deal with it, then advised to use condoms and read the pamphlets available in the waiting room. I went into work, apologising repeatedly, painfully aware that I really did look as though I'd been hard at it with a bottle of Drambuie and a few older gentlemen all night.

At lunchtime I was still pissing toxic sludge but the lacerations inside me seemed to be healing, to my great relief. I checked my phone, I had a message from you. It said: *For fuck's sake Bibby I can't believe you gave me an std.*

I thought you were joking, so I called you later, from outside the coffee shop when I went to pick up the team caramel lattes, our Christmas treat from head office.

'Hey, hi,' I said, trying to keep things light in spite of how bad I felt.

'For fuck's sake Bibby,' you said. 'You calling to say, "Hey hi" when you've given me the fucking clap?' It was clear from your tone that you were serious about this, serious and unforgiving.

'Tom,' I continued, 'I don't think I gave it to you.'

'Yeah you did,' you said, 'you probably picked it up from slagging around with all those Diegos in California. I don't know who you've been shagging.'

I was unprepared, I thought we were in this misfortune together. I said, 'That's a horrible thing to say. Why do you say that? "Diegos", Tom, that's so rude! It's just racist really, racist and rude and untrue.'

'Sort it out Bibby,' you said, 'I know how you put it about. Fuck's sake.'

I maintained my composure a moment longer, I didn't want to heap a fight on top of the flaming skip of builders' refuse this day had already become. I didn't want to embarrass myself in the doorway of Starbucks, I didn't want to turn to insults to medicate this affliction.

'Look it doesn't matter who gave it to who does it?' I said, hopefully. 'We both have it and it's easily treated.'

You replied with ire, 'Well we wouldn't have to treat it if you weren't such a slut though would we Bibby? If you weren't fucking every bumboy in LA.'

Then it all caught up with me, quick as a bullet to the head. I finally lost my patience with you, a year or so too late.

'You are *such* a cunt,' I said. 'I had sex with one person, *one person* the whole time I was away, and we were both so high neither of us could get hard, so I think it's very unlikely it's me who gave it to you isn't it?'

'Yeah, whatever, Bibby,' you said, 'I've got to go to the fucking clap clinic now so I don't have time for this shit,' and you hung up.

I was blindsided, I couldn't even find the words to curse you. I don't think I've ever been so devastated by a simple phone call. At least not since my little sister called to tell me that my mother's boyfriend had taken the dog into the garage and broken his neck.

When I took the coffees back to the shop, they were already getting cold. I realised I'd been gone for more than three quarters of an hour, so I apologised again.

'Sorry,' I said. 'The queue in there was endless today.'

I was shaking a little, from the cold of the doorway, from the medication, from the lack of sleep and our altercation.

'Still feeling a bit *unwell*, are we?' my boss asked, bitchily.

'A bit,' I said, 'but I'll be fine tomorrow.'

IX

Getting over gonorrhoea is a little like recovering from a bout of food poisoning, the untrustworthy body leaking poisonous muck at all the most inconvenient times, leaving you disgusted by your own corporeality, unable to imbibe the French pleasures of fucking and eating, until such time that the spasms and writhing have been forgotten, by the muscles at least. It took a week or so, but I came around to bodily existence again, eventually. I didn't try to address the hostilities which had opened between us though. I hoped that you'd at least send me an email, asking if I was feeling better, though I knew an apology was completely impossible.

Musing on this anger, I came home to Adam's empty flat on one of many dismal evenings, flooded with an erotic exhaustion, and found myself alone. Having worked from 7 a.m., I immediately fell onto the sofa-bed and wrapped myself in silence. Yes, the flat was exceptionally quiet, no neighbours heaving furniture about, none of the eternally ascending scales coming from Sarah's room, no traffic even, just a remarkable pin-drop stillness. I had intended to nap, but my flesh had another opinion of how I should use this time. I felt myself get hard seemingly without reason, and winced in preparation for the blade of agony which had accompanied all my erections since I acquired that unfriendly, bacterial life experience, but no pain came. Still, I pulled the bed sheets up to my chest and lay with my arms flat above them, like a hospital patient, as boys at boarding schools are told to sleep to show that they aren't abusing themselves.

Somehow, in straightening out the sheets like this I uncovered a pair of Adam's discarded underwear, left behind as he'd rushed off out, I supposed. I reached for them, initially to toss them onto the floor, but slowly my movements betrayed a different impulse. I brought them to my face and inhaled, the smell of his arse and his ball sweat very present, further swelling my convalescent dick. Of course, I began to masturbate, letting the undies rest on my face, with my nose pressed up against that strip of the crotch which had rubbed up against his hole. Yes, I felt a little disgusted with myself, but already I was too far gone to stop sniffing those most intimate scents. The smell of missed opportunities, of full balls and a firm arse, I had been taken too far out on this jet stream of pheromones to look back now. He had been so sweet to me when I told him about the STI, he hadn't even flinched, though surely he must've felt a little revolted. When I told him how cruel you'd been, he said, 'What a bastard,' and held me close again. I felt a burning ignominy at the thought of him catching me here, sprawled out on his bed, stroking my cock and sniffing his dirty undies, but that only made me more excited. I was struck all over with guilt; this was how I was repaying all of his kindnesses, jerking off in his bed, disrespecting him and his privacy? The combination of humiliation, and exhibitionism, and the smell of his sweaty arsehole was completely overwhelming, and I came hard, all over myself, ten days of repressed ejaculate splattering my torso, and then, I don't know why, but I started to cry.

Sobbing, soaked in my own semen, slowly cooling, tears rushing from my eyes in a way I had only known once before, when my first real boyfriend admitted that he had been fucking our flatmate. The same sense of brutal exposure too. I was hunched up on myself in waves of unexpected emotion, I thought I might puke, and when I tried to get up it was all I could do to sit upright and steady myself on the wall. At the time I thought I must be crying because I was tired, because I'd accidentally fallen a little bit in love with Adam, because I'd come back to an England of ever-increasing unkindness and abandoned my dreams in California. I thought it was the lack of light in London in the winter, waking up at 5 a.m. to flog perfume to sociopaths, waiting on a forever-delayed pay cheque and scraping by on a tenner borrowed here and there from anyone I could beg it off. Now of course I realise that I was crying purely and simply for you, my own wide-eyed whore, for the unnecessary viciousness you'd shown me, and for the realisation that yes, you really were bad news, the worst.

Joan Didion said that a novel is like a painting, that the first daubs define the work, that even if you try to rework it *the original strokes are still there in the texture of the thing*. The same is true for relationships, and at a certain point it's too late to overpaint them, the foundational brushstrokes have decided. I had allowed you to act the way you did for too long. I thought by ignoring your nasty remarks, your lack of grace and manners, your casual racism, and your occasional outbursts of internalised homophobia, that I would appear unassailable, unmoved by you or your childishness, robust, and above politics, like a constitutional monarch. But in allowing it, I fostered it.

Love is like learning a foreign language, a new tongue every time. You have to study the rules and the grammar, but until they become instinctive in you, you will always be fumbling to conjugate, incomprehensible and confused. Until the language is alive in you and automatic, and you can skip between tenses with ease of motion, you remain nothing but a child whose words cannot be taken seriously. Until the day arrives when you can talk about what you have, what you have had, what you once had, without stopping to run through *Yo tengo, Yo tuve, Yo tenía*, then you are lost in illiteracy. Love has to be intuitive, second nature, a reflex, but I hadn't reached that point with you yet. I wasn't at one with the logic of the language, so I could only feel pained, I couldn't ask what it was that had wounded me. I couldn't formulate the question, I could only sob and offer more inexpressible groanings.

I had just enough time to dry my eyes and clean myself up, to toss the underwear back in amongst the bed sheets, before Adam arrived home. He was tired, quieter than usual. He said hello but not much more, he showered and ate, silently. He was also thinking of how to say something.

I was sleepy, so I brushed my teeth in preparation for an early night, but before we turned in, he said, 'Liza, I have to talk to you.'

I froze where I stood. It couldn't be about the underwear, could it? He couldn't have seen, could he? Was it possible that he'd detected traces of cum, or noticed that his underwear was screwed up where he hadn't left it?

'OK,' I said, laughing nervously, my face maybe reddening.

'I'm sorry Liza,' he said, 'but I'm afraid I'm going to have to ask you to leave. I love you, but you've been here for quite a lot longer than I'd expected, and well, Sarah's a bit fed up too. It is only a small place.'

'Yes Liza,' I said, almost relieved. 'Yes of course. It's been a bit of a tough time. But then when is it not?'

'Exactly,' he said, 'that's sort of the problem, isn't it?'

I faked a smile, I thought I might cry again, but I didn't, thank God. For the moment I was all out of tears.

'Could you stay with Thomas James perhaps?' he suggested. 'Or is it still a bit weird between you two?'

'It is a bit,' I said. 'But I'll work something out.'

What did it matter where I lived really? As long as I was in London I was within striking distance, I was contactable by telephone, I could bump into you on any given street, at any number of parties, and I was so deeply disconcerted by that proximity. I went to stay with Elsa for a while, back on that couch where I'd first daydreamed of loving you, more than aware of the heavy-handed dramatic irony of my situation.

Elsa said, 'It's good to have you back, Liza! I don't know how long I can have you for this time, because my landlord is getting quite strict about guests,' and here she changed tone, not wanting to seem insensitive, adding, 'anyway I'm sure something better will come along. Any minute now Lady Astor, you sexy croque madame!'

As it happened, I didn't stay long, I didn't have to. I was spared the embarrassment of being asked to leave another friend's house, by an email from Morgan.

She wrote, *I'm so, so sorry that I've been so lousy at keeping in touch, but you'll never believe what happened! The apartment fell into the laundromat downstairs, like just literally collapsed! Isn't that insane? That landlord was always so shady. Luckily nobody was at home at the time — don't worry we're fine! It was such a mess though, and we couldn't go back inside so I couldn't write to you to explain. I've decided to go to New York, I think that this was a sign to move out of the Bay Area. You know that saying, 'If you could be happy in a bubble but never leave — would you?' Well, I don't think I would. Robert is staying but I'm not! I have a job interview in New York next week to manage a 'boutique hotel'. Seriously! I already Skyped with the guy and he seems cool, so look, I was thinking about something. You don't seem very happy in London, so why not come to New York with me? We can get married, and you can get your visa, I'm sure I could find you a job at the hotel pretty easy, at least to begin with. Then you'll find something better, you're so good at so many things. What do you think? I know it sounds insane, but I think it could work. Don't you want to live in the rotten apple, at least for a little while? It would make a great chapter for your book!*

So I was saved. Saved from a life of crying over you, and wanking off into my best friend's underwear, saved from the indignity of finding another temporary job in retail once my seasonal contract was up, saved from sleeping on couches and subsisting on supermarket meal deals. London was not for me, no, London was a mirage offering everything, giving nothing, a party I was always outside of, looking in on, through a plate-glass window.

I accepted Morgan's proposal, as transparently flawed as it was, if for no other reason than the shoddy belief I held that anything was better than this mess I'd found myself in. What had I achieved since coming back to England anyway, besides overstaying my welcome? Besides having earned just enough to leave again, by working a job not even worth writing about? As soon as I received my long overdue pay cheque I wrote to Morgan and said, *You're on! See you at JFK on the 23rd!* Life is what happens whilst waiting on wage slips, it seems.

Elsa was surprised, maybe relieved, but she said, 'Oh Liza! You'll be singing on Broadway in no time! How exciting! I'll have to come and visit you and your new wife, the future Mrs Lady Astor, Liza Minnelli the Fourth!'

She threw me a going-away breakfast party, on the morning of my flight. It was a subdued affair, not unlike a wake, or the last visit to a relative on their deathbed, and equally full of hard-to-consider memories. Adam came, and Jovian came, Lulu called to say she hadn't been to bed yet and would have to miss it. She wished me well though, and said she'd see me out there.

Elsa opened two of the relics she'd stashed in the kitchen for just such an occasion: a jar of foie gras from her grandmother, and a bottle of champagne left over from Christmas. You were noticeably absent. I hadn't asked you, I hadn't even told you I was leaving this time. Everybody else had (I presume) silently agreed, on my behalf, not to invite you, though in reality this was really a party in your honour; this trip, this new chapter was dedicated to you, or rather to putting the continents back where they belonged, between us.

Adam and Jovian and Elsa came with me all the way to Heathrow, trying to allay my nerves, to buoy up my mood with their projections of how incredible everything would be for me now.

'A new life, a new wife, a New York!' said Jovian. 'And if you can make it there – you'll see us all coming to stay with you!' he broke off with a laugh.

One of the wheels came off my suitcase. I panicked when I thought I'd lost my passport. The lady in blue and red at the American Airlines counter let me check in with 10kg of excess luggage without charging me extra. I boarded the flight with no regrets. Eight hours later I landed in New York, satisfied that I had now done enough to be rid of you for good.

X

I loved Morgan, more than enough to have married her, and I believe that she loved me, that we could have made a perfectly happy couple (all the happier since we didn't fuck), lost amongst the millions of immigrants who come to New York every year, on a sea of forged social security numbers and healthcare dodges, to get swallowed up in menial jobs and rent spikes. We might have settled into an unremarkable, haphazard existence, fraught with panic and fervour, hustling for better prospects, our beggings and ravings ringing harmoniously within the city's eternal hymn of honks, howls and hallelujahs. We might even have found our way to respectability, had Morgan's job at the boutique hotel worked out. I might have made a go of life as a concierge or a chambermaid, like Sophie Calle but without the family money. We might have become eco-tourism start-up billionaires, we might have become friends with Oprah, converted to Buddhism, collected a few Rothkos. Might might might, I might have married Morgan and lived happily ever after in spite of everything, and you, in turn, might have lived to be thirty. Might, might, might, one more word for the bonfire.

Instead, Morgan's hotel management ambitions came to a sudden sodden end when a water main burst and the whole place flooded, three days after I arrived in New York.

'Honestly,' she said, 'it's like I live under a Biblical curse – ceilings collapse, buildings flood. What next? Locusts?'

No one walks out of an old life and into a new one, all neat and square at the corners just like that. It was all too good to be true, of course it was. Did I really believe that I could turn up, no papers, no savings, no plan, and just make it work? Was I really still that naive?

I'm sorry to say it now, but yes, I think I was.

With the brief dream of home and employment washed away before it was ever really realised, Morgan and I were at the mercy of the city, entirely. We knew some people in Park Slope, friends from Berkeley who had a couch they let us crash on, and we were grateful, though it wasn't big enough for us both to lay out flat on, so we took turns sleeping. One of our hosts was now a celebrity journalist, who spent her days cornering teen pop stars in supermarket car parks, and tailing them to restaurants to stake out their dates for gossip magazines. Her suggestion was that we move in to the Chelsea Hotel, as we were *quite bohemian*. We did actually go over to check it out, but even that old flea pit was now well out of our reach when we considered our meagre pooled resources. An artist we had introduced ourselves to once in a cafe back in SF let us stay in her studio above the Museum of Sex. It was a nice set-up, until she tried to strong-arm me into becoming her unpaid intern, and started inflicting erotic massages on Morgan. Occasionally she'd burst in, coked up to the eyeballs, with a harem of gay men, at 2 a.m., waking

Morgan and I up, insisting we all go to the club. It was entertaining for a while, but entirely unsustainable.

The only place we could afford, when we'd hocked everything of value, was a hostel in Harlem, where we shared a double room, and amused the boys on the corner to no end.

'You girls ain't from round here, are you?' they yelled, but not unkindly.

'No,' said Morgan, her hair whipping about her face in the brisk winter breeze, 'we're from California.'

I liked Harlem, it was full of ghosts, and I made friends with them as they flew between the brownstones and the still-jumping jazz clubs. In summer school I had read Nella Larsen's Harlem Renaissance classic, *Passing*, and had become enthralled both with the notion of passing (then entirely new to me), and with the tragic story of a woman who becomes what she is not against the odds, only to plunge to her death (suicide? murder? accident?) from an open window right there, above 125th Street. I was passing myself now, as a woman. My hair reached my shoulders and men would sidle up to ask, 'Hey beautiful, can I uh, get you a drink sometime?' It was only when I spoke, in an unexpectedly low register, that they recoiled, saying, 'Oh, uh, sorry I didn't realise.' It made me miss you a little, their lack of imagination, their rigidity, their failure to see. Hadn't any of these clowns ever watched a Lauren Bacall picture?

The neighbourhood, with all of its nineteenth-century splendour, now reduced somewhat in circumstance, made me homesick for the Saturday afternoons I spent as a teenager roving around Liverpool city centre, looking for lax off-licences, and derelict buildings to fuck in. If I looked due east I could almost imagine that I was seeing the port of my hometown, the Liver buildings, the Georgian museums, the bomb damage, the two Cathedrals, and the old girls in market cafes chain-smoking Benson & Hedges as they fried eggs. A seven-day crossing, an Edwardian pleasure cruise on a Cunard liner would have taken me back there at another point in time, and out ahead of me I knew there was a place in the future when I would have to return, but at that particular point, I was stranded in the present moment.

My dominant memory now is how tired I was throughout that first winter; the city wore me out, wore me down, with infinite, arduous subway journeys, horrible, terrible weather, colder than London, skeezy odd jobs, and the almost constant ache of missing everything I was so desperate to flee from. Morgan, far quicker off the mark here than in comfortable San Francisco, had found a job in a shoe shop. Since I still didn't have any visa paperwork, I couldn't get such a plum gig as this, so I fell back on my old habits of hunting through Craigslist for desultory work and cash-in-hand situations. I gave out giant dollar bills as part of a lottery promotion, I sat for photographers who were building their portfolios, I dressed windows in a vintage store, and I had sex in prearranged threesomes with other roving waifs, to titillate wealthy older men. Truly, New York is a city where a lack of morals goes a long way. Through it all my heart throbbed and my ego smarted, when I recalled your spiteful tone and your easy smile. I was still embittered, still in love. New York was purgatory to me, for a long time.

Daily I took the endless subway down from Harlem all the way to Williamsburg, where Morgan's shoe shop sat in a strip of slowly gentrifying storefronts, druggists and bodegas, still almost entirely untroubled by upmarket shoppers. A few doors down there was a Salvation Army with the most esoteric of opening hours, and a little further on was a bar which held amateur burlesque contests. Sometimes, after shutting up the shoe shop, Morgan and I would go in and scope out the gaggle of strippers competing for the grand prize of $200 cash and a plastic tiara.

Morgan said, 'You could do that.'

'What, strip?' I asked.

'Yeah!' she said. 'You're a performer, aren't you? You should *totally* enter.'

I giggled, sure she wasn't serious, and said, 'I don't think you just, ta-da, become a stripper.'

'Burlesque artist,' she corrected.

'Yeah, exactly,' I said. 'You need, I don't know, an act, or some experience, a gimmick.'

'Oh honey,' she said wryly, 'if anyone's got a gimmick it's you. You are *all* gimmick.'

I glared and said, 'I'm a writer, I want to be a writer.'

She looked at me as though I were just being prissy, and said, 'Come on, you spent literally the entire summer running half-naked through the streets of San Francisco. What's the big deal? There might even be some decent cash in it.'

The inevitability of it all.

We rigged up a number in the course of an afternoon, a naughty schoolkid routine, set to Doris Day's *Teacher's Pet*. And though I played it down, as just a laugh and nothing serious, if I'm honest, I was excited by the prospect of being onstage again, by the possibility of being in some way creative again. The whole time I was in London, I had been so wound up in you, nothing else had registered as having any importance. I hadn't written a line, I hadn't worked on anything, I had almost totally forgotten that I had any potential, any dreams. Now I felt like something inside me, some will to live, some artistic impulse, was waking up, coming out of hibernation, showing its head above ground.

Unbelievably I won the contest, and the cash prize, though I lost the crown in the cab home. Possibilities stirred. I rejoiced at my surprise victory, a week's rent at the hostel paid, and I smirked to myself all the way back up to Harlem.

'I guess I'm just a natural,' I said to Morgan.

She was tired. 'It's not exactly difficult,' she said, then rolled down her window to smoke.

'Hey, hey lady,' said the cab driver. 'No smoking! You can't smoke in my car.'

'Oops,' she said sarcastically, 'sorry,' flicking the cigarette out into the street.

Morgan's cynicism didn't faze me. I had $200 in my bra in untraceable cash, a bundle of dollar bills, and a promise that there was more where that came from. One of the other girls from the contest asked me for my number and said that she'd call at the weekend because she knew a few more clubs I could perform at.

'You're pretty slick,' she said. 'We don't get many Londoners here, it's a good act.'

I always thought it was funny, that to so many Americans, England, London and the UK are all the same thing, but I also recognised the credibility and cachet this conflation gave me. Here nobody recognised that I didn't differentiate the 'a' sounds in 'bath' and 'trap'. That I only had the Northern working-class æ didn't register at all, but the fact that I held my 't's at the end of each 'what' and 'cut' framed me as an elegant British subject, a classy broad.

The emcee said I should come back next week and do a guest spot, guaranteed fee, drinks tickets, the works. And they were all so kind to me, so sweet and welcoming, flattering even. I felt just a little like Lana Turner, discovered at Schwab's drugstore, and saying 'Well why not? If you *really* think so.'

Legitimate employment was out of my reach, but bumping and grinding on bars, stages and tabletops across the five boroughs, go-go dancing for $10 an hour was not. I was willing to work for very little, and until very late, I was a fresh face and nobody ever knew if I was a man or a woman. In my strips I always kept the truth of the matter to myself, and found a nice little niche in the market. You see, every single significant moment in my life had been purely accidental, the result of my tripping over and falling into some new, unexpected situation, and hoping I would be alright when I stood up again. This episode was no different, finding my underwear stuffed with singles and thinking, *Well it's better than the perfume shop*, and it really was. The hours suited me, since I hate having to get out of bed before noon, and the money was roughly commensurate with the effort exerted. If it wasn't exactly what I'd pictured when I thought of my new life in the Big Apple, at least it was something, and compared with those last three months in London, it was really quite alright. I had my own bed, I had money for the subway, I drank for free, and I could eat every day. Well, most days. What were my other options anyway? By March I'd overstayed my tourist visa without having filed papers for marriage, and from a purely practical point of view, I had become an illegal immigrant, literally unemployable. I knew other aliens who worked in restaurant kitchens, but I didn't ever pass a single trial shift. Instead I worked with what I had, serving myself up to the great American public: European cuisine, à la carte.

Since the shoe shop was always empty, Morgan was free to sit behind the register all day, leafing through the stacks of old magazines, *Vanity Fair*, *Harper's*, *Elle*, that we had found in the basement. Whoever had accumulated them had been a very diligent reader; it seemed as though they hadn't missed a single issue of their favourite titles between 1977 and 2001, when the collection abruptly broke off. I often thought about who this avid mag fiend might have been, wondered how they lived their life and what had happened to them at the turn of the century. Did they move to a care home, convert to Mormonism, go blind, die on 9/11?

'You know,' said Morgan, 'when you look at all these fashion magazines lined up like this, you really get to see that it's just the same old crap going around and around again.'

All the same, we mined this maligned library for costume inspiration; Morgan picked out looks which suggested routines and I found complimentary songs on YouTube. Still puzzled that this was my life now, I tried out new numbers in front of the shoe shop mirrors, whilst Morgan sewed up costumes at the cash desk. With a length of Velcro in one hand, and a bagel in the other, she oversaw rehearsals, intermittently catcalling, 'More! More ass! Big smile!'

If ever anybody came in, I would pretend to be a customer twirling around in a new pair of boots, so she didn't look quite so slack. This happened so infrequently though that most days we had the rehearsal-studio-come-atelier to ourselves and we made good use of it. I didn't have a cell phone, so I had to give out Morgan's number. She handled all business calls, talking me up and leveraging better bookings. She was a surprisingly good manager, a real little showbiz Svengali; New York suited her.

'Of course, in London, the performances are always the highlight of any party,' she'd say, 'so I think it's fair to say $250, right? Right! Thank you darling!'

'Thank you darling,' I guffawed. 'You are too much!'

'Shut up and dance, Gypsy!' she cackled.

We made a good team I admit.

'You should do Cher,' she said. 'If you do Cher you can do gay clubs, and they pay better.'

Because I believed that Morgan was always right, I did Cher, dressed as a mummified pharaoh, peeling off my bandages to 'If I Could Turn Back Time'. I made a Victoria sponge onstage whilst stripping to 'If I Knew You Were Comin' I'd've Baked a Cake'; I disrobed from a hot pink swimsuit decorated with gumballs to the tune of 'Surfin' USA'; I tore off my cocktail gown amidst a diva fit in time to David Bowie's 'Fame'. I worked in gay clubs, in strip clubs, in sex clubs, in theatres, at pharmacies, at restaurants, and once in a ten-pin bowling alley in Jersey City where the bowling balls actually rolled through the dressing room.

When I crabbed to Morgan that exotic dancing wasn't exactly why I came to New York, that I felt perhaps I was being blown off course, she said, 'You have to *live* first, before you can write.'

I nodded, 'I guess.'

'You know what Penny Arcade said,' she declaimed, 'there *are* no child prodigies in literature!'

Morgan and I had been fans of Ms Arcade since we were at Berkeley, largely because she was quotable on every topic. She had lived through flower power, disco, punk, AIDS and gentrification; if anyone should know about life on the underground it was her.

Morgan continued, 'There's no writerly equivalent to Mozart, you know? None. Even JT LeRoy was a fake.'

'Not quite a fake,' I said, but she wasn't listening.

'And what else would you write about anyway?' she asked. 'Your depressed mother and your life on a dreary council estate? Come on Bibby Elliot, get your ass in gear.'

I resigned myself to the lunacy of the situation and set about figuring out how I could pull party poppers from my bra without giving the gag away too soon, comforting myself with the thought that if this reality wasn't my dream, at least it was all a good laugh. And it's how I made all of my friends in New York, it's how I began to imagine that I could make a new life for myself, it's how I saved enough money to present my first piece of writing onstage, at a tiny theatre (really no bigger than a living room) on the Bowery. I was proud to have lived through a flood, life in a crummy hostel, and the pain you inflicted on me, all in the course of my first year as a New Yorker.

Naturally, I shared pictures and videos frequently with friends back in London; I am a citizen of the twenty-first century after all. I dotted them all along the information superhighway, to say, *Look! I didn't fail.* It didn't matter that Morgan and I had entirely underestimated the expense and complexity of nuptial law and immigration requirements, and had never made it down the aisle. It didn't matter that I hadn't the legal paperwork to be there, or a plan for how to get hold of it. It didn't matter that I lived in fear of deportation, in a room so small that the door would hit my bed when I opened it. No, all that mattered was that I hadn't failed. That I had been right to disavow you, to leave London and not look back. Somehow I was standing, upright, onstage, a stripper, an illegal immigrant, a refugee from gender totality, in a city where my accent read simply as *European*, rather than underclass. I could smile in photographs, and know that my former acquaintances would be looking at my pictures in another time zone and thinking to themselves, *Well, I guess she really went and did it!* Not that I would care, because I was gone, and the people I had known before were gone, too. And though it wasn't like writing, though I hadn't ever longed to do it, in a way I came to love this life, being onstage. I prized the applause and the affirmation from strangers because it made me feel like I was capable of something, finally.

'The reluctant star,' said Morgan, 'so timid at first, now look, you can hardly keep your rigging on!'

Before I was even aware of it, a new life had grown under my feet, and I had begun to walk the length of Manhattan, not out of sorrow but out of joy.

There's a photograph somewhere, taken a good while after I'd settled into my new life in NYC. It's digital, motion-blurred, and in it I'm twirling a bikini top above my head, my face blanched out with clown white and redrawn in fuchsia and violet. I can remember changing and making up for that gig, sitting on a beer crate in the back office of the bar, knocking back a vodka tonic, and patiently explaining the cues on my CD to the DJ. The bar was not very busy that night, but I was getting a flat fee, so I wasn't unduly perturbed. I did my thing for the indifferent audience, chalked it up to experience, and then went off to sink the rest of the bottle with Morgan and Jonny and Billy, once it was over.

Morgan said, 'Billy kinda looks like you'd look, don't you think? If you were, you know, an actual boy?'

Billy was a writer. He discreetly distributed a zine across Brooklyn and the Lower East Side twice a year, which people scrabbled out to try and grab, as soon as a new issue was said to be circulating. It was a very popular publication, because it was hilarious, and full of psychedelic sex stories, all drawn from real life interactions and recounted without expurgation. Shape-shifting and very dry, there was an almost comic book quality to it, and the irresistible invitation to 'Be Billy'. As he said, 'It's a verb not a noun.'

Everyone had a crush on him, everyone wanted to go home with him, to fuck and find themselves very thinly disguised in his next batch of dirty stories; boys were caught up as much by his prowess on the page as by his good looks, everyone wanted to be memorialised in a fantasy. The true delight of the zine was the feeling that even if you were unlucky in real life, you could at least take some version of Billy home with you to jerk off with, which is, I think, the highest acclaim an author can ever hope for.

Billy and I were introduced by a party promoter, Trent, who wanted to hire two redheads in underwear to hand out shots at the opening of his new gay bar. It was an unusual context to meet in, stripped down to our undies and holding a platter of shot glasses each, but if it felt weird, well, we were both getting $150 and all the booze we could handle, so we rolled with it.

'You're not actually a redhead though, are you?' I asked Billy.

'No,' he said, 'sorta strawberry blond, but Trent's colour-blind.'

Some way into the night we struck on the drunken ruse of telling people that the free shots were actually $2 a pop, and pocketing all the loot, stuffing it directly into our underwear. By closing time we were wasted, flush, and friends for life.

In turn Billy introduced me to Jonny, whom he'd been in a play with. Jonny was androgynous, a little gothic, 'ethnically ambiguous and polymorphously perverse', as he put it, an opera singer, entirely nocturnal. He could impersonate just about any person he'd ever met, or seen or heard, as well as countless stock personae drawn out of the cultural repertoire. He would mimic Morgan or Billy for me when they weren't around, and I guess would mimic me to them too, only he had a very strict rule about never impersonating anyone who was in the room.

He said, 'I'm calling their spirit up, and if they're already here, well then, I couldn't do that, now could I?'

Billy, Morgan, Jonny and I trooped around every-where together, from fancy Upper West Side recitals to filthy Lower East Side cruise bars, never formally pledging allegiance to either life. Often, we'd simply gravitate towards whomever had the drinks tickets or the guest list that night. Like that random Thursday when I was stripping out of my pink bikini in front a half-empty room somewhere in Bushwick, and they all came to see me, and someone took a picture and posted it online a week, ten days later. I snorted when I saw it. I said to myself, *Jeez that was dismal.*

Then right below the picture, an hour or so after it appeared, came one waggish line from you, *Another packed crowd there I see Bibby.*

This was the first time you had written, in how many months? Six, no eight, no, could it possibly have been a year? Until I read that limp gibe, I hadn't stopped to count.

Morgan was reading over my shoulder. 'He is such an asshole,' she said.

I wasn't sure I agreed with her, though. I thought I detected something like trepidation there, some gentle footsteps, a tiptoeing on your part towards an apology, a gentle invocation, *How are you doing?* A timid *I miss you*, dressed in the glad rags of a taunt.

But Morgan said, 'Forget that. Let's go,' and we were off in a cab to Times Square.

She had booked me a gig, performing as a silent rococo nymph, in an installation for a hotel swimming pool, where I would ring in a new era.

'This is perfect for you,' she said. 'And a gig uptown is a step in the right direction, Gypsy!'

She had made me a set of waterproof baroque bloomers, and a boned corset in peach, she'd styled me an enormous Louis XVI wig, all of which would require hours of torturous getting-into. I was already anticipating the feel of the bobby pins scraping my scalp and the bruising of the corset. I hadn't the time to translate your salty one-liner.

I had the crosstown traffic to consider because it was New Year's Eve, almost exactly one year since I'd left, and I had a new life now, one full of straight-talking, overly friendly Americans, to inhabit. I was glad to be insulated from you, between us there was the thick and brittle Styrofoam wall of time, keeping both the chill of your contempt and the warmth of your touch away from me. I did not reply, I would not respond.

The New Year was arriving on angel's wings and I intended to greet her with a kiss full on the mouth, to lay myself down in her arms and listen as she prophesied, to surrender to her embrace and let her swoop upwards with me, out over the city, out into the night, out into whatever lay ahead, unconcerned with you and your fumbled nonsense.

During dress rehearsal, as I lay on my back in the warm water, I found myself hanging in a prolonged moment of silence, waiting for the lights to be focused on the pool, waiting for the technicians to find the right levels for the music, waiting for the host to finalise the running order, waiting. In the pool I thought about the scene with the transgender mermaids in the aquarium, in that stupid Jeffrey Eugenides book, and how much I disliked it. I recognised that if I took slow enough, deep enough breaths, I could float on the surface of the water, barely moving, suspended outside of myself.

It was like returning to the womb for twenty minutes; I thought about my mother. Weightless and free from gravity's despotism, like cheating death, I was buoyed up on the knife-edge of each breath, midway between Heaven and Earth, an act of surrender. As I drifted, as I dreamed, the lights dimmed all around me, leaving only a phosphorescent blue, issued, I understood, from the underwater lanterns below. I allowed myself to slip backwards. *Just for a moment*, I told myself, *I'm strong enough now*, and I thought of you, lying on your stomach, propped up on your elbow, your hair plastered to your face, sweat running between the cheeks of your perfect cyclist's arse. I pictured you jumping up and striding towards your bedroom door, still half hard, whistling 'Laid', rubbing your face with a towel, then throwing me a smug unspoiled grin of satisfaction, a post-coital benediction. Then a golden halo of light found me, and I bent to the thrill of its warmth. It picked me out like the searchlight from a police helicopter, that spotlight from the technician's desk, illuminating my body, floating in the pool like the stiff in the opening credits of *Sunset Boulevard*, shaking me from my reverie.

'Ready when you are,' I heard the technician call.

'OK, great,' I said, pulling myself out from this aquatic daydream and into the time I was physically inhabiting.

My feet felt for the tiled floor of the pool, my shoulders shuddering a little from the cold collision of these two temporal fronts.

Calmly, I spoke out into the darkness, 'If you take it from the first track, I'd like to mark it out a few times in the water.'

'Got it!' came the reply.

Then the music played through the speaker system and I was lost to the present moment once more.

XI

'Back now.' I think about that line a lot.

'Back now,' you wrote that to me in a letter, when I was away in California.

'Back now,' you scribbled without explaining where you'd been or what you'd been doing.

The phrase draws me back inside itself again and again; something in this line is mellifluous, mesmeric. I can't hold out against the summons of these words, I roll the phrase around in my mouth like a pearl. 'Back now,' double-loaded with meaning: the now you came back to is long gone, and yet it remains to be experienced. Each time I reread this letter, it calls me back to a now I was never even involved with.

I know my now is not the same now as yours, but sometimes it feels like it is, or I like to imagine it so. I make believe that the afternoon you sat at your desk to write me that letter is the same afternoon in which I am writing this out, that somehow our nows will intersect once again. Buddhist teaching says all that exists is this present moment, nothing else. Theoretical physicists say even that is a fiction, there is no present moment, only subtle granular divisions in the field of space-time; now is a moving target.

I'm here at this kitchen table ten years since we first met, six years since we last spoke, four years since your death. When I count out the interceding years like this, over and over, it starts to sound like prayers on the rosary, *As it was in the beginning, is now and ever shall be. World without end, Amen.* The energy and attention I've poured into this writing has eaten away at my now (however theoretically flawed the poor moment might be I'm still fond of it). The present day is full of moth holes, it has been too long neglected in favour of my journeying back into the past. But as Father Ignacio said at Mass last week, 'We must think of ourselves like arrows, God draws back the string so that we may fly forwards.'

'Back now' is what I say when I'm trying to force myself to get back to work, back to the business of writing this out. It becomes a bigger challenge, a bigger ask, the further I go, the closer I get to the end (your end).

'Back now,' I say, like a television newsreader, 'to our correspondent in New York City.' *It's necessary for the narrative,* I tell myself, *to revisit life there.* And I concur with myself (even though I know I am hastening you towards your demise) because NYC is a moment in time in which I'd managed, if not to forget you, then at least no longer to ache for you. It's an instant that suggests that things could have been different, could have worked out better for us both.

Morgan and I found a room, in an apartment on Hope Street, Brooklyn. After leaving the hostel in Harlem we had stayed with another friend from college for a while, but then his girlfriend moved in, and she did not dig us at all. Our friend was exhaustively but furtively queer, and the atmosphere was really very tense. When we saw the ad for the room on Hope Street, we were at peak desperation so we ran right over the minute we were offered a viewing. It was the only residential building on a street otherwise full of dry-cleaning warehouses and mechanic shops, and the front door was bolted with such a flimsy lock that you only had to push to get in. Two crackheads sat on the doorstep pensively smoking a pipe, hunched like gargoyles on a cathedral's lichened facade.

Entering into the murk of a very dim hallway, we called out, 'Hello?' and a voice hissed back, 'Go away! No one lives here!'

'Sure,' Morgan said, 'but would you please tell whoever doesn't live here that we've come to look at the room upstairs?'

The landlord came down the hallway staircase smiling and said, 'Don't mind them, they're illegal. Let me show you around!'

'Hope Street!' Morgan said, 'The irony is too fucking much!'

We moved straight in, into a weird little lilac room with two twin beds. We lived with Eddie, a theatre promoter who managed a few cabaret acts; Jackson, a law professor with an incredible capacity for whisky and grace; Katie, who worked in entertainment PR; and Selena, whose grandfather had made a multimillion-dollar fortune canning barbecue beans. Even with our rent subsidised (I suspect) by Selena, it was more than we could afford and we were late with the payments almost every month, but really our other options were non-existent. There were only so many parties to perform at, and cabs and costumes ate up much of my tawdry income. Morgan herself was moving closer and closer to losing her job at the shoe shop, because, to be fair, she wasn't any good at it. They were lean times, leaner even than the days of reading *Crime and Punishment* in bed in San

Francisco, waiting for our daily burrito, because at least back there it was sunny, and we always had Robert's credit card to rely on.

We ate a lot of Little Debbie snack cakes, we wiped out all the canapés at every function we crashed, we made a lot of pancakes at home. We figured out that we could feed ourselves on $2.75 a day, which made us feel a little proud even, like we were getting by. We knew it couldn't last, this subsistence, but of course, Morgan and I were still banking on some sort of big break, some wealthy bisexual lover coming to scoop the pair of us up. We were quite convinced that it was only a question of when. At the risk of repeating myself, was I really so naive?

Well, yes, and no. I did believe that struggle would purify me, and that hard work would pay off in style eventually, but in the meantime I was more than willing to be pragmatic, and work at any cash-in-hand chore I could find. So, I called a number that I'd found on a poster in a video rental store, and asked about the position advertised, selling clothes downtown on Saturdays. Memories of my job at the perfume shop came back to me, of soggy sandwiches eaten in the stockroom, of leaving work exhausted at 8 p.m. and heading straight over to you. As unpleasant as that episode had been, it was at least experience in a *high-end retail environment*, and so helped me land this new job – it's strange how things work out. I hardly minded that gig at all, because there was zip all to do, and I could go on kidding myself that I was having my Crystal Allen moment, that I was a pretty little shop girl on the precipice of hooking any number of affluent married men.

The boutique was in Chelsea, the designer was Turkish, and I was surprised to see, when I googled her name, that a whole bunch of Oscar-winning starlets wore her frocks on the red carpet. Only ever for one night though, to an award show or a premiere; nobody ever wanted to keep the dresses for good it seemed. But then, I guess movie stars don't ever wear the same thing twice, do they?

My job was to clean the dresses up a bit, before they went back to being pawed at by tourists and half-hearted window shoppers, on the rail where they remained throughout my tenure, and probably remain still. They weren't (entirely) bad, just a little too expensive for the casual middle-income buyer, and not nearly expensive enough for the rich. One of Helena Rubinstein's quips comes to mind here: 'Of course that face cream was a failure – we made it too cheap!' Something to that effect, the details are lost but the sentiment holds.

I also enjoyed the task of sending out invites to sales and shows and previews, to the designer's client list. They were beautifully printed on a heavy card stock, artfully chosen, bearing a *malocchio* design, the big blue evil eye that wards off bad luck across the Mediterranean. As almost all of the designer's clients were uptight Upper West Side Presbyterians they were oblivious to the meaning of the message, and would call upon receipt, in a blind panic, asking why we had cursed them. The designer believed the evil eye would bring her good fortune, and so would never change or replace it. Instead she simply told me to let anyone who was upset know that in Turkey the *malocchio* brought good luck, not bad.

'But this is not Turkey!' came the frantic response of distressed customers. 'This is America!'

Much like Morgan's shoe shop, my Saturday job rarely brought me into contact with the actual task of selling anything. I was puzzled as to how these places stayed in business. Were they simply vanity projects floated on the mysterious wealth of their owners? Probably. Morgan explained that her boss was actually a celebrated mathematician who had made his money elsewhere, before ever getting into the stiletto racket.

'If you notice,' she told me, 'all of the heels are at specific heights. One and a half inches, three inches, five inches, none of which put the back into tension. These shoes are all mathematically designed,' she smiled, 'that's why they're all so ugly.'

I had a lot of time on my hands on Saturdays then. I dragged myself in to open the store, usually hungover to Hell after performing the night before, and much later than my boss would have liked. If it was an especially exciting day I might help somebody try on a gown, or give them a business card, or confirm that yes, this was the model worn by so-and-so to the Golden Globes. *No pictures please.* Sometimes Billy came to visit with a pair of iced coffees, occasionally one or two of the girls I knew from the burlesque clubs would come to say hi whilst out shopping with a sugar daddy, usually though I was quite alone in the store. I browsed online for pictures of Joan Crawford, and more dodgy gigs from the etc. sections of the internet's slimier websites. I was also free to chat via the miracle of messenger services, with friends back in London and in San Francisco, with Jovian, sometimes with Finley, a friend from Berkeley who was studying painting in Berlin, and with Robert, who was finally graduating. He kept promising to come and see us in New York.

'We miss you!' I wrote. 'Come visit!'

'I want to,' he replied, 'but I have so much debt, you wouldn't even believe.'

I felt guilty, I said nothing.

Did you ever experience the ludicrous £1-an-hour joy of the internet cafe with its grimy signage: PLEASE DO NOT USE THESE COMPUTERS TO VIEW INDECENT MATERIALS, hand-written and eternally ignored? No, maybe you hadn't ever had to stoop to that greasy indecency. Perhaps your gainfully employed father bought a home computer for business and allowed you to go online after school, but not until you'd finished your homework. I can't ever imagine you finishing your homework though, I only see you wanking off your schoolmates after P.E. or printing off pictures of shirtless boyband singers. All the same, you must remember when chatting online meant loading a CD-ROM into the computer and sitting through the ear-piercing twitterings of the dial-up connection?

All these little technological steps that we took independently, towards each other, towards the primordial swamp, the early outcroppings of the world wide web and the prehistoric social media sites, where we first connected with dirty, precocious messages (misspelled and badly punctuated in your case). Do you know (now that you're dead) that Hedy Lamarr invented the internet? That we are sitting in an electromagnetic field at all times, that we always were, even before we knew it? Has Heaven or whatever revealed it all to you? Radio waves, television, phone calls, the internet are all just ways in which we've hacked into this field, piggybacking on its fluctuations to whisper *Hello* to each other when we're out of earshot, to touch each other when we're out of reach, to send each other pictures of our open, waiting orifices, to say *Fuck me, I need it.*

The internet is a lot like praying, isn't it? A means of connecting to a higher power, of asking for help, of bringing the things we need into being. I've even seen people use the computer screen as an ersatz altar, and give YouTube videos the same function as chapels, as a place to offer votives and prayers to saints and martyrs. Under a video on the life of Joan of Arc, I saw a long list of comments, including *Dare to die for Jesus* and *I have already passed from death to life* and *Pray for us Joan*. I wondered, how often does St Joan stop by to check out the feedback from her fans, and when she does, does she act on it?

I should not have been surprised then, when you popped up on my screen in a little box in the bottom right-hand corner of my browser, there amongst all the other open tabs and unanswered emails, saying 'Alright Bibby' (no question mark). I was in the middle of a conversation in another window, with Adam, who was making toast in his little flat in Waterloo. He told me he missed me, he said that he'd been drawing on huge eyebrows, like my beloved Joan Crawford, for all of his violin gigs.

I was busy, so I ignored your message, left it to flash insistently for a while, and chatted to Adam about which brow pencils were worth robbing. I complained to him a little, about how silly it was to have crossed the Atlantic only to find myself behind a shop counter again. He made a joke about the time he and I and Elsa had improvised a truncated, musical version of *The Odyssey* in a supermarket, with the security guard following us about saying, 'You really can't do that in here, sir, we don't have a licence for live music.' I grinned and it was nice to think of London without feeling embarrassment or disgust. When he disappeared to butter his toast, I casually clicked on your message, typing a simple, stupid 'Yo.'

And there we were, leapling, with a simple New Wave jump cut, back at the beginning, at that point at which we talked convivially from a distance. Like the old days after graduation, when I lived in a different kind of penury at my mother's house, and had to log on at the library, and hide my erection behind *The Brief History of Lancashire*. You asked what was up, you told me all about your cyclical intimacy with Lucy Dear, about your upcoming trip to Brazil, about your misadventures in China, all the photographs you had taken, the boys you had fooled around with, and the Turner Prize winner you were occasionally assisting now. How busy you had been. A lot had happened in a year and a half.

It all came streaming out as if there never had been any bad blood between us, no STI, no unkindness; or rather as if it were all very far behind us now – and yet it felt as though we'd spoken only a week ago. It was as simple and sure as a musical theatre set piece, almost as if we'd never said goodbye, it was all just as it always was. Just as we'd always found each other at those parties in London, here we were, colliding without comment, seemingly unruffled. You couldn't have known I would accept your invitation to chat. I hadn't taken the bait when you'd commented on my photo, I could well have just continued to ignore you. Were you second-guessing me, calling my bluff? Was it really no big thing to you either way, if I answered or not?

Casually, effortlessly, my Saturday job became our spot in space and time. Like adulterous lovers who know to go to a certain hotel at a certain time on a certain evening of the month, whilst the children are with their grandparents, whilst the other half is studying for a driving test, we started coming to the screen to chat, every week, same Bat time, same Bat place, another unspoken arrangement.

I spent the rest of my week running around town on an endless wild goose chase, rehearsing, stripping, and picking up odd jobs, meeting Billy and Jonny for huge slices of Mexican cheesecake that tasted like hair mousse with a hint of lemon, and drinking until we fell into a pile on the street, so really I hadn't any other time to talk to you. Besides Saturday afternoons when I was ostensibly working. I actually came to look forward to going to the boutique, if only to talk with you, when our time zones overlapped just long enough to poke fun at each other and share links to dirty videos. So many details of your life, typed out pell-mell in those online conversations, all kinds of irrelevant bits and pieces about buying new undies, and your new favourite ale, but not a word about the affair on which this whole sorry story would come to turn. Why was that? Guilt? I doubt it! Forgetfulness? Maybe. Or the feeling that it wasn't worth mentioning? No, that can't be it.

Adam surfaced with the same frequency. Every Saturday he wrote from the sofa-bed as he prepared for his early night ahead of another Sunday morning's teaching. He filled me in on what Elsa was up to, mentioned all the dates he'd been going on which somehow didn't ever pan out, told me about work, and wrote that he had bumped into his Parisian ex after three years, and wondered what he had ever seen in him – besides his charming mother. He even suggested in one chat that he might visit me, saying that he needed a good old-fashioned adventure. I treasured the prospect, but had the foresight, at least, not to get hung up on it; like Robert's forever-delayed trip to New York, Adam's was built more on hope than on any functioning reason. All the while, over in a neighbouring window, you were dishing up your own casserole of petulance and philosophy, slandering whoever had pissed you off and praising the graft of whoever was putting out.

Quite contented, I would lean on the cash desk (which never saw any cash) typing with one hand, and dreamily chewing the nails of the other, alternating my attentions between the two of you, firing off a quick :p or :) or :(when necessary, to keep the less captivating stream of conversation flowing when the other exchange offered more exciting fare. I didn't ever mention to you, of course, that I was simultaneously chatting with Adam, nor did I tell him I was talking to you. I thought it might've seemed rude that I wasn't giving my full attention to either discussion, and besides, I wanted to revel in this secret synchronicity. I was also very aware that you two didn't exactly think the world of each other. I clearly remembered you saying, 'You shagging? No? Well then!' and him saying, 'I really don't get what you see in him.'

I got the feeling though that you both knew. Perhaps you felt duplicity oscillate through Hedy Lamarr's electromagnetic field, ardour passing through the three of us? For example, the conversations often turned spicy simultaneously, which I simply ascribed to the phases of the moon over London, or some such metaphysical erotica. You told me that you missed my dick (though you never said you missed me) and said you were waiting to feel it in you again. And Adam, in spite of how clear he had made it that my muliebrity did not get him off, sent me pictures of himself shirtless, smirking, maybe aroused by distance, or simply turned on by posing, naked with one hand behind his head, his pecs pert and tensed. What a funny tangle it was. I felt like Catherine shared by Jules et Jim, I was all caught up and flattered, so I barely considered who else you might be chatting to in between tossing smutty sobriquets my way. Was it Lucy Dear or Paulette or Lulu or Leo on the other line? And Adam, who was he writing to? The French ex or some online flirt? I don't know, I didn't think to ask, I just thrilled in the sensation of being pressed up between your spectral bodies like some Lucky Pierre, and though it wasn't real, it was real enough.

Adam still sent me letters, lovely little notes and post-cards. There was always the hint of romance to those mailings, in the way that there is when schoolchildren send their mothers notes on Valentine's Day saying *I love you the most.* We seemed to have matured in reverse, grown up backwards. A harmless, hardly sexual love, but a feel-good love. I have to wonder now, how that love survived so long, and ask what we lost when we finally stopped sending each other mail.

You and I didn't write to each other anymore, we had fallen out of the practice of sending letters long ago. Perhaps it would have been too painful a reminder of how things had once been progressing between us, or maybe we'd grown up enough now to know that all those things you write out by hand, and then post off in a passion, aren't guaranteed to hold true by the time the envelope is opened on the other side of the ocean.

So we made do with this less lovely, but more instan-taneous, messenger. It felt safer like that, less likely to blow up in my face again. Sometimes I'd get an unscheduled email too, often just a line, *What you writ-ing now Bibby?* or *When do I get to see your cum shot?* Sometimes a longer message, like when you thought you'd be visiting New York, or when you wanted to put me in touch with Leo, who was in town performing at a book fair. Usually though it was Saturdays, amongst the unsold dresses and the fake smiles I gave the ladies who came in seemingly just to taunt me, and giggle, *Oh, just looking thank you!*

I was glad we could be friends again, and yes chatting with you was quite a nice way to pass the time whilst earning a slice of the rent, but of course, the designer had to let me go. She said that one of the clerks from the neighbouring boutique had told her, 'Every time I go out for a smoke I see that, erm, person who works for you, just leaning on the counter, ignoring the customers, *clearly* browsing the internet!' I'm pretty sure he was angling for my job, because it paid cash, but still, it was a lousy thing to do.

The designer looked almost genuinely sorry when she said, 'It's just not how we want to represent the brand.' As always she discreetly handed me my $80, but this time it came in a notecard which read *Sorry to See You Go,* with the infamous evil eye stamped on the reverse.

You're fired! God bless you.

I didn't dwell on this piece of bad luck for long though, because Finley was in town. He was stopping off in New York, on his way back from Berlin to California, because he wanted to join the overnight protest-vigil outside the gallery which was hosting a show of Carl Andre's work. 'He killed his wife,' said Finley, 'he pushed Ana Mendieta out of a window and got away with it! Where's her retrospective, hey? Why isn't she on the cover of *Art in America*? Why is he internationally *celebrated* when she's dead?'

I remember we were hosting a pre-party for the protest on Hope Street, because what could be more fitting? Finley and I went shopping for refreshments at the cheapest local liquor store. He was wearing a gingham dress and my fur stole, which caused a savage man to accost us outside the store. He started calling Finley a *disgusting faggot asshole*, and Finley, riled up with an indignation only someone raised in a deeply religious family can muster, swung at him with a cut-price bottle of Prosecco. He was screaming, 'Not today – this is the one day I won't put up with this shit.' Actively fearful of the outcome, I held him back, pleading with him to recognise that no good could come of this, that he could seriously injure this man, and in all likelihood, standing there in that red check dress, would probably be the one to suffer for it. Cursing, he backed down, and the aggressor slunk away, obviously scared.

At the time I thought this a victory for pacifism, a virtue I had never, truth be told, extolled all that often. I felt I had done the right thing in breaking up this fight, but then I am a terribly sanctimonious sort of person. Now, when I look about at the constantly rising levels of fear and abuse and actual physical harm perpetrated against queer people, all of which was promised to be washed away in the stream of progressive society if we would just be patient long enough, I have to wonder if maybe one less homophobe blighting the earth wouldn't have been the truer victory. We went home, still shaking, and in confused aggression, fucked on the bathroom floor before the guests arrived. At the party we got so black-out drunk that we missed the evening's main event, the vigil itself. Morgan or Eddie must've seen we were too wasted to go anywhere and put us to bed.

We woke up the next morning surrounded by the wreckage of a party we could not remember. I was in

my underwear, but Finley was still wearing the gingham gown. I scooped up the discarded fur from the
floor, draped the stole around my bare shoulders, and
stepped into the empty living room. On the couch
someone I did not recognise was dead to the world, a
single sleeping body on the sofa. The rest of the house
was abandoned.

'Fuck,' said Finley, 'this place is a mess.'

I was quite used to waking up in such circumstances.
I simply croaked, 'Surely you're used to it, living in Die
Hauptstadt and all?'

He scanned the room looking dismayed, and said,
'This is way worse than Berlin, you people are crazy!' as
if he had not been a participant himself.

We decided to watch a Cassavetes movie, because
neither of us ever had. Eddie had a whole stack on top
of the TV, and this seemed like the perfect opportunity
to get a cinematic education. I don't remember the plot,
though I do remember the atmosphere, so saturated
with misplaced romance. I think I fell back asleep a few
times, not out of boredom though, I was simply under
hypnosis.

The room is warm, the soundtrack is terribly slurred
because we're watching an old VHS copy of the movie,
naturally I think of you and your video tapes. Some way
in, the kid on the couch wakes, quiet and confused. He
sits up to watch the film with us without saying a word.
He's skinny and shirtless, he's wearing Bart Simpson
boxer shorts. Because it's getting quite hot in the room
now, I ditch the fur, and Finley takes off his dress. The
three of us sit together in our underwear watching
things slowly unfold.

Onscreen, Gena Rowlands says, 'Love is a stream. It's
continuous, it doesn't stop.'

I think about you, leapling, your dirty smirk and your *Come on then*, and Finley starts making out with this stranger on the couch. I think about you and your vertical blinds and your blue eyes and your beautiful nose and someone's hand reaches to caress my chest. I'm pulled backwards into a warm, amorphous pool of desire. Haven't you noticed how hangovers always make people so horny? The three of us, me and Finley and this unknown soldier, are fooling around on the couch, naked and curious, and the film keeps rolling.

Sitting across a desk from her, Gena Rowland's co-star refutes her assertions on the nature of love. He shakes his head and insists that love does eventually cease.

'Oh no,' Rowlands firmly replies, 'it does not stop.'

XII

I'm dipping fries in mayonnaise one morning at Kellogg's Diner. Morgan is looking wan and restless, occasionally tracing loops on her plate in ketchup. Her job at the shoe shop has come to an end. Not because she was fired, she is keen to explain, but because the landlord was raising the rent on the store. Now that it has become such a prime spot, her boss could no longer afford the lease.

'Just think,' she says, 'two years ago it was all thrift stores and strip clubs.'

'It still is,' I say.

'Yeah, but now a second-hand blouse costs $180, and the strip club has a wine list,' she snarks.

The diner is just one street over from our apartment, it's open 24/7, and so we often end up at the table in the window if we can't sleep, if there's something playing on our minds. The menu is famously bad and the service is worse, but it's deeply soothing to slide in at 3.30 a.m., slurp a chocolate shake and doodle on napkins.

Because it's cheap, and because it's right off the L-train, and because you can always get a spot, all sorts of people turn up. Performers come in after gigs, and ravers come after clubs, subway drivers come in before their shifts, mourners hold all-night wakes over refillable cups of dishwater coffee, and taxi drivers stop by for breakfast before they go to bed. In amongst the insomniacs, adolescent hair metal fans, and hustlers in repose, there's often an actor from TV trying to lay low in the corner, or a drunken downtown luminary squawking and holding court over a coterie of acolytes and half-cut twinks. Sometimes we see a few of the burlesque girls too, coming in late after a show, dressed down in athleisure wear, but with their stage make-up and extravagant wigs still on. Sometimes they just wave, more often they come over and air kiss us, ask how things are going, and order a few new rhinestoned bras from Morgan, her sideline in underwear-for-strippers having boomed exponentially.

This morning though, it's unusually quiet, just Morgan, me, and someone's lonely *abuelita*, struggling on a grilled American cheese sandwich, with Celine Dion drifting through the diner on the airwaves. We finish our fries and ask for some water, the waitress sloshes our plastic glasses three-quarters full with disinterest, then departs.

Morgan plonks a big fat book on the table, a huge 1980s volume on Mexican history, all laid out in coffee and cream, which she found lying in the street earlier in the evening. Unable to ignore it, she had scooped up the book and lugged it about all night, clinging to it like a Kisbee ring. She's dying to crack it open, and though I'm not really all that interested, I play along because she seems sort of blue. She sweeps our dirty napkins and empty condiment sachets aside, clears a space for the book, and begins to read, poring over the soiled pages, though many of them are stuck together and tear as she flips through. She has to skip several states entirely, before she lands on Mexico City and gasps, 'Let's go!'

I smile, I nod, I'm tired.

'I want to go there so bad,' she says, 'I've wanted to visit my whole life! I'm sure my real family are Mexican. I can feel it.'

'Yeah,' I say, 'it looks incredible, but I—'

'Oh right,' she says sadly. 'You can't go anywhere – without papers.'

'Yeah, if I go to Mexico, I won't be able to come back to New York so…' I trail off, feeling for maybe the first time the real limits of my situation.

Morgan looks like a little girl whose birthday cake has plunged off the table, face-down, and I feel as though I'm the one who has pushed it. I feel so guilty I can hardly sip at my water glass. Fool that I am, I had been thinking all night that she was just feeling bummed about losing her job at the shoe shop. She hangs her head low over the book, and I can see from the mist that has entered her eyes how she longs to be gone.

Until this morning I had completely forgotten about that particular dawn at Kellogg's, had entirely neglected *The History of Mexico*. It was only when I took myself downtown to see the Cathedral, the Zócalo, and el Templo Mayor for the first time since arriving in Mexico City, that I remembered, and felt the uncanny shudder of a prophecy run down my spine. I entered the Cathedral, dipped my fingers in the holy water, and thought of Morgan, heard her again, as if we were together in the diner.

'La Catedral Metropolitana de la Asunción de la Santísima Virgen María a los Cielos was constructed from the ruins of the Mexica people's own temple after the Spanish conquest,' she says. 'It's believed that they buried sacred idols in the foundations to consecrate it to their own Gods. Isn't that amazing? Somewhere, under there, are all of these sixteenth-century sacred Mexica carvings, still vibrating.'

I walked around the perimeter of the cathedral, mixed in with all the Scandinavian gawpers, clutching their baseball caps reverentially, Canons and Nikons hanging from their necks like millstones. By casting my eyes down, I tried to signal to the assembled faithful that I was not there to rubberneck, as they crossed themselves and kissed the plaster feet of saints. I had never seen such living glory, not even in Rome, where the Vatican's greatest treasures are displayed, but where the security guards and the inhuman level of order and cleanliness make the churches feel like winter palaces long vacated. The monumental gold-leafed altars; the graphic, mutilated life-size Christ; the miniature votive offerings of tiny metal ears, legs, heads; a living, breathing cosmos watched over by a mystical vision: Cristóbal de Villalpando's *Woman of the Apocalypse*. In the painting, the Virgin stands on a cloud, crowned with stars, surrounded by a heavenly orchestra. She raises her eyes towards God the father, whilst below her the Archangel Michael dispatches the Devil. She ascends, body and soul, into Heaven, and simultaneously announces the coming of God's kingdom on Earth; time is happening all at once.

Truly the Virgin is loved here, she is now more Mexican than tequila, she belongs to this country. No hospital hallway, no mechanic's workshop, no bus driver's dashboard unadorned by her presence; she is conquest, consolation and liberation. The story goes that, barely a decade after La Conquista, Mary appeared in the New World to an indigenous peasant, speaking in Nahuatl. She asked him to build her a house right there, on the spot where once there had been a temple to Tonantzin, the Aztec mother Goddess. (The Virgin can be very proprietary.) I imagine the conquistadors must have taken this as assurance that the native population had been subjugated; they could surely never have conceived that men like Hidalgo and Zapata would carry the image of Our Lady of Guadalupe into battle, when they rose up to free themselves from Spanish rule.

I picture Morgan, she's leaning on that melamine tabletop at the diner, looking up from the book. She says, 'Walter Benjamin was right, huh? About history being an angel, only she is not being blown backwards any place, she's looping, looping, looping. And of her own volition.'

I rest my head on the table and she reads aloud, the city's founding myth. 'The Mexica wandered in the high desert for almost a century,' she says, 'watching for a sign before they built their home.'

'Yeah,' I smirk, 'I know the feeling.'

'After roaming for a hundred years,' she continues, unfazed by my sass, 'the Mexica finally saw the symbol that was presaged to mark the site of their new citadel, an eagle perched on a cactus, with a snake in its beak. There they broke ground, and built Tenochtitlan, the most splendid city on earth, bigger than any in the whole of Charles V's Holy Roman Empire. When Cortés arrived with his troops, the architectural marvels he saw there left him, quote, "So amazed as to be unable to comprehend their reality."'

With these words pealing in my mind, I left the cathedral, eager to see these marvels for myself. Weaving between the surging crowds of tourists, dodging the perspiring organ grinders, and the street performers dressed as Aztec warriors, Minnie, Mickey and the Mario Brothers, I zigzagged over to the temple. Even in excavated ruins, it remains a thing of wonder. I was agog in the sun, astonished by the scale of what is in fact six concentric ancient temples, stacked on top of each other through time, like a megalithic matryoshka, built and rebuilt over the two hundred years of the old city's expansion. Unbelievably it had all been lost for half a millennium, presumed buried under the cathedral. I read on a stark museum placard that even in the 1920s, when the south-west corner of the temple was rediscovered to the north-east of the cathedral, the prevailing opinion was that it was all better left buried. If workers from the electricity company hadn't accidentally turned up an enormous Aztec carved stone disk, too astounding to ignore, the whole lot, the entire antiquarian city, would probably still be underground. Of course, in the process of building the new temple museum, a number of art deco mansions and a few nineteenth-century villas were demolished, but that's just another one of history's dirty tricks, isn't it? Looping, looping, looping.

In the temple I found myself stuck behind a large tour group, irritated by their slowness in the heat, but occasionally gleaning little bits of info dropped by their guide.

He said, 'It seems that it was only after the ruin of the Mexica people that the capital was given their name, Mexico City.'

One of the visitors in his group said, 'You mean like how Athens is named after the Goddess Athena?'

'Well yes, mythologically at least,' said the guide. 'Though historians now believe that *Athens* is not actually a Greek word. It's probably a corruption of *Attica*, a fragment from a forgotten language. Most likely then, the Goddess is named for the city, *not* the city for the Goddess.'

There was a collective enthusiastic murmuring of *you don't say!* and I thought about the strange coincidence of my mother having wanted to call me Thomas. I thought, *If I ever have a son that's what I'll call him.* Clearly the city I inhabit is consecrated to you. Glazed over, ignoring both the tour guide and the strict prohibition on bringing food and drink into the ruined temple, I saw a little girl eating a bar of chocolate. I recognised the red wrapper and cartoon king on the packaging straight away, because it was one of my favourites, a Carlos V bar.

I slowed my pace, aware that it was beginning to look as though I were tagging along with the tour group, uninvited. I stopped entirely, to muse on the gargantuan and frankly terrifying faces of the stone snakes carved into the temple stairways. I wondered if I might see a real, shy little lizard squeeze out from between the stones, if I waited still enough, for long enough. Instead, a plane soared overhead, above me, above the ruins, and I turned to follow its path over my shoulder, watched it disappear out of sight, behind the huge flag (the largest, they say, in the country) which flies over the main square of the capital. The national crest fluttering high above the city on a merciful breeze, majestic: an eagle perched on a cactus, with a snake in its beak, just as Morgan had foretold.

I realised how long it had been since I'd written to her, I hadn't even told her where I was yet. I felt sheepish about that, and so I determined to email her, to say, *Remember that book on Mexico you found in the street? The one with that long chapter on temples which you insisted on reading aloud in Kellogg's Diner? Well, guess where I am right now?*

This city is a boundless palimpsest; all of its history, pre-Columbian, colonial, Napoleonic, Aztec, Catholic, revolutionary, deco, authoritarian, is evident (often simultaneously) at every turn. The baroque convents are now museums, there are galleries dedicated to everything from the history of the post office to folk art. Art nouveau mansions rocked by earthquakes reopen as Prada boutiques, and the Russian malachite doors on display at Chapultepec Castle, gifted by Tsar Nicholas I, still draw gasps of admiration.

So much is preserved like this, by curators and conservationists, that it forces the question: what about the treasures lost for good in war and fire and coups? What happens to that which is looted and levelled, can no longer be excavated? Does it all fall out of time? What other stories might we tell ourselves about the past if other artefacts were still in circulation? And how many of these antiquities are we misunderstanding entirely, or worse, bending them to mean what we wish them to mean?

When I got home from the temple I was intending to write to Morgan, but a caffeinated flash of inspiration sent me scrabbling in a different direction, back towards the birthplace of our affair. As if off on my own techno-archaeological dig, I travelled to that old platform where we first got to know each other, in words at least. I wanted to see if I still had time, if it wasn't too late to sift through centuries-old messages and excavate you. I had hoped that what I found would help me know you again, know you better, help me write this all out with a greater truth, but all I found was another dead end in the labyrinth, another brick wall. From my kitchen table I returned to that site (for the first time in what, a decade?), but to my soft-hearted horror, discovered that *all of the unsaved message content dated before July 2013 has been erased.*

For the longest time I had taken comfort in thinking that I could always crack into the cache of communication held there in suspended animation. I believed that (were I to recover my password) I could descend again into the past, as if the internet were a royal tomb. I imagined it to be cold there in the crypt, that my eyes would struggle to adjust, probably I would sneeze a few times on account of the dust, but surely it would be quiet, and undisturbed by anything but spiderwebs. I expected a stillness of possibility, to hear a few beats of silence before I broke fully into memory, hurrying to read the solemn inscriptions, to uncover what we had said to each other, but it was not to be.

How I would have relished reading some of your lame jokes again, restoring the finer details of your poseur banter, or even looking at your more innocent pictures. Because, fuck, I am so sick of the useless six images which my search engine returns. Google, like a dopey Labrador always coming back with the same stick or tennis ball. The past has been paved over. When did you know you were dead?

Technically you and I are millennials, having grown up in a VHS childhood and come of age online. Our lives are uniquely comprised of CDs and MP3s, Walkmen and laptops, payphones and smartphones, these are our artefacts. Unlike our parents or elder siblings, technology didn't alienate us, it gave us a frame of reference, to note how digital culture makes life seem even more illusory, even more hallucinatory.

Analogue life (as wasteful as it was) at least left physical traces, carved stone disks, flags, churches. Perhaps
not permanent traces, photographs fade and facades
degrade, but at least we had the chance to watch them
turn yellow. Everything physical decays and decom-
poses, yes, that is natural. Once a Polaroid is gone it
cannot be replaced it's true, but the frailty of the physical was also its protection. Knowing hard copies to
be frail, to be prone to crumble like a saint's jawbone,
we protected them in shoeboxes and dresser drawers,
kept letters and snapshots safe. Now with all our faith
placed unquestionably in URLs, we don't notice as it
all vanishes into a jumble of corporate databases. We
forget where we might have uploaded what, we forget
passwords, or worse yet, forget to back up our data
before Flickr, Tumblr, Hotmail change their terms of
service, before they are steamrollered by a bigger business, erased from the internet, built upon.

This afternoon in my treasure quest, I have unearthed
a lost picture of your dick in your hand, a find of
great significance. Close-up, hard and fleshy, mouth-
watering really, the foreskin is pulled right back, the
frenulum stretched tight, and just below it is that quiz-
zical pink squiggle, which I loved. That raised smudge
of illogical skin on the underside of your cock, where
the shaft met the tip. A beautiful picture of a beautiful
penis. You sent it to me via messenger when I was in
New York, along with a few lines to say that if I ever
came back to London this *fit bod* would be ready and
willing, and that if I ever wanted a place to stay, you'd
make some space available, for a price. 'Used undies
would be a good start,' you wrote. The psychic I sows
all of this together, and although I did not remember
receiving this message, when I rediscovered it today, it

came with an immediate sense of recognition. I had stashed these words and images like carved idols, deep in my subconscious, so that I might shape the future in your likeness.

The aggressive delicacy with which you gripped your dick in that photo made it look almost like a bouquet of flowers, and I could tell from the way it was swollen and shiny that you undoubtably came hard very soon after modelling for that picture. Did it turn you on to strip and pose for me? *Was* it for me?

It's maddening to know that there were other pictures, many more, now destroyed. I wish I had click-and-dragged them all onto the desktop, opened up a new folder, and stashed it on my hard drive along with all the filth you sent me in private messages. Now it's all gone. But why should a Myspace profile be preserved when whole civilisations have been annihilated to boost the egos of European monarchs? When currently the whole planet is being destroyed? Everything is momentary, a digital life is wiped out without any more ceremony than a physical life, it is simply so.

I try to take comfort in the contents of my heart, but I can't help mourning for all those silly online back-and-forths, the attachments you sent me, your attempts to aggravate me, my attempts to seem unconcerned. Just as you reach for the telephone to call someone (and it's only halfway through dialling the number that you remember they couldn't possibly answer), one day you attempt to summon up the words and pictures you most want to see, only to find they are long gone. I find myself cursing technology now, I do not have Job's patience, I cannot reconcile myself to his mantra, *the Lord giveth and the Lord taketh away*. I can't always trust my memory, and letters are too rehearsed. I wish I had something hard, cold and misspelt, something instantaneous, something typed out whilst you were eating cereal in your underwear, something you assigned no weight to, to tell me who you were. I want it all back, everything that has been taken, wiped away from where it should still be. I want it all back, I want your nasty remarks and your explicit images and your hit-and-miss poetry back, I want you back, leapling, I want your body, and I know I can't have it.

I've catalogued all the conversations known to me studiously, but they are not enough; so I continue obsessively trawling through long-since-abandoned group chats, and social networking sites which have dwindled to spam-filled ghost towns, and through old email accounts which I'd forgotten I ever had, until *finally*, I stumble upon something new, a sacred parchment buried within the substratum of this story. It's just an asinine little nothing of a message, but I've begun assigning great meaning to it, reading and rereading it aloud, so many times now that it has almost become a chant, a string of sounds which have shed their meaning. It's a meagre, pedestrian email which has somehow survived overlooked, to mock me, to comfort me, and which I now cherish and display under glass, bowing low before it, crossing myself like the colonised peasant I am, as though this snippet of text holds the living word of God Himself, rather than some crude flirtations dashed off by you a decade ago.

It reads:

supppose
maybee
iam playing cricket in essex sunday
willbe back maybee 9pm

so late sunday could be fine
call me first should be ok

In the diner, Morgan closes the book reverently, her eyes damp, but now more luminous. She raises her hand, waves to the waitress and says, 'Cheque please.'

XIII

We were heartbroken, and wildly jealous, when Katie, our favourite roommate at Hope Street, was promoted and relocated to Los Angeles. Her room was filled by a permanently disgruntled grad student, who was not as hardcore as he believed, and subsequently took shelter elsewhere most nights. We would call Katie long distance, and alternately plead with her to come back, or else find a place with a second bedroom so we could come live with her. Morgan especially longed to be back in California.

'I love you guys! That would be amazing!' Katie said. 'I think that it's only artists who ever *really* understand me. Everyone in PR is so square, it's like, where's the fun guys? This is *supposed* to be show business.'

If she felt too full of homesickness, out there on the West Coast, Katie would spontaneously hop on a flight from LA after work on Friday afternoon, and crash-land back in New York at 2 a.m., gleeful and ready to party. Whenever she blew in for a visit it was always in a snowstorm of cocaine, 1970s-style, blizzards of the stuff, obliterating the sunlight for days and days. She'd take a cab with her suitcase, straight from LaGuardia to the club, to meet our roommate

Eddie because he always had the lead on where to get drugs. She'd hunt him down, sometimes DJing in the East Village, sometimes out with one of the acts he managed up in Midtown, sometimes at an after-party with some of the trust fund performance artists he knew, and a few curators from MOMA. Wherever they met became ground zero for a weekend of libellous chaos; Katie and Eddie hit the town hard. They were impressive in their scope and scale, racking up more bar visits in a night than most poseurs managed in a month; certainly they made Morgan and me look like lightweights. They ran from leather bars to lesbian bars and back and always, every time, at the stroke of 6 a.m., Eddie would disappear into the dawn with some unsuitable twink, and Katie would find her way back to the apartment alone with her suitcase, give the front door a kick, and collapse on the couch with a deli sandwich in her hand.

One Saturday morning, maybe two or three months after she had left for Los Angeles, I woke with a violent start to the reverberations of *The Sound of Music: Live!* exploding from the stereo in the living room. Clearly Katie was home. It was early, maybe 9 a.m., and in addition to the joy of Julie Andrews at full belt, what sounded like a brawl between cartoon hoodlums was taking place across the length of the apartment – Hope Street was always such a bicoastal flophouse.

A knock came at my door. I was not ready for this, whatever this was, and Morgan (always better qualified to handle a crisis) had not yet come home. I thought, *I'll just lie quiet and surely they'll go away.* But the knocking continued. When I opened the door, with red-eyed dread, I saw Katie alone on a comedown, crying, half in half out of her clothes, having turned the place over looking for a benzo or two. Standing in my doorway she looked all in.

'JJ baby,' she said, 'I need something to take the edge off, I've been up all night, I did way too much and now I'm like freaking out, so do you have something for me because I am, I don't even know, I am *not* feeling good.'

'Come here,' I said, and she sat in a heap on my bed, whilst I rifled through the mock-croc purse where I kept my stash.

Luckily for her, a week earlier I had performed at a private party, in the home of a wealthy Upper West Side psychiatrist. He had built a theatre in his lounge, and invited forty close friends over to celebrate something or other very special with him. To this end he had hired me and a ballet dancer (*a very odd combination,* I admit) as the entertainment. We were well paid but under strict orders not to mention the party to anyone, and to remain hidden in his ensuite until he gave us the cue to come out. We were to be a surprise, you see. Not used to being sequestered in a powder room like this, the ballet dancer and I quickly grew anxious – *Had we missed the cue?* – then bored, *Could it just happen already?*

We sat on the edge of the bathtub playing I Spy. I guess we could have had a fuck, only he was worried about making a mess of his lovely ivory pouch, and though I presumed my own genitals were somewhere under the mounds of tulle I was wearing, I couldn't be exactly sure where. So instead we rummaged around the bathroom, operating under the premise that, as we were in the home of an upmarket shrink, there was bound to be a supply of quality pharmaceuticals in there somewhere. Indeed there was, and we each discreetly selected two of everything, wrapping the loot up in tissue paper so that we could research at a later point exactly what each pill was, and thus imbibe responsibly.

So, when Katie burst into my room at that ungodly hour a week or so later, I had some blue capsules which, according to the internet, would help cool her heels a little. I had been stripping the night before and had woken up with a headache, so I took one too, for good measure. We decided that since it was such a beautiful morning, we would put on some nice clean dresses and sit on the stoop to enjoy the sunshine.

'Oh JJ!' she said, 'We look just like princesses! Are we princesses?'

'Sure we are,' I said. 'You and I are the Princesses of Hope Street.'

She squealed with joy and said, 'You know what princesses love? Hopscotch!'

Whether this is true or not I don't know, but all the same she drew out a grid on the sidewalk, with a piece of chalk left out by some of our non-existent neighbour's children. We played for a happy while; the beautiful morning seemed like a dream as we skipped up and down in our gowns outside the dry-cleaning warehouses, and became dreamier still when the tranquilisers caught up with us.

'JJ,' she said, 'I think I need to lie down.'

So we did, right there in the street, in our princess gowns.

The rest of the weekend continued in a similar vein, dressing up, getting high, occasionally vomiting, running over to Kellogg's Diner to satisfy a craving for a chocolate malt, climbing in and out of cabs, posing for pictures at parties we'd crashed, making big plans, crowding into toilet cubicles, swapping our clothing, and scooping up more and more friends and lovers into this higgledy-piggledy parade. My recollections of that weekend are a fluorescent haze, as is much of my time in New York. I know I was at one point crawling around the floor, very distraught at having lost a false eyelash, accusing a cockroach of having stolen it, and I recall someone booking us all into a hotel near Times Square. I remember lying on the bed, looking up and seeing myself reflected in the mirrored ceiling, in pink bikini briefs, falling in and out of sleep while Morgan read sections of the children's Bible out loud, asking in irritation, 'Hey! Are you listening?' The rest is lost, fuzzy; we didn't even have the benefit of Baby, our old camcorder, anymore – she was long gone.

Jonny, Eddie, Morgan, Billy, Katie and me, a few go-go boys and a woman we'd met at an ATM. When Monday morning came, we were all sitting on the floor of the enormous shower in the hotel bathroom, trying to console Katie over the fact that she'd missed her flight back to LA, trying to dissuade her from calling her boss and confessing it all. Some bright spark amongst us said, 'I know! Let's all tell each other one thing we love about each other!', which distracted her enough to forget Los Angeles and her responsibilities for a little while longer. We clung to each other, extolling our mutual virtues all over the floor, with passionate relish, clammy and quick, hearts beating and eyes darting, gilded with tender tears. At a certain point I panicked because I could not remember how long I had been there, and it seemed suddenly imperative that I know. I didn't want to spoil the game by interrupting it, so I quietly went over the experiences and occurrences in my head, trying to settle up my accounts with time, but it was all just too malleable. *Well then, let's start at the very beginning*, I said to myself. *How long have you been in the city?* But when I tried to connect the dots all I got was a tangle of scribbles, no conclusive image, no steadfast answer. The psychic I was jammed tight shut with narcotics, and I was forced to ask aloud, 'Guys, how long have I been here?'

'In the shower?' asked Katie.

'No, no, *here*,' I said. 'In New York.'

There was a general totting up, a lot of humming and hawing, several suggestions, but the pile of bodies heaped on the bathroom floor could not reach a unanimous verdict. So we turned to Morgan, who alone had enough authority to make a final decision, and asked her to tell us.

'Well, if you include your weekends in Atlantic City, and those two trips to LA, your time in New York comes out at a grand two years and six months!'

A collective gasp, *Really? That long? But it feels like only yesterday when we first met! Are you sure? Wow!* and then Katie started crying again.

To me, though, it seemed an impossibly short epoch, a ridiculous, petty, penny-pinching slice of time. How was it possible, when I looked at this drooling, sleep-deprived huddle, whom I adored to the depths of my weather-eaten soul, that I had only had the luxury of their love for two years and six months? Impossible!

Time is a fraud, of no use to me! I thought. *It's not fit for purpose, it must be leaking!* They all went on gabbing around me, some threatening to go home, some demanding room service, some suggesting we might do just one more line, some talking about bringing in blankets to make the shower floor cosier, all buzzing with the crazed hum of a beehive.

I couldn't conceive that each of these little bumble-bees (and more) could have played together in my garden for just two years and six months. How was it that I'd ridden on the back of a motorbike across Lower Manhattan with Jonny, and watched Eddie pour that glass of milk on his own head on the dance floor at Julius', that I'd been seated at dinner next to my heroine Penny Arcade at a dinner for Holly Woodlawn, that I'd clutched Billy's hand in the front row of the opera on opening night, and exclaimed, 'This is our life!', all in such a brief time – two years and six months?

And what about all the boys? The lovers I had put in your place, leapling. Were they also the product of two years and six months? Impossible. The scrawny, long-haired boy with all the tattoos and the bullet in his hand, the trans boy I was crazy about who told me I was *really fucking beautiful* then promptly broke my heart in a bagel shop, the guy I slept with just to get back at his journalist boyfriend who'd written something mean about me in a magazine column, the straight room-mate from our apartment, pre-Hope Street, who would come into my room silently when he knew Morgan was out, always chuckling the next morning and saying, 'Oh man, I hope I wasn't sleepwalking again last night!'

All of this in two years and six months? No, I refused to believe it. Seconds and minutes and hours and days and weeks and months and years had proven themselves false. From now I would only believe in the passing of time as measured in friends and lovers, people, bodies, headaches, irresponsible clinches, the passage of heat towards cold, happy coincidences and tragic accidents. I swore it to myself.

'*You know*,' slurred Billy, 'Henry Miller said that being happy and knowing it, is the greatest thing one can ever experience. Ever.'

'Is he the guy who makes the beer?' asked one of the go-go boys.

'No dumbass,' said Eddie, 'he's the writer.'

'And having *experienced* this happiness,' Billy continued, 'all that you can do is kill yourself, so Henry says anyway.'

'Bummer,' said Morgan, but so earnestly that everyone broke out into wild laughter all around her.

Myself I was ecstatic, and I knew it, but not weighing up my options for suicide, rather I bathed in the reflected light of this life I'd staggered into and squatted for so long. It didn't get better, I knew, than being high and half-suffocated by all of these people whom I loved so dearly, it couldn't.

At 2 p.m. the hotel staff asked us to either check in for another night, or to check out immediately. Nobody knew whose idea this had been in the first place, or who was going to pay; I'm still unsure who did pay, if anyone. It was not a courteous ejection – we were practically thrown out onto the street by two hulking doormen, with the manager yapping, 'Y'all are damn lucky I don't call the cops!'

We were kicked to the kerb, in a state of some dissolution, crawling out into the early afternoon, horrified by the noise, the pollution, the heat, the crowds, stumbling into taxi cabs, crying *Call me!* as we split into smaller groups. In our cab, Morgan sat up front next to the driver. I squeezed into the back with Jonny and Katie. As soon as the car got going they began making out with gay abandon, French kissing with skills refined through years of practice on both coasts. The mood was one of syrup, submission to the universe, smelting, a synchronised decomposition, ineffable, then Morgan turned and spoke to me. Through the hatch in the Plexiglas partition, she sighed, looking tired, looking mournful, and of course I knew what was coming.

'I have to tell you something,' she said.

'Oh yeah?' I asked, though she didn't need to spell it out.

'I'm leaving,' she said, 'for good. *This* is too much, all this, this city. It's not for me. I miss San Francisco.' She looked dead beat.

I asked, 'Are you sure it's not just the coke?' and the taxi driver's eyebrows shot up in the rear-view mirror.

'Of course,' she snorted at my indiscretion. 'I just can't see it ever being any different. Honestly, can you?'

'Does it have to be different?' I asked her, but I knew I was being stupid. 'You'll feel differently tomorrow.'

'I've known for a long time,' she said plaintively. 'I didn't want you to think I was leaving you.'

'But you are,' I replied, trying not to sulk.

'Everybody has to grow up sooner or later,' she said tersely, and I knew the argument was lost.

She wanted to leave at the end of the month, back to California where things grow, where you can breathe the air, back to apartments with secure front doors, where cockroaches are an optional extra. She had to go, she said, while she was still enough of a whole person to make such a decision with a sound mind.

'I mean, how long can this go on for?' she asked.

She said she didn't want to wake up at forty, sharing a roach-infested shoebox with a rolling chorus line of strangers, getting by sewing G-strings and rip-away panties. She said she wanted to leave with *some* dignity intact, to go back to SF, to the good weather, before it was too late for her to straighten herself out, to learn new skills, to get a job with health insurance.

'I don't want to be calling my mother begging for a plane ticket home because I'm sick and can't afford to see a doctor,' she said.

I said that maybe she was right, perhaps it was better to return while she was still in the pink flush of youth, rather than in the yellow hue of hepatitis.

'And you?' she asked.

'I can stick it out,' I said.

'But do you want to though?' She sighed, 'Don't you have aspirations for more than this?'

'Of course,' I replied, 'you know that this isn't what I want to do forever.'

'Well, you know you'll have to be in the country for a minimum of ten years right, before they'll even *consider* giving you any kind of legal status? That's like *eight more years* of this. So, what? Are you planning on dancing on tables for the next decade? What about real work, real life? When was the last time you wrote anything?'

I couldn't answer.

In the course of our taxi ride across the bridge, she put it to me plainly, and perhaps I was coming down too hard, harder than expected, but my situation suddenly did not seem so gorgeous. I reeled my responses off, cold, hurt. *No, this was not a surprise, yes I had seen this coming, no I didn't want to admit it, yes I'd just have to accept it, no I didn't want her to go, yes I would miss her, no I didn't hate her, yes I still loved her, no I wasn't lying.*

'I'm sorry it didn't work out with us,' she said. 'I mean, I feel guilty. Sometimes I feel like it's my fault, but honestly what did we think would happen? Neither of us can even keep a job.'

I pressed my mouth shut very tightly and nodded.

She sighed and said, 'You have to understand, *this* just isn't what I want. I don't want to make silly costumes and live off pancakes anymore. Does that seem selfish?'

'No,' I said coldly, 'You're being very pragmatic.'

She yelled, 'Oh my God, what is it with you? Why can you never say what you feel? You *can* be angry, you know! I'd understand if you were pissed with me! But I hate this fucking stuck-up British attitude, *"You're being pragmatic."* Fuck you're so annoying sometimes. Ugh!'

She was flushed with a temper I'd only ever seen once before, when she got into a fight with a landlord who had tried to scam us out of a deposit by claiming that we'd never paid him one. I remember how she lost it with him, turning scarlet and screaming, 'That's bullshit Jeremy, bullshit!'

She asked, 'Hey. Can I smoke out the window?'

The driver, who looked a little afraid of her, nodded silently 'yes', and so she lit a cigarette. She took a few drags, breathing out blue streams of smoke into the street as it streaked past, then picked up her monologue where she'd left off.

'What is it with this weird passivity of yours? Did you lose any capacity to think for yourself? Are you just going to wait around for someone else to tell you what to do with your life when I'm gone? What are you, a professional girlfriend?'

Then I lost my cool, I said, 'You have some motherfucking nerve, girl! You invited me here, you said it'd be *no problem*, that you had it all lined up. You brought me here and now you're telling me I made this mess for myself?'

'Oh fuck that,' she said. 'You have and that's life! I mean, get a fucking grip!'

She turned and looked straight ahead, assuming that aristocratic air which was never too far away, and the cab became completely quiet. Jonny and Katie were sleeping in a heap, the taxi driver was silent, he had turned off the radio, had fallen into rapt attention, straining to hear every word of this insane conversation. Morgan was right, of course, I was entirely passive, I never made decisions for myself, I just let myself be tossed around like an old football by whoever picked me up. I'd never had the strength of personality to say *this is what I want*, so I just found myself in one stupid, precarious situation after another, irresponsible and airheaded.

I felt very lonely. To me Morgan was New York, she was America, and even though we weren't married, she was my wife. That hollow feeling that Jarvis Cocker sings about in 'Sorted For E's & Wizz' crept over me, and I read between the lines. I knew I wasn't being invited back to San Francisco, and recognising that, accepting that I wasn't going back with her, that the apartment above the laundromat was lost for good, things really did seem bleak.

There's a William Burroughs photograph which I love, it's taken from a balcony, looking down from the second floor onto the cold pavement of what seems to be the East Village. The street is barely populated, the few figures captured seem to be vanishing, moving further away, the railings of the fire escape in front of the camera lens becoming prison bars framing a world outside that is abandoning the photographer. I saw it with you in fact, at the Photographers' Gallery in London, sometime after that dire taxi ride, and it summed up quite perfectly how I felt in the back of the cab, it took me right back to that atmospheric sensation of being left behind.

Looking out of the taxi cab window, dismal in spite of the fair weather, all I saw ahead of me were years of dodging Homeland Security, persuading friends to cash pay cheques for me, writing to my mother to say *Maybe next Christmas*, rent hikes on illegal sublets, missing my sisters' weddings, dancing at bars for seventy-five dirty dollar bills, hangovers, and more hangovers, paving over squalor with delusions of grandeur, and the occasional casting which could never hope to match the rocketing cost of living in NYC. That was what I had to look forward to, unless, unless of course, I chose to cash out now, while I still had this charmed present, before the inescapable future, the destiny I had been running away from all this time, caught up with me, and I found myself an addict, or a convict, or both. In a way, I guess I was taking Henry Miller's advice after all. I acknowledged that I had been happy, and that this probably couldn't be bettered, and though I didn't decide to drown myself or jump in front of a train, I did surrender to a certain kind of destruction.

Back at the apartment Morgan and I tucked Jonny and Katie into bed, and talked it over, over tea. I agreed that when Morgan left for California, I would leave for London.

'I love you, you silly tart,' she said. 'I'll miss you.'

She looked so beautiful that afternoon, even on the harshest of comedowns, she was so stately, so lovely. Sometimes I even ask if it's possible that Morgan was the man who got away, and not you? If in fact this book should be addressed to her? Yes, it strikes me now, writing this out, looking back on the whole sordid thing from the Mexican present moment, that Morgan could've been the love of my life. Well, maybe, leapling, maybe. Perhaps in a mirror universe where you are still alive and out there photographing abandoned Soviet buildings, that's how it happened.

I said that I'd go back to school in London. She said that she'd get a job and save up, and follow me there, and we'd go up North and I'd introduce her to my family. They'd all be so grown up by now, old enough to understand. There was still hope.

So why then, rather than meetings at the National Theatre and book readings at Foyles on Charing Cross Road, why was my mind only filled with one vertiginous image of disaster? The picture from the ceiling of Chapultepec Castle which Morgan had shown me in *The History of Mexico*. A painting of the boy hero who threw himself from the walls of the castle, clutching the Mexican flag, defending it from the invading US troops to his last breath. I too was going to fall out of this life now, not to die, but to disappear all the same. Someone told me insistently on a dance floor once, 'One can't *be* dead, death is not a state one can exist in,' and this proved him right. Surely enough, though I went on living I ceased to exist, I wasn't dead, but I was headed quite outside of my life.

What was it to be? Back to Adam's sofa, back to temp jobs, back to boiled eggs and sausages, as though everything that had happened since was entirely without worth? No. I refused to allow these past two years and six months to die in vain, to have meant nothing. I would learn this lesson if it killed me. *This time it's going to be different*, I promised myself. But how?

In the week after Morgan announced her departure I started looking at writing programmes, something I should have done when I was eighteen instead of allowing myself and my good grades to be shunted against the cold walls of academia. I found that I was still in time to apply to the experimental writing programme at Central Saint Martins, which I took to be a most fortuitous sign, and repeated my newly minted mantra, *This time it's going to be different*.

I wrote you an email to say that yes, I was coming back to London actually, and that I'd gladly take you up on your kind offer to free up a little space in your flat. 'Just for a few days, maybe longer if there's a room going.' *This time it's going to be different,* I said, and it was as if I believed it. As if I sincerely hoped I could find redemption by stepping out of this havoc and into your mayhem, as if this sleight of hand was enough. Looping, looping, looping.

Then I was packing up my meagre, flamboyant belongings, waving Morgan off, booking my flight, promising my friends I'd be back soon, hosting a hushed going-away party, everyone on their best behaviour, calling Billy at his office and crying on his voicemail, allowing Selena and Eddie to put me in a cab to JFK. Why did it all seem so familiar? It hadn't been two years and six months, no. It couldn't have been more than a week or two since Elsa and Adam and Jovian had put me on that flight from Heathrow.

I could have allowed myself to imagine that I was just dreaming in reverse, if not for Jonny, who was going to Dublin to sing in a festival of new opera. I arranged to take the same flight, to travel over the Atlantic with him, doped up on the last of the Iranian psychiatrist's tranquilisers, so it wouldn't feel as hard to leave. He entertained me through the long wait in the departure lounge with impersonations of all our friends, saying, 'Don't worry, you'll see 'em all again in no time!', coaxing chuckles out of me until it was time to board.

Somewhere over Nova Scotia, we hit turbulence and woke with a fright. Amid the shaking and shouting, we both reached out for the other, each of us attempting to break the other's fall from within the panic of our own gentle comas. We clung to each other all through the night, and when we landed in Ireland we were still in each other's arms.

PART THREE

'Fortunately I am not the first person to tell you that you will never die. You simply lose your body. You will be the same except you won't have to worry about rent or mortgages or fashionable clothes. You will be released from sexual obsessions.'

— COOKIE MUELLER

I

Recently I dreamt of you. It's hardly a surprise that, since you're at the forefront of my consciousness during all my waking hours, you'd take a nocturnal detour and wander through the moonlit passages of my sleep. Or perhaps it was more of a hallucination, since I had the feeling you were absolutely there. Stood at the foot of my bed, you were saying, 'You're Miss Ramsgate, aren't you?'

It was as if you'd solved a long-standing riddle, glee-fully cracked a code, finally figured out my true identity (something I have certainly never achieved). I wanted to argue my case with you, but I felt bound by a deli-cacy, a diplomacy. I was aware that you had died, and I didn't want to cause you any further upset; just as when you tell a lover you've found someone new, the sight of their pain bestows on you a supersensitive tact, which makes you act far more kindly to them in your final moments together, than in many of the preceding years. I think I was also aware of not wanting to make you angry, in part because I've seen enough horror movies to know that enraging the undead is always mighty foolish, but also because of a fear of my own temper, unstoppable once the fuse is lit.

So when you said, 'You're Miss Ramsgate, aren't you?', I simply smiled meekly and pieced together the vague and blameless reply, 'I think we've taken different things from this story.'

I woke from this dream into the strangest of worlds, one in which the Emperor of Japan had abdicated, and Notre Dame was on fire, and tweets demanding the immediate reform of US gun laws kept on coming from my friend Hattie, even though she'd been dead since January. The last time I saw her she was dressed as a naughty nun, smoking an illicit fag outside Rapture Cafe on the Lower East Side, pure Irish-American charm, smiling coyly, and wishing Jonny and I a safe flight to Dublin.

After leaving New York, I stayed in Ireland for a week, strolling aimlessly and alone, while Jonny did press interviews and charmed the festival directors. I spent my time staggering from church to church in a jet-lagged fugue, weeping with separation anxiety, saturated by the foggy chill I felt on this side of the Atlantic. I can remember kneeling and praying in a pew, in an otherwise desolate nave, remaining there all afternoon, sobbing interminably until the cleaning ladies came in. They were surprised to see me there, and I heard them talk in low voices, about whether or not they should ease me out, so that they could shut up shop. The hushed discussion built in whispered intensity, coming to a terse conclusion when one of the unseen guardians hissed, 'Oh leave her be Mary, she's obviously having a hard time!'

With that they trundled off to the vestry with their mop buckets, leaving me undisturbed a little while longer.

Later that evening I saw a group of people watching a pair of muscular acrobats climbing up and over each other in the street; they were wearing Union Jack underwear and bowler hats. I stopped briefly, if only to feel myself part of a crowd, and heard the old lady in front of me say to another, 'Oh would you come on now Mary? When you've seen one you've seen them all.' I left the small scrum of onlookers, feeling much the same sentiment, and wondering if every woman in Dublin over fifty was called Mary. I found that a soothing thought, it made me giggle even, made me think of the habit Billy and I had of calling each other Mary, in homage to the archetypical old queen, whom we adored and channelled, and who we imagined would always call *everyone* Mary.

Jonny was staying in Dublin until the end of the month, to finish his run of shows, but I had no real reason to be there, I was only delaying the inevitable. I was in limbo between the lost paradise of New York and the awaiting hellfire of London, plus it seemed to be inexplicably expensive there. Some starry-eyed kid, who was fawning over Jonny, explained it to us in a drag bar, 'Sure, the city hasn't been the same since the boom. The Celtic Tiger was off the leash for a while there, and didn't the prices show it?' Then he went in for the kill, as if this well-worn tale of economic instability had pushed him over the edge of desire. Drunkenly he poured himself into Jonny's lap, seizing him by the lapels of his leather jacket, and prompting me to make my excuses and leave. Half-cut, cold and worn out, walking back to Jonny's festival flat I decided to linger no longer, to throw myself into the future, which was also my past. When I got in, I used very nearly all the money I had left in the world to book my travel onwards to London. Then I wrote to you. You replied briefly, promptly, you were a little crude, you wrote:

ok Bibbs
a week in my room
comes at a cost
yet to be established
but you need to do better to please
see you in a bit
x

I flew on a tiny plane, two days later. It hardly even seemed like a commercial aircraft, more like something for real estate reconnaissance, or for ferrying back-bench MPs to party political conferences. We landed in Blackpool, in sight of that most British of mock-eries, the Blackpool Tower, that ungainly musical star in Parisian drag, who seems forever to be saying, 'No love, we don't need no Europe here!' I took the train straight on to London, arriving after dark, half out of my mind with fatigue and culture shock — nothing had changed. Euston was still the squalid teeming horror of Burger King wrappers, pigeons and furious travel delays. The underground was still overcrowded, over-lit and festooned with free newspapers, abandoned half-read. Old Street station, where I emerged with my suitcase, was still a piss-reeking rabbit warren, spew-ing out travellers from those many grimy exits studded with hopeless junkies and beggars. It struck me how little I had missed the city, and concomitantly, that I had already set about romanticising the superior filth of New York.

We had arranged to meet at an old haunt. Since you were finishing a job late, and as it was something of a crossroads between the studio and your apartment, we chose the Joiners Arms as the X to mark the spot. I lugged my suitcase up Hackney Road, cursing its weight every three steps, a cold sweat trickling down my back, the September air crisp. I was worried that I'd have kept you waiting for too long, that you might have already left, cycled off in a blue huff.

As it transpired I arrived before you, stumbling into the largely empty pub, luggage in tow. One of the bar staff immediately started shrieking, 'You can't bring *that* in *here*!' as if I'd dragged my suitcase into St Paul's, rather than this decrepit gay bar with its puke-stained carpets. The Joiners was just the same as ever too.

The landlady, Beverley, ever-regal, came out and contradicted her barman.

'It's alright love,' she said, 'you're fine with it.'

She dismissed the disgruntled employee with a wave, smiled to me and said, 'Been a while hasn't it, dear?'

'Yes, Bev,' I exhaled, 'it really has.'

And in you strolled, like a cowboy too skinny for his own movie, swaggering over the sticky floor, nothing but undulating limbs all held together by a smirk. My heart ran straight to my mouth. I swear it took every shred of my remaining will to prevent it from bursting right out of my maw and across the room in a geyser of hot blood. With that blasé, pacific entrance the whole interstitial period, two years and six months, fell away for a moment. You were wearing a pair of Exeter University Rugby Football Club shorts, which really were short, shorter than your boxer shorts, which peeked from beneath them, five or six centimetres further down your leg. There was something aristocratic about that, something of the eighteenth-century lace cuff erupting from a sleek embroidered frock coat, like the foam on the head of a wave. Effortless, inelegant, succinct and of course, adjusting your junk, you gave me that nod, and there it was: 'Alright Bibby?'

I put my arms around you, you were damp from the cycle, and you smelled a little like cradle cap. We sat down at a table just off from the dance floor, the three of us: you, me and the suitcase. You eyed it up and asked, 'What's all this?'

'My stuff,' I said, worrying that I hadn't made the situation clear enough. 'I'm back, I'm looking for a place.'

'I see, I see,' you said, furrowing your brow in mock contemplation, 'Bibby needs a place, eh?'

'Uh-huh,' I replied, flavouring my response with an undertone of *you know that.*

'Hmmm,' you said with the same facetious expression, 'Bibby's back in town.'

I felt pressed at being toyed with so soon. I tried to put my cards in order. 'I did tell you that I needed somewhere to stay for a bit.'

Bringing your face right into mine, you nodded lazily, 'Oh yeah? So when you gonna shave my arsehole then?'

I hadn't heard that word for so long, it zipped through me like a hit of poppers. The Americanised 'asshole' is so ubiquitous and inoffensive, it doesn't carry any of the original word's puerile eroticism, so when you uttered it I was hit full force with its thrilling Georgian vulgarity, and disarmed to the point that I blushed and snorted, like a schoolgirl flush with half a bottle of Nana's sherry.

'Whenever. Any time you want really,' was all I could manage by way of response.

We talked some more, mainly about your strangely esoteric job in that famous photographer's studio, where you were charged with both utterly anodyne tasks, such as photocopying broadsheet reviews, and missions of real responsibility, like being sent off to Brazil to lay the foundations for a whole new body of work. You were quite careful to mystify it more than was probably necessary, though I couldn't work out if you were trying to exaggerate your own importance, or play it down. You didn't ask me much about my time in New York, you just made a few crass remarks to the tune of, 'I bet you've been handling a lot of big black cock haven't you, Bibby?' I rolled my eyes and declined to dignify your provocations.

A few pints in, the night wore on, and the bar began to fill slightly. The same pick-n-mix as always, of casual alcoholics, PhD students never any closer to their doctorate, shy kids on first dates, emotional drunks and screaming queens spilling out of cabs and into the exact same scene as last night. Amongst them was a suave middle-aged man whom I recognised, perhaps from Brooklyn, perhaps from Bethnal Green. The sort of man who seems to have been forty-five for the past decade, always wearing a pale blue shirt with the sleeves rolled up, unbuttoned to the sternum, looking like he might direct a show on French television, or be readying himself to acquire a tech start-up.

'It's you!' he exclaimed, throwing his arms out wide.

'It is,' I said, rising awkwardly to accept his embrace.

With his utter lack of self-awareness he seemed like a peer of the realm, and he dropped down onto the stool next to me, ignoring and immediately enraging you. Hoping to draw his name out subtly, I gestured to you and said, 'This is my friend Thomas James.'

'Is it?' he replied, barely looking at you. Instead he took hold of both of my hands, folding them into his lap as he regaled me with sighs of how he'd been hoping to run into me again.

It was not how I had imagined the evening would progress. I could feel waves of antagonism radiating from you. I tried to turn in your direction but I was held entirely in place by this not unhandsome interloper, until he stood up and offered to get me a drink.

'Yes, sure, great, thanks.' I rattled off a series of agreements to encourage him on his way to the bar.

When I turned to face you, you gave me the most deathly of stares. I thought that you were going to tell me to fuck off and find somewhere else to sleep. I knew you were capable of that, and I was afraid of what the consequences of my unwilling extramarital flirtations would be. But, in fact, when you spoke, your tone was almost mournful, and you said in a low voice, 'I don't like him touching you.'

What was this? Jealousy? Possessiveness? A flash of some true silver feeling on a riverbed perpetually concealed by the muddy waters of your swift-flowing self-presentation? I sat up a little more erect, and allowed myself to luxuriate, for just a moment, in the feeling of power your unwitting admission had given me. When my friend returned (with a drink for me and one for himself) I could have let a haughty little laugh fly, but I knew that would've been cruel, so I kept it for myself, like a jewel. But I revelled, all the same, in the sensation of being sat between the two of you, knowing that it was entirely possible that you'd come to blows over me, if I were to nudge things in that direction.

Out of boredom, I suppose, or the sting of being slighted, you sank into yourself and looked gloomily about the place, your eyes resting first on the pool table, then on the bar, then on a lonely-looking boy who was doing his best not to appear lost. Wickedly perspicacious, my gentleman caller poked me and said, 'Oh, it seems like your friend likes the look of that one over there.'

He sniggered, and to your pink-faced horror waved to the boy, beckoning him over like a waiter. I had to admit it was a clever plan. Palming you off on some clueless undergraduate in order to clear the way, now that was pleasingly devious. If I'd had a lace fan about my person, I would have brought it out, simply to underline my delight at all this double-dealing.

This poor puppy-faced kid blushed all the way across the dance floor, shuffling over the gruesome carpet with such timidity I had to wonder if he'd ever spoken to another human being in his life. My would-be suitor said aloud, quite brusquely, 'Our friend here thinks you're quite fit, don't you, dear? He wants to buy you a drink.'

You whipped your head around with speed and rage and growled, 'Fuck off,' with a vitriol no one could have read as playful or shy. The scowl on your face, the way you spat out the words, your whole body flexed in tension, ready to rise up and knock him sprawling across the carpet, making such a tinderbox of the situation. And this crestfallen, scarlet-faced boy, blinking at the bewildering scene, staring slack-jawed, like he didn't know whether he was about to cry, or cream his pants.

'Let's go,' you said, drawing yourself up to your full height.

I followed you out the door without looking back.

We walked home under a moon brilliantly luminous, and fully visible from Earth. Her light was startling, perhaps providing that flicker of lunacy with which the evening had been irradiated. In her nearness and nakedness, truly she seemed like a crazed woman seeking everywhere for lovers, but to what end I could not say: to fuck or dispatch? As we walked, you catalogued aloud all the slights you had suffered since I'd been gone. The people who had disrespected you, overlooked you for jobs, snubbed you socially, and how you would pay them back tenfold as soon as you had the chance. You lived on perpetually thinning ice, but instead of treading carefully, moving slowly, you were forever thundering down on the verglas, hard as Hell. Your fury shaved a full five minutes off the journey (in spite of my heavy suitcase and your always unwieldy bicycle), though by the time we arrived at your apartment it was approaching midnight.

In the stillness of the night, the old faithful fluorescents still buzzed too loudly as you flicked them on. It was all as I had pictured it, those hundreds of times over since we'd last seen each other, on that evening we'd spent watching your VHS tapes, and losing our youthful illusions. The place was the same disarray of junky paraphernalia and kitsch of genuine value, all displayed without design. The tap at the kitchen sink still dripped with certainty into the grey plastic washing-up bowl, and the turquoise linoleum still longed for repair or replacement. Perhaps you had new roommates sleeping in their secret chambers behind the plywood walls, but I had never really known your old roommates, so such a change was negligible, if it registered at all. The only thing that had changed in all the time that suddenly rolled in to fill the void between then and now, was your bedroom doorway. I had only ever known there to be a rudimentary plank, haphazardly used to seal up your room when it was time to sleep or fuck, but now there was a door. An actual door, hung on hinges, standing ajar now yes, but its very openness suggested such a situation might not always be the case, it hinted that some things may have changed after all.

A little shudder ran through me, and when I looked into your room it was like looking into an open grave. I stepped in, kicking a few of the T-shirts on the floor to clear a path. A scent, a cologne I recognised lingered in there, not yours, you didn't wear any. It irked me that I couldn't figure out where I knew this fragrance from because I have a keen memory for these things, but then perhaps it was only the scent of the past? I ran my fingers over a large-format black and white photocopy of two teenage boxers mid-fight, and toyed with the dusty collection of plastic figurines on top of your chest of drawers. You moved past me, sat down on your bed and opened your laptop, slipped your right hand into your underwear and began chewing the nails of your left, as if unaware I was there at all.

'I'm going to brush my teeth,' I said.

'Alright,' you said, paying no attention.

In the bathroom I rifled through the collected cosmetics in the cupboard above the sink. It was an incongruous assortment of cheap supermarket products and toiletries from the gentlemen's perfumers of Jermyn Street, expensive floral shaving soap from Trumper's and grimy plastic bottles of Nivea aftershave balm. There were at least seven toothbrushes in various stages of decay, a few disposable razor blades glinting on their backs like dead flies, and a beautiful blue plastic comb, far too handsome to have been made this side of the seventies. I perused this biography in beauty products whilst I brushed my teeth, closing the cupboard when I was done, and moving on to stare at myself in the dirty mirrored door. I remembered one of Jonny's stories, about how he watched himself weep in a mirror streaked with toothpaste and spit, after hearing of the death of his favourite aunt. *Such a tender tale*, I sighed. Had he told me this in person? Or was it just an anecdote from his show? I couldn't be sure. My head was foggy, my eyes looked slightly bloodshot, my complexion a little sallow: despondent at this sight, I turned off the light and left the extractor fan droning.

My suitcase was still in the living room, lying on its side looking listless in the middle of the floor. I pulled out something to sleep in, then tried to tuck the case away neatly behind an armchair, but that served only to make it look more obtrusive, more cumbersome. One tattered corner sticking out hatefully, announcing itself as both an accident waiting to happen and as a situation far beyond my control. Coyly, I re-entered your room.

And there you were, sat on the end of your bed, lit only by the desk lamp. You were barefoot in a T-shirt, your rugby shorts had been discarded to the floor, and your cock was hard, tenting your striped boxers.

'So Bibby's back in town, eh?' you said quietly, almost to yourself.

I stepped towards you, kissed you and you fell backwards like a corpse onto the bed, pulling me down with you. The inevitability of it all. At once we fragmented, flying out in a shower of limbs, our component parts scattered in all directions by the propulsive forces of desire, only for our outlines to contract around us again sharply, reassembling us in the demi-darkness as an erratic pattern of touches, gasps and fumbles, our torsos scorching against each other, teeth colliding, erections smashing together. Sex made us a Cubist masterpiece, flattened and dislocated, seen with new eyes, yet still so familiar, sprawling in all directions at once, a spasming frieze of warfare and pleasure.

I raised your head up off the pillow, clasping my hands behind your dirty blond skull, like Salome kissing the head of John the Baptist. I had put from my mind the pain and distress which came as the direct result of our last encounter, I wished to be washed clean in this renewed intimacy, this new River Jordan. I wanted you to tell me it was all better now, but of course you never did.

You were breathing heavily through your nose, and your kisses grew impatient, you couldn't be satisfied with these alone, you needed more. With your hands flat on my flat chest, you pushed me up and back so we formed a capital L, and smoothly you curled yourself up so you could bring your wet mouth to my hard dick. I wonder still what powered this frenetic, vampiric sexual drive of yours. Were you maybe hoping that by imbibing such quantities of freshly delivered sperm you might somehow gain eternal youth? No. You were just an insatiable, lustful bastard, who liked the taste of cum, so I gave you mine. You swallowed it silently, skilfully, and spat out my softening cock like an unwanted pacifier when you were done.

I straddled you, resting my ass on my heels, tugging on your balls with one hand and jerking your dick with the other, letting a long chain of saliva slip from my lips and drizzle your hard cock with glossy lubrication. I stroked your dick for a long time, while you lay back, strangely stiff and still on the bed, pale and inflexible, your muscles rigid with the hunger for orgasm, and the subservient thrill of having surrendered your power to me. I think if I had tied your hands together that would have pleased you greatly. Instead you reached your bleached white arms out towards me, pulling my face towards your gaping mouth, your gasps and inexpressible groanings obstructing my attempts to kiss you again.

Still I kept on wanking your dick, exhausted from the day, my wrist beginning to cramp, my mind beginning to wander. Though I hate to admit it, I did wonder, self-ishly, how much longer it would take. How foolishly we wish our lives away. Now that I know how fragile all of this is, I cherish even the most unpleasant of moments; even when having a cavity filled, or crunching my way through abs exercises, I say, *This is my life and it is precious*. But back then I was only impatient, and out of ennui itself, I bit your left nipple, hard. The arrival of this pain caused your body to finally tremble, you bucked your pelvis up against me and spurted spunk all over your-self, with one long, inarticulate moan.

When it was over, without any pause for reflection, you reached for your T-shirt and used the balled-up fabric to clean your stomach, with the same sort of motion you'd use to scoop up guacamole on a tortilla chip, so that it had the effect of smearing you in semen, rather than actually wiping up the mess. And with that you switched off the desk lamp, said, 'Good night then, Bibby,' and rolled onto your shoulder facing the wall.

I lay looking at the ceiling, needing to take a piss, wondering where my clothes were amongst all the mess. I was about to slide out of bed to put myself back together, when you reached for me. Perhaps feeling my intention through the shifting of my weight on the mattress, you reached over your shoulder, caught my arm and pulled me to you. You drew me close against your back, the bony notches of your spine making themselves known in turn against my breastbone, the strangely pronounced triangles of my upper abdominals and the softness of my belly. You used my arms to hold yourself tight, to comfort, to reassure yourself of your place in the universe, and almost immediately your breathing became deeper and slower, how quickly you had fallen asleep. I felt a little cold, and I still needed to pee, I wanted to close the door properly, but couldn't bring myself to disturb you. So I crawled up even closer to you, sharing your warmth, silently astonished at how two such creatures could have found their way back into each other's company.

II

When I told you the next morning that I had plans to see Adam, you registered it with only a short bob of the head, before you gave me a frugal, matrimonial peck on the lips, and cycled off to the studio. I spent the morning rummaging through my belongings, trying to find something acceptable to wear from amongst the acres of tired rags in my suitcase. I thought about borrowing a shirt of yours, but I didn't think you'd find that very endearing.

I checked my emails, hoping to see a message from Morgan or Jonny, neither of whom had written. I did have a notification, however, from Central Saint Martins, inviting me to an interview later the following week over in Clerkenwell. It seemed possible that I was about to embark on a master's degree in experimental writing, a course of study which seemed inherently contradictory, but that itself appealed to me, so I grinned, and puzzled at the workings of the universe.

Had I really needed to waste all that time running around America in my tawdry Sunday best, hustling for sex and drugs, when right here I had the makings of a real, tangible life? Morgan had been right, yes, it was time to grow up, and I guess without even knowing it, I had. So, I'd study, I'd write, maybe work on some new performances, I'd toil away at my school desk until it was time for me come back home to the warmth of your bed. There I'd unburden myself of the day's stresses and you'd renew my strength, each and every evening, through the satiating power of your beautiful body. Life could be just that simple. It may have been all the coffee I sank, or the jet lag, or simply the hypnotic brightness of that new September day, but I believed in this fairy-tale for almost the entire morning.

I felt nervous and excited at the prospect of meeting Adam; I had missed him more than just about anyone else whilst I'd been away, and I wanted to see him as soon as I could, now that I was back. I loved him. It felt like we were more than just buddies, we were co-stars, novitiates in the same order, circling potential lovers, though it still ran me through to remember him saying, 'I just don't see you like that.' Knowing that my femininity was such a boner kill for him was a hard pill to swallow, perhaps I had never quite outgrown my desire for him. I ask myself now, *Wouldn't it have been more appropriate, and perhaps less painful, to accept that maybe it was time to stop pining after gay boys who were themselves pining after gay boys?* Well, yes, but you see, I still had that particular lesson to learn.

I was standing outside Charing Cross station waiting, smiling, aflutter, scanning the crowds continually for the first sign of Adam, when he pulled up next to me on a blue-framed bicycle. He had come from the opposite direction, I was startled because I hadn't seen him arrive, and the joy and the surprise made me all tender and silly and qualmish. Surely we hugged, maybe I cried, but from amongst these jumbled emotions I can't seem to summon up the details, not with any real clarity. I remember a goofy mood of flushed pink cheer, but the particulars are unavailable to me now, and it's as if I'm trying to pick out information from a document obscured by the thick black strokes of redaction.

I know that we had no fixed plans, because we never really did. We were usually so broke that even stopping for a cup of coffee would've been a significant extravagance, so most often we just walked about together, it's what we had always done. I suppose it gave us a sense of ownership over the city; sometimes we could cover great swathes of town, ambling seemingly aimlessly, though I always had the feeling that Adam knew where we were going.

I'm pretty sure that we took a walk through Trafalgar Square and up along Charing Cross Road that morning. I remember it because it seemed a funny route to choose, a promenade for tourists and sightseers, so why were we there? Gaggles of day-trippers following the raised umbrellas of their tour guides, Adam wheeling his bike through the multitudes, and me twittering on inconscient, describing in great, gaudy detail my adventures in the USA.

Here the details come back into sharper focus.

I'm reeling off my many indiscretions: three-ways, online hook-ups, a $300 fuck, drunken shags, secretive liaisons with my roommate while his girlfriend slept in the next room, kerb-crawling taxi drivers, all the *has anybody ever told you you look just like a real woman*, and the eternally wandering hands of Manhattan's patrician class. I always wanted to impress Adam, to shock him, to make him giggle and blush a little, to make it clear that even though he did not see me as an irresistible object of lust, plenty of others did.

I go on and on in this vein, until we're way past Leicester Square. I barely pause for breath before I commit the cardinal sin, and say, 'And of course as soon as I got here, I went over to Thomas fucking James's place, and the first thing we did was shag, so Liza I am exhausted!'

Adam comes to a sharp halt somewhere in Chinatown, and looks at me, not in shared amusement or modest fascination, but horrified, disbelieving. He stands stock-still, his face screwed up in confusion, mouth slightly open, unable to scrabble for words, turning a bloodless shade of white. He clutches his chest, a sudden sweat beading his brow, he looks pained, like he is having a heart attack, and then it hits me.

It hits me.

'You're seeing him, aren't you?' I say redundantly. 'You're seeing him? Fuck.'

Adam nods, 'Yeah.'

Sat at the kitchen table, whilst writing all of this out, I streamed a story on NPR, about two academics who have recreated the sound of a choir in the Hagia Sophia from six hundred years ago. They did this by recording a balloon bursting inside the building. From the quality of that tiny instance of sound they captured all the sonic information of the old church. Likewise, when I recall Adam's agitated, bewildered 'Yeah' from that early afternoon in September, the tone it comes back with is loaded with more history and ire than a single throwaway word could feasibly be expected to hold.

'Yeah,' he says. 'For a year already.'

Still standing still, amongst the fluid crowds of Chinatown, I notice that my own heart rate is accelerating too, even as I try to keep calm.

'And didn't either of you think it would be a good idea to tell me this?'

I want to be harsh, but I don't have it in me, and besides aren't I the one who's come crashing into this happy little set-up, wilfully ignorant of anything but my own wants and needs?

So I continue more kindly, 'I didn't know. He didn't say anything about it.'

Adam takes a deep breath and says, 'I told you, in a letter.'

I cast my mind over all the mail we'd shared, the silly postcards and the heartfelt missives that sprawled on for pages. The psychic I runs across a notecard in the shape of the London skyline on which Adam had written of going out in Manchester in a silk bow tie and being asked if he were in fancy dress. Runs over a white rectangle of card, posted from France, reading only, 'Minimalism is the key!', and a letter which asked, 'I wonder how you'll have changed and if you'll find me changed?' And yes there it is! A quip in there amongst it all, yes, a line about *seeing Tom*, but how could he have meant that Tom, my Tom, Tom whom we always called Thomas James? Tom who he always said was bad news, Tom who he'd watched me cry over, and rail against?

Adam was never wildly promiscuous, too busy, too sensitive, but he was embroiled in a constant pantomime of passionate moonlit clinches, and unrequited love stories with gooey-eyed boys, with whom he'd canoodle for a while before reaching the conclusion that it would never have worked. So this line about *seeing Tom* was obscured by all the other midweek heartaches and boundless hopefulness, lost in a long list of affairs with handsome, Nordic Stefans and Christians, and boyish, laddish Joes and Jacks. It was buried amongst all sorts of gossip, about his mum, about the weather, and the several simultaneous platonic romances he was leading, in a letter I'd received from him amidst all the depravity of my life on Hope Street. *I've been seeing Tom*, discreet, ambiguous, no big shakes, it had not exactly been an open admission. Or perhaps I had simply shut it out of my mind as soon as I read it, maybe Socrates was right when he insisted that the written word induces only forgetfulness into the souls of those who learn it.

'I'm sorry,' I say. 'I really am. I didn't put it together.'

'It's fine,' he says, an angry vermillion creeping up from his collar to replace the lead white on his face.

'No, but, really,' I try.

'It's fine,' he repeats testily. Then more gently, 'I know you didn't know. I can see that from your face. It's fine, it's not your fault.'

'What a bastard,' I say. But Adam looks hurt, so I add, hopefully, 'Or do you two have some sort of arrangement?'

Then, just for a second, I think that he's going to crack a joke, make a light-hearted reference to that scene in *Cabaret* where Liza Minnelli and Michael York discover that they're unwittingly participating in a ménage à trois, that they have both been played by their duplicitous lover. But, no.

Instead, he says, very gloomily, 'No. No, there's no arrangement.'

He grips at the handlebars of his bicycle, as though it is the only thing keeping him from breaking into a million tiny pieces on the street. I realise that I've never seen him ride a bike before. Was it a gift from you, leapling? The front wheel takes on the cartoonish form of an engagement ring. I recognise his cologne as that

247

which had lingered in your room the day I got back, a fragrance from my old job at the perfume shop, which I'd stolen and gifted him. I feel sick to my stomach. We walk a few paces on, then I try to make a joke, see that it's not going to work, ask instead if he wants to sit down and talk about things.

'I don't want to discuss it,' he says coldly, definitively, then, trying to modify his tone, he says, 'let's talk about something else. Have you seen Liza yet?'

And so we continue on through Soho, chewing over gentler topics, the comings and goings of our mutual friends, plans for new work, our sisters giving birth. The conversation is functional, unremarkable, calm; to all extents and purposes it is a dialogue between two friends catching up, but I can tell he isn't really here with me anymore. His mind is somewhere else, frantic, fluttering like a frightened sparrow, desperate to get free from this strange human environment into which he has mistakenly flown.

I realise that if I'd have chosen to come back and sleep on Adam's sofa-bed again, rather than shacking up with you, this whole situation might've been avoided. Surely Adam would have told me straight in those circumstances? I keep thinking how much easier everything would've been then, and yet I can't help but wish that I was still in the dark about it all.

'I should've come to stay with you, Liza,' I say. 'And saved all this trouble.'

I pause, hazard a smile, aware that I'm also flushing pink. I say, 'But I couldn't ask. I still felt too ashamed.'

Adam doesn't answer.

He strolls with me far enough so as not to seem impolite, then says he's feeling tired, has to teach at three. He gives me a brief, too distant goodbye, then jumps on his bike and heads back to the apartment in Waterloo, saying he'll call me the next day. He looks as though he is about to disintegrate, and I have never forgotten that expression of hurt and bewilderment, or the guilt that it caused me, never. That look of betrayal he tried so desperately to mask, as if I'd told him, *I just don't love you anymore.*

I am alone and nearing Tottenham Court Road, wishing that I had the cash to go get plastered. An unexpected image rushes into my mind from one of the old video tapes, of Robert and I lip-synching in the streets of the Mission, to a song which is playing from a laptop just out of shot. Morgan is filming, and as the song moves towards the dance break we'd practised so hard for, you can hear her squeal, 'Oh my God! That's my laptop! They're stealing my laptop!' The camera drops and the tape catches only the pavement and her blurry sneakers, coming in and out of the frame as we run after the would-be thieves who had tried to rob us. This is how I feel now, stunned by the intrusion of uninvited elements into this frame I have so carefully devised. This time it's going to be different.

I call Elsa, she doesn't answer, perhaps she's already speaking to Adam, maybe he got in there first. Then it starts to rain.

'Fuck it,' I mutter to myself.

I trudge back to your place in an unequal, befuddled headspace, because of course I do, and besides, where else am I supposed to go now?

III

You were at home, two glasses of cider and a big bag of crisps spilled open on the table; the September sun had returned. You were moving a piece of furniture with your roommate onto that morbid grey tarmacked area outside the kitchen, which you rather pretentiously called the terrace. The immoveable article got jammed in the doorway repeatedly, and you swore at it, kicked it. Your roommate did his best to keep the peace between you and the wardrobe, or the sideboard, or whatever it was; I was too dazed to properly comprehend. We didn't say hello when I came in, rather I went straight to my case, took out my notebook and started scrawling, so that I had something to busy myself with, in order to stop myself from crying.

Like any bound novice, my notebook was a hothouse of manifestations; here I jotted down journal entries and sketched out short stories, helter-skelter, hoping that by committing the ideas to paper I would gain power over them. Between the pages I had stashed endless bits of rubbish: Metro tickets, fliers for gigs I'd never made it to, the foil from Kinder Eggs folded out neatly in squares, post-it notes with unplaceable phone numbers scribbled in red biro, information on vaccinations, a gift tag from a Christmas long past, prayer cards, and obscene doodles on cocktail napkins; in short, a life's work.

I found a clean page and started a letter to Morgan which I knew I'd never send, it began: *Oh my fucking God, you WILL NOT believe the mess I've gotten myself into this time. Well you probably will but...*

You looked at me, sitting on your sofa, ignoring your struggle, and commented, 'Bibby's not offering to help I see.'

I didn't reply. It would have to wait until later, until we were alone, if there were to be any possibility of navigating this situation with the slimmest hope of a happy outcome. Brushing off your dig I returned to the page.

You grunted away on the terrace, forcing the furniture out to pasture, then, sweaty and flushed, sat back at the table, to finish your cider and crisps with your roommate, who was seemingly in no hurry to be on his way to meet the friend he had already kept hanging for half an hour. It was almost unendurable, this wait to be alone, and even then, once he had finally shuffled off, you stepped outside onto the terrace again to chat with your neighbour for ten more insufferable minutes. Finally you came in with a grin on your face, saying, 'Good man. Good man,' then put the empty glasses in the sink.

Gesturing to your neighbour's flat you said, 'He's a scientist, works with noise. Weaponising it.'

I said, 'What? Like the Kate Bush song?'

You continued, 'Yeah. He has this one sound that would make you shit yourself straight away.' And here you grinned wider. 'I would love to use that sound, play it in the middle of a DJ set at BoomBox and just watch all those wankers shit themselves.'

You were picturing it, standing in the kitchen, smirking as you envisioned victory over your mortal enemies, that is to say, everyone who hadn't acknowledged your greatness with the required gusto.

'I saw Adam today,' I said.

'Oh yeah?' you replied. 'How is Ads?'

Ads, you say, and I recognise the sound of that balloon bursting again. *Ads*, that proves it.

'Well,' I said, 'he told me that you and he have been seeing each other. That you've been dating for a year, in fact.'

'Did he?' you asked nonchalantly.

'Yes, he did,' I said, and felt my colour rising again. 'And he was not exactly pleased when I told him that we were fucking.'

'Well why'd you say that?' you said gruffly. 'That was stupid.'

I snorted, 'I told him because I tell him everything, Thomas, because he's my friend.'

You cast a look over your shoulder, back towards the door which opened onto the terrace, and said, 'He doesn't own me.'

I admit I was taken aback by that. I said, 'No, but he thinks you're in a monogamous relationship.'

You shrugged, 'Yeah, well we're not.'

'Clearly!' I snorted, but it was, as my mother would've said, like arguing with the wall.

So I tried a different tack: 'I guess that's really for you and him to talk about, but why didn't you tell me?'

'Because it's none of your business!' You lost your temper, and scoffed, 'Bibby comes sidling in here after years, wants a shag and can't handle the consequences. You need to grow up!'

Now I was shouting, 'But he's my best friend, you dick, you know that! And *clearly* he's in love with you.' I could feel all the nerves in my body steel, ready to throw something at your head.

'So?' you said.

I gasped, 'I'm here fucking my best friend's boyfriend, without even knowing it! I mean can't you see what a lousy situation that puts me in?'

You spat, 'Oh piss off with your hippie bollocks.'

I spat back, 'Do you have to be such a bastard all the time?'

Your face contorted into an expression of genuine surprise, then registered sorrow, then flushed a hateful rouge, and swiftly you were on the attack again.

You hissed, 'Yeah well, Adam, your *best mate*, said that all you ever did was use him. He said that you stayed with him for months, didn't give him anything, just slept in his room, didn't even pay any bills – just used him.'

I think I actually took a step backwards, staggered slightly, flailing as if your words were a mirror showing me the true, putrid state of my soul. I was lost for a moment, scrabbling for a comeback, flailing, hardly able to believe that Adam would have said that about me, knowing that he had, imagining the two of you picking over my many failings together, laughing at me. It was like a kick in the balls, a slap across the face, a punch to the gut, all at once and worse. The emotions caused me almost to double over; you saw this, and wasted no time in driving your stake home into my heart.

'He said that you took over his space and you wouldn't leave,' you sneered. 'I guess that's what you thought you'd do with me too, eh Bibby? You saw a soft touch, and you were going to try and rinse me too, eh?'

'No,' I stammered, 'I just needed to stay until I could find a place, it's not easy.'

'Never is though, is it, Bibby?' you said, truly nasty.

My head was reeling, like I was coming up too hard on a pill, or I'd just been smacked in the face by one of my mother's boyfriends. How was it possible that my lover and my best friend had a thing, where they got together to trash me as, what, foreplay? How self-absorbed was I that I hadn't seen any of this coming? Blindsided, I dropped down into a chair, faint, like I was already hearing that voice saying, 'Yes, he's dead.'

I cleared my throat, you stood there staring at me. I said, 'I think you two should talk about things—'

'I think you should keep your nose out!' you barked. Then you snatched your keys up off the table, sniping, 'I'm going out.'

I sat there for a while telling myself it wasn't so bad really, that it was all just a big misunderstanding. I wished I had Billy or Jonny or Morgan close by, I wished that I'd never come back. I wanted to call Adam, but thought better of it. I dialled Elsa again instead. She answered this time, more sombre than usual, no laughter in her voice when she said, 'Hi Liza. Sorry I missed your call, I was, ah, working. Are you back now?'

'I am,' I said, 'I'm back.'

We made loose arrangements to meet over the weekend, maybe to go to a gallery, maybe to see her cousin and the new baby. She was living in West London now, and I was in the East End, further apart than I would have liked at that particular moment. Midway through our meandering conversation I asked the question I had called her to have answered.

'Liza,' I said, 'Did you know about it, about the two of them?'

'Yes,' she said soberly, 'I'm sorry I didn't tell you, but—'

'It's OK,' I said, 'nobody would want to be in the middle of all this.'

A silence came down heavy between us, like a plush velvet theatre curtain. I wanted to let it settle, to hide my shame in its shroud, but the stillness only made me more uneasy, so I continued.

'Is it general knowledge then?'

'I think so,' she said. 'It's been a while.'

It was just like when I told a friend that I had been molested by my doctor, and he replied flippantly, 'Oh yeah, he does that to everyone. He's notorious for it.' That ho-hum admission that terrible things happen in plain sight. Presidents assault businesswomen on first-class flights, and children are trafficked out of their homes by TV personalities, and we all shrug, *Well, what are you gonna do?* and anyway what was my problem compared to any of that?

As we were both still using pay-as-you-go phones we didn't talk for much longer. We agreed to firm up our plans before the weekend arrived, tried our luck with a few memorable puns from back when, and then said a timid farewell. Elsa's 'Goodnight, Liza Minnelli' disappeared into the night, mixing with the faint echo of Adam's mumbled insistence, 'I don't want to discuss it,' and the reverberation of your loud order, 'Keep your nose out!'

One of Mexico's daily newspapers recently ran a photograph of a dead whale, which had been discovered in the Amazon. Nobody could figure out where it came from, this enormous beast, stranded in the rainforest, inexplicable. When I saw this picture, I was awed by the magnitude of its strangeness, and by the way it matched, so exactly, my feelings on that night years earlier; the sensation of being washed up, beached on your sofa. It's a small sorrow, or a universal jest, that we often don't have the images we need to help us understand certain situations in our lives, until much later, when the need is gone, and the image can only bring us backwards in a dizzying state of reverie, to a moment we had tried so hard to forget.

I must've been in the exact same spot you'd left me in, because when you came back, hair tacked to your forehead with sweat, smelling of four quick pints, you said ironically, 'Busy night eh, Bibbs?'

'Something like that,' I said, sulkily. 'I had a lot to think about.'

You pulled a mocking, moody face, your big bottom lip stuck out, a childish leer ruined only by the huge comic hiccup that ripped it apart. I could see that you were tight; you sat down next to me, patting my knee over and over again, saying, 'Bibbs, Bibbs, Bibbs.'

'You're drunk,' I said with a roll of my eyes, 'go to bed.'

'Yeah,' you said. 'It's late.'

You stood up and walked towards your bedroom. I thought that you would surely just crash and leave me to my own devices, but as you pushed the door, you turned to look back at me, your eyes lingering on my face.

'I'll sleep out here,' I said, maybe just a touch too dramatically.

'Don't,' you said. 'You don't have to, it's not comfortable.'

I didn't reply, didn't move.

You looked apologetic, you said, 'Sleep in here Bibbs. Nothing funny like.'

When I was five or six I was given a bar of soap in the shape of a red racing car for Christmas. I sniffed it frequently. It was so beautiful, I imagined it must taste delicious too, that if I bit into it, it would be full of chocolate. Even though I knew it was soap I convinced myself that I was being lied to, that this car was actually full of lovely, gooey chocolate, just waiting for someone brave enough to bite through the glossy shell. Following you inside that night, stepping into the deep ocean blue of your bedroom was just the same, I remained a child.

We climbed into bed quietly, politely, discreetly, as though we were sales execs on a somewhat awkward team-building trip, camping in the forest, lying back to back and perfectly still. But soon enough you rolled over and I inevitably felt your fingers slip under the waist-band of my underwear, sliding them down, and then the insistence of your hard prick, through the cotton of your underwear, rubbing up against the firmness of my arse. I knew this wouldn't end well, it couldn't, it was bound to leave a bad taste in the mouth. But like that racing car soap, I could not resist your beauty, so I bit into the bar, because I had to know the truth of the matter.

I fucked you stupid. I fucked you so hard you looked panicked. I fucked you with every atom of anger and hurt and betrayal I had at my disposal. I fucked you like you were Adam. I fucked you like I hated you, like I loved you, roughly, from behind, and you gasped, 'Fuck fuck fuck – are you gonna cum?' You clawed at the pillow under your head, pushing yourself back on me deeper, deeper, 'Ah! Ah! Ah!' and the way your arse contracted around my cock told me you had unloaded your spunk all over the bed, and so I fired my own cum inside you, into unplumbed depths, as far I could go.

Dogs fuck for dominance, what was my excuse?

IV

You wanted us to go outside into the world and spend the afternoon together in the oncoming wet weather, like two regular people. I wasn't so keen, I was suspicious, I thought it was a little late for us to start going on dates now. Besides, I was pressed with the practical concerns of preparing for my interview at Saint Martins, and helping Jonny to find a hotel room within his budget for when he arrived in London – plus I just wasn't in the mood. I put forward several excuses, time, money, the weather, but oblivious to my disinclination, you listed ideas of how we might spend the day. Regent's Park, Hampstead Heath, Camden Market, all of which seemed unsuitable, all of which I declined, and so you became bellicose.

You said, 'Don't you care about what I'm interested in?'

Maybe I didn't. Maybe I was only in it for your body, after all. Would that change anything? If it was just sex I was using you for, then so be it, people do act like that, don't they? They get fuck-drunk and lie to themselves that there's something more. People want to feel that they share more than just muscular contractions and heavy secretions, because it gives meaning to what can seem so meaningless, and what's wrong with that? But if this were merely a physical thing, just a joy bang, would I have allowed myself to be so carried away? Would I have put up with all the rest of it? I don't think so. Clearly I was in it deep enough to love you, if not expressly to like you all that much.

Your insistence on us going out felt familiar; my step-father would often behave in the same way. He would demand that he and I spend time together bonding, though I had no interest in that either. When I was fourteen or so, we'd go to football matches, or bars, not really because he wanted to get to know me, but so he could use my presence as a foil for his alcoholism. If he took me out, and told my mother it was for the purpose of providing me with some obviously needed male socialisation, then she couldn't be angry when he came back pissed, could she? Even if I had homework to do, or just wanted to spend my free time learning the Janet Jackson dance routines I'd taped from TV, he'd insist, the argument being that it would be good for me, that I'd benefit from this masculine exertion.

I hated spending time with him. I hated how pleased my mother looked each time we went out together, I hated being away from my sisters, and I hated the condescending expression that would crawl across his face when he put me in the car. The sneer that said *I'm doing this for your own good.* Not that I had any hope of arguing with him, I'd tried saying no before, and it hadn't taken him until the count of three before he'd smacked me hard across the face, saying, 'You ungrateful little bastard, who the fuck do you think you are, eh? I'm trying to be *nice.*'

I think it's obvious that this tension has carried over into my adult life, that this horror of being controlled, this refusal to be held in place, has made me light on my feet, but heavy in my heart. I simply do not trust men, I am always on my guard with them, one eye on that wandering hand, waiting to see if it will settle as a caress on the small of my back, or a slap in the face. But believe me when I say, I hit back now. I strike back hard, and low, and I do not hesitate to use whatever I can lay my hands on to protect myself.

My stepfather would get me a couple of drinks in a bar where they turned a blind eye, get himself several more, we'd eat crisps, I'd squirm. He'd give me the *man of the world* bit about his vast life experience: 'I graduated from the school of hard knocks, me,' etc. etc., and then when he was sufficiently sauced we'd really get to the heart of the matter. Those much-cherished sleazy stories of how he and his RAF buddies would get together and masturbate. How they'd play games in the barracks, which somehow always ended up with someone eating someone else's cum. Conveniently you see, as well as a screen for his heavy drinking, my obvious teenage queerness provided the perfect cover for the murkier recesses of his own sexuality. It was the first time I understood the precarity of the situation my sexuality placed me in, how I was from here on out to be burdened with the erotic projections of men, or else face their violent retribution. By telling me how he would hold and stroke his best friend's hard dick, my stepfather could get a dirty kick out of sharing the goods with an audience both captive and (so he presumed) appreciative, circulating his precious smut like a schoolboy passing around a degraded copy of *Razzle*. But of course it was all just banter, just shenanigans, just lads-lads-lads, just getting a fourteen-year-old drunk and talking about how you liked to have your cock played with. No one could ever say that was inappropriate, could they?

Inevitably after a few hours' drinking he would get impatient that I wasn't playing along, his sour breath in my face, saliva dribbling off his bottom lip. Did he imagine I was going to ask, 'Please Daddy, show me how it's done?' I really can't think how the scenario was supposed to reach a satisfying conclusion for him. Frustrated, he'd spot a woman in the pub, any woman, put me in a black cab home, and tell me to tell my mother that he had some work to do. He'd come back very late, splattered with vomit, having lost his keys, kicking the front door, waking up the baby, my mother throwing his belongings out of the window and swearing that this was the last time, and all the nurses from the care home across the street chorusing, 'You tell 'im girl – tell 'im to fuck right off!'

In the same way, I felt strong-armed into spending Sunday afternoon with you, and it was only from a weighted sense of obligation that I agreed. Certainly if you had squared up to me I would have broken a bottle over your head, so it wasn't physical violence I feared. But there was that same contempt to your voice, this same implicit declaration that I was yours to command as you would. Knowing I was currently dependent on your kindness made you imperious, and made me recoil. I felt that I owed you something for letting me stay, that in fact you might kick me out if I didn't go with you, and then where would I be? I didn't feel I had very much choice then but to leave my student loan paperwork half complete, and go with you, to Speakers' Corner of all places.

Besides one or two early morning trips down Brick Lane, we had never even seen daylight together. We had only ever been nocturnal, finding each other after dark in nightclubs and dive bars, more often than not right there in the sepulchre of your bedroom. I think I preferred it that way, I liked the silence and the isolation. I don't know what it was about that Sunday that made you so desperate for us to hang out, but it seemingly gave you a spring in your step to see that I wasn't so into it. It made you feel tough.

Why was I so reluctant anyway? It could be that I was afraid of what the light of day would show me, that it would prove us to be incompatible, or incontestably destined for each other, unpleasant to discover either way. And then, I was trepidatious about us being spotted together. I hadn't really seen any of my old friends since I'd been back, and it would've been very poor form to bump into one of them, strolling down Piccadilly arm-in-arm with my best friend's boyfriend.

I was jumpy on the journey. I froze when I thought I saw Lulu on the platform at Marble Arch, but it wasn't her, just a lovely doppelgänger. I blushed all the same though, at the memory of running into her at the Joiners a few years back, and sheepishly admitting that yes, it was you I was waiting for. I remember how archly she had replied, 'Oh but I thought he was a, wait, what was it? A boring lanky bastard?' I guess it hadn't really been that long since you'd broken up.

We travelled unseen, nobody clocked us on the tube, no gossip spread; thankfully everyone we knew suffered through Sundays on an M-cat comedown, and besides what was there to see? You weren't one for public displays of affection. You were the William Burroughs type, macho and masochistic. You had sex in a certain way, but you weren't defined by it, certainly you had no loyalty towards other queer people, and absolutely no interest in the fight for visibility or equality. You were mean about anyone campy or swishy, unless they were nailing you, of course.

I remember lying next to you, silently skimming over the very, very long list of your (known) sexual partners, and as I considered them, I thought I saw a pattern emerge. You often formed attachments to, and shared something, let's say, romantic with expressly feminine lovers, and frequently these bodies flaunted a transfemininity. Some of us outgrew it, some of us grew further into it, but unmistakably it was a hallmark of your taste, just as your own big nose and blue eyes were testament to mine. I took comfort in this, I felt protected by this desire, I don't think I ever considered that it was maybe just a fetish. I suppose that's why I was so shocked then, to see that you were dating Adam. He was so square-shouldered, he couldn't even walk in heels. So, what did he have that I didn't?

I asked you, lying there after fucking you, 'Do you think that you pick up so many femmes because you're uncomfortable being gay?'

You curled up one half of your mouth into a little hare-lip smirk in the slowly disappearing darkness and said, 'Probably doesn't take a genius to work that out, does it?'

I consider it an honour to have served alongside them, those beautiful epicene creatures. Paulette who almost caricatured the female form; Leo with his Chalayan bubble dress and his bright red lipstick; Anders impossibly slender, all cheekbones and eyelashes; and of course, radiant Lulu, who, if the truth be told, and we agree this is the time to tell it, was the real reason I ever gave you the benefit of the doubt. You didn't know that, did you? How could you when I am only now really learning it for myself? (This text continues to surprise me, it is smarter than I am, it knows more than I do, the book I thought I was writing is somehow writing me).

The first time I saw her onstage, taking off her clothes inside an enormous white balloon, I felt that I would rightly be struck blind for staring at her lunar beauty. When she had stripped down to almost nothing, she burst the balloon, showering the crowd with glitter, and came forth like Athena from the head of Zeus, fully formed. I can only liken it to the thrill young cinema audiences must have felt, sitting alone together in the dark, and seeing Louise Brooks onscreen for the first time. The rush of *I must know her, I must have her, I must be her*, a collision of desire and jealousy and admiration, founded entirely on these four enthralling unexpected drunken minutes (so then, not so very unlike a fuck). All I knew of her back then was that she never performed for free, that every pop star wanted her in their music video, and that she was dating you. You, the lumbering smartarse rocking up to every party and always trying it on. You suddenly became illuminated for me with another kind of light, silver, flickering, reflected from the big screen.

Would it insult your pride to know that I began to entertain your advances because I wanted you to replace Lulu with me; so that I could, in a way, become her, even if only in my mind and in your arms? So that I could take on the beautiful transgender body that I still could not admit to wanting. It's almost evil. She was one of two, maybe three, people I remember you ever speaking fondly of, and I'm quite sure that you were unaware at first, at least, that I was looking over your shoulder when you embraced me, hoping to catch her eye. I'm appalled to admit this now, but there it is. The psychic I has always been watching; to finally acknowledge this as my motivation is almost enough to excuse your own behaviour. Almost.

We all have our own nocturnal, amphibious reasonings. In going to bed with you I was both becoming Lulu and having her for myself. You went to bed with me, and all the other transdrogynous pretty young things, according to an anacreontic logic of your own. Think about it for a moment, that spectral projection, that dance we do when we're fucking. We like to think our congress is private, but it's wide open to the public, we think it's a *pas de deux* but it's a pile-up, a mosh pit, not a ballroom. It cannot be delineated by space, nor by time.

Last night, from the window of a cab, I saw a subway train burst out from the subterranean darkness and appear above ground. I was travelling back to Tacubaya, it was dark, and the radio was playing that one indefatigable hit, which I know all the words to, but still can't name. I watched as the train overtook me, sliding by the cab like a well-oiled phantom, and briefly I was parallel to the last carriage, contemplating a group of men fucking on the seats, and against the windows. That Frank O'Hara line came to mind, 'subways are only fun when you're feeling sexy,' and I grinned. For a few moments, maybe twenty or thirty seconds, the carriage was alive to me with casual fucks and random encounters, sex made brilliant by the yellow lights overhead, the train convulsing with desire before it disappeared back underground. It was like a visitation, the cab driver did not acknowledge it, the men themselves seemed unaware that they were visible from the highway, and so I was left to wonder if it was for me alone. Should I build my church here?

Your hand reaches out now, from the past, to touch my chest and it finds the flesh of the future, because I have outlived you, and so you linger in my sexual vocabulary, haunting my orgasms. But even when we were in bed together as two living breathing bodies, we were still not alone, never alone. All of those hands that had guided us to each other, that had caressed and abused us respectively, pleasured and aggrieved us, were with us, their ghostly fingers pulling our hair and finding their way inside all of our fleshy openings. Moreover the boys you wanted me to be more like were in bed with us too, along with the boys I wanted you to be more like, and the boys we mistook each other for. For all the intimacy they professed, the nights we spent together were actually public orgies, psychic sex parties with an open-door policy, with each of us alternating between the desired and the desiring. The two of us in an endless closed loop, you becoming Lulu for me, me becoming Adam for you, you becoming Adam for me, me becoming Lulu for you. Occasionally we would even settle into ourselves, like moths alighting on the bare bulb of your desk lamp and promptly expiring.

You saw your sexuality as more of a kink than an identity. Adam too always said, quite frankly, that he was gay, but not queer, just a man who had sex with men, that's all, and maybe that's why you liked him? I was unsettled by this positioning, it made me feel that I was overreacting to the cavalcade of casual homophobia I endured every time I took a bus. And how strange then, that I should be the ambiguous third point in our triangle, the unsexed missing link, the plastic junction which connected you two in your apolitical coupling. You were the kind of gay man who would have said that refugees who drowned crossing the Mediterranean had only themselves to blame, who would have agreed that all those UKIP dickheads were simply saying what needed to be said, and sometimes I'm almost glad you died before you had the opportunity to vote for Brexit, or start bemoaning the destruction of the English language as brought on by people who used neutral pronouns.

You had a definite streak of misogyny to complement your internalised homophobia, as well as that Southern contempt for the working North, and a deeply unpleasant attitude to race. You had often peppered your letters to me with advice to 'watch out for those sleazy Latinos', but I honestly thought you were just joking. Though now I see that even if you were, they were jokes in extremely poor taste. I would ask Adam, 'Do you think he really means it, when he says the sight of a mosque makes him sick?'

And Adam would smile patiently and say, 'No, he's just trying to get a rise out of you.'

How can I regard Adam and I, now, as anything but two wilful idiots? So ready to be blind to all your many faults. You constantly teased me for my left-coast leanings, for my socialism, my vegetarianism, my feminism, and undoubtedly you saw my attempts at anti-racism as part of the same bogus liberal pose. I thought that you were just puncturing my right-on ego, mocking that uptight, holier-than-thou face I put on when I felt someone was being treated poorly, satirising my white saviour complex. Your insults were like the 4,000lb blockbuster bombs scrawled with 'TO ADOLF' I'd seen in *Time* magazine. Loaded onto Lancaster bombers, ready to be dropped on Berlin – they had clearly defined targets, yet I stubbornly figured myself as the subject of these assaults. Now I'm aghast, when I look at your letters, or think back on our conversations, and think how, laughably, I even made your racism all about me. When you said the things you did about how 'bangla boys' were the ruin of the nation, I responded as if it were just another example of you taking the piss out of my *hippie bollocks*, that is to say I ignored it. And in my silence I was so often complicit, very rarely did I argue with you. I think I was trying to use the same method on you my mother told me would work with playground bullies: 'Just don't give them a reaction and then they'll go away.' It hadn't worked in secondary school and it didn't work with you.

But wait. I have wandered too far along the waterway now, I have followed the S-shaped curve of my self-pity too far out, I need to bring myself back to the page, before I lose myself forever. Maggie Nelson uses the clever little conjuration, 'place me,' when she is jumping between theory and memory. She is speaking in the first person to her own 'you', her own husband, her own reader. 'Place me,' she asks him, and he does, we do, so now I ask the same of you. Place me on that Sunday in September, as the good weather comes to an end. Place me on that afternoon when you are amenable but restless, and I am still in love with you. Place me in that moment when you take me by surprise, and insist we spend the day outdoors together, and I as always fold.

It was drizzling, an apathetic, brumous rain. To protest being dragged along to Speakers' Corner, to this carnival of clowns, I wore an oversize fun fur coat and a pair of huge Versace black-out shades, a gift from an old boyfriend. I was hoping to make it clear that I didn't want to be there, that it was all a great inconvenience to me, to underline my distaste for the scene by refusing to make eye contact with it. But standing in the drizzle, under an umbrella in sunglasses, there was more than a hint of Margot and Richie Tenenbaum's illicit love to the scene. Or maybe I'm back-projecting romance onto the blank and meaningless surface which the past almost certainly is? Perhaps you were only thinking, *What the fuck are you wearing now?*, not at all charmed by the misplaced allure of the sequence.

I trudged along behind you, ogling one fringe lunatic after another, this monkey house of freethinkers howling at the tyranny of popular discourse, and flinging the shit of Fundamentalism, Flat Earth Theory and Anti-Vaccination rhetoric around. The bad weather made the situation less pleasurable yet, and the Hell and damnation speeches of the Pentecostal preachers genuinely frightened me. I was brought up to fear God and still it does not take much to have me on my knees begging for forgiveness. Chilled and huddled under the brolly, I shuddered from the cold, from guilt, from fear of objurgation.

The crowds gradually began to thin on account of the steadily increasing rain, and the soapboxes started to sag, looking ever more unstable. And yet, the claptrap of the cockamamy theologians who bristled on, demanding the government bring back hanging, fox hunting and national service, seemed to put a sparkle in your eye. You'd go right up to a speaker, acting like you were absolutely enthralled by what he had to say, then turn to me, and gesture with your thumb and say, 'Look at this wanker!', the brim of your hat bowing with the weight of the rain. Was it a prank you were pulling? A way for you to say, 'Yeah I know all of this is rubbish, but it's a laugh'? Or was it simply proof that you had absolutely no principles at all, besides your unswerving belief in your own incontestable superiority? Baudelaire, the old bastard, came to mind. His summation that morality is what's truly wicked, because it stifles the creative impulses that only illegal, immoral thoughts and deeds can foster. Perhaps this is proof that your own vile logic was correct, or maybe I am still wildly spin-doctoring your reputation in order to clear my own name? I know I am destroying you, you as you were, by trying to preserve you as I wanted you to be.

I could see that you longed to be up there on your own platform, spewing your own illogical broth of communism, ethno-nationalism and free-market terrorism, into the soup bowl minds of the hopeless and hungry. I'm sure you saw yourself in the lineage of Marx and Orwell and Morris, standing before a huge crush who had all come to hear you talk of your plans to remake the country. Unlike those men however, you didn't have any real, defined policies, or a debatable manifesto. With your portfolio of quips, your unsupported accusations and your charismatic grandstanding, you were more a Webster than a Lenin. Yet your politicking was strangely prophetic; looking around the world as it stands now, your deliberate aggravations and your lashing out at whoever was currently most unpopular would have been very welcome here today. But on that Sunday, with the crowd paper-thin and the sky a cruel gunmetal grey, you realised the pickings were slim, so we disappeared to find protection under the russet canopy of a weeping beech.

The rain did not relent, in fact it worsened. It came down in sheets, the tree was not shelter enough, so we hurried towards a bus stop and took the number 6 down to the Royal Academy. This rainy-day jaunt, the idea of just *popping in* to the RA, clearly made you feel jocular, and foppish, a laddish Beau Brummell, a man of fashion and taste taking in the arts quite without ceremony, casually, the way a bon vivant might neck a bottle of Montrachet at lunch, without thinking much of it. In spite of being wet through you seemed uncharacteristically blithe there on the bus. Indeed, amidst my own Weltschmerz there dawned the vague hope that this afternoon out might mark a turning point for us after all; that in leaving the conflagration and heading for the museum, we could possibly be moving towards something reasonable, less acrimonious than we'd ever had before. That maybe we'd even discover some shared interests outside of nineties pop and anal sex.

I had never actually been inside the Royal Academy, I didn't know about the public galleries you could visit for free, and I had always been far too afraid of the £18 exhibition price tag to forge the courtyard. But here, you looked quite at ease, striding up the stairs as if it were your grandparents' house, and you were bringing me back with you from school, to spend the summer holiday throwing stones at squirrels, and fucking in the attic. Here on this miserable Sunday afternoon, waiting decorously, was the whitewashed world of a stable society, where money flowed freely from an unseen spring, where one knew what was what; it was the world that you, you phoney anarchist, secretly dreamt of more fully inhabiting. I felt horribly out of place, I felt both overdressed and underdressed, definitely inappropriately dressed, amongst all the ageing enthusiasts of nineteenth-century portraiture. We were very much in the presence of people who go to galleries mainly for the scones, who think that Monet was pushing it a bit, who look to art for a moral uplift when they've run out of patience with Radio 4. You looked smug.

I said, 'This lot look like angels compared to that rabble in the park.'

You said, 'They talk a lot of sense.'

'You are joking,' I laughed, 'they didn't have a decent idea between them!'

'I don't know,' you said, 'this country is becoming a shithole. Somebody's got to do something about it. You're English, remember that, don't be deceived by the bullshit, Bibby.'

Though it was hardly the place to hash this out, I figured that since the heavy rain was going to hold us hostage a good while longer, and we were obliged by the protocols of our surroundings to keep our voices down, that this was as good a time as any to push back. 'Do you really believe that, though?' I asked. 'Do you really believe that immigrants are the problem?'

'Yeah,' you said without flinching. 'I want to be able to walk down Brick Lane without being sexually assaulted by some hairy bastard from Crete.'

'Why do you have to say things like that?' I said with disdain. 'It isn't funny, you know.'

'So?' you shrugged. 'I'm a racist and I'm proud, I'm gonna be piling it on. Can you handle it?'

'You're not a racist,' I snarked. 'You're a bad comedian.'

I caved so quickly. I walked as swiftly as I could in the opposite direction from you, needing to take at least a minute to gather myself before we set to it again. With enough distance between us I did my best to regulate my breathing and steady my rising heart rate. I would not give you the satisfaction. I repeated my lines, *He's just trying to get a rise out of you, trying to get a rise out of you, trying to...* I still refused to believe you were the thing you were telling me you were; I'm told they call this cognitive dissonance.

The lies you tell yourself when you love someone, the excuses you can make for them, for yourself, to avoid an argument, are astounding. He doesn't really mean it, you whisper, he's just saying this to upset me. I can remember all the countless excuses my mother made for her violent, womanising boyfriends. How she'd tell me it was down to stress at work, or money troubles, and that they were going to start seeing a counsellor, and that she had to give them the benefit of the doubt, one last time. How she double-folded her faculties, like a contortionist's limbs, in order to avoid the simple, honest truth of saying, 'I know he's a bastard, but I love him, and it's beyond my control.'

My behaviour was not dissimilar, and just as I now have to hold my mother responsible, at least in part, for the physical and sexual abuse my siblings and I endured as children, I have to accept that by never really challenging your poisonous opinions I let them flourish. Yes, leapling, restoring you to your full and ugly height shows me in a very harsh light too, and I have to acknowledge that. I think that in trying so hard to know you, now you're gone, I've come to encounter myself clearly for the first time, peeling paint, unflattering angles and all. If you were a Duke of Windsor in waiting, blaming it all on the Jews and the Reds, then I have, in my refusal to reproach, exposed myself as your would-be Wallis Simpson. I wish I could say this argument is the reason we broke for good, but I can't, and I'm disgusted with us both, I want you to know that.

Shrill and ill-mannered, my phone rang out in the gallery. It was an Irish number, and when I answered it took me a second or so to recognise Jonny's voice. He was sobbing, I thought maybe he was distressed by a bad review of the opera, but that seemed completely out of character. Stifling his tears he took a deep breath, and asked me, very calmly, 'JJ, do you think I have the mark of death on me?'

I made my way hurriedly outside and assured him that he didn't.

'No,' I said, 'you absolutely do not. I have never seen anyone as vital and full of life as you. You're just fine.'

'Really,' he asked, 'you really think so?'

'Yes,' I confirmed. 'Really. When will you be in London?'

'Tuesday,' he said. 'How is it? Glad to be back?'

'No! Fuck, it's a nightmare,' I said. 'I wish I'd never left New York.'

V

The day Jonny arrived in London was also the day of my interview at Central Saint Martins, another convenient narrative beat. I was going to meet him straight after the interview; irrespective of how it went I'd need to see him, either to celebrate or commiserate. I dressed with slow purpose that morning, careful to allow myself plenty of time, to fix my face and run over all the possible lines of discussion in my head. Why did I want to study at an art school and not a drama school? How did I see myself making the move back into formal education? What did I hope to achieve from a master's? In reality, going back to school was simply how I'd justified my decision to cash out on New York, but I thought that answer needed a little polishing before I presented it.

I remember what I wore that day because Jonny took a picture. Burgundy flat-front slacks, a seventies viscose shirt with a repeating Pre-Raphaelite print of a bare-breasted mother clutching her child, a paint-splattered raincoat and a pair of Salvatore Ferragamo tasselled loafers, which I had found for an unreal $25 in a thrift store. I had padded my bra just enough, and undid my shirt one button further than usual, so that it fell open mid-breastbone. It was, as Jonny said, whilst snapping with his smartphone, 'Quite a look.'

Somewhere out there, there are pictures you took of me. I've never seen them because I never wanted to be the subject of those point-and-shoot portraits to begin with, I found them too exposing, too brutalising. Your pictures stripped away a person's armour with their invasive front-on flash, and I don't think I want to go as far now as seeing myself as you saw me. Everything you did had such a mocking tone to it, I never did appreciate it when you tried to overexpose my particular composure.

You should know better than anyone how cruel the camera can be. Didn't the tabloid newspapers run only the most unflattering pictures of you to report your death? Didn't they choose the ones where you looked the most strung out and red-faced, the most like a party boy fuck-up? They didn't source a picture of you looking handsome and hopeful, only half-cut and hedonistic, deserving it. Photographs impose a truth on their subject, even if what they report is false.

I had built myself up out of council estate squalor and adolescent acne, into something lithesome and arcane, but your photographic style was deliberately designed to find the chav inside the woman I was trying to become, and to expose him. It turned you on to have this sorcery at your fingers, to know who it was you were *really* spreading your legs for, just as it excited you to submit sexually to someone so unmanly, so broke. I have no doubt you looked at both 'feminine' and 'working class' as interchangeable and equally loathsome, and that it was a source of great eroticism for you to be taken by someone so debased, in the same way homophobic, racist white men fantasise about being fucked by broad-shouldered black studs.

Sitting on your bed, I attended to the side-parting in my hair with your beautiful blue wide-tooth comb, using it to tease out the Rita Hayworth wave I'd been cultivating at the front, then dragging it back, to give the curls a little separation. My hair is very thick, at that time I wore it shoulder-length and your comb struggled to make it through all this glory. I pulled it down through the red waves which pooled about my neck, trying to marshal some order into this wayward mass. I was quietly pleased with how it was coming together, then, with the most sickening crack, the comb snapped in two in my hand, and I jumped up in fright.

You were already gone for the day, thank goodness, because I knew you would freak the fuck out if you saw this. That comb was obviously precious, it vibrated with the aura of having belonged to some much-loved long-gone grandpa, of having been placed into your life at an uncharacteristically sentimental moment. But now my right fist was closed around one half of it, while the other half remained lodged by its teeth above my left ear, like a turquoise studded Navajo barrette. I took both pieces, grabbed my bag and ran straight out of your apartment, as if hounded by the demons, released from your now shattered comb. I took the tube to Farringdon and only there, on some unassuming street corner, did I drop the poor broken thing into the bin. In case you were wondering, my dear long-lost sparring partner, now you know.

I continued towards my interview, spooked, utterly convinced that this was a very bad omen, and yet it was a breeze. The head of department told me there and then that I had a place if I wanted it, and even though two friends had told me that it was a lousy course that they both regretted taking, I enrolled. I figured, *Well between them they have a record deal with RCA and a run of sold-out shows at Carnegie Hall – so it obviously can't be that bad.* I thought that if I wanted to prove myself as a serious practitioner, if I wanted to legitimise myself, then studying for a master's degree in experimental writing at a prestigious art school was the smart thing to do. But the comb was right, and fools never listen.

I went towards Soho to meet Jonny. We had agreed to meet under that horrendous Freddie Mercury sculpture on Tottenham Court Road, which had been erected to promote the seemingly immortal, yet totally lifeless Queen musical. My friend was a dresser on the show, I knew how horrible it was, but Freddie was as good as any other landmark to convene beneath. Certainly better than all the other statues of tyrants, rapists and genocidal maniacs which decorate that strip of Central London. I was very happy to see Jonny, I felt that since he'd ferried me over the Styx to the UK, he might be able to take me back. At the very least he offered a tangible reminder that I had a life far away from and unconnected to you.

'JJ bebe!' he shouted, waving and running right across the road, 'I'm so glad to see you!'

'How are you?' I asked, embracing him. 'Are you feeling better now?'

'Huh?' he puzzled, and for a moment he seemed lost. 'Oh yeah! The phone call, sure,' he smiled. 'That was the shrooms talking.' He shrugged, and smiled again.

Jonny was staying in a pitiful hotel in Vauxhall, so when we met in the West End I think he must've been pleased to see that not all of London looked like South Lambeth Road. And I must've been feeling mischievous because I suggested we go to the Stockpot for lunch. Jonny was game.

I told him, 'It is quite terrible,' but he wasn't put off.

The Stockpot was one of those old-school joints which had inexplicably survived successive waves of recession and gentrification, and sat there on Old Compton Street, seemingly as solid as ever, all pine-panelled walls and hand-written menus, serving the sort of pre-war British food I had never known anyone outside of a Graham Greene novel to eat. I can only ascribe my desire to visit the restaurant to a secret nostalgia for this, Grandma's England, which I had unknowingly harboured throughout my time away. Certainly I wasn't sadistic enough to take Jonny there for the sake of the food, for the broccoli cheese, liver and onions, or grilled sardines, their misshapen portions all served with boiled potatoes, with rice pudding or jelly and UHT cream following for dessert.

I think I wanted to share something real with Jonny. In such a rich city as London, a place like the Stockpot, with its chipped mugs, and tables pressed so closely together that you could hardly get by, seemed shabby and not a little grimy. Reminiscent of those market cafes in Liverpool where a cup of tea was 50p, there was something reassuringly low-rent about the place. It felt a little like falling out of sight, down the cracks, which, as our friend and teacher Penny Arcade said, is where everything interesting happens anyway.

The Stockpot had the same soothing quality as Kellogg's Diner, or El Farolito, its unchanging atmosphere suggested that it was outside of time; because it was already so out of place in the city, it simply couldn't be displaced. I know permanence is an illusion, I know perpetuity is a myth, but I chose to hold on to that feeling. The way you cling to one bassline when you're rolling, playing it and replaying it, until you realise you've listened to the same track thirty-three times straight in the course of a night.

I'd call the Stockpot authentic, if the word hadn't become so coloured now with all the acrylic phoniness hyperreality can paint with. I'm sure anyone who encountered the place for the first time today would be appalled that there was no Union Jack bunting on the walls, and no scones on the menu, or gin. The simulation has so entirely replaced the reality that even people who have lived their whole lives in Britain now think of Britishness as some composite of *A Clockwork Orange* and *Howards End*, a never-ending dipsomaniacal tea party.

The Stockpot didn't ever really feel like London, it seemed more like something that came out of the dreams of AI software, as though it were the product of rapidly amassed and massively misunderstood input data. The fading, grubby glory of the place, the waiters in old-fashioned Soho black-and-whites, the squeezy plastic bottles of sauce, and the jumble-sale mixture of diners – academics, artists, old queens and new lovers – made me feel as at home as a stranger in a strange land ever can be.

An American friend once laughingly rebuffed your statement that London was 'the most metropolitan city in the world' with the quip, 'Please, it's the Cleveland of Europe.' God, you hated him. For someone who was always away travelling, you loved Britain (well, Kipling's Britain at least), and I wondered if all of your journeying wasn't only a way to prove your heartfelt belief that it was the finest country in the world. In contrast I was always running away because I was pretty sure you were wrong, and felt the pressing need to collect anecdotal evidence that anywhere else was preferable.

In truth, the further away I get, the more at ease I feel. In places where I am an obvious outsider I can at least relax into the pose of stranger, because it's much more acceptable, more comfortable, to be an outsider in a place where you aren't obliged to feel at home. I think that's why I've come to love Mexico City so much, because I'm deathly pale and speak terrible Spanish, and am so clearly marked as *extranjera*. And, sometimes when I'm eating an eighty-peso lunch of pork and beans off a plastic plate at the *fondita*, I almost feel like I've come full circle, back to the Stockpot again, though I know it has long since gone out of business.

After our late lunch Jonny and I walked about, and he entertained me with his uncanny impressions of all our friends. The voices and mannerisms would suddenly come over him, as though he were an Edwardian medium, and right there on Regent Street he'd conjure up Morgan or Billy, seemingly without any effort. As always, I begged him to do me, and as always, he refused, maintaining his prohibition on summoning the spirit of those already present.

I wondered why Jonny and I had never fucked; there'd been enough late-night phone calls between us, and certainly a good many opportunities. Once when we were in LA together, bored and horny, we found a boy called Jay on Craigslist who was looking for a threesome. We decided to go over and show him a good time, only Los Angeles is a horribly confusing city for out-of-towners to negotiate, and so we found ourselves endlessly driving in the wrong direction, up the wrong freeway, and no matter how many times we called LA Jay to ask for clearer directions, we didn't ever seem to get any closer. After a few hours of being caught up in what might've been David Lynch's most tedious masterpiece, LA Jay texted to say he was bored and going to bed. So Jonny and I likewise went home, too tired, too dispirited when we returned to do anything besides lie about on the floor and listen to Concrete Blonde. Maybe we had a lucky escape.

I spent some time trying to explain to Jonny the travails of my first weeks back in London. It was such a long, convoluted story, requiring me to jump back-wards and forwards, through the recent past, and over the Atlantic several times, that I thought I might have lost him on the details.

'No, no,' he said, 'I get it, I get it. You were in love with this guy, you went away, now he's dating your best friend, and you're both fucking him.'

'Pretty much,' I said. 'And I feel bad.'

'Uh-huh,' he said.

'For myself mainly,' I continued. 'But for Adam too, and for Thomas even.'

'Yeah,' said Jonny, 'it's a pickle.'

We turned in at one of those glossy Mayfair galleries, the blue-chip sort that has a location in every major market, and represents artists who represent watertight investments. We were buzzed in; of course, the place was empty. They were showing an untitled video work by Bruce Nauman in the main gallery space. Two projec-tors threw the same image onto the floor and onto the wall in front of us, of two figures in black, rolling away from each other whilst reaching towards each other with fingertips outstretched. They journeyed clockwise inside a white circle delineated by black lines, so that they had the effect of appearing as the hands of a clock scrolling through the hours.

As the video was projected in the same direction, but from two different angles (onto the ground from above, and onto the wall from behind us), the doubled moving surfaces formed an uneasy right angle, a hard corner, a vanishing point, into which these two sets of twisting, rotating bodies seemed capable of drawing the unwary viewer, black hole-like, towards destruction. Watching these spiralling bodies moving as watch faces, mimicking time, made me feel as though I were falling headlong into a whirling nothing, as though I were plunging face-first into infinity. Seeing them tumble, and turn around and around and around, made me panic, because although these four lithe figures seemed to beckon me into this shared abyss, they themselves remained deceptive, and untouched by the vortex which their hypnotic bodies opened up. They were two pairs of sirens, a quaternity, calling me into the whirlpool, like a deadly mirage composed of my own paranoiac desires. I realised they would keep on rolling around and around long after I was gone, like time in action, disinterested, unmoved. It struck me that this projection was more than apt, and I recognised something in these untouchable bodies, bound up only in each other. I saw a reflection of you and Adam tumbling together, and accepted that there was simply no way into the image for me, without facing my own obliteration.

I remembered how Robert had a strange habit of being extremely specific about the time in between things. How he was always saying, 'JJ, can you believe it's already been five and a half hours since we left!' or, 'I've only been awake for thirteen hours, there's no need for me to feel so sleepy.' With him *a little while* or *earlier* or *sometime this morning* never came into play, he only ever dealt in these countable units. The memory of this particular quirk, which I had grown first to accept, then to love during my time in California, took me right back there. As I stood watching Nauman's performers corkscrew I had the sensation of lying next to Robert in his bed the last time I saw him in San Francisco. Place me, in the bedroom, all soggy on E, with Robert telling me tenderly that he loved me, but like a sister, that when it comes to romance he needs someone strong, and manly. I saw a now painfully obvious sequence of events revealed, staggered throughout my life: Robert letting me down easy; the Latvian boy I was fucking, who told me I didn't smell enough like a man (though I had never advertised myself as such); and then Adam, who made it clear to me that he saw me as a beloved gal pal but no more.

There in the gallery, I think I finally began to understand that you and Adam really were just what you said you were, just two gay men, just two guys who have sex with guys, that's all. I had thought that your predilection for transfemmes and androgynes would serve me well, keep me safe, but in reality you didn't ever consider any of us as serious candidates, did you? There was no place for us in this mirror world. My own incongruous physicality, flat chest, long hair, the feminine dominance I possessed, marked me as an intruder in this uncomplicated universe of bromance and doppelbangers. I felt timid, humiliated but somewhat enlightened. Your sideline in amorphous bodies like mine was just that, an after-dinner kick, just like your foray into fucking real girls, the product of an erratic libido. Dare I say that I can now accept things as they are? Even if you had parted ways with Adam, it wouldn't have been on my account, would it? Yeah, you'd keep me in your macho-lite orbit, but there was about as much chance of you giving me any real consideration as a partner as there was of Morrissey apologising for his racist outbursts; as there was of Adam or Robert or any of the rest of them acquiring a sudden taste for femme tops.

Like all moments of revelation, this did not come without pain. I was made aware of my shortcomings as both a man and as a woman, with incandescent lucidity, in the light of that untitled video piece. Nauman's human automata continued to turn on their fixed axes, and the gallery attendant, seemingly forgetting we were there, made a long, and loud, and very personal phone call, looking extremely embarrassed when we passed her desk on the way out.

As we left Jonny said, 'Usually I get a laugh out of ol' Brucie, but that video, I don't know...' he trailed off.

I nodded in agreement, 'I think I was more in the mood for some illuminated puns, myself, some neon blowjob sculptures.'

'Yeah, the video kinda bummed me out,' he said, and we stepped into the early twilight.

We walked all the way down to Vauxhall, stopping in at the Tavern just as it opened for one quiet drink. As ever, when the phrase 'one quiet drink' is uttered, 8 p.m. suddenly becomes 10 p.m. and 10 p.m. immediately becomes midnight, and out you stumble onto the pavement wishing you had a fag, staggered by the late hour, asking 'When's the last tube?'

This then became my accidental homecoming; I realised I'd been hidden away in shame in your flat ever since I'd come back. No one had seen me. People rushed up to me all night, saying, 'Oh here she is!' or 'Where've you been then, la?' and 'I didn't know you were back!' Onstage, the compère welcomed me home, and declared that he'd seen Jonny perform in Dublin, that he had one of the greatest voices of his generation. In the swarm of attention and alcohol I almost felt like I belonged. The two of us enjoyed quite a regal evening of it, warmed in the glow of speculation about our wildly fascinating New York lives, graciously receiving a steady flow of visitors at our table, and drunkenly disparaging the live acts which we thought were impossibly old hat. I was sorry when the lights came on and the security guard asked if we needed a cab.

Outside in the purple velvet of an autumn midnight, Jonny and I said goodbye. He walked back to his hotel, and I took the Victoria Line to the District Line, back East in your direction, grateful that on this Tuesday night at least, the tube was almost abandoned.

I crept into your apartment, as quietly as I could, drunk but intent to cause minimal disturbance. The light was out in your room, I could hear that you were asleep in there, snoring softly. I stripped to my underwear, then tiptoed towards your door, but only to take a look. What were you dreaming of leapling? I gazed for a minute at your long lovely body, your limbs sprawling out from under the covers in the milk of the moon, then I pulled your door shut and I lay down on the sofa. I made my bed under a thick orange blanket, falling asleep immediately.

VI

I woke up because you were slamming things around in
the bathroom. I sat up on the couch, slowly. You came
out and threw me a look of ice-cold fury.

'Bibby's awake,' you said.

I replied, 'It was kinda hard to sleep.'

You glossed over that detail, it wasn't of interest. You
asked, 'Have you seen my comb?'

'No,' I said, trying to reach for some composure. 'I
don't think so, what comb?'

'Blue, plastic, 1950s,' you sighed. 'It was in the bathroom cabinet.'

'No, sorry,' I said.

'Fuck's sake Bibby,' you snapped. 'I need my comb.'

You went and hammered on your long-suffering
flatmate's flimsy door, and I panicked for a moment
thinking there was some way he could've seen what I'd
done. I knew that that was impossible of course, but all
the same I took the opportunity to slip into the shower,
to revive my aching head, and to ask how I was going
to survive this.

I stripped; the bathroom resounded with the low,
maddening hum of the extractor fan, a particularly
irksome complement to my well-deserved headache.

The water took forever to get hot, so I stood huddled under the shower head, amongst the armada of half-empty bottles which lined the floor of the cubicle. The plughole was clogged with hair, the shower wouldn't drain properly and within a few minutes all of the tubes of shampoo and shower gel began to bob about at my feet in the greying water. I wanted to dissolve immediately and forever.

I let my mind wander to the night before, I attempted to narrativise it, I had sunk a lot of booze. I tried to figure out who had actually paid for those bottles of lousy red wine, I wondered if Jonny had invited anyone up to his hotel room, I scrolled through hazy recollections trying to remember who it was I said I'd meet up with at the weekend. The evening had been an unexpected pleasure, a joy I was not prepared for, and I would have stayed in my reminiscences, under the warming water, safe from your temper, for far longer, but the shower was threatening to overflow.

I stepped out onto the cold bathroom floor, and reached for a less than fresh towel, shuddering as the September draught came in under the door. I prayed that I'd still have enough cash in my coat pocket to go out and get some breakfast, to stay clear until your bad mood had receded, or had at least fastened itself on some other target.

Wet, cold, hungover, I come out into the living room, shivering. You're sitting on the sofa, scowling.

'Did you find it?' I ask.

'What?' you say.

'Your comb,' I reply.

'No,' you say, 'and I'm pissed off.'

I say, 'It's probably in your room somewhere.'

I'm surprised at how easily this line of lies comes to me. I put it down to your nefarious influence, unfairly perhaps, and a Nine Inch Nails lyric comes into my head, Trent Reznor mocking me as all your most hateful qualities become my own. I'm anxious, and I go as far as to hum this very bleak song cheerily, so as to seem innocent and bright, masking my hangover, my guilt, as I sift through my suitcase for something to wear. But this morning nothing's where it should be, everything seems to be in an even greater state of disarray than usual. By and by I pull a few low-impact garments from the case so that I may scarper pronto, then as I pause to consider where it would be best to dress, you turn to me with a stealthy, knowing look.

'Out late, eh, Bibby?' you say.

'Yes,' I reply. 'My friend Jonny is here from New York.'

'Oh yeah?' you say. 'Your friend Jonny. Stayed out with your mate Jonny all night, did you?'

'Not all night,' I mumble, 'I was back before one.'

You ask, 'So why didn't you get in bed with me then?'

And rather than antagonistic, you look mournful, sitting there clutching a stuffed toy owl, as though it were you with the sore head. I'm so primed for another squabble, so fretful about the stupid comb, and so ready to fight with you over it; I'm not at all expecting this sudden streak of sadness from you; you catch me off-guard again. You look like a little lost boy, no comb, no one to tuck him up in bed at night, all petulant and sob-faced. For a second I think a tear has come to my own eye, before I realise that it's just the water dripping down from my hair.

'I didn't want to wake you up,' I say.

'Yeah right,' you say, and I catch your drift.

I laugh, 'I'm not sleeping with Jonny. I don't actually fuck everyone I know.'

'Near enough,' you say sulkily.

I pause to wonder – what are you expecting from me here?

'I don't understand you, Thomas,' I say. 'What is this situation we're in?'

'It's not a situation,' you answer, 'I'm letting you stay because I'm nice, but what's in it for me, eh?'

'Well obviously,' I begin, 'when I get my student loan I'll give you something towards the bills...'

'That's not what I mean,' you cut me off and glower. You lean backwards in your seat, letting your arms rest wide on the back of the sofa, looking down at your crotch, then over to me, then back to your crotch. You don't speak with words, but I know what you're saying.

I stand in my towel, cold water trickling down my bare torso, holding a handful of creased clothes by my side, my hair slicked to my aching skull, last night's mascara ringing my eyes, a pitiful sight. I clear my throat and I say, 'I, erm, I'm just not really in the mood right now.'

You rise from the sofa, a smirk of excitement playing on your lips. I can see the outline of your hard cock pushing against your shorts. 'Come on Bibbs,' you say. 'We haven't done it for ages.'

I flush, and fold my arms and all the clothes up in front of me. Embarrassed, I say, 'We had sex like two day ago.'

You dismiss this and say, 'Well, sort of.'

Striding the short distance between us in two steps, you come toe to toe with me, face to face. You grab hold of my balls through the towel, I'm getting hard now too, and when I step back I can feel the coolness of the wall caress my bare shoulders. I hold the clothes to my chest with my right hand and instinctively secure my towel with the left. You press closer. I'm trapped, I can't get away, but the very taboo nature of this situation, this suggestion of sexual assault, is impossibly arousing and I feel doubly ashamed.

You lean in to kiss me, your eyes closed and your mouth open, one hand on my chest and the other loosening my grip on the towel. But I don't let it drop.

Instead, I say, 'We can't do this anymore.'

You scoff, 'What?'

I say, 'We can't have sex anymore.'

'Why not?' you ask.

'For a lot of reasons,' I reply. 'Mainly Adam.'

'I can do what I like,' you say angrily.

'Yeah, well, I can't,' I snap. 'I love him, and this will hurt him, so we just can't.'

You sneer, 'So that's how it is, eh, Bibby? You're just looking for a free ride, are you? Staying here, not giving me anything in return.'

You turn away and pace the floor. I try to hide myself behind this huddle of crumpled clothes, I look for modesty, and fumble, 'I told you… I'll give you something when I get it.'

You drop, white with a cold temper, back on to the sofa. You take a deep breath and say with casual, offhand aggression, 'I was thinking, yeah? What if, what if my dick is just a metaphor?'

I feel the blood drain from my own face now, because that is a line from my notebook. There's no way it's a coincidence, no way that you with your uncouth and cumbersome language could have stumbled upon that specific phrase in any other way besides by flicking through my journal. The glint of malice in your eyes is further confirmation.

'What?' I ask, dumbfounded, and you quote, or rather misquote, more of the text back to me.

I didn't even really know what I was doing on those pages; I was just following Martha Graham's advice. I was letting the vitality translate through me, keeping the channel open, I wasn't judging it, I certainly wasn't ready to share it. It was defenceless, in utero, sacrosanct.

'That's from my notebook,' I splutter the obvious.

'I was looking for my comb,' you gloat, 'and it looked interesting, so you know.'

You pull the notebook out from underneath the corduroy pillow beside you, casually leaf through it, then begin reading out loud, choosing the more intimate scenes from this very private text, but mangling the words I have spent so long adjusting, reassembling them to better suit your own vindictive needs. Still standing before you basically naked, absolutely exposed, I redden with anger and humiliation, but I'm tethered to the spot. I can't actually believe that you would do this to me, but, of course you would.

'Nice bit of penmanship here, Bibby,' you say scornfully. 'I see that you're writing some sort of book. Some kind of memoir is it?'

'No, it's not, it's new writing, it's autofiction,' I say stumbling for words. I feel so stupid, why am I trying to explain myself? But I keep talking to buy myself time; this is exactly the sort of situation for which I've been primed by Saturday afternoons with my stepfather. I'm hypnotised by the scene, wanting to get out, but unable to think clearly enough to even dress myself.

If you had decided to rifle through my emails, or my post even, I would have been put out, yes, but we would probably have maintained some sort of relationship afterwards. What you were doing here was something else though, it wasn't just greedy curiosity, it was a deliberate attempt to violate me, to mock me, to subdue me, to punish me for my insubordination, to demean me with the thing most precious to me. Though I'd never admitted it to you, you knew how important my writing was to me, you could smell it. Big cats stalk their prey for great distances, I knew that from the natural history documentaries I watched with my granddad. You'd seen me bent over that notebook, scribbling away at odd hours, brow furrowed in concentration. You'd pried before, but unlike with Morgan, I'd swiftly shut the book on you. My insistence that you leave well alone had clearly apprised you with the knowledge that there was something of great value to me there. Big cats locate the weakness in the herd, and that's when they strike.

You cough, a parodical little hem-hem, before you begin to read aloud again:

'My mother actually divorced her second husband because he was run out of town. He was babysitting the neighbour's kids, the parents came back early and found him... Well, no one ever completed that sentence but my mother kicked him out anyway. My mother only told me recently the real reason for her divorce. She only told me, not my sisters. She only told me because I have a penis and I'm capable of hearing stuff like that, because I have a penis and need to hear stuff like that. Was it a warning of the dangers of a *man's body*? Did she expect me to perpetrate a crime myself, to perpetuate the family line? To fuck a little girl for myself? Too bad I can't get it up for babies, huh?'

As you reel off these lines, I feel such deep disgust, you snort derisively, and then I lose my cool.

I throw down my clothes, lunge towards you, and hiss, 'Give me that,' but you are too quick.

You bounce up from the sofa and escape my swing. You laugh, hide the book behind your back, and start snatching at my towel with your free arm, long and lithe like a championship rower.

'Come on then,' you say, and lick your lips.

I step back to regroup, I honestly think that I'm about to start crying for real now, I can't bear this. I need that book back, but I can't trade it for the towel, for my one remaining scrap of dignity.

You continue your assault, 'I bet the Booker Prize judges don't see many stories about transvestite strippers do they, eh? Bet they'll love this.'

I snarl, 'I'm not a fucking transvestite, you stupid fuck,' and you light up with the thrill of landing another clean blow.

'Oh, right yes, you're some kind of woman now are you, Bibby?' you snigger. 'Want to tell that to the beast between your legs then, eh?'

You grab again at my towel; stepping back neatly I narrowly manage to avoid your grasp. There's a ringing in my ears, a cold sweat washes over my entire body. I lay my eyes on the large pair of fabric scissors one of your roommates has left on the table. I consider it, for a moment I consider it. I have the makings of a killer leapling, and God knows you're marked for an early death. I could do it, if not stab you I could at least strike you, but no, I'm crumbling under the weight of my own body. I'm destroyed. Where is all of my strength now? All I say is, 'I have to get dressed.'

I pick up my clothes and take myself back into the bathroom, cursing you under my breath for your stupid, childish behaviour, damning you for forcing the event. If I don't pick up and go right away, I will have to accept any and all degradations you force on me from this day forward, I know this, I'm certain of it. I'm furious with myself for allowing this to happen, and more so for losing it like this, over what is really just an adolescent prank, after putting up with so much worse from you, for so long. I bang my head on the cabinet above the sink, *Motherfucker! Underhand motherfucker!* and I put my fist in my mouth to stifle a scream. I'm angry beyond understanding, I'm shaking all over, but I refuse to show you that, refuse to give you any more of myself. I check myself, steady myself, and put my clothes on.

When I emerge again into the living room, you are still on the couch, and I masquerade as unmoved. If it were not for the penumbra of passive aggression I cast around me, it would surely appear as if nothing of any importance has happened. Or so I want to think, though I know my emotions jump off me visibly, like sparks from an angle grinder.

You have one hand in your underwear as always, you're reading something on your phone. I collect the few items of mine that are dotted about the place, and put them into my suitcase, tying my wet hair back with a ribbon someone looped about my neck the night before. You seem not to notice me packing, or if you have noticed, not to care. You act as though you're ignoring a child's bad behaviour so as to avoid rewarding them with any attention, negative or otherwise.

When I was a child I hated to be tickled, I couldn't stand the way it made me spasm and flail, how quickly and completely it made me powerless. I detested the way my stepfather would pounce on me, and tickle me until I almost puked, and when I called out for him to stop everyone around me would say, 'Don't be a baby, he's only playing with you!' So one day I told myself, *I just won't be ticklish anymore*, as simple as that, and it worked. The next time he tried to tickle me, I didn't respond, I didn't giggle, I didn't try to wriggle free. I just went as limp as boiled spaghetti, and let him do it. He quickly gave up when he saw there was nothing in it for him. I guess he was just looking to get a rise out of me too.

I do the same with you, I use the same spell. I say to myself, *I will no longer care about him*. I make this incantation in absolute seriousness, and absolute silence, as I fasten my bedevilled suitcase shut. Then I rise, put on my coat, and say, 'I'm going now.'

You're actually quite startled by this. You say, 'Look, here's your book. Here it is, have it back. Come on, I was just taking the piss.'

'Right,' I say without emotion, and take it from your hand.

'Well, call me then, or send a message, yeah?' you mumble.

You're crestfallen.

I've won.

No.

No one wins here.

'Sure, yes, of course,' I say, but I am already on my way out.

It might've looked like I was just having a Maria Callas moment, simply performing petulance, you would've been forgiven for thinking so. The cause of this upset was so pathetic, so teenage. You'd read a private notebook, and teased me with it, so what? Maybe you comforted yourself with the thought that I'd walk about for a bit, hissing, then realise how heavy my case was, remember how fine your arse was, and come back at the end of the day, with downcast eyes and a murmur about *getting carried away*. I'm sure you felt quite satisfied even, Onassis, flexing your own prowess. And it's true that I was at a loss, a disarming dread like a cocaine comedown took over me as soon as I reached the end of your street. Jonny only had a single room at his crummy hotel, and Elsa had a cousin on her couch, I knew there was only one possible option: I had to reach out to Jackie Kennedy herself. Without much joy, I paused outside Tesco, and called Adam.

'Liza,' I said trying to be personable, 'I need a favour.'

He didn't sound at all surprised to hear this from me. He asked, 'What is it, Liza?'

I told the truth, 'I can't stay with Thomas James anymore, I just can't. Can I come to yours for a few days?'

Adam sighed, and said, 'OK Liza, but it *will* be just for a few days this time, won't it?'

Why on earth Adam agreed I don't know, hadn't enough trouble triangulated here? Perhaps some people are just irredeemably good.

I took the longest, most circuitous route possible over to Adam's house, two buses rather than the tube. It felt worse than the prospect of taking the Megabus back to my mother's house, so maybe I should've just done that? I dawdled to delay my arrival, I had to give myself a little time to think. How could I explain or describe what had happened? I needed some extra padding around this sore spot, to help me flesh out the cadaverous unreality of the moment. Is it even possible to break up with someone you aren't in a relationship with? If not, why did I feel so bad, and yet so strangely liberated?

The bus threw me about, I was shaken to the quick, I had walked out of your apartment, knowing it would be the last time. I felt a very real loss, cut through with choler, and a molten sadness. A not unfamiliar cocktail of sentiments when it came to you, only now I was taking this vodka stinger on a buffed silver tray to quaff in the company of my best friend, who was, inconveniently, also your boyfriend. Whatever I was feeling, I realised, should not be spilled directly onto Adam's carpet, and so I slapped a tempered face on things. I chose to think of this as a sleepover, as being just what he and I needed, some time together to process the emotional molasses we were wading through, knee-deep.

Adam greeted me at the door with cordial, if strained, hospitality. He made tea, and we made small talk about the onset of autumn, about Elsa, about Jovian, all our old friends, but not about you. He asked me about my interview at Saint Martins, and explained to me that Leo had asked him to join his new theatre company – he was going to be the musical director. Elsa and Lulu were also involved; they were trying to blend drag and soap opera with live art and contemporary dance, in a sort of soup of camp hysteria. I smiled and nodded, and tried to pay attention. I didn't quite get it, but then when do I ever?

There was a neat pile of embellished bodysuits on his desk, which he had obviously been working on before I arrived. Being a classic millennial multi-hyphenate creative, Adam was also helping to make the costumes for the troupe, as well as assisting with the make-up design; it often seemed as though he found the very idea of free time almost mortally frightening.

Knowing me too well, he said, 'If you have anything that needs mending, put it in the pile and I'll fix it for you.'

To be polite, to fill the air, to play my part as a grateful guest better than I had done previously, I took a pair of jeans out from my suitcase, which had torn at the crotch. Adam assessed the damage, and said, 'Oh Liza! What have you done here?'

'I was running for the subway with my friend Cody,' I laughed, 'and they just ripped.'

'Subway,' he snickered at this Americanism, then said, 'who's Cody?'

'Trouble,' I said.

Cody was a long-haired, tattooed, skinny little bad boy who looked like a member of the Manson family. He made porn, he arrived at bars strung out, in just a jockstrap. Obviously I was obsessed. To avoid talking about what was really on my mind, to prevent myself from asking *Why did you say all of those awful things about me?* I told Adam about Cody as he sat to sew my jeans. I told him the story of how Cody and his friend Ricky had been held up at gunpoint in Los Angeles, because I knew how Adam loved a good yarn.

'Instead of putting up their hands and dropping their wallets, Cody said this friend of his, this Ricky dude, just *queened the fuck out*, and so they both ended up getting shot!'

Adam gasped, 'No!'

'Yeah,' I said. 'They survived, but Cody still has a bullet in his hand.'

I could see Adam was deep into it, so I continued. 'He used to let me play with it. Push it around under his skin, when we were drunk. It was right there between his thumb and index finger.'

Adam, slightly queasy, asked the obvious question: 'Why didn't he have it removed?'

I explained that his doctor had said that it would be difficult, and possibly dangerous, to go into his hand and take the bullet out. 'They said it would probably cause less harm to leave it there, and wait for it to work itself out.' As I said that I chuckled a little and added, 'I think I know the feeling.'

'What?' said Adam.

I gave in and said, 'Thomas.'

For a while, he didn't reply. He had his head bent over the crotch seam of my jeans, patching it up from the inside with a strip of silver fabric. He looked angelic, like an Edith Wharton heroine, darning by the fireside, awaiting the return of the philandering lover she hopes to set right through her tender devotions.

'What happened this time?' he asked patiently, with just a shade of vehemence.

'He just went too far,' I sighed. 'He went through my belongings and read all my notes. And he kept trying to manipulate me into having sex, he just wouldn't lay off. So yeah, just being Thomas James really.'

Adam looked embarrassed. 'Oh,' he said, and swallowed hard.

'I told him he should show you some respect, you know?'

His brow had clouded with stormy indignation, he looked hurt.

I began to say, 'I don't want to interfere...'

He countered with, 'So don't.'

And I shut my mouth.

I remember sitting in my mother's car when I was nine or ten, she was kissing her boyfriend outside the place they both worked. When she got into the car she looked very sorry, and I asked her why.

'We aren't going to see each other anymore,' she said.

I was confused. I said, 'But you were just kissing.'

She nodded, 'That was a kiss goodbye,' and we drove off.

On the way home she told me that she wanted to try and make things work with her husband. She said,

'I have some things I need to talk about with your dad first.'

I looked out of the passenger window in chagrin: that old chestnut. My scorn was only softened ten minutes down the road, when she said, 'They say you can't love two people at once, but I don't think that's true.'

Not every child has the advantage of such an honest and forthright mother, I really should be more grateful.

Adam kept his focus on the sewing, he wanted to deny this situation was even happening. It was, unsurprisingly perhaps, symmetrical with your own need to ignore the complications of the circumstances. Ultimately it was Adam's refusal to talk, as much as your own insistence that there was nothing to talk about, that pushed me towards the recognition that I could love either one of you, but not both. And I chose him, not because I loved him more, but because I felt he was more deserving of love. In leaving you that morning I had deliberately taken myself out of this messy equation, and unlike all those times before, there would be no backsliding. Yet I still wanted the impossible, I desperately hoped that Adam would put his arms around me and say, 'I understand, I know how he is. I'm sorry he hurt you.'

But that gentle comfort would never come, we were long past the age of innocence now. If it was not the done thing to talk of consensual non-monogamy, or the intricacies of queer intimacy, or to try and navigate a new understanding of these relationships, then I would be quiet on the matter, silent of my own free will, without having to be told to shut up again. Even if these mores seemed ridiculous and unfair, I decided I wouldn't jeopardise anyone else's shot at love with my own whorish ways.

'We're not going to see each other anymore,' I said, out loud, but mainly for my own benefit. It was the final line of my incantation.

But as any witch will tell you, the key to performing an act of magic is that the sorcerer must entirely believe in the spell they are casting, if it is to be successful. This is crucial, because without this unshakeable belief the spell will not bind. I think this was my mistake, that I didn't believe it was over, not truly. I watched Adam finish mending my trousers, and told myself I had made the right choice, even with you still lodged in there: my very own bullet, taunting me from inside myself, the sacred idol speaking from deep within.

VII

In the time since you've been gone, you haven't really been gone at all; if anything you've become more ineluctable than ever. While you were still alive and I was still trying to get over you, I only had to avoid certain places, certain people, certain parties, and I'd be safe. Now, however, that you are no longer hidebound to your mortal form, you can appear anywhere. These manifestations are totally unpredictable, and made always more startling by the fact that you should be gone for good.

In the weeks after you died I was afraid to open a newspaper, lest I be faced with your photo under another sensational headline, hemmed in by the insinuations and exaggerations regarding the circumstances of your death. The first time I saw you in a paper, which I had absentmindedly picked up off the seat next to me on the tube, I was very frightened. Seeing you there, below a piece on Prince Charles's trip to meet some despot in the Middle East, just another face amidst the rabble of celebrity love triangles, political gaffes and heart-warming stories of heroic pets, was so disorienting that I had to drop my head in my hands, and my hands between my knees, causing the other passengers to panic that I was either in the middle of a fainting spell, or else mumbling a prayer before detonating a bomb.

After the initial shock I became wary of newspapers, immediately turning my eyes away whenever I encountered one. But some scandalous new revelation about the late great Whitney Houston, or a glimmer of hope offered by a left-wing politician's sudden surge in popularity, was usually enough to lure me back in, and caught off-guard I'd see you again. Your picture in amongst the others briefly brought you back, with whiplash effect; it was as if there'd been a clerical error, as if you hadn't died after all, but rather had become so successful as a photographer that tabloids wanted to print sleazy pics of you to stoke their circulation. The coverage you generated almost made me feel proud. I wanted to stand up and say, 'Look! That's my friend!' Even though I knew you weren't being spoken of with kindness or respect, still I felt that it was something to see your picture in the papers, that you had been recognised, finally, by the world. They had referred to you as a 'Photographer' after all.

The story stayed hot for quite some time, it had all the ingredients of a successful red top intrigue: you were handsome, talented and white, on the precipice of great things, killed in such a tragic, public way, and in the presence of all those famous, wealthy people too. Truly, your death was a brilliant stone in a gorgeous setting, and readers on the overground loved to see it glitter as they scarfed down prawn mayo sandwiches.

I passed through the stages of grief in jumble-sale order: shock, bargaining, denial, acceptance coming pell-mell as I followed your progress through the news cycle, until anger rushed to the fore and annihilated all other feelings. The more I read retellings of the night in question, stories written to keep bemused commuters up to date on the legal fall-out of it all, the more enraged I became.

I recall foolishly reading a highly moralising piece which suggested that you were high when it happened, and that your death had been a direct result of your sexual advances towards a handsome young model, that your boozy lechery had in effect been repaid in full. Knowing, from people who had been with you that night, that you were in fact sober, brought me into a state close to homicidal rage. Why should it matter? It didn't. But how could people be allowed to write these things? Pure speculation and scandal, based on nothing but homophobic projections and an entirely fictional implication that the good and the bad are always punished and rewarded appropriately.

That it wasn't necessary to have known the deceased in order to have an opinion on him was proven by the decimating comments left below promulgating articles by perfect strangers, who chipped in with summations that your death was God's verdict on your disgusting lifestyle, and on all people like you, with tactless readings of the situation as a prime example of society's decline, with almost illegible insults, and heartless, brainless jokes. One would have thought the defiled body in question was that of Oliver Cromwell, rightfully dug up and hanged in chains from the Tyburn Tree, rather than that of a 27-year-old boy who died a needless death after a brief and unremarkable life.

When did you know you were dead? I've asked myself, and indeed I've asked you, speaking aloud when alone, if you would have found all of this funny, flattering even. Goodness knows you loved attention of any kind, you weren't selective, and were equally smug when slandered as you were when praised. Would you have loved the light which those bonfires of indignation and exasperation threw on you then? All the scurrilous drivel from those dirty little red top rags. The only thing worse than being talked about, etc., etc. I swear I could feel you leaning over my shoulder as I scrolled through the comments section, tapping the screen, saying, 'Look at that wanker,' and grinning.

I remember skimming another newspaper article over someone's shoulder on the bus, and having to get off on Hackney Road, because I couldn't bear to sit there in silence anymore. I was nowhere near home but I needed to scream. I called Elsa and shouted and sobbed, asking, 'How could they say this? This is all lies. How could they say this?' I couldn't tell which way I was walking, my eyes were red and prickling with tears, mucus was pouring from my nose faster than I could suck it back into my skull. I staggered around in the street sure that I would go completely mad, shouting incomprehensibly down the phone, with Elsa occasionally punctuating her silence with, 'Oh Liza, I'm so sorry.'

The way she spoke, her words so full of remorse though I knew she couldn't stand you, cast an insane shadow of mistrust, as if she were somehow liable. Not that I imagined her guilty of your death, rather it felt as if she'd always known that this was how things would end. As if blessed with a second sight, my own Cassandra had foretold it, and I wondered if this gift was maybe the source of that strange sadness which had always seemed to dog her, trailing her even as she posed in Prada for *W Magazine*.

I have to ask, whilst walking the streets, did you ever see me in a magazine and miss me? While I was still at Central Saint Martins I wrote a play that became a small success, and earned me a few nice spots in the arts press. But maybe it passed you by, this dainty first step?

My mother somehow read about the play, and was unhappy with how I had presented her.

'I'm sorry if it hurt you,' I said, 'but I just wrote it how it was.'

'No,' she replied. 'You wrote it how you *remember* it was.'

Surely you must've seen me turn up in *Time Out* or *Exeunt*, when the play became a legitimate fringe hit, and it was written up in the nationals and nominated for awards? Did you see me, leapling? Smiling up at you out of the *Metro* in a borrowed dress and a vintage fur? Were you proud? Or were you still angry? I'm not asking out of any sense of self-satisfaction, I just want to feel like I didn't vanish from sight completely, the morning we fought over my notebook. I want to have lingered in your life, like you've lingered in mine, causing you complicated feelings of anguish and delight, anger and arousal, and occasionally maybe even joy.

Gradually, the story of your death slipped from the front pages and further inside the newspapers. Receiving less and less attention, it shrivelled up, becoming smaller and smaller, occupying less and less print space, until eventually it vanished completely, before you were even cold in the grave. That was just as bad. It was like they were done with you, though no one had been brought to justice, no one held responsible, but then that never really was what those hacks were interested in, was it? They'd simply wrung your corpse of all the juice they needed, and once you were bone dry, they left you to desiccate. Other stories took your place, Christmas grew nearer, and so your death was replaced by the traditional festive reportage on how many OAPs would die from being unable to afford heating that winter, and how much the wife of a famous footballer had spent on hair extensions, and exclusive snaps of a teen YouTuber's family vacation to Barbados. Your dying had been just an interstitial variation.

Your social media profiles were mercifully deactivated, eventually, though the network continued to send out such celebratory spam as *Today is Thomas's birthday!* for a long time. It wasn't inaccurate, of course, today was still your birthday, even if you were no longer alive to mark it. Your account was memorialised, and through some petty bureaucracy allowed to hang inactive in cyberspace, as a kind of cork noticeboard for people to pin sentimental memos on. The profile *Thomas James Rip* sits there still, dormant and decorated by pictures of flowers left on the spot where the paramedics failed to resuscitate you, a perfect simulacrum of a grave. I don't think any tomb was ever daubed in such inanities as yours though. Dictators, paedophiles, and now-unpopular social thinkers: all have had their graves smashed and graffitied. Holocaust survivors have had theirs defaced with swastikas, and AIDS victims have had theirs spray-painted with FAGGOTS; desecration is not new. But my asinine contemporaries and their torpid attempts to articulate loss, my God, it all makes me feel so hopeless.

We will miss u Thom
Thinking of you x

Why even fucking bother?

When I visit this page of sorrows, as I do, the miserable outpouring of insipid anguish, emojis and misspelled epitaphs almost drowns your memory out entirely. *RIP Tommy :(* and *Thomas James is dead? WTF? I'm in shock* and *Thomas James was one of the only people who got one over on me, gonna miss him.* This lukewarm sniff-fest, this mediocre line-up of gawkers who reacted to your death as they would react to a clickbait article head-lined *These are the kids from* Saved by the Bell *now – feel old yet?* Was this your cortège? People posted pictures of you, or you and them, as if to stake a claim on this facsimile of grief, and legitimise their self-indulgence, using this terrible thing as a honeytrap to catch their daily dose of *U OK huns.*

Most horrifying of all, the friend you were with that night posted a picture of you, which he took moments after you died. It was removed for violating community standards before I saw it, and I'm grateful for that, because when Jovian described it to me, he looked as though he would truly have given anything not to have seen it. I thought often about asking to see the picture, I thought that maybe that would bring me closure, but luckily I was too much of a coward to go through with it. Too afraid to pore over that final image of you, blond, bloody and sprawled out on the pavement like Princess Di, those invasive pornographic pictures which violated you, and all that was sacred in the moment of your passing.

Many prurient articles came up in subsequent waves, and stimulated new rounds of discussion across my news-feed. Friends would share and reshare, and comment on each other's reposts, delighting the algorithm which guerdoned the propagated content with greater visibil-ity and a broader reach. Our age of screens has brought about something new and previously impossible, digi-tal grief, in which we commune via computer with our emotions, in order to circulate them more widely.

We other Victorians had learned to keep our lamentations to ourselves since wailing in the streets had fallen out of fashion. But then, with Wi-Fi came the return of the collective ritual, and it is now common practice for people to stop by these computerised stelae to grieve publicly, in between shopping for discounts on handbags and skim-reading think pieces on meditation, flicking between browser tabs mindlessly.

Grief is long. People still share memories of you when they come to them, posting a picture or a few erratic lines about you, tacking them up online a little thoughtlessly. The network generates and celebrates anniversaries for engagement, and another picture from the past pops up, uncalled for. This rivulet of images has never really stopped; perhaps it has slowed but it still flows, finding its way up through the ground in surprising places, where the earth is weak, like a spring of miraculous water, a shrine to Our Lady. 'Love is a stream,' said Gena Rowlands, remember?

Still now, like Fred and Ginger dancing the last waltz down a supermarket aisle, still now, ten years since we met, six since we last spoke, four since your death, still now, something arrives totally out of context and bowls me clean over. Last month, the *Guardian* ran a piece on the phenomenon of cyclists lashing out at careless drivers, drawing a comparison between bike-riding aggression and road rage. They illustrated the article with a picture of you, entirely unconnected, whizzing between buses down Regent Street. Did anyone in the chain connecting the photographer's agent to the photo editor to the subeditor know you had died years before the picture ran? When I opened the paper in my hipster expat cafe, I gasped. There you were, racing towards me at top speed on your bike, out of the past, and there was no then and there was no now, every-thing was eternal, *And I saw a new heaven and a new earth: for the first heaven and the first earth were passed away; and there was no more sea.*

It goes on, the world online and off is studded with unexploded landmines. I've been talking with a theatre in London about the possibility of re-staging one of my plays. The artistic director is called Tomas, and the producer is called James, and so each time I get an email from them it appears, at first, to be sent from you, Thomas James. This has happened several times now in the course of our discussion, and each time, a few palpitating seconds pass, while I wonder if your old account has been hacked, or if your parents have written to me for some unknown reason, or if you've accessed Hotmail from the afterlife, before I realise the trick my overeager eyes have played on me again.

All of these mistakes, these mirages, have ultimately driven home the truth of the matter, have ensured that you remained permanently in the present tense. Unwilling to dissipate into the past, forever forced back into the now, you have become suspended as what you were then, eternally stunted. Present tense Thomas will never be replaced by any Thomas of the future. The reformed Thomas, the pleasant Thomas, the vegan Thomas, the polite Thomas, the monogamous Thomas will never come to be, but then neither will Thomas the Deliveroo employee, or Thomas the racist taxi driver, or Thomas the Brexiteer. You have been pinned down in time, you have become a meme, like the lady on the internet espousing her endless love of discount curtains, or the badly repainted face of Jesus on that infamous fresco, or Grumpy Cat, or the Ermahgerd girl, or the fist-pump baby, all of whom only exist for us in that moment. The circling sightings of you at twenty-seven, embarking on your Saturn return, the posted and reposted pictures have kept you in your grave, as a brick in the mouth of a vampire ensures he does not rise again.

VIII

I've been reading Ocean Vuong. There's a second-hand English bookstore above the American Legion of Friends, they deliver by bike because Mexico City is both alarmingly contemporary and pleasantly antediluvian.

'Let me begin again,' Vuong writes, at the top of a new chapter.

He's asking not simply to pick up from where he left off, he's not just saying, 'back now,' he is asking for a chance to start again from the beginning, to change the course of inevitable tragedy. As if this line, 'let me begin again,' were a spell, or a speech act, capable of erasing the filthy grey slush that has covered the ground, of replacing it with a sheet of fresh white snow, ready for inscription by clean new boots. This is a fantasy I need to indulge in, just for a moment.

I know I cannot avoid hurtling towards your death, I realise that this is impossible. Just because I haven't written it up yet doesn't mean it hasn't happened, won't happen, can be averted, I know that. But I also know that in this act of writing I am making something new: one part biography, one part fiction, two parts slash, and in this new world, the world on the page, the world the writer has so steadfastly overseen, you are still alive. You are still walking around London with one hand in your shorts, casting aspersions, and causing adolescent shelf stackers to blush under your coruscating gaze and question their sexuality. You are still at large, and so before I rush into murder, let me begin again. Place me. Back now. I need more time to say goodbye.

I stayed only a few days with Adam after our fight. Quickly I found a room on the Caledonian Road, determined to build a life outside your sphere of influence. My apartment was ugly, I was living with strangers for the first time in my life. We didn't share more than a cursory nod in the kitchen, and every morning on the bus to Saint Martins I mourned the lives I'd left behind in America. Throughout this transition I'd clung steadfast to my one remaining hope, that Morgan would follow me to London as we'd agreed. That she would arrive back in my life, all guns blazing, telling me to forget you, waving off my heartache with her own incantation, 'Throw a little glitter on it, darling.' I waited on Morgan, ready to populate London with insane propositions and life-changing whims, full of that Yankee magic with which she'd transform my life from black and white to glorious technicolour once again. I waited on her appearance, but instead received an email, quite scant on detail, telling me that I was on my own.

I'm so sorry darling, she wrote, *I've been so busy, I haven't had a minute to write! I found a new place on 24th, and I have an interview next week at a tech start-up, working on fabric development which I'm really excited about. I haven't been able to save much for a ticket to London though, but really I've been thinking, maybe I should stay in California a bit longer? At least until the winter is over, I mean London in December sounds hellish! But maybe next year?*

Jonny had left too, back to New York. I didn't cry when we said goodbye, at least not until he said, 'Don't sweat it JJ bebe. I'll be back or you'll be back, one or the other.'

I tried making friends at school, but I was too wrung out, I had too little to offer. I was the only student who was interested in the experimental possibilities of text in performance, everyone else seemed to find the form redundant. They were all crazy for haiku and concrete poetry, their optimism was exhausting; watching them plan for a future that would never arrive made me despair.

Hearing them talk about how the internet offered radical possibilities for disseminating new writing caused me to sink deeper into the black funk that was swallowing me. I wanted to say, 'You're deluded, the only way you're going to succeed in the arts is if your father bankrolls you and your mother pulls in a few favours at the *Telegraph*!' But I didn't, of course, I simply smiled and waited for the end of the seminar, aware that I was being marked down for my lack of constructive input.

I had almost no interest in school, I felt I could have taught the classes myself, but then again nothing new there, I've always been pretentious. The only times I had ever felt I was being taught anything worth knowing was when I had been gifted lessons from the muses in the guise of those old queens: Penny Arcade, Bambi Lake, Rumi Missabu. Stoned, I had sat with Jonny and Morgan in the apartments and dressing rooms of these stars (to me the *greatest* stars), and listened to them talk of when the world was young, of how everything was an illusion, and how to present one's self most strikingly in it.

In comparison all Saint Martins could muster were ephebic discussions and dreary class trips to public museums. We went to the new Saatchi Gallery in Chelsea to look at an exhibition on Russian contemporary art. We were accompanied by two members of staff so that we might get a handle on thinking critically, instead of just mooning about the place daydreaming and anticipating the joyful moment when we'd get to the gift shop and finally be free to buy pencils. I hate visiting museums with a crowd, I'd much rather dawdle or power through as suits my own mood, without the pressure of coming up with anything clever to say mid-mooch. For this reason I decided to work from the top floor down, more or less against the flow of the exhibition.

Upstairs there was a whole room given over to the simple brooding pleasure of Vikenti Nilin's monochrome photography series, *Neighbours*. In the images, residents of a Soviet tower block sit on their windowsills, dangling their legs right over the nothingness; naturally I thought of you and your love of Socialist architecture. I wondered if you had ever photographed these same buildings yourself? (Stupid, I know, when Russia is so huge.)

I wish I had one of your pictures now, to frame and rest on this kitchen table, not of you but by you. A photograph you'd taken would make me feel closer to you, because it would be an image as you'd seen it with your own eyes, I'd be inside you again. Should I ask then, after all this time? Ask to see the pictures you took of me, when I was caught off-guard? To maybe see what you saw in me as I was then, uncertain, morose, and always overdressed.

The subjects in the gallery portraits were mere millimetres from certain death, but they didn't look afraid, no they hardly looked more than bored. It was as if for some

reason they had had to spend a lot of time in this perilous position, had grown accustomed to it, and no longer
feared it. The angles Nilin had chosen to shoot from
were almost journalistic, as if to document suicides that
never happened, to record protestors waiting for a news
crew that never came. There's a sense of something being
rehearsed, or rather that the actors are in repose between
scenes, there's never a suggestion that a Dionysian impulse
might kick in, that they may all throw themselves to the
ground, no. The pictures are calm, yet still they terrified
me, the same way the famous picture of builders eating
sandwiches atop the half-built Rockefeller Center always
does. Although I myself was on firm ground, the gallery
floor solid beneath my feet, the vertigo I felt looking at
the photographs was very real, and still I could not look
away. It seemed there was something prophetic to those
pictures, something struggling to communicate itself to
me; I sweated trying to hear it. Eve Kosofsky Sedgwick
talked about how clearly the voice of destruction speaks,
didn't she? So why wouldn't these pictures pipe up? The
peace of the images, so at odds with the reality of the
precarity the subjects faced, made me want to shout *Look
out!* How could they not know the danger they were in?
When do we ever?

I skipped out on most of the other class trips, melan-
choly, potentially on the verge of a breakdown. And
really, I have very little else to say about my time studying experimental writing; it provided no consolation,
and very little distraction from the pain of everything
I had lost. I had come back to London with less than
I'd left with, which was no mean feat considering the
infinitesimal resources I had taken with me when I
absconded to New York. Here, in London, there were
no tables to dance on, no chance to do three routines

a night and take $200 or $300 home. Living as an illegal alien in New York had pushed me deep into the murky world of cash-in-hand jobs, and all the madness of stripping, posing for questionable photographers, and running illicit tasks. Back in London though, I couldn't ever manifest those pathways. I guess I'd lost my mojo, my magic, my drive – everything I touched had fallen apart. It was a year of pure subsistence. I gave the school's finance office the run-around for months, promising I'd pay the fees the very next week, right up until the point they threatened to lock me out of the studio. Eventually, Jackson, my old law professor roommate from Hope Street, paid the fees for me when his salary cheque cleared with an erroneous extra 'o'. He had grown up Baptist, he said it was obviously a sign, so I was spared one indignity at least, though the school administrators forever regarded me as some sort of international huckster. Clearing this debt should have been a cause for great celebration, but who was there to celebrate with? I couldn't bear to be around people, and when I told my mother about this fluke prosperity over the phone, she said, 'Yeah, and what's he going to expect in return, this *Jackson*?'

From October to December I was starving, hungry and always cold. My means of getting by was to walk around supermarkets filling up a basket of groceries, posing as a casual shopper, while eating as many donuts, croissants and Danish pastries as I could. My trick was to approach the checkout calmly, but whilst waiting in line to suddenly receive an urgent phone call, drop the basket at the register, and dash out saying, 'Oh my God! Where are you now? I'm coming – hold on!'

I met Jovian for tea in Soho one faceless afternoon. He took a quick look at me and said, 'You're not in a good way, are you?' Elsa had told me, too, that I looked too thin; but I took it as a compliment. This return to London was not enlivened by parties with the great and the good, no rubbing shoulders with the literati this time, just months' worth of stolen baked goods, stuffed in my mouth in the supermarket aisles, which Lulu joked probably goes to explain why I can't digest wheat or dairy anymore.

I saw you around a couple of times. Once in Clerkenwell, you walked towards me and I crossed the road before you noticed, and once from a bus window, I saw you cycle past in the opposite direction. I wondered if perhaps you had seen me too, from a distance, or on other occasions, and I decided that it was best to leave the space between us wild and full of strangers. I was deeply, deeply unhappy, broken up about you and broken up about Adam and broken up about having left all my friends in New York.

When I looked around London, with its museum cafe culture, its desperately imitative aesthetics and its thirst for the premium mediocre, where the avant-garde was really just a place for rich kids to tread water until they signed lucrative sponsorship deals, I conceded unconditional defeat. It was a city built to look like some flabby-minded fool's vision of Ancient Greece, with endless allusions to its age-old cultural foes, France and America, dotted about artlessly. In short, a city that could have been built outside Shanghai purely for the purpose of souvenir photographs, and every sham breezeblock reminded me of you. The endlessly lauded YBAs of the nineties had been the overwrought funeral wreath on the city's claim to being a leader of world culture. As the perfect Thatcherite bastards they were, they had skipped all the way to the bank with the loot of radicalism, taking the city's credibility with them. Now all anybody wanted from art was a six-figure salary, and to be guaranteed a reservation at Sexy Fish. Just like Penny Arcade had told us, 'Artists are the new pop stars.'

I acknowledge now that this is probably an unkind view of the capital, unfair and petty, but the impression formed of a city is always more truly a reflection of the inhabitant's state of mind. London was Hell for a time; I despaired of the city, I despaired of school, I despaired of anything you might call creative.

I maintained a dutiful exchange with Robert, or tried to; distance sometimes only makes the heart grow weary. Morgan was always so busy now she was back in California, feeling guilty, maybe feeling relieved. Katie I knew was more of an in-person friend, and Jackson, aside from working occasional financial miracles, could never return an email. Billy and I chatted a lot, from the school computer room, sometimes I spoke with Jonny too, or Eddie even, occasionally with Elsa who was away a lot, working in Sweden, but not you, never you.

I did keep up my peppy correspondence with Finley, though. He was still painting in Berlin. Glad to have me back in Europe, he invited me to stay with him during the Christmas break. At the time you could get a return ticket for €35 in the dead of winter, because Berlin hadn't yet become the sixth borough, the prime location for Scandinavian real estate speculation, the hen party hotspot it is now. The German capital was so underpopulated then it was almost eerie, whole apartment buildings lay empty and abandoned, squats and co-ops were still very common, and anyone who did have to pay for a room paid no more than €300 a month. It was also freezing, colder even than those New York winters, which I had never learned to love.

Finley had just gone through a break-up, he was limp with hopelessness too, so we spent most of our time in bed under three duvets. His boyfriend had been a trauma medic; they broke up because he was just too deeply disturbed by the things he saw on duty to maintain any sort of romantic relationship. Finley said his job consisted mainly of attending to people who had been hit by trains, and giving them huge doses of morphine there on the tracks, to keep them as calm and as comfortable as possible until the train could be reversed off of them. 'At that point though,' he said, 'the wheels are basically all that's holding the body together. When the train backs off, they come completely apart.'

'Yeah,' I said, grimacing. 'That does sound pretty traumatic.'

Finley and I held each other, tried to soothe each other, didn't fuck, barely moved. Although it was my first time in Berlin, I was more than happy to just lie down, warm and sheltered. I didn't have any real desire to find out if there was life outside so the winter weather suited my mood just fine. In hindsight I see now that I must have been very depressed.

On one of the few occasions we did leave the apartment, Finley and I bundled up with practically all the clothes available on his floor. The amassed sweaters, scarves and long johns reminded me of buying donuts late at night in San Francisco. Now, my overwhelming memory of that trip to Berlin is of having completely fallen out of time. Finley showed me a graffiti doodle of a ghost on the wall in his hallway; it had been painted over twice already by the *Hausmeister*. He looked at it quizzically and said, 'I don't know how, but it just keeps coming back.' I didn't know any German then, so all of the language around me, spoken, and written on the few sparse billboards I saw, was completely beyond my comprehension. It was a kind of therapeutic sensory deprivation, I walked next to Finley, numb from the cold, unable to understand barely a thing for the whole week.

Finley lived over in Friedrichshain, in the old Russian East Berlin. The walk to the U-Bahn took us through the neighbourhood some wags had nicknamed Stasi Town. A long white avenue, almost like a Haussmann boulevard, running down towards Frankfurter Tor, flanked on either side by enormous Soviet apartment blocks, solid, square, identical. Before the wall came down, these had been the homes of party members; they were quietly opulent, and deeply oppressive. I felt flattened by their scale, and disorientated by how they seemed to run on into eternity in all directions.

It started to snow very heavily, and suddenly we couldn't see more than our hands in front of our faces, unable to tell which way we were walking, as the snowflakes whirled around us in this endless tunnel of white on white on white. I had the strangest sensa-tion of floating, of having been entirely removed from the clutches of gravity, inside this dizzying isolation booth. Occasionally we were able to glimpse beyond the curtain of snowfall but all we saw was the endless stretch of Soviet buildings, smooth, and offering us no means of knowing if we were still walking in the right direction. I lost sight of Finley even; he had stepped too far ahead, out of my limited field of vision, or maybe I had moved too far ahead of him and he was now behind me? I turned to look, and turned again, but now I couldn't be sure where I had come from and where I was going, so I just stopped walking.

This blizzard picked me up and set me down outside of space, and because time and space are actually space-time, when the snow displaced me physically, it took me outside of temporality too. I entered into eternity, right there in that sentient snow globe. I wondered if this was what death was, white noise and suspension, being outside of everything but simultaneously a part of everything. I can remember feeling that all the people I had loved and lost were there wheeling around my head in the snow, even those who hadn't yet died. I threw my arms open to receive them, to join them, they were everywhere around me, and I was illuminated with a gentle sense of joy reviving. Then Finley's gloved hand broke through my whirling vision. He grabbed my arm and led me into a bakery, to sip a 70c coffee until the weather calmed.

We sat and he said, 'What were you doing out there? Are you crazy? You were just spinning around in the middle of the road!'

'Was I?' I asked confusedly. 'It felt like I was in Heaven.'

IX

That first trip to Berlin intensified the desire, seemingly endless within me, to be gone again, for good. I wanted to keep running without direction, to start again somewhere else unsoiled. Instead I returned begrudgingly to London and school, and all the rush hour shoving, the constant rain, and the maddening chorus on the street, 'Sorry, excuse me, sorry.' I never went to parties, never to the theatre, just back and forth like a phantom, to school, to the supermarket, to bed. Every day the same, yet every day somehow worse.

One afternoon, I came home to my miserable shared apartment, and there was a letter from you waiting on the carpet. It had been maybe four months. No apology of course, no attempt to explain yourself, but a very funny bit about your plan to take a trip to the Deep South in summer. You wrote, *I suppose having survived Russia and Mongolia alone, I should be able to outwit a bunch of inbred evangelical asparagus farmers.* Did I even hazard a smile? I don't know, but I saw something I'd never noticed in your letters before: you wrote in cursive, yes, but in all capitals. If you had asked for forgiveness I would have been bound to give it to you, it's in my restless Catholic blood to forgive anyone who asks to be forgiven and means it. As you hadn't asked, I wasn't obligated, and honestly I was relieved.

I told Adam about the letter next time I saw him, and asked, 'But how did he know my address?'

Adam said, 'I gave it to him, I hope that's alright.'

I was surprised, but not upset. I thought that there was even something sweet, something tender about that, something selfless. But still, I left the letter unanswered.

I was doing my best to repair my friendship with Adam after the turbulence of my return. We were working through things by working on things – art therapy, you might call it. He came into the studio at school and improvised on the violin, underscoring my unwieldy, meandering texts. For my mid-year review Elsa joined us too, to paint me, herself and the stage, whilst I read; we were all three regrouping somewhat, a family healing after estrangements.

Between us we spoke an impenetrable hobgoblin language which we had patched together out of French, English and Italian (only Elsa being fluent in all three) plus some long-standing slang, and plainly fictitious words. We all still called each other Liza, this was the house Polari with which we tried to hold each other close. Of course, now our family had this hairline fracture, and there were some secrets which could only move, like a bishop on a chessboard, along the diagonal, which could never triangulate. Intrigues that almost always concerned you.

In private I told Elsa, 'I feel like such a child, just ignoring his letters, and pretending that I don't see him in the street.'

She was sketching with a notebook on her knee, backlit by the sun. We were in the room she'd moved into, over near Notting Hill. She asked me, 'Why don't you just say a quick hello and then keep on walking?'

'Oh Liza,' I said. 'A single word would be just the start of, I don't know what, but I know it wouldn't be good.'

Looking up from the page, she sighed, 'What is it you both see in him?'

She carried on with her drawing. I chewed a hangnail dolefully, and said, 'I'm too weak, Liza, that's the problem,' and I laid it out for her, as plainly as I could.

'If we spoke one word we'd speak more, and I don't think I have the strength to turn away from him again. He has the morals of an alley cat, and I'm not too far behind him, so I have to handle it this way. I have to role-play a vigour I don't really have.'

She asked, 'What do you mean?'

I said, 'It's just how things are. Adam will always choose Thomas, and ultimately, Thomas will always choose Adam, and if I get in the way I'll lose them both.'

'Men!' she said. 'I always wished I could've been a lesbian.'

'Me too, girl,' I chuckled. 'Me too.'

She told me a story about Brigitte Bardot complete with a very campy impression. How the great sex kitten had announced, 'I gave my youth to men but I give my old age to animals.' She laughed and added, 'That's the way to be, Liza.'

I lay back on her bed, staring at the ceiling, reminding myself that I had to make sure to back up the hard drive of my ailing laptop before it finally gave out. My mother had told me about an article on cyber data she'd read. I didn't know she was so well informed, but she'd given me the stark warning, 'If data doesn't exist in three places, it doesn't exist at all.' It sounded like a line of copy she'd recycled verbatim, but it panicked me into setting up a free online storage account, and buying twenty-quid external hard drive, hoping that these digital amygdalae would keep me safe.

I must've dozed off at some point, because I began dreaming that I was onstage in a top hat and tails, like Dietrich in Morocco, but singing 'Falling in Love Again', a song which I knew came from *The Blue Angel*. Then things took a very strange turn. In my dream I unzipped my fly, and hung the tip of my penis out of the zip. I carried on singing, pulling it out of my trousers only to reveal that it was in fact a sausage, one of a long chain of sausages, which I pulled out though my fly link by link, eventually draping the pork and beef around my neck, like a boa. I found this image simultaneously disturbing, and very amusing, and woke myself laughing. Elsa was no longer in the room, she must have slipped off to make a cup of tea or call her mother, but on the pillow next to me was the sketch she'd been drawing. It was a picture of my sprawling, languid self on her bed, which she had titled, *Liza in repose*.

X

It feels especially cruel that when you died (when you went out like that – like a light), you didn't take everything with you; you linger in your emails and your hand-scrawled notes. And what are we supposed to do now? All of this writing won't turn the light back on, no matter how long we sit under the bare bulb and pray. Instead the dubious treasure trove you left taunts me, tempts me to crack it open and revile myself further: *Why did I say that? How did I misunderstand what is written there clear as day?* And when I read over my own letters, those I wrote to you in candour, which found their way back to me after your death, I feel almost compelled to burn them, to hide my well-earned shame.

I can remember vividly the last time we spoke, or rather the last time we had anything that could be considered a two-way conversation, and even then only just. It was in Peckham, my first and only trip. I was running late to see the new company that Leo had created with Elsa and Adam and everyone else. They were performing at a gallery opening, it was around March maybe, a few months after my trip to Berlin, and your unacknowledged letter. I had been held back at school, in a very heated group crit which dragged on way past six, and to compound my troubles I had taken the wrong train from London Bridge. In Peckham I then walked in the wrong direction for twenty minutes before I realised, almost as if I didn't want to arrive at the gallery. Several people had shouted unkind things at me, and now distanced from the insults, I wonder, *Why is abuse from strangers always so unoriginal?*

It was getting dark, even before I arrived, and I was irate with myself for being so incapable of even the simplest of missions. I hustled down the high street, hoping that the performance had been delayed, willing the venue to reveal itself to me sooner rather than later, there amongst all the vegan fast-food joints and beauty supply stores.

The psychic I opens on our final scene.

When I finally find the gallery I'm amazed to see how empty it is. I walk about the virtually forsaken space, through one room to the next, circling the lonely sculptures, and only slowly realising that there is another area, outside at the back of the building. I still feel uneasy in social situations, but I follow the murmur of the crowd all the same. Out here it's a scrum, elbow to elbow, a few hundred people in a big concrete courtyard watching our friends writhing on ten square metres of scaffold, lit by macabre red lights. They are all here, Adam, Elsa, Lulu, Leo, on their makeshift stage, mouthing the words to a show tune, played at half-speed so the lyrics sound like they are being sung by a chorus of Satanic voices all slurred on ketamine. Ticker tape is being fired off, and tinsel is being thrown about, and it's immediately clear that I am witnessing the finale. I can see the climax has been reached before my arrival, and all that's left for me is the slow deflation of manic egos, the waves of congratulations which I'll have to bend to, or else risk seeming disinterested, or jealous.

I notice something odd about one of the lights. At first it seems like a badly focused spot, but then I realise it is actually the light from a bedroom window, glowing from behind the performers. The disgruntled residents, I presume homophobic (but maybe that's projecting too much?), are heckling the cast. The leotards, their wigs and fishnets, and their big red overdrawn mouths are a particular provocation. I can't hear the people up there, but they're passionate. Mounted up high, outlined in bold by their window frames, they look like silent movie stars, gesticulating wildly and without reserve. I'm watching the angry neighbours throughout the curtain call (there are no curtains but convention still demands). They are pouring something out from their window, splattering the performers with, what is it? Milk? Water? Piss? For a second I am afraid, acknowledging how high up they are, how treacherous the scaffold is, how long the drop. By the time the performers have all safely disembarked from the shaky stage my heart is in my mouth, right up there with a rising feeling of panic, and something like agoraphobia at the sight of such a crowd after spending so long in relative social isolation.

It's cold, so the applause is briefer than seems fair, and quite quickly the whole tide of the audience turns towards me and the direction I had come in. They're intent on hurrying back inside, to the slightly warmer embrace of the exhibition space. I cast about for Elsa or Adam, or Lulu, to present myself and prove my existence, to show that I am a good, faithful friend. Instead, almost comically, I collide with you. You, wheeling your bike through the dispersing crowd; you, lit in the grisly red floodlights. You don't say hello, of course, you just get to the point directly, you go straight for the kill.

'So this is how it is eh, Bibby?' you say.

Not meeting your eye, I reply, 'How what is?'

'I see, I see,' you continue, aiming for enigmatic but landing on inelegant. 'This is how it is.'

'Whatever,' I say, knowing you hate my Americanisms as much as I hate your likely lad affectations.

'So you're just gonna take what you want and that's it, is it?' you say. 'Not going to call, not going to ask how I am? I see. I see how it is.'

And you say this seriously, as if you yourself hadn't pushed me into this bitter corner.

Time is all mixed up now, elements from disparate eras of my life rush in too often and colour the scene. Because as a child I was crazy about the Doris Day movie *Calamity Jane*, but couldn't work the VHS player, each time I watched it I started in a different place, and now all the narrative is wiped in favour of freewheeling images and arbitrary musical moments. Let me begin again. Because I once cooked a vegan chilli whilst listening to a documentary on Georgian London, any time I eat aubergines I think of the Prince Regent sitting out the battle of Waterloo. Place me. And every time I hear Streisand, I expect to find myself waking up in a make-up chair, shaken from a dream by Morgan. Looping, looping, looping.

Many, many memories have likewise been restored to me partially corrupted, but this night, this sorry occasion in Peckham, I can see with such clarity, it could be an insect preserved in amber. Back now.

People peel past us, knocking your bike. You hiss, 'Cunts.'

'What do you want from me, Thomas?' I ask with shotgun honesty.

And it's like watching you die in my arms; I feel I could buckle under the weight of your body, fall to my knees covered in your blood. That familiar look of pain is plastered on your face, the same one you'd worn when you had realised I was planning to leave for California without telling you, the same one you'd worn when you asked, 'Why didn't you get into bed with me then?', when you told me, 'I don't like him touching you.'

Yet, there's some wicked glee mixed in with the hurt, isn't there? It shimmers in your infernal blue eyes. You're like a fiend returned, like one of Catherine Deneuve's skeletal ex-lovers in *The Hunger*, rising up from a coffin to avenge themselves. It's scary yes, it's grievous, but more than anything, it's just very sad.

You say, 'No, I see how it is, Bibby. I see how it is.'

I turn on my heel and leave.

I forget my desire to see Elsa, or Adam or Lulu, or Leo. I leave them all to the night, and to the photographers, and to packing up their kit, and rinsing the water or milk, or whatever it was, from their costumes. I go straight out through the gallery, looking directly ahead. In my peripheral vision I can see people waving to me, but I do not stop. Outside I can already see the rain starting to fall, and all of those people along the street from the gallery to the train station, waiting to jeer me. I can see the arduous journey back home on a Friday night full of insensitive drunks nudging their friends, chuckling, goading each other to ask, 'Eh mate, are you a woman?', and laughing wildly. I can see my scarlet cheeks, aflame with shame and anger and a desire to kill, and I can't see an end to any of it. And above all this, as I hurry through the oncoming drizzle, towards my flat on the bad side of King's Cross, I see, superimposed over everything else, your face, illuminated in that gruesome crimson, with your tensed mouth muttering, 'So that's how it is, eh Bibby?'

It's a vision that has always haunted me.

XI

I could have chosen to stop writing by now. I should leave it here, wrapping the story up with this last encounter, our final slanging match, the conclusion for which we were always headed; but I can't. I'm not ready to finish yet, I'm not ready to let go, because I know that with this book I will kill you, for good.

When Virginia Woolf's beloved brother died of typhoid, she kept him alive by writing in her letters that he was recovered and slurping chicken broth, that he'd be up and about before Christmas, although he'd been dead for a month. I think what I'm feeling now, this impulse to write onwards, is something similar, a comparable strategy, a traumatic response, though heavily delayed. A recondite sorrow which can only be expressed through the rigour of putting words on the page.

I can't stop writing yet because until I put it down on paper, the accident hasn't happened, and I feel obliged to be with you at the end this time. Your death has become the fault line that runs through me, it's the hard border that breaks my life into two halves, *before* and *after*, and you have ever since remained 'the most plaintive and poignant of a line of ghosts'.

It is ten years since we met, six years since we last spoke, four years since your death, and I still grieve for you. I had lost people before you and I have lost people since you but somehow your loss has proven the hardest to bear. Harder than my dear old Nanny who loved me without condition, harder than Martin who died instantly of a heart attack on the studio floor, harder than my neighbour Johnathan who overdosed, or little Charlie dead of a brain tumour at eleven years old, harder than Brian who walked out in front of a train, harder than Rachel who died alone at Christmas, and harder than Auntie Viv, who went out resplendent like a saint with the family all around her.

The night before I left London for good, before I took the trip which brought me to Mexico City, I went to a private view in Bethnal Green. It was a show of new images by the photographer you had worked for. There was one enormous central image of the ocean, where the border of two nations met on water, large photographs of empty desks, and sculptural foliage, and then, there at the back, amongst a series of 4x6s tacked to the wall, was your beautiful grinning face. Truly our lives do not belong to us, they do not belong to the future, or to the possibilities tomorrow might bring, no, they belong to the dead. And when I think of that small company of dancers, comprised of the fallen whom I have loved, you are still the premier danseur noble, they your corps de ballet.

When did you know you were dead?

The day I found out, I understood what grief was, grief that is not sorrow. The other deaths in my life had been accompanied by a sadness, which was right and just. I could accept that old age and suicide and cancer were all logical conclusions to human existence, horrible yes, but understandable. But your death was unscripted, it came out of nowhere, in the middle of so much, and it cut me up so badly that the scars are now a distinguishing feature of mine.

The day I found out you were dead I finally understood the Prince song, where he cries for Tracy because he wants to see him again. Previously I'd always thought it was an unnatural, selfish sentiment, creepy even. When Auntie Viv was nearing the end, with my mother weeping at her bedside, saying, 'I don't want you to go!', Viv, propped up on pillows, already laid out in state, replied, 'If you knew the pain I was in, love, you wouldn't ask me to stay.' I agreed with Viv, and her right to bodily autonomy, and it was a rational death. But when you died I cried for Tracy too, because you'd gone out without knowing it, without needing it, with so much left unsaid. I didn't care that it was a greedy desire and I didn't care that I had no right to it, because that's what grief is, as all-consuming as a drug addiction.

The day I found out you were dead I wept like you can only weep once, doubled over in the emergency brace position, gasping for breath in between heaving sobs, dragging myself up to standing, clinging to the wall retching. And after that passed came the long slow blindsiding numbness, and then this desperation, almost a mania to see you again, which has never really gone away. Ultimately I suppose that's why I have written this, so that I might see you once again, clearly and wholly. I've tried to reform the molten glass of memory, blow it, shape it, and take the diamond-tipped cutter's tool to it, so that I have you forever, cut in crystal. Though now I hold it in my hands, I see how this figure refracts the light and obscures everything behind it.

In the months following your death, I started compiling a list of all the times I had avoided you, willing myself to reimagine each of these as the site of a beautiful reconciliation. I began having conversations with you out loud, I told you what I thought of you, I called you a rotten cunt, I asked you for forgiveness, I pictured you naked and splayed on your bed besmirched with my semen, I saw you vividly, dancing (badly) in one of your stupid outfits, saw you smirk, 'Come on then,' saw you spit, 'I see how it is Bibby.' Of course I became obsessed by the thought that it was my fault, that if we'd have been on better terms you might have been somewhere else that evening, or that at least I might have been with you when it happened. Maybe I'd have saved you, maybe I'd be dead too, or maybe I'd have been the one kneeling over you as the light faded from your eyes, gripping your collar and whimpering, 'I don't want you to go.'

You had been dead for fifteen hours by the time I knew it. Why hadn't I felt it when it happened? Why hadn't I dropped whatever I was holding, knowing something was wrong? Why hadn't you come to tell me you were leaving? That photograph of you dead in the street, awaiting the powerless paramedics. I have still never seen it, but I have spent a long time imagining how you looked lying there. I want to picture you peaceful, still, and still gorgeous, like Evelyn McHale, the world's most beautiful suicide. That eerie black and white photo, which shows the twenty-something's lovely body in repose, one gloved hand holding her pearls as if taken by surprise. Her mouth and eyes are closed, her shoes are off, her stockings rolled down and her skirt hitched just above the knee. She has thrown herself off the Empire State Building, but if it weren't for the crumpled roof of the car her body lies on, and the broken glass scattered around her, you would think this woman is simply tanning her legs on her lunch break. The passive prettiness of Evelyn McHale, now beyond whatever pain had brought her here, this pure, iconic loss of an innocent, is surely what Edgar Allan Poe was driving at, when he said that the death of a beautiful woman is the most poetic thing in the world. Which is maybe why it doesn't work so well for you.

I torture myself with gruesome images of you bloody and unrecognisable, split open, disfigured by the violence of your death. I think about that fine body broken, the blond hair caked with brain matter, the blue eyes filled with blood. You appear to me torn apart and spilling your insides out, like Zola's Nana reduced to 'a shovel-ful of corrupted flesh'. And my basest instincts stirring in me the desire to see you again, hold you again, fuck you again, make me into one of Nana's cigar-smoking lovers, not with her at the end, but outside her window, decrying the waste of pleasure her sorry end consti-tutes. I force myself to stare at this nightmare image, the same way I forced myself to stare straight at the blood-ied, suffering, crucified Christ above the altar when, as a child, I prayed. I refuse to allow myself to look away, I insist that the truth of the agony be acknowledged, be respected.

Even as I try to form these images, the final picture of your life, I'm aware of the process by which image becomes icon, how one picture, even on a page, can become the repository for a person's whole life. I don't want to do this to you, I don't want to take you as Warhol took Ms McHale and screen-print the life out of you, but I know that just as memory is created by the act of remembering, so is the story created by the storytelling. From this point in time I'm seeking to represent the reality of a life (though not a death) I witnessed; but the wicked medium I've chosen, this narrative prose, has more power than me, the writer, and will go on to replace the reality it sought to represent. Perhaps that's why I didn't ever ask to see that conclusive photograph, because it would reduce you to one devastating finality and I want to resist that. Recently I saw the remarkable short, *Reality Fragment 160921*, and a certain line in it grabbed me: 'I will never be able to remember you accurately, but infinitely.' *Yes*, I thought, *that is how it should be.*

My friend Moritz lost his father around the same time you died. His dad was not a very nice man either. We bonded over much shared grief, and a lot of hash, sitting in his bed making extremely tasteless jokes, getting very stoned and watching whatever came up next on YouTube. At some point he showed me a video he'd made when he was twenty, of himself in his first apartment in Cologne, lying back against a wall painted aquamarine, masturbating. He's completely naked in the video, he's smoking a cigarette, there's no sound on the tape. Bette Davis said that silent movies always had a dream atmosphere to them, and I think she's right. The Moritz in the video looked like the Moritz I knew, only not so furry and with much more hair product, perhaps a little slimmer, definitely paler, though that could have been just a trick of the light too.

There's a lava lamp on the bedside table, and a radio alarm clock, everything looks fantastically ancient, the way the recent past always does, and the footage is terribly poignant. He skilfully exhales a curl of cigarette smoke, the fingers of his left hand snake down towards his pink hole, and slip inside. His cock gets very hard, he fucks himself with a flesh-coloured dildo, rides it for close to thirty minutes, before, sticky-faced, he unloads thick wads of cum; it spurts up like a baroque fountain of pleasure, and he licks his fingers clean.

Throughout he has made constant eye contact, as though the camera were the lover for whom he was performing, so now we have this unedited record of his twenty-year-old self, his lust for life, and his desire to be seen long into the future. The video acts like a time capsule, it's as if he had the foresight to say, 'When I'm sixty I'll be glad to look back on this.' It's a covenant with eternity, an act of queer futurity, a generous offer to curious unknown voyeurs of the future, inviting them to take pleasure in the display of this willing, wanting body. It's a cinematic expression of Walt Whitman's suggestion that maybe the grass is just the chest hair of young men (whom he may have loved, if he had known) and I want so badly for you to have just such a future.

So I doom myself to wander on.

XII

After our run-in, I tried to keep a low profile for the rest of the school year. When I summoned up the spirit to socialise again I was careful only to go out in West London, to arts clubs and members-only joints, boring places where Elsa's model agency had arrangements. I wanted to stay clear of the South and the East, and of you, so I ended up in places where I had nothing in common with the other guests, getting paralytic on a series of anonymous bar tabs.

During an argument once, my mother told me that I live my life like a sunbather in the park, forever moving the blanket to chase the sun, desperate to catch just another five minutes of self-indulgence before twilight. I think she's right. I have chased every high, every dopamine hit, every good time I could get, I have decried my most heartfelt desires as the hallucinations of a drug-addled brain, I have tried to outrun myself indefinitely, but still life has led me here. The inevitability of it all.

My memories of that last semester at Saint Martins are as blurry as any I made in San Francisco or New York, a smear of selfies in the bathroom of Sketch, of men in white button-down shirts and too much cologne asking, *Did anyone ever tell you you look just like…*; of Elsa singing the Queen of the Night aria wherever she found a hallway with good reverb. In this idiotic miasma, of goofing off and smoking too much weed with an obnoxious photographer I had met on the night bus, I parsed out my time, and I believed that I was beginning to see the light at the end of the tunnel.

I took a trip with Finley to Greece, whilst I should really have been at work on my thesis, figuring that the Mediterranean, though East, should be far enough beyond your reach. It was an early summer holiday, funded by some money my mother gave me when she remortgaged the house, and by the proceeds of a painting Finley had sold. We met in Athens, buoyant in the June sun, a world away from the blizzard of sadness we'd shared in Berlin. We ate, we drank, we picked up boys in Zappeion Park and barely slept. Even when we were in bed we were either gossiping or fooling around. I sent Morgan a picture of the two of us in a naked, drunken embrace, tagged with 'We Miss U!!!!'

She replied archly, 'Have you two ever heard of *platonic* friendships?'

Finley and I took a ferry and swam off the coast of Agistri, where we found a beautiful beach, empty besides one sun-bronzed dyke, topless in a visor. We took off our swim shorts and declared that this strip of sand was now a gay nudist beach. I think we even planted a flag (my Madonna T-shirt tied to a plank of driftwood) to make it official, but there wasn't really enough of a breeze to make it flutter.

It was an outrageously hot day, we had slogged across the island at noon to find a place to swim, and so throwing ourselves about in the turquoise Mediterranean was wonderfully reviving. We splashed each other for a while, pissed about running in and out of the sea, so as to feel the sun scorch our arses and have the water kiss it better. Although I had grown up in Liverpool and had come of age in San Francisco, I had never before swum in the ocean. Both Northern England and Northern California have beaches, of course, but the water is cold, and polluted. On family holidays I had splashed in Spanish swimming pools maybe, or paddled ankle-deep in Welsh rockpools, but I had never been out in the open water. Never been taken by that azure expanse, carried off my feet and out towards the horizon, and allowed to feel the freedom that only floating on your back in the ocean can offer.

The weightlessness felt like a bump of aircraft turbulence, only much more pleasant, like the split-second or so you are out of your seat, but still belted in. An almost ghostly feeling of gliding without propulsion, lingering over a fathomless drop when there is nowhere to fall, most definitely present in the world, but still outside it, endless stasis yes, but in motion. This effortless rise and fall on the waves took me back to the New Year's Eve I spent in a hotel pool in New York, performing as a rococo nymph. Once more I felt that the temporary defiance of gravity's rule was also excusing me from existing in time. I wondered, *if one could float forever would one live forever?* It was like that familiar sensation in which I had delighted as an adolescent, of skipping out of school early and without permission, stepping into a world strange and delicious. Like walking onto an empty theatre set, like a snowstorm, like returning to the womb, being the first one awake on Christmas morning, or coming to in someone else's life. For fear of burning under the hungry Greek sun, Finley and I swam back to shore to reapply some SPF.

As we emerged glistening and pinkish from the water, Finley shrieked, and said, 'Oh my God! JJ! What the fuck happened?'

When I looked down I saw that my left leg, from the knee to the foot, was covered in raised red welts, where I had obliviously become entangled with a jellyfish. I hadn't felt it before I saw it, it hadn't hurt at all, and so seeing must surely be believing, because it immediately became very painful.

I was hopping about, still naked, not knowing if I should dress or not, rest or run back to Athens, yelping, but not really distressed. The topless woman who was sharing our beach came over, attracted by the commotion; she was smoking a cigarette, shaking her head and tutting. She said something in French, but neither of us understood what she meant until she pantomimed it, and I said to Finley, 'I think she's saying you should piss on me.'

'Oui!' she exclaimed, pivoting emphatically between Finley's junk and my disfigured leg. 'Pissez sur lui!'

So he did, he pissed down my leg as the topless French lady finished her fag, looking on to ensure that we did as we were told. If anything I was quite thrilled, isn't that sick? Maybe I missed my calling as a masochist. My first swim in the ocean, my first jellyfish sting, it seemed like a good thing, that I'd been kissed by Mother Nature, and in kissing me below the knee she'd spared me a lot of the pain that she might've unfurled higher up. The throb of the jellyfish sting flooded me with adrenaline and endorphins, and the rest of the vacation passed in a steady flow of mastic ice cream, late-afternoon strolls through antiquity, and obscene flirtations with desperately handsome Greek boys. The wounds themselves lingered briefly, as strawberry flecks of temporary discolouration along my calf and shin bone, then after a fortnight they were gone. I hardly thought about it afterwards, and when I did it was with a smile, because it made me feel very alive.

But that was my life before you died, when I was robust enough to laugh this sort of thing off. Since your death, every slip, or trip, or coughing fit, makes me so painfully aware that we live on borrowed time, and any moment, really any moment, could wipe us out without warning. Last month, I was travelling in Jalisco when a stranger held out his arm and prevented me from stepping on a scorpion in my sandals.

'Gracias!' I exclaimed, petrified.

'They don't kill you,' he said, 'but it hurts.'

I clutched at my neck in panic and asked, 'How much?'

He shrugged, 'It depends how much pain you can take.'

I thought I would puke with fear, but it wasn't the sting I was afraid of, not really. What truly scared me was how close I had come to an accident without knowing it. The nearness of the scorpion, standing in for the nearness of death, an anxious fear ever present these past four years.

When I got back from Greece, I had tanned for the first time in my life, and Elsa told me that you'd left on your trip to Appalachia. I felt safe enough, knowing that I wouldn't run into you, to venture back over to our old haunts in the East End. I surely couldn't have returned without the assurance that you were gone. We went to see Adam perform in some little club space in Mile End; he said he was trying to make some text-based performance work. *Naturally*, I thought, perhaps a little unkindly, perhaps still a little sore.

Adam was playing violin in a huge skirt made from musical scores; he was shirtless for a balanced silhouette. His face was bleached with pressed powder, and his muscular torso was smeared too thickly in white face paint, as if to make tasteful his flaunted sex appeal by degrading his lovely face and body. He played a collage of original compositions, some refrains from pop standards, some Ligeti, and a few snatches of Bernard Herrmann's *Vertigo* theme – in between, he delivered snatches of the poetic wandering texts he'd written. He played in the round, turning slowly to face the full circumference of the audience, moving at a butoh pace, giving his muscular shoulders and back to the audience for long stretches. It was only when he turned one final time in my direction that I saw his face was streaked with tears. He set aside his violin and sang a very plaintive version, a cappella, of the Chet Baker standard, 'I Get Along Without You Very Well'. I understood then that your departure for America was the moment we were all marking here, and felt a little resentful, damn me for my pettiness.

After the performance I sat with Adam as he wet-wiped off the clown white. His eyes were very red, he was withdrawn, I couldn't understand why he had put himself through that.

'He'll be back, Liza,' I said, misunderstanding things as always.

He started to cry again, very quietly, and I realised that this was an exorcism, not a *bon voyage* party; he was trying to rid himself of you for good. He was utilising Chet Baker to manifest this vision of a new life, the song was his spell, his version of *I just won't be ticklish anymore*, he was using the words 'I Get Along Without You Very Well' to make it so.

'Oh,' I said, as the penny dropped. 'Is there someone else?'

'Several,' he said.

'Oh Liza,' I sighed, but I did not feel vindicated, only very sorry for all three of us.

I pitied the lot of us, because it seemed clear that this was still far from over. Even then, watching Adam summon up the full strength of this resolution to banish you, seeing him brim with sorrow and hatred, and swear he'd never see you again, I knew it was untrue. I'm sure he knew it too. He couldn't go on with the way you lied to him, treated him, fucked him about, but then he couldn't go on without you either. It was the eternal lover's bind. Paul Preciado puts it nicely: 'Couples are governed by a law of quantum physics according to which there is no opposition between contrary terms, but rather a simultaneity of dialectical facts.' Though maybe Erasure were more succinct when they sang, 'Love to hate you'.

'Maybe you could work something out?' I said, cringing even as I spoke the words.

'How?' he asked, looking incredulous, looking angry, striking a tone which I didn't respond to at all well.

Exasperated I said, 'If you're going to love someone, you have to love them for who they *actually* are!' But I immediately regretted it. It sounded so patronising, what right did I have?

You would come back after two or three months, with a tan of your own and a chipped front tooth which made you sexier than ever, but then Satan was always the most beautiful of all God's angels. The two of you would fall back together, just as surely as a right-wing government replaces a left-wing government, you'd make your pledges to be a better man, he'd go to great pains to help you heal yourself, and I'd watch from the sidelines, hear it on the grapevine, grateful at least that from the shadows, I had come to some understanding of it all.

As I left Adam's little makeshift dressing room that night, he was trying to put a happy face on things, talking to some well-wishers who had barged in: a boy who was crushing on him, and someone or another from a record label who was raving about the purity and beauty of Chet Baker's voice.

'Is he still alive?' asked someone in the party.

Adam shook his head, 'He died in the eighties. Heroin overdose.'

'No he didn't,' someone else corrected, 'he fell out of a hotel window.'

XIII

When I heard that you had been killed I was more or less inconsolable, not that there was anyone at hand to offer consolation. My new boyfriend was out and I didn't much like his roommate. It was a year and a half since I'd seen you at the gallery, an age since we'd fought over my notebook, decades since we'd shared gonorrhoea, a lifetime since we'd met. After calling Adam to confirm that what I'd read was true, I simply fell back on the bed in a ball of blistering sorrow. I was home alone all day, I cried until I was hoarse then fell back to sleep, streaked with snot. When I woke the room was dark and my phone was ringing, the number was unlisted, I was afraid and confused. I hung up but the call came again, and again, and I started to think that maybe this was all just a horrible joke, that you were calling me from a payphone in Belarus to say, 'Don't be like that, Bibbs, I was just taking the piss.'

So I answered, with trepidation, but of course it wasn't you. It was Morgan. She said, 'Oh my God. I just heard. Oh my God are you OK? I've been trying to call you for hours. I'm so sorry, are you OK? This is so awful, I'm so sorry. I know how much you loved him. I'm so sorry.'

I didn't attend your funeral, instead I went to Istanbul, with this new boyfriend I had, who always thought that getting away from it all was the answer to everything. I wasn't amongst the mourners who put you in the ground. I didn't meet your parents, I didn't offer condolences, or pocket tissues to the stranger sitting next to me, or greet once-familiar faces with the standard-issue line about how sad it was to meet again *under such unhappy circumstances.*

I stayed in Istanbul, that seat of three empires, for almost the whole of the autumn. I tried to find solace in a city that seemingly never ended, seemingly staked a claim on eternity with even more credulity than Rome. The apartment we had was on Istiklal, the pedestrianised heart of the city. It afforded a beautiful view of the neighbourhood, the holy domes and the Galata Tower, which became my cynosure in the city, the beacon by which I found my way home. The tower has been standing since the fourteenth century; it once housed the mechanics that controlled the great sea chain which defended the Golden Horn from enemy vessels, and they say that a seventeenth-century inventor leapt from the observation deck and glided across the Bosporus on a pair of artificial wings. To me it always looked like Leonora Carrington's *Tower of Nagas* rising up from the waters of the past into the pink and blue smoke of the future. All the funny little monsters dotted in front of the painted tower seemed so fittingly medieval, borrowed from a Bosch even, standing in for all the odd characters, the tourists, the beggars, the old men spitting out the husks of sunflower seeds who now populated the surrounding Galata plaza.

Most evenings I sat smoking endless joints, glued to the TV news stations, as they described in relentless detail the latest manoeuvres of ISIS. Probably the most infamous crimes committed by the Sunni militants, in an expansively appalling catalogue of atrocities, even more shocking than the wilful destruction of libraries, temples and Assyrian statues, were their executions of gay men. In front of TV cameras, these men, blindfolded and with their hands bound, were thrown from the roofs of tall buildings and if they didn't die on impact, they were stoned to death on the ground by a leering mob. Truly the death of Christ himself could not have been more pitiful. I watched these murders over and over, the news media was in love with them, because they offered the perfect chance to showcase the liberal values which wars were allegedly being fought to defend, and simultaneously to revel in the sight of bloody, homophobic violence. I can't say if it was pity, or a morbid fascination that kept me watching, maybe a sense of connection I couldn't feel any other way. Strangely, even though I was now in a country which bordered the Islamic State caliphate, I felt no closer to the war; it was all mediated through the cold spectacle of the screen. Sitting in front of the TV, stoned and goggle-eyed, this is what I did, leapling, while our friends said goodbye to you.

I stayed away from your funeral out of cowardice, out of shame. I had the ridiculous fear that people would scorn me and say, 'How dare you show your face here?', that they'd despise me for having ignored you, for having wasted my chance to be reconciled, and now you were gone. I was also paranoid enough to think that, as our separation had been so ugly and hardly private, I'd arrive and find the door slammed in my face, like Queen Caroline at George IV's coronation. And anyway what right did I have to be there?

Adam was the official widow. Even Maria Callas had enough dignity to stay away when they buried Aristotle Onassis. I wasn't present for the ceremony which officially recognised your passing, I wasn't there for the funeral rites, I didn't come dressed in black to kiss your coffin, but here, with this book I bury you.

When I got back to London it was late November. It was one of those freakishly warm weeks with which we are now unfortunately becoming so familiar, and the temperature allowed me a gentler return from Istanbul than I might have expected. I made a point of calling in on Jovian, who always felt like Father Confessor to me, like the Friar who married Romeo to Juliet in secret. Maybe I wanted his forgiveness for missing the funeral, maybe I wanted to hear him describe it, though I couldn't bear to ask him my questions about who had been there, and who had cried loudest.

He had always lived in the same apartment, a few minutes away from the Joiners, a dark one-bedroom place behind a row of shops, which was stacked practically floor to ceiling with VHS tapes. You and I had spent many long hours there, watching pop culture thinkers spar on late-night TV.

Jovian asked me how I was.

'OK,' I said.

He gave me his solace, but cynically, I couldn't help feeling that to him, this was another perfect twist in the clubland autobiography he was never going to write, another hardship he could share with the chat show hosts he'd never encounter, another sorrow endured on his long, slow climb to the top. I couldn't otherwise explain the faraway look in his eyes, how he seemed to be addressing an unseen cinematographer rather than me.

He asked how Adam had taken it.

'Badly,' I said. 'I'm seeing him later tonight. For the first time.'

'For the first time, since...' he asked.

'Yes,' I answered, and felt full of disgrace.

I should've been there to hold Adam's hand at the funeral, to help him shoulder the loss, but what could it matter now? Life went on whether you liked it or not. I started to cry just a little, and Jovian, never desperately comfortable with physical touch, put his arm around me awkwardly and whispered, 'I know, I know. It's a terrible thing...'

He broke off for a moment, I didn't know if he was about to cry himself, or retch. He looked strangely blank, pale, panicked, and when he continued, the real sentiment became clear. He was all adrift, he wasn't ghostwriting his memoir, he was lost.

He said, 'I keep thinking to myself, we have today and he doesn't. We have this morning and Thomas doesn't.'

I wept for just a minute longer, for you and everything we'd have to live without now. I thanked Jovian for his understanding. He handled grief with a great reverence; that's not to say flashy, but with a sombre understanding of the duties to be performed. He was after all like me, from that old Irish Catholic stock. As I was back in London now, we talked about seeing each other more regularly, but I don't think either of us had any real desire for that anymore, or the faith that it would be so. We said, 'We must get together again soon,' only to formalise the agreement that we never would. I cast a parting glance over all the video tapes, *Cher on Wogan '91*, *Bowie Cracked Actor*, *Dynasty Season 6 Pt2*, and left his apartment that afternoon, with an image of us – you, me and Jovian – eating M&Ms on the couch, watching late-night TV, knowing that moment would never come again.

I met Adam that evening on the bridge at the bottom of Broadway Market. It was still very warm, in fact I sweated slightly in my black angora sweater. When Adam arrived on his bike, he was all in black too. He was wearing a fluffy cardigan; we must've looked like two giant grieving *Sesame Street* puppets. We didn't talk at first, but we held each other and cried, his sobs becoming more and more violent until it seemed as though he would shake apart. I remember the weight of his body in my arms on the bridge as I struggled to keep us both upright. I pressed him closer to me, to show him I was strong enough, that I could take it, but also to protect him from the small group of boys who had gathered on the corner. They were laughing, making fun of him.

'I'm sorry, Liza,' I said, 'I'm so sorry.'

He looked up, his eyes bloodshot, big blue bags underneath, sitting sharp and hollow against his deathly white skin, his face stained with tears, chin smeared with thin pale mucus. He took control of himself, dabbed at his face with a tissue, coughed, seemed almost to collapse again, then pulled himself up, like a drunk who has decided enough is enough.

He said, 'That's it, Liza. That's the end of our youth.'

Where were you when Kennedy was shot? Do you remember the fall of the Berlin Wall? Your death had become a moment like that, already, a moment like the moon landings, or 9/11 or Princess Diana's death, a bookmark in time, caged in speculation: *before* and *after*. Let me begin again.

He asked, 'Do you want to come back to the flat?'

I recoiled, and spluttered, 'To Thomas's flat?'

'Yes,' he said, quite calm now. 'His parents thought it would be a good idea for me to take over the lease.'

I couldn't picture Adam living anywhere besides that apartment in Waterloo; it was almost beyond comprehension that he would've moved anywhere, but moving into that place, your place, seemed especially fantastical.

'But what about your flat?' I asked.

'The landlord wanted to sell it,' he said. 'It just worked out this way.'

We walked back through Haggerston, through Bethnal Green, through Whitechapel, the three of us: me, him, and the bike.

'Funny weather,' he said, and that nonchalant aside, that casual bit of small talk, made me feel afraid, paranoid, like this was all a set-up, even. Through a cold sweat, I began to feel that this scene, the two of us going back to your apartment together, was unavoidable now, the inescapable end point, the inevitability of it all. I was being forced there in the same way the eye is forced, by disciplined perspective and the stark white of a tablecloth, towards the diminutive, haloed Christ in the background of Tintoretto's *Marriage at Cana*. No, there was to be no turning away now.

I expected the apartment to be a gruesome mausoleum, icy, the rank smell of decomposing flesh spilling from underneath the front door, the furniture beginning to cobweb. I half wondered if I would find you laid out on your bed, stiff and vacant. Adam led the way, and I followed up the stairs as I had always done, but when he slipped the key into the lock it all became too much and I gasped, 'I can't.' He took me by the hand and led me inside. Place me.

And it was so startlingly clean, and new, and tidy-looking. Everything had been organised, everything was in place, everything was so meticulously presented that I wondered if Adam was maybe putting it on the market. It was such a sterling, effective change, a total remodelling of an atmosphere I thought could never be renovated. I felt as though I were in the penultimate scene of *American Psycho*, comic and uncanny. Having prepared myself to walk into a charnel house, I instead stepped into *World of Interiors*. Adam dropped his bag on the couch and went directly into your bedroom, his bedroom now, I suppose.

I lingered in the doorway, unable to cross the threshold without an invitation. Adam beckoned, 'Come in.'

Back now.

My eyes are already brimming. I step into the bedroom, on a wave of perspiration and nausea. I want to steady myself but I can't bear to touch anything, for fear it might be coated in some slime or ectoplasm. It's like walking into an empty museum, or the Paris Catacombs after hours, looking about the place by torchlight, afraid of what you might glimpse next. I want to sit down but there's only the chair at Adam's neatly cluttered desktop or your bed, the source of all this trouble.

Let me begin again.

The dimensions of the room are the only thing that remain the same, everything else is gone, has been replaced or rearranged. Where is all of your stuff? The VHS tapes, the stuffed owls, the dirty pictures? I feel Joan Didion's indignation swelling up in me, *What if he comes back?* Wouldn't you need it all; all your stupid outfits and your broken cameras?

I notice that Adam has also put up a working set of blinds. At first I feel there's something disrespectful in this, but on reflection, I accept that it's ultimately a peaceful gesture, a new solution to an old problem. I can remember seeing Dominik Lang's *Sleeping City* a few years later and having the exact same feeling again, seeing how he'd repurposed his late father's studio as a sculpture, as an installation. I was crying then too. I turn my back to Adam, pause for breath, my hands clutching my own shoulders, my head down. He says, 'Liza?' and when I turn I see that he's offering me a plastic packet of papers, holding them towards me, with the same gesture employed to serve legal documents. They're my letters to you, all of them.

You always seemed so careless, so haphazard, I thought by now for sure they'd be long gone down the back of the sofa, in the bin, left on a table in a pub, but you'd saved them because they meant something to you, and this final realisation, of the longevity of your love, makes me crumple up completely. It's too much. I want to leave. I wish I had never come. I turn towards the open door, but the room stretches out before me like an endless black corridor. I take a step towards the living room, unsure if I'll make it. I stumble.

It's Adam's turn to hold me now, and I lose all composure, lose all pretence, lose all claim on being OK. He takes me to sit on the sofa and lets me wear myself out a while in all-out hysteria. I cling to him like he's the only thing that will stop me from drowning, fingers digging into his flesh. I'm howling into his chest, repeating, 'Why did I have to be so stubborn?', and he holds me like he used to each morning after his alarm went off.

There's a novel by the German movie star Lilli Palmer, called *The Red Raven*, in which the main character is willed a box of letters, detailing the affair between her husband and her best friend, who has thrown herself out of the window in despair at the situation. It came over earlier this week, with another bike messenger from the English-language bookstore. The protagonist, a thinly veiled version of the actress herself, is left to deal with the emotional wreckage of her husband's betrayal, compounded by her friend's death. Reading it, whilst writing this, has made me grateful that there were no such secrets to be discovered in our letters, that I have myself at least been spared half a heartache.

In the packet of papers Adam gave me, in amongst my letters to you, was one from you, unfinished. Though it was barely half a side long, you had added P.T.O. to the bottom of the page, as if you were embarking on a missive that you knew would run on and on and on. The letter isn't dated, but in the top right-hand corner there are those two teenage boxers, like a coat of arms, photocopied, black and white, and in the envelope is a sachet of lube from Denmark. There's a line asking me for a photograph which I would never have sent. You had written, *Send me a picture of your body. I've forgotten what you look like naked, well I haven't but it would be nice to be reminded.*

How wish I could remind you.

You died before I fell out of love with you, you see, unlike the other lovers I was done with when we broke, and of whom I hardly ever think. With them the end had come, and whether with flaming acrimony or soppy forgiveness, we had accepted it. But with you there was so much left undone, so much unaccounted for, and that's why I have never managed to fully absolve myself of you.

When I left the apartment Adam was folding bed linens quite absentmindedly; he nodded goodbye but barely registered my departure. I think he was still in shock. The evening air had not yet cooled, and so I walked home, clutching your letters as though they were pages from a missing gospel, hoping the sweat from my fingers would not permeate the plastic wallet and smudge the ink.

I wasn't in a hurry, I took the long way round, took the route we used to take from your place to the Joiners, strolling plangent. I ask myself now why I would deliberately extend my agony, by walking this road to Calvary, but as our friend Maggie Nelson says, 'such revisitations constitute a life.' I passed through Bethnal Green, and saw Lulu from across the street, in costume, smoking outside the Working Men's Club. I tried to pass by unnoticed, only she saw me and called out, 'Eh la, over here!', and so I had no choice but to cross over and say hello. She looked tired, and thin, a little less lustrous, and I felt that I was to blame.

She said, 'I heard you went away again.'

'I did,' I said, 'I just got back.'

'We missed you at the funeral,' she said, dragging on her fag.

'How was it?' I asked sheepishly. 'Was it OK?'

'Yeah,' she said. 'It was fine really. Everyone was very supportive. I think his family were shocked to see so many of us there,' and she chuckled softly.

I felt choked, and a little castigated. 'I'm sorry,' I said.

'Well, we all deal with things differently.' She smiled, faintly, but genuinely.

'No,' I said, 'that's not what I mean.'

'Oh,' she said, 'right.'

'I feel like I took him from you,' I said. 'And I'm sorry.'

She laughed more robustly this time, and said, 'Oh la, no one really ever belongs to anyone, do they?'

She took one last puff on her cigarette, flicked it to the ground, and crushed it with the tip of a golden stiletto.

'I better go back in,' she said. 'Doors'll be opening soon.'

'Sure thing,' I said.

'See you la,' she said, and waved as she disappeared inside.

Walking home, I remembered watching one of Jovian's old video tapes with you at his place years ago: an interview with Madonna on the Arsenio Hall Show from the early nineties, which you suffered through less than gracefully.

She comes on resplendent in a white pantsuit, huge shoulders, bold red lips, corkscrew perm, and the crowd goes wild. You say that she's ridiculous, but the studio audience is freaking out, yelling her name, shouting *I love you*, and she looks amazed, as though this has never happened to her before, and she's totally real. She almost looks a little afraid of it all, she waves to the audience timidly, gratefully. You can see the thought run across her face, *Is this my life?* She sits on the sofa opposite the host, the crowd is still screaming and crying, and then Arsenio gestures to them, seemingly saying, *Take it all in baby!* She looks so happy, and when they finally abate, he says something like, 'One day, when you feel blue, you can put the tape in and look back on this moment!'

When a dying star finally collapses it contracts to a point so tiny, but so massive, that it warps the time-space field itself. The famed black hole hereby created exerts such a force as to annexe and repurpose time. Inside, the machinations of the black hole are so immeasurably slow that they appear to us, on the outside, as stasis. To our poor, weary, useless eyes, nothing is happening up there, we cannot perceive that in fact the frozen star is rebounding outwards again, ready to throw out a whole new universe.

Ten years since we first met, six since we last spoke, four since your death, and what is there to show that this ever happened? No tapes, no monument, no commemorative china, just this book, and our letters, which will themselves all crumble to nothingness. But that's OK, because I read that nothing really exists anyway. All that is real is the relationship between things, things that don't exist, or rather things that only exist because of their relationship to one another. Now there's no you, eventually there'll be no me, but everything that has happened between us is how we have come to know ourselves.

Last week was Easter Sunday. During Mass, Father Ignacio told us that we can only know the three persons of the Holy Trinity in relation to each other: God the Father, God the Son and God the Holy Spirit. At least I think that's what he said, my Spanish comprehension is still lacklustre. What I have learned though, for sure, is that the word for 'sentence', *oración*, can also mean 'prayer', and I know that every line of this book is both.

Epilogue

It's London Fashion Week, it's always London Fashion Week. You're invited to a party in Shoreditch, hosted by a PR company to showcase their clients and woo journalists with free booze, the usual bullshit. You're going because you're in a good mood, you're up for a laugh, and a load of people you know are going to be there. 9 French Place, a four-storey warehouse space with a roof terrace. Not so very different from your own building, though in a better area and in much better nick. Another famous photographer owns it, he doesn't live there though, it's an investment property. *Fair enough,* you think, but also, *wanker.* Some posh bitch in a little black dress looks you over with disdain, your denim knee-length cut-offs, your scruffy vest, your cap. You chain your bike to a lamppost and walk towards the door. The woman asks, 'Are you here for the event?'

You say, 'Yeah,' she takes your name, and regrettably, lets you in. You go up to the fourth floor.

Inside you see a few friends, you see that dickhead – whats-his-name? – that DJ you hate, a few fashion people you recognise from *i-D* or the *Evening Standard.* You see a tall, very handsome boy over by the window. The blinds are drawn, pulled down to keep out the glare of the paparazzi, always hoping to get a candid shot of Kate or Cara at a party like this. This boy stands alone, framed against the tasteful cafe-au-lait cotton. From where you're standing the blind behind him looks like a photographer's backdrop, and you think, *He is fucking fit.*

The friend who invited you comes by with a beer in his hand, and says, 'We're going up to the roof. Get a drink and join us, yeah?' You nod, you look in the direction of the bar, there's a small crowd, you think, *I'll wait.* You turn back to check out this boy again. *So fit*, you say to yourself, *he must be a model*, and you realise that he is, and that you've met him before, you've worked together, and this is your in with him.

'Alright?' you say.

'Yes, I, erm,' he says, just happy that someone's come to talk to him.

He doesn't know how lovely he is, doesn't realise that people are intimidated by his beauty, he's only nineteen. He's spent his whole life so far being taunted for his strange looks, his scrawny limbs and ungainly height.

'We did that thing together, few months ago,' you say.

'Oh yeah,' he smiles. 'Oh yeah! With that girl from the agency, what was her name? How've you been?'

He's nervous. This puts you at ease. You've been cycling, you're hot, you can smell your own sweat, so can he and he's still smiling.

You talk a while, in vague, flattering terms, careful not to say too much, keep it smooth. The trick with seduction is to let the object of your desire do all the work themselves, tire themselves out, then fall into your arms in a dead faint.

You tell him about an exhibition of your work, which you're putting together with guidance from your mentor, your celebrated boss.

He can hardly believe he's here in this world. He says, 'What? You work for *him*? That's mad!'

You both laugh, and he says quizzically, 'I never laugh.' You say, 'Oh yeah?'

And he tells you a story, far too personal, about growing up in Macclesfield, how all his classmates teased him because he giggled like a faggot, so he'd trained himself only to smile quietly.

Emboldened by this closeness, aroused by the casual schoolboy homophobia, you say, 'I bet I can make you laugh,' and you let your tongue play, visible inside the corner of your mouth.

'Oh really?' He blushes hard.

'Yeah,' you say and you reach forward, towards his exceptional beauty, to tickle him. He's wearing a flimsy, expensive grey T-shirt, obviously given to him by the PR, so when you put your fingers on his chest, you can feel the warm skin and hard bone beneath, there's nothing between you now.

He laughs, and it *is* a very effeminate giggle, he raises his hands and very half-heartedly says, 'Don't,' but he is still beaming, and makes no attempt to take your hands off him.

'Don't what?' you say, taking a step away from him in mock innocence.

'Tickle me!' he says, looking confused.

And, set-up perfected, you pounce, saying, 'Alright, then!' and begin to tickle him again, up the ribs and under the arms and he's chuckling now, squirming in pleasure, wriggling with desire and this new awareness that people are looking at him. It becomes almost too much, he puts his arm out behind him to steady himself against the window, but it's wide open behind the blind, and he falls backwards, he can't regain his balance, he reaches for you, and you fall out with him, out of the window. He lands on a classic white Spitfire Triumph, it breaks his pelvis, but it breaks his fall. You hit the pavement and smash open your skull.

There's a scream from above and someone yells, 'Tom's gone out the window!'

There's a short moment of confusion, as you try to understand what's happening to you. You hear this boy crying in pain somewhere out of shot, the September sky above you is black, but there don't seem to be any stars up there, and the last thing you see is the flash of a camera in your face. The psychic I closes. I ask myself, *Is that when you knew?*

Credits

Page

1   Joan Didion, 'Why I Write', *New York Times*, 5 Dec 1976.

33   Agnès Varda (dir.), *The Beaches of Agnès* (2008), made by Agnès Varda.

36   Friedrich Nietzsche, *The Will To Power* (1901; Penguin, 2017).

71   Iris Murdoch, quoted in John Haffenden, 'Interview with Iris Murdoch', *Literary Review*, April 1983.

97   Daniel M. Lavery, *Something That May Shock and Discredit You* (Simon & Schuster, 2020). Quoted text on p. 97 from *Something That May Shock and Discredit You* by Daniel M. Lavery (2020), reprinted here with permission.

158   Joan Didion, quoted in 'The Art of Nonfiction', Philip Gourevitch (ed.), *The Paris Review Interviews, Vol. I* (Canongate, 2006).

194   John Casavettes, *Love Streams* (1984). Reprinted with kind permission of MGM Studios.

225   Cookie Mueller, 'Walking Through Clear Water in a Pool Painted Black', *Collected Stories* (1991; Semiotext(e), 2022).

265 Frank O'Hara, excerpt from 'Five Poems' from *Lunch Poems*. Copyright © 1964 by Frank O'Hara. Reprinted with the permission of The Permissions Company, LLC on behalf of City Lights Books, citylights.com. All rights reserved.

339 April Lin and Jasmine Lin (dirs.), *Reality Fragment 160921*, (2017).

347 Paul Preciado, 'The Losers Conspiracy', *Artforum*, 26 March 2020.

356 Joan Didion, *The Year of Magical Thinking* (Vintage, 2006).

359 Maggie Nelson, excerpt from *The Argonauts*, page 112. Copyright © 2015 by Maggie Nelson. Reprinted with the permission of The Permissions Company, LLC on behalf of Graywolf Press, Minneapolis, Minnesota, graywolfpress.org.

Acknowledgements

I extend my heartfelt thanks to the early readers of this book: Ali Smith, Sophie Iremonger and Chris Brett Bailey, and most especially to Olivia Laing whose fervent encouragement throughout the process made the writing possible; to my friends Sarah, Max, Matt, Joseph, Chanell, Helen, Kat, Jordan, Anna, Gina, Beau, Stevie and Rhyannon for years of international magic; to my sweet pals at Malpas who so kindly put up with me skulking about for months at a time whilst I wrote this; to my family, especially my sister Nicola who has saved my skin more times than I care to remember; to Zoe Ross for believing in me and helping me find my way in the big bad world of letters; to Paul Baggaley for championing this book from the start and to Allegra Le Fanu for her unending insight and patience as an editor; to Scott Elliott and the team at HSK for giving me time and space to work; to Michael Bermudez for allowing me to spend two tropical months writing in his garden; to Laura and Ash at The Uncultured for helping me restructure my practice and allowing me to grow as an artist; to the Society of Authors, ACE and A-N for the generous funding which supported the writing and research of this book; to Our Lady of Perpetual

Succour for her blessed guidance, and of course to my darling Felix whose enduring love, compassion and understanding underpins the very fabric of this book, and indeed my life.

A Note on the Author

Lauren John Joseph was born in Liverpool and lives in London. They are the author of the plays *Boy in a Dress* and *A Generous Lover*, and the experimental prose volume *Everything Must Go*. Their film and performance work has been shown internationally across the UK, US, Europe and Asia. This is their first novel.

A Note on the Type

The text of this book is set in Bembo, which was first used in 1495 by the Venetian printer Aldus Manutius for Cardinal Bembo's *De Aetna*. The original types were cut for Manutius by Francesco Griffo. Bembo was one of the types used by Claude Garamond (1480–1561) as a model for his Romain de l'Université, and so it was a forerunner of what became the standard European type for the following two centuries. Its modern form follows the original types and was designed for Monotype in 1929.